THE STARS UNDYING

EMPIRE WITHOUT END:
BOOK ONE

EMERY ROBIN

orbitbooks.net

SF

This book is a work of fiction. Names, characters, places, and incidents are the product of the author's imagination or are used fictitiously. Any resemblance to actual events, locales, or persons, living or dead, is coincidental.

Cover design by Lauren Panepinto
Cover illustration by Marc Simonetti

Orbit
Hachette Book Group
1290 Avenue of the Americas
New York, NY 10104
orbitbooks.net

First Edition: November 2022
Simultaneously published in Great Britain by Orbit

Orbit is an imprint of Hachette Book Group.
The Orbit name and logo are trademarks of Little, Brown Book Group Limited.

Library of Congress Cataloging-in-Publication Data
Names: Robin, Emery, author.
Title: The stars undying / Emery Robin.
Description: First edition. | New York, NY : Orbit, 2022. | Series: Empire without end ; book 1
Identifiers: LCCN 2022022409 | ISBN 9780316391399 (hardcover) | ISBN 9780316391597 (ebook)
Subjects: LCGFT: Space operas (Fiction) | Fantasy fiction. | Novels.
Classification: LCC PS3618.O317586 S73 2022 | DDC 813/.6—dc23/eng/20220513
LC record available at https://lccn.loc.gov/2022022409

ISBNs: 9780316391399 (hardcover), 9780316391597 (ebook)

Printed in the United States of America

LSC-C

Printing 1, 2022

To the Rockridge Branch of the Oakland Public Library,
which to me was as great a wonder as Alexandria.

THE STARS UNDYING

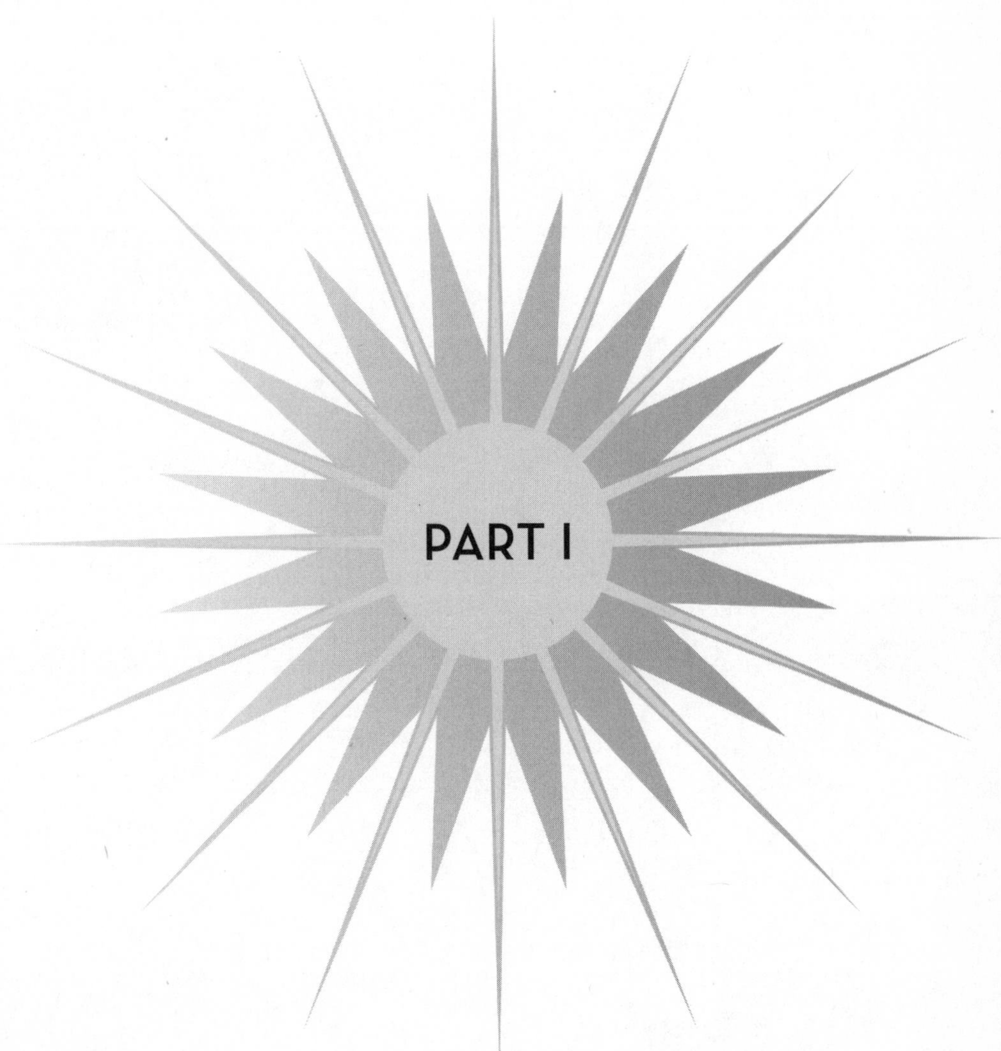

PART I

CHAPTER ONE

GRACIA

In the first year of the Thirty-Third Dynasty, when He came to the planet where I was born and made of it a wasteland for glory's sake, my ten-times-great-grandfather's king and lover, Alekso Undying, built on the ruins of the gods who had lived before Him Alectelo, the City of Endless Pearl, the Bride of Szayet, the Star of the Swordbelt Arm, the Ever-Living God's Empty Grave.

He caught fever and filled that grave, ten months later. You can't believe in names.

Three hundred years is a long time to call any place Endless, for one thing. Alectelo is no different, and the pearl of the harbor-gate was cracked and flaking when I ran my hand up it, and its shine had long since worn away. It had only ever been inlay, anyway. Beneath it was brass, solid and warm, and browning like bread at the edges where the air was creeping through.

"It needs repairs," said Zorione, just behind my shoulder.

I curled my fingers against the metal. "It needs money," I said.

"She won't give it," Zorione said. She was sitting on a nearby crate already, stretching out her legs in front of her. She had complained of her old bones and aching feet through every back alley and tunnel in the city, and been silent only when we passed under markets, where the noise might have carried to the street. "Why would she?" she went on, without looking at me. "*She* never comes to the harbor. Are the captains and generals kept in wine and honey-cakes? Yes? That keeps *her* happy."

I said nothing. After a moment she said, "Of course—it's not hers," and subsided.

I knew I ought to be grateful for her devotion. Nevertheless it was not a question of possession that stirred me, looking at the curling rust on that gate framing the white inlet where our island broke to the endless sea. Nor was it a question of reverence, though it might have been, in better times. It was the deepest anger I had ever felt, and one of the few angers I had never found myself able to put aside. It was the second time in my life I had seen the queen of my planet be careless with something beautiful.

"It wouldn't matter, anyway," I said, and let my hand fall. "This is quicksilver pearl. It only grows in Ceiao these days."

It was a cool day at the edge of the only world I had ever known. The trade winds were coming up from the ocean, smelling of brine and exhaust, and the half-moon-studded sky was a clear and cloudless blue. At the edge of my hearing was the distant hum of rockets from across the water, a low roar like the sound of the lions my people had once worshipped. I took it as an omen, and hoped it a good one. Alectelans had made no sacrifices to mindless beasts these past three centuries. But if Alekso heard my prayers, it was months since He had last answered them, and I needed all the succor I could get.

"How long until the ship?" I said.

I had asked three times in the last half hour, but Zorione said patiently, "Ten minutes," as if it were the first time. "If she hasn't caught it yet," and she made a sign against bad luck in the air and spit over her shoulder. It made me smile, though I tried not to let her see it. She was a true Alectelan, Sintian in name and parentage but in faith half orthodoxy and half heathenism, in that peculiar fanatical blend that every born resident of the city held close to their hearts. And though she carried all unhappiness as unfailingly as she carried my remaining possessions, I had no interest in offending her. She had shown no sign, as yet, of being capable of disloyalty. Still: I had so little left to lose.

The water was white-green and choppy with the wind, and so when our ship came skipping across the sea at last, it was only the sparks that gave it away, meandering orange and red toward the concrete shore like moths. At the very last moment it slowed and skidded onto the runway in a cloud of exhaust, coming to a stop yards from our feet.

My maid was coughing. I held still and listened for the creak of a hatch. When the smuggler appeared through the drifting grey particulates a moment later, shaven-headed and grinning with crooked teeth, Zorione jumped.

"Good morning," I said. "Anastazia Szaradya? We spoke earlier. I'm—"

"I know who you are," she said in Szayeti-accented Sintian. Her eyes took me in—cotton dress, dust-grey sandals, bare face, bare arms—before they flicked to Zorione, behind me. "This is the backer?"

I kept my smile wide and pleasant. "One of them," I said. "The rest are expecting our report from the satellite in—I'm sorry, was it three hours? Four?"

"By nightfall, madam," Zorione said, looking deeply uncomfortable.

I gave her an apologetic look behind the smuggler's back. If I had had a choice in who to play the role of the backer, I would not have chosen Zorione, who as long as I had known her had despised deception almost as fiercely as rule-breaking, and rule-breaking like blasphemy. But she knew as well as I did what a luxury choice had become for us. "By nightfall," I repeated. "Shall we board the ship?"

The smuggler narrowed her eyes at me. "And how long after will the pearls be sent to the satellite?" she said. "You said three days?"

I flicked my eyes to Zorione, who cleared her throat. "A week," she said. "The transport ship will bring them, if they find her safe and sound. *Only* if," she added, in a burst of improvisation. I rewarded her with a quick nod.

"A week?" said the smuggler. "For a piece of walking bad luck? Better I should be holding a bomb! Was this what we agreed to?"

Zorione's face went blank. "You know," I said hastily, "you're very right. Speed *is* of the essence. I would personally prefer to leave the system as soon as possible. Madam Buquista, might your consortium abandon the precautionary measures we discussed? I understand the concern that the army not trace the payment back to Madam Szaradya—of course the Ceians might trace it, too, and come to investigate her—but is that really *my* highest priority? Perhaps instead—"

The smuggler snorted. "Hush," she said. "Fine. Keep your precautions. *You*, girl, can keep your patience. Meanwhile"—she nodded at Zorione's outraged face—"when your ship comes for her, we discuss delay fees, hmm?"

Zorione looked admirably unhappy at this, and I would have nodded at her to put up a lengthy and losing argument, when there was a low, dull hum, akin to the noise of an insect.

Then the sky wiped dark from horizon to horizon. The sea, which had been glittering with daylight, flooded black; the shadow of the smuggler's ship swelled and swept over us, and we were left in darkness. The smuggler swore—I whispered a prayer, and I could see Zorione's silhouetted hands moving in a charm against ill fortune—and above us, just where the sun had shone and twenty times its size, the face of the queen of Szayet opened up like an eye.

She was smiling down at us. She was a lovely woman, the queen, and though holos had a peculiar quality that always seemed to make it impossible to meet anyone's eyes, her gaze felt heavy and prickling as it swept over the concrete and the sea and the pearl of the harbor-gate below. She had braided her hair in the high Ceian style, and she had thrown on a military coat and hat that I was almost certain had belonged to the king, and she had painted her mouth, hastily enough that it smeared at her lip as if she had just bitten into raw meat. Around her left ear, stretching up to her hairline, curled a dozen golden wires, pressed so closely to her skin they might have been a tattoo. An artfully draped braid hid where I knew they slipped through her temple, into her skull. In her earlobe, at the base of the wires, sat a shining silver pearl.

She said, sweetly and very slowly—I could hear it echo, as I knew it was doing on docks and in cathedrals, in marketplaces and alleyways, across the whole city of Alectelo, and though I had seen the machines in the markets that threw these images into the sky, though I had laid hands on them and shown them my own face, my breath caught, my heart hammered, I wanted to fall to my knees—

"Do you think the Oracle blind?"

She paused as if for a reply. There was none, of course. She added, even more sweetly, "Or perhaps you think her stupid?"

"Time to go," said the smuggler.

We scrabbled ourselves up the ladder as quickly as we could: the smuggler first, then me, Zorione taking the rear with the handles of my bags clenched in her bony fingers. Above me, the queen's voice was rising: "Did you think I would not see," she said, "did you think the tongue and eyes of Alekso Undying would not *know*? I have heard—I will be told—where the liar Altagracia Caviro is hiding. I will be told in what harbor she dares to stand, I will be told in what ship she dares to fly. You are *bound* to do her harm, all you who worship the Undying—you are bound to do her harm, Alekso wishes it so—"

Zorione, swaying on the rungs, made another elaborate sign in the air, this time against blasphemy. "Please don't fall," I called down to her. "I can't afford to lose you. But I appreciate the piety." She huffed and seized hold of the ladder again.

When we had all tumbled into the cramped confines of the ship, the smuggler slammed the hatch shut above my head, and shoved lumps of bread and a pinch of salt into our waiting hands. The bread was hard as stone and tasted like lint—it must have come out of her pocket, a thought I immediately decided not to contemplate—but I swallowed it as best I could, and smeared the salt onto my tongue with my thumb. The queen's voice was echoing even now through the walls, muffled and metallic. I heard *worship a lying* and *demand by right* and *suffer the fate*, and turned my head away.

The smuggler had gone ahead of me, through the bowels of the ship. I made to push past Zorione, but she caught my arm at the last moment, and stood on her tiptoes to whisper into my ear, "Madam, I'm afraid—"

"I know," I said, "but we knew she would only be a step behind us—we have to go." But she shook her head frantically, leaned closer, and hissed:

"What is the thief going to do to us when she finds out there isn't any consortium?"

My first, absurd impulse was to laugh, and I had to clap my hand over my mouth to stifle it. When I had myself under control, I shook my head and bent to whisper back: "Zorione, how can it be worse than what would have happened if we hadn't told her that there was?"

She let me go, her face pinched with worry. I wished I knew what to say to her—but I had a week to find an answer, and here and now I made my way through sputtering wires and hissing pipes through the little hallway where the smuggler had disappeared.

I found her in a worn chair at what I presumed to be the ship's only control panel, laid out in red lights before a dark viewscreen not four handspans wide. "How long until we're out of the atmosphere?" I said.

"It'll take as long as it takes," said the smuggler. "If you have any service complaints, you've got three guesses where you can put them."

Three guesses seemed excessive, but it was more munificence than I had been offered in months. "If I stand here behind you," I said, "will I be in your way?"

"You're in my way wherever you are," she said, and shoved a lever forward. Beneath us, the engines coughed irritably to life. "Don't go into the back, it's full of Szayeti falcon jars. Eighteenth Dynasty."

I would remember that. I let it settle to the floor of my mind for now, though, and tucked myself into what little space there was behind the smuggler's chair. We had begun our journey back across the water, bouncing over the flickering waves. The spray threw rainbows around us, so bright my eyes streamed, and my first warning that we had arrived at the launch spot and begun to rise was a hum in my ears, low at first and then louder—and then a pain in my head, as sharp as if someone had clapped their hands to my temples and squeezed. The smuggler was mouthing something—I thought it was *here we go*—

—and then the sky was fading, blue into colorlessness into a deep indigo and the ocean was shrinking below, dotted by scudding clouds. The floor of the ship shook, then coughed. My ears popped.

"Simple part done," said the smuggler. I was beginning to believe she liked having someone to talk to.

That, at least, I knew how to indulge. "Simple part?" I said, as bewildered as if I did not already know the answer. "What comes next?"

"*That*," said the smuggler, pointing with grim satisfaction. I allowed myself a moment of pride—it had been excellent timing—and looked past her pointing finger to where the Ceian-bought warship sat black and seething like an anthill in the center of my sky.

"We can't answer a royal customs holo," I said, making myself sound shocked.

"Wasn't planning to," said the smuggler. "Imperial pricks already gave the queen my face. Do you know, three decades ago, I flew six times a year through thirty ports from here to Muntiru without stopping to tell any man my name. Now every asteroid twenty feet across is infested with barbarians in blue, asking for the sequence of every gene my mother gave me." She paused. "Wonder whose fault that is."

It took a great deal of faith to attribute that kind of influence to any Oracle, let alone the Oracle she meant. But faith, unlike warships, had never been in short supply among the Szayeti.

"What will we do?" I said. "Speed through the army's radar?"

"Better," said the smuggler. "We outweave it. Hold on."

That was the only warning I got. In the back, I could hear Zorione yelp as the ship spun like a top, suddenly and violently. The smuggler shoved a lever forward, yanked it to the left, and pushed three sliders on the control board up to their highest positions. A holo had sprung to life on the dashboard, a glittering spiderweb of yellow lines delineated by a wide black curve at their edge. Within it was a single white dot: our ship, I guessed, and the edge of the atmosphere.

"What's that?" I said anyway, and let the smuggler explain.

She liked explaining, and it distracted me, which I knew after only a few seconds I would badly need. Flying with the smuggler was not unlike being a piece of soap dropped in the bath. She might have lost control of the ship entirely and I would never have known the difference, except for the unwavering fierceness of her smile. "How many times have you done this?" I attempted to ask through rattling teeth as we swiveled and plummeted through empty air.

"At least twice!" she said with malicious cheer.

It was difficult to tell when we passed the warship. Certainly the smuggler did not seem to know. I think she must have thought that, were I sufficiently bumped and jolted, I would give up and go join my nursemaid in the back, but I hung on stubbornly to the back of her chair, and stared from the control panel to the viewscreen to the holo and back again, matching each to each in my mind. It was an old trick I had, when fighting off illness or pain or plain misery, to focus on something at which I felt very stupid, and learn each detail as if it were another tongue. At other times it had served me well. Now, hungry and tired and nauseous at once, it was more difficult, and by the time the ship turned one final time and settled into stillness, I was clinging to the smuggler's chair as if it were my father alive again.

The smuggler smirked. "Twenty minutes," she said. "New record. Hey," she added in Szayeti, mostly to herself, "maybe she carries good luck after all."

"I try to," I said, in the same language, and caught the flicker of her first true smile. Below us, I could see the broad white edge of the planet, beginning to shrink against the darkness. I had seen it from this distance only once before in my life.

My people are a people of prophecy. Long before Alekso Undying came from old Sintia to our shores, long before my ten-times-great-grandfather, weeping, bore His body from the palace at Kutayet to the tomb where I grew up, my people spoke with the voices of serpents and lions, falcons and foxes, who roamed this world and who saw the future written in blood. The people then said what was, what is, and what will be; and though Alekso's beloved and his descendants are their rulers now, and though they have had no god but their conqueror for three hundred years, they have not forgotten that they once told the future as freely as any queen. They never will.

The queen of Szayet had prophesied, these last eight months, that she was the only and rightful bearer of the Pearl of the Dead. She had prophesied herself the heir to the voice of Alekso our conqueror, the Undying who had died all those centuries ago. She had prophesied that her words were His words, and her words were the future, and that there was no future in them for Altagracia Caviro Patramata, father-beloved lady of Alectelo, seeker of the god and friend to the people, her only rival, her only enemy, her only and her best-beloved sister.

As the rust-green coin of Szayet receded before me, and the night crept in from every corner of the viewscreen, I leaned across the smuggler's shoulder and pressed my fingers to the glass as I had to the arch at the harbor, and I whispered: "I will see you again."

My sister had called me a liar today.

I am a liar, of course. But I meant to be a prophet, too.

CHAPTER TWO

CEIRRAN

I had loved Quinha, more's the trouble.

In the whole Empire of Ceiao, for all its rabble and reputation, there's only a fistful of citizens who have the born-or-bred true talent of a military general. Fewer with the charisma and the money to handle the populace, and fewer still who have any head for politics, and only a sprinkling, only enough for me to count on the fingers of my good right hand, are that rarest of things: a damn fine pilot. Quinha had been all of these, and a friend besides. I'd fought with her, I'd plotted with her. I'd cared for her. I hadn't *wanted* to kill her.

Nevertheless.

She was coming up the meteor bank when her ship slipped into our sights: an imperial dreadnought twenty klicks wide, blooming on our radar screens as a mass of shifting yellows and reds. In the darkness of the accretion-tide she was hardly visible. If I'd been in my fighter I might have caught her and picked off her cannons, one by one, and my fingers itched for the controls. But those days were gone and had been for many years, and I had my governorship to think of, and my dignity besides.

"Let me at her," said Ana, who had neither. She was sprawled in a curved white chair at my right hand. She liked that sort of thing, Ana did. If she had ever been able to find the patience for subtlety, she wouldn't have looked for it.

I considered the thought. Ana was no ace, but she was a quick draw and a vicious brute in battle, and it paid to indulge her, more often than not. But I shook my head in the end.

"I want her pinned to a planet," I said, "and coming out ground fighting. Bring the soldiers their force-shields, and pull around *Laureathan* to port. We'll drive her up the bank toward the star-well."

"Like conquerors we'll do it," said Ana. "Bring her corpse before us to the city gates."

That wasn't why. Quinha's ship was borrowed, a colony-made pirate thing, but I feared her guns. If I had no choice but to fight her in open space, I'd send in a dozen fair-size destroyers, and do her damage enough to make her hesitate at coming within our cannon range. For now, though, there was choice, and I would have been a fool not to take advantage of it. And there was another reason, too, which Ana would have had no stomach to hear. "Yes," I said anyway. "She'll search some near planet for safe harbor. We'll carry her in the brig for the home journey."

I had not known, at the time, what planet she would seek out. Even had I known, would I have cared? The hand of the empire reaches far and wide, from old Cherekku's stone mazes to the sulfide storms of Madinabia, and I had not been to this arm of the galaxy since my childhood. We make a point, in Ceiao, not to be overcome by decadence. Even the name of Alekso of Sintia means little to us.

It meant little to me, in any case, at the time.

We surged after her. It was a great ship that I was riding, built under my eye at Ceiao's own river docks by a thousand trained workmen. Quinha's wasn't, and she knew it. We could see her struggling to dart and weave among the asteroid storms, her aching-slow banks and turns up the gravity curves. If she'd charmed the builders, or bribed the navy, or besieged the dockyards, or had her men installed among the magistrates—but she hadn't. She hadn't, and I had, and she had lost Ceiao, and I had won the war.

It made me ashamed to watch her fly. She was the one who had taught me, all those years ago, never to respect a commander whose fighting begins on the battlefield.

When she gunned her engines, I hesitated. This was her corner of local space, and she knew it like the back of her hand. She might have been leading me into the path of a comet, or some trick of local gravity that would have sent half the fleet tumbling into a newborn star. But her dreadnought was shrinking in our sights, and Ana had risen from her seat and was pacing the viewscreen like a lion.

"Chase her," I said, and shut my eyes as the great warship shuddered underneath me. Betting against Quinha's long experience had failed me in the Merchants' Council once. Betting against it a second time on the battlefield had won me a city. Best of three, as they said in Ceiao, made fortune.

I needn't have worried.

The system rose up in our viewscreen all at once. It was an old star we were looking at—life-bearing, naturally, but reddening and rusted around the edges. There were only a few planets, idly flung out beside it at haphazard angles. Nearly all were ringed; only one, a little blue-green thing with a patchwork of cloud atop its surface, was surrounded by a sprinkling of moons, and even they were peculiarly shaped, knobbled and jagged at odd edges. I thought of a rogue planet plowing through the orbit path, until Captain Galvão Orcadan said behind me: "Szayet, sir."

Szayet! I exhaled. "Prepare the rafts," I said, and a few lieutenants sprang up and disappeared down the ladders. "Get ahead of her, if you can, shunt her toward Medveyet—but if you can't, press her in hard. The less time she has to disembark, the better. She's got seaships in that hold, and provisions for weeks. I don't want her hiding out on the water there."

"She'll need to make landfall, sir," said Galvão, "or try to exit the atmosphere again, and we're sure to see if she does. She can hide on the water, but she can't hide for long. We may not need to chase her down at all." His voice crept up at the end, uncertain.

"I have no intention of letting every cynic in Ceiao watch me spend thirty days blockading the richest treasury in the Swordbelt Arm," I said.

Galvão subsided at once. He was in the right, of course, and if I could, I would have told him so. But there was a reason I wanted to meet Quinha planetside, and it was a reason I had already kept from Ana.

There was a veneer of ships overlaying the planet, thicker than I had expected. If I hadn't known better I might have thought she had steered us into a trap after all—they were our make, each of them, good Ceian steel gunboats and galleons and blue destroyers dodging in and out of the ports like flies—but this was no ambush, only the local government's fleet. Bought at a premium, most likely. I might even have sold some of them myself, back in my magistrate days.

Nevertheless I held up a hand, and the ship slowed and pulled up into a reluctant orbit. Quinha was barreling forward, past the gunners, past the cargo ships, toward the thick, drifting air of the planet. The ships made no move to stop her as she grew smaller and smaller, like dust, and finally popped out of eyesight. Still I watched, and still I waited, and when Galvão grew restless and said, "Commander Ceirran, you said—" I held up a hand again.

"I know," I said. "One moment more."

Ana had gone dead still. Only her eyes were moving: from me to the viewscreen, from the viewscreen to me, her head cocked like a dog that had scented prey. I caught her gaze and held it, telling her *Wait* and *Yes*, and her lips parted slightly—

There it was. I took an involuntary step forward, and Ana's head whipped round: a Szayeti destroyer, peeled away from the nearest warship, was dropping like a stone toward the planet.

"Is it—" said Galvão.

"It is," I said. "They're going after her. Someone find the lieutenants and tell them to hold our ships."

Ana said nothing. She followed me back to my quarters, though, as I had known she would, and when we arrived she shut the door behind her and threw herself into the chair across from my desk.

"Fortune's tits," she said. "You'll give up a prize we've chased down half this spiral arm? And for what—*politics*?"

"Will I?" I said mildly, easing myself down across from her.

"She'll raise an army," said Ana, "and stretch out this war for another three months, and send half my men to the void, and they *will* rake you over the coals at home, and I'll be stuck on the inside of a cruiser, poking at radar screens and driving you mad with complaining. Not a chance! Let me at her, and to hell with Szayeti sovereignty—what good has it ever done them, anyway?"

"Your grasp of foreign policy is remarkable," I said. "Tell me, what is your opinion of the Oracle of Szayet?"

"The girl?" said Ana. "I'll tell you this much, I'd have bet my captain's pin she'd be a poor strategist, but I was wrong. Another reason you should let me take twenty men and—yes, all right. Good-looking. Parochial. A bit of a complainer, to my mind. Young to be queen. Hope she's more careful about eating bad meat than her father was. Why?"

"I met her father, once," I said, "but never her."

"Well, I never met her, either," said Ana. "What of it?"

"I know," I said, and picked up a stylus and rolled it over my fingers thoughtfully, knuckle to knuckle. "Has Quinha?"

That stopped Ana in her tracks. She leaned back in her chair and looked at me with narrowed eyes. "You think she hasn't," she said. "You think Quinha can't manage her?"

"I am not," I said, "entirely sure that Quinha knows what she is managing."

"How old *is* she, fourteen?" said Ana, who knew very well Casimiro Caviro Faifisto's daughters were only a few years younger than she. "That'd be old enough to go to war at home. How childish can she be?"

Back the stylus went, over the same four knuckles. "Are you in debt, Anita?" I said.

"That's a personal question," said Ana, and when I looked at her, "Yes, and you know the amount to the centono."

"So is Szayet," I said. "By several orders of magnitude more than you, I hope. From simply buying the Ceian ships they needed to defend themselves, at first, and then from buying Ceian weapons, and then her advice, and then her aid. Faifisto nearly tripled the debts in his lifetime, but he inherited them from his aunt, who inherited them from her mother, who inherited them from her grandfather, and *he* used Szayet itself as collateral against them when he put down a civil war." I tapped the stylus on my desk, and it woke into a shivering sea of maps and waiting holos. "Quinha bought the bulk of them," I said, "not long after we met."

Ana stared, then swore.

"Then you *will* give up the prize," she said. "She won't need to raise an army—the queen will raise one for her! What in the world are you thinking?"

"I am thinking," I said, "about diplomacy. Do you have your dress uniform?"

CHAPTER
THREE

GRACIA

When I was young, I went with my father to see the empire.

My sister cried. My sister rarely cried; I was the one who sat and screamed over every scraped knee and torn skirt, the one who our father fluttered to and swept up in his arms and kissed on the head and called *mia Gracino* and *mia trezoro* and *mia karulino* in the Malisintian tongue of our ancestor, taking little notice of the fact that despite all my howling, my eyes were always dry. But on the day we left for Ceiao my sister had wept at the runway in the harbor as the ship heat curled up around our feet, face red and silent, her mouth a flat line and her eyes so hot on me that I was afraid my hair would burn.

"Don't leave me," she said.

"Sweeting," said my father warmly. "Are you worried? Zorione will take care of every little thing. You'll be safe and sound and ready to welcome us back to Alectelo when we return."

"I'm not *scared*," said Arcelia scornfully. My father chuckled and ruffled her hair.

"What shall I bring you from the city?" he said. "A silver dress? A jewel? A little cuckoo for a pet, hmm?"

"Nothing," said Arcelia. "I don't want anything—I don't *want* to welcome you back to Alectelo—I want to *leave* Alectelo—"

"Leave Alectelo!" said my father, laughing. "Listen to the child. What about this, darling—do you want to touch the Pearl before I go? How would you like that?"

This was a rare privilege, and one that both of us sorely coveted. But when he bent his head down Arcelia shied away.

"I want to *go*," she repeated. Her eyes were fixed on mine like stars.

"You know what the Ceians told me. If I could take you both, I would, sweet," said my father, but he was already drifting away from her, toward the waiting entrance of our ship. It was never safe to rely on the length of his attention. Even my sister knew that. But she only clenched her fists at her side, and her gaze flicked away from my face to his retreating back. Though her expression had grown no less dangerous, I shrank back in relief.

"I don't *care* what the Ceians want," she said.

My father turned back then, and he walked to her and knelt over her so that his long, rich red cloak pooled around her little body, and he rubbed the pale pad of his thumb very softly over her temple.

"Unlearn that," he said to her, "or I'll make you sorry." Then he kissed her on the top of her head, and drew away. I ran after him, toward the open mouth of the ship where our servants waited with bread and salt. I was too afraid to look back.

I had never in my life before been in a ship. As young as I was it seemed as large as the world. I was in awe of everything: the mazelike blue Ceian mosaic patterned under my feet; the high narrow windows, through which at any moment I felt I might witness a comet or a neighboring planet or an asteroid storm; the broad silver ceilings curved like the vault of heaven, so closely and intricately carved that I wondered they did not shatter onto our heads. Every inch of the ship's walls glittered with light, holos and radar displays and dozens of thickly jeweled control panels, each accompanied by red-cloaked, pinch-browed pilots, who sprang off their chairs whenever my father passed them and fell to their knees on the floor, murmuring obeisances. The king did not greet his people in return. He could not have if he wanted to. He did not speak a word of the Szayeti tongue.

Nor had I ever before in my life been allowed so much time alone with my father. I was determined to take full advantage of it: Each of those ten days spent journeying through the star fields I clung to his side, sat by his red-robed knees as he held court in the captain's chair, chattered to him endlessly at breakfast and at suppertime. I watched him as devotedly as a cat watches a bird, while he spoke of trade and politics with the captain, and frowned over holo recordings and tariff agreements, and charted our path on the great sparkling map in the navigation room. I loved to walk through that map with him, to reach up for his arm as he led me through spiral arms and nebulae. In the darkness, his round face seemed like another celestial body, lit in the low soft reds of dying stars.

My sister and I had already begun our formal education, lessons in rhetoric and mathematics and languages from a sour-faced old tutor who had come cheaply from Sintia and whose Ceian was scarcely better than ours. To see my father rule, though, was an education of an entirely different sort, and I drank it in like water. Everything he did, from how he oiled his beard in the morning to how he read his books at night, was a source of fascination. What I loved most of all was to see him in judgment: how the officers would come to kneel before him, how he would hold himself proudly as they told him their disputes, the stern and solemn set to his mouth. Then he would take off his glasses, and close his eyes, and put two fingers to the Pearl in the lobe of his ear—to me, it felt as if all the ship froze at those moments, when my father listened to the voice of our god who had conquered their planet those centuries ago, the dead man who slept in a tomb twelve thousand light-years away—and when he opened his eyes again and spoke, they sighed a little, as if my father's prophecy were like honey, as if his justice were like sweet wine.

During sleeping hours, when the day crew had gone to bed and only a few of the thin Szayeti servants crept like shadows from the engines to the oxygen ports, I would sit at his feet in the ship's great hall and demand he tell me the stories of the carvings above us.

"Surely you know this, Gracino?" he would say to me each night, a ritual just as solemn as all his others. "What has Zorione told you in that nursery?"

"But I want to hear it from you," I would tell him, and lean contentedly against his knees and follow his gaze upward to where the armies and the mountains and the reaching hands of the moon shifted in the low lamplight. "I want to hear the truth."

And so he would tell me again: how Alekso had come from the high black heavens to Szayet on the first day of summer, fleet stretching behind His crown-ship in such size and quantity that they had blocked out the merciless sun, and at the sight of Him lions had fled, and serpents had wriggled into the earth; how Alekso had seen that the Ostrayeti, who came from the great green moon where quicksilver pearl first grew, had lured our people into worshipping them by offering sophisticated ships and computing, and then had made them slaves; how Alekso had cast them down in fire and thunder; how they had rushed to their pearl ships and tried to flee, but at Alekso's command that selfsame green moon had splintered and cracked and burned for seven nights and days, and the waters of our ocean had come up from the deeps and closed over the Ostrayeti soldiers and generals, and drowned all the gods and cities of the old world; and how the free Szayeti people had come in their multitudes and knelt before Him, to worship Him as their new god over not only Szayet but His whole empire, from generation to generation. He was a wonderful storyteller, my father. In his voice each part of the conquest was alive and breathing, sky and fire so real that I might have been there—as, in a way, my father had. He pointed to each part of the story in the ceiling in turn as he told it, every night. I loved all those carvings, angular and flat in the old Szayeti style. I could not have told you a single detail of them afterward, though, because I was always watching his long-fingered brown hands, and each night all I thought of was how proud I was that they so nearly resembled my own.

"Did He know He would become a god," I asked him one of those nights, "when He came to our planet?"

"Not at all," he told me. He always sounded distant when Alekso was speaking to him, dreamy, as if a part of him had wandered away. "He had conquered dozens of planets before ours, sweeting, don't forget that. If our people hadn't chosen to worship Alekso, He might never have thought to want divinity at all." He paused, then. "You'll want to remember that," he said, "when you're queen."

"Or when Arcelia is," I said sleepily.

I felt his hand, which was stroking my hair, stop. "Altagracia," he said, and it made me sit up, for he hardly ever called me by my name. "I said when you're queen. I mean what I say."

I twisted my head to stare at the broad circle of his face. "How do you know I'll be queen?" I said. It sounded childish, and I was young enough that knowing I sounded childish still angered me. "Arcelia told me Zorione told *her* Alekso only tells the king who'll be the next heir when he's—" I did not like to say *deathbed*. My voice seemed abruptly too loud, in the quiet of the sleeping hold.

He looked at me awhile, and then he sighed.

"The people believe a prophet's business is to say the words of the divine, dear heart, and it's as well that they do," he said, and his hand resumed stroking my hair again. "But it's not true. A prophet's business is a translator's. A prophet's business is to take His words, and to make them into something the world can bear to hear. You'll remember that one day, too."

It would take me many years to understand what he meant, and by that time, I would already be at war.

There was one other moment that unsettled me in those ten days of travel, and I did not think to remember it until I was long returned to Alectelo. My father did, on occasion, manage to slip my devoted regard. There were no nursemaids on the ship, but I had no hesitation in demanding the attention of the pilots as if they had no work but to entertain me. I would point to dials and radar screens and demand in Szayeti *Szedo? Szedo? What?* the only word I had learned from the kitchen girls. In this way my earliest education in my people's language began as a hodgepodge of astronomy and technical terms, so that I knew *gravitational warp monitor* before *orange*, and *phototachometer* before *speed*. The pilots were tremendously patient with me—they had no choice—and so on the afternoon of the seventh day, my father had been attending to his own business for many hours before I grew bored and fled to find him before dinner.

A friendly ensign said he had gone to meet with the captain in their quarters, so I trotted down the hallways until I reached the door. My hand was on the door when I stopped: I could hear my father speaking.

He said: "... doing our best, Admiral, and Szayet expects you to understand—"

There was a staticky rush of speech, too soft for me to make out. I hesitated, then crouched at the door and put my eye to the crack. I could see my father's chair at his desk, and the bald spot at the back of his head, and the gold gleam where the wires of the Pearl came over the shell of his ear. Beyond him, so pixelated that her head was hardly recognizable as human, was a grey-haired woman with wide, pale eyes. It was she who was speaking, and whatever she was saying was making my father's fists curl and uncurl just below the surface of the desk.

When she was done he laughed, though I was not sure if he was amused. "I wish for that, too, Admiral. But please assure them once again that any—investment—remains as sound as it might have been ten years ago, or twenty. Even a hundred. In fact, if they *were* to personally speak with me—"

Another murmur of static. My father said, "No—no, not at all. Not at all. I don't mean to give that impression. Of course I'm very satisfied. I have every intention—" The woman said something else, ending in a lilting question, and my father's head bobbed up and down. "Thank you," he said. "I'd be in your—" He hesitated. "The delegation would appreciate it."

The blur of pixels shifted, a flash of white teeth, and said something, and raised its hand. My father coughed. "Oracle," he said. "The title is Oracle. If you please."

The head replied—was its tone apologetic? I couldn't tell—and disappeared.

I turned, then, and crept back down the corridor. I did not understand, and I did not want to. I must have mistaken him, or my eyes must have failed me. I had not seen my father bury his face in his hands.

We arrived at Ceiao on the morning of the eleventh day. It

was a harbor not at all like the one we had left. The Alectelan royal port was always near empty, crisp and clean and covered in quicksilver pearl and silent servants. It adjoined my sister's bedroom, and I had spent many a hot afternoon with her there, watching the ships heave across the ground away from our little palace toward the horizon.

But my first glimpse of Ceiao made my stomach jolt. There was *land* in that harbor, so much land that I thought I could run right off the edge of the planet and keep going. At home, all you would have needed to do was walk up a hill and look around, and you would have known at once how far you were from the sea—there was no question of where the world began, and none of where it ended. Ceiao had no such humility. The farther I looked, the farther the city spilled, toward and toward the sky and the horizon, tower over tower, courthouses and market roofs and gleaming video screens, belches of smoke that must have been factories, the distant glimmers of bridge and river and metro-track and street.

The port itself seemed like an anthill: not only the blue-cloaked Ceian soldiers, who I recognized at once from their constancy at our court, but Sintians, Itsaryeti, Medveyeti, the Cherekku with silver-painted lips who at home only emerged from their quarter to trade, Tllacah in knit caps and wide black skirts, Diajundot with braids reaching down to their waists, even a few tall white-booted women from far-flung Muntiru who I had only glimpsed before in our tutor's glitching holos. I tugged at my father's arm, wanting to ask if I could look at their tattoos, but he shrugged me off at once. He was scanning the docks, his jaw tight.

"There was meant to be an attendant," he said to one of our captains, a stiff-lipped woman whose name I never remembered after. "She said she would send an attendant—do you see someone? I can't read any of this damn signage, it's been years—is there an announcement on a video screen? Are we to be brought into the city?"

"Faifisto!" said a pleasant voice, and a Ceian woman shouldered past me. I say a woman—in reality she could not have been more than a few years older than me. But she was dressed in the blue cloak and tunic all the soldiers wore, and she stood at attention as straight as any of my father's men, and there was a golden pin on her shoulder to signify she was an officer. I stared up at my father, waiting for him to explain. This was some sort of joke, I thought—a costume—or this girl was some inadequate playmate, sent for my sake?

"I'm here to escort you to customs," said the girl. She had a wiry build, and straight hair cropped close to an angular, square-jawed face that might be called striking several years in the future, once the pimples had ceased to lay siege to it. "I was told you were the arrival from Szayet, yes? I'm not mistaken?"

Abruptly I was very sure she already knew she was not mistaken. Beneath the suggestion of prettiness there was a sharp amusement in her eyes, which I had seen before only when Arcelia and I went to the palace gardens to pour water into anthills. It was a look I distrusted instantly on another girl's face.

But my father only shook himself and coughed. "Yes," he said, "yes, erm—" I had never heard him stutter before.

The soldier girl's expression was perfectly courteous, except for her eyes. I thought unexpectedly that if she were truly my sister, I would have kicked her in the shins.

Instead I said, very loudly, "This is the Oracle of Szayet, and the voice of Alekso Undying. He is the lord of Alectelo, and king of the sunken cities, and the one who by blood and by prophecy carries the Pearl of the Dead. Who are *you*?"

The soldier girl's eyes crinkled.

"Oh," she said, "yes. They told me there would be a child. Fortune smiles. Well, Oracle, if—my mistake, Oracle of Szayet and...I'm terribly sorry, I promise Sintian was very amusing in school...voice of Alekso the Undead? Is that right?"

My cheeks went hot at once. My father coughed again, and glanced at me for just a moment. I had never seen him look at me like that.

"I understand you're my escort," he said shortly.

"No," said the soldier girl to me, "please, I don't want to offend. Say it again for me. The Oracle of Szayet and the voice of Alekso Undying." She said His name strangely, slurring the *s*, so that it sounded soft and mocking in her mouth. "And—now what else was there? Lord of Alectelo, and king of the cities in the kitchen sink?"

"May I ask whether Admiral Semfontan sent you?" my father snapped.

"Of course," said the soldier girl in a tone of mild surprise. "She said she'd be happy to speak with you in the next few days, if you happened to be able to fit her in. Is that important to you, then?"

My father bit out, "I would be honored."

The girl's face broke into a smile. "What good fortune," she said. "My name is Lieutenant Decretan, then. It's a pleasure to meet you." She stuck out a hand, and I watched in horror as my father took it and shook. "Let me escort you to customs."

The customs bay was a squat little room at the edge of the dock, occupied by a desk and glaring white lamps and a short, grey-haired official, who pushed her glasses up her nose and stared coolly at us as we swept in like a rain of gold. "The ship from Szayet, is it?" she said. "And Lieutenant Decretan."

The lieutenant smiled at her with the same mocking glint that she had shown us. "These are particular friends of Admiral Quinha Semfontan," she said. "If that makes a difference to you, Inspector."

The official shut her eyes. "And I expect in the name of the admiral they should be allowed to bring all sorts of disease through the city gates?" she said to the lieutenant, and smiled tight-lipped at my father. "My apologies," she said, "if Admiral Semfontan has told you differently."

"I have never—" my father began.

"I'm sure," said the official curtly. "You would've visited fifteen years ago? Twenty? I'm afraid the damsel plague was after that. We simply can't be too careful with foreigners these days. Well, Master—Caviro Faifisto—ah, the Oracle of Szayet, is it? Well, Master Oracle, have you or your party any food, plant material, animal products, wildlife products, laserwort, moneys in excess of five thousand dekar, maps or literature containing maps or literature referencing maps—"

Her voice droned on. I stood beside my father, feeling as hot as if I had been dipped in boiling water. No one had bowed to the two of us. No one had knelt. No one had even offered us bread and salt.

"Well—that's all of it," she said at last, jolting me out of my stupor. Lieutenant Decretan peeled herself off the wall, where she had been lounging with offensive casualness. "Last item. We'll need the cult paraphernalia, of course."

My father's soldiers, who had been pulling themselves sluggishly to attention, went still. The lieutenant's expression did not change, but she blinked very slowly. It was I who said, my voice as childish as it had ever sounded: "His what?"

The official bent over her desk to see me and raised her eyebrows. "Cult paraphernalia," she said slowly, sounding as if she were talking instead to a girl of four or five, and tapped her ear. "This is a *disestablishmentarian* planet. Have you heard of *disestablishmentarian* before?"

I had not. "Of course I have," I said.

"We'll keep your jewelry very safe," said the official, "don't worry," and bent back, and raised her eyebrows. "Master Oracle?"

My father put his hand to his ear, as if to take his glasses off. It was only then I understood what the little woman was demanding of him, and I gave a cry and sprang at the desk—but before I had gotten more than a foot closer, my father held up a hand, and one of his soldiers caught me around the waist and lifted me without effort so that I was kicking my legs fruitlessly into the air.

"Father," I sobbed, "Father, Father," but my father glanced at me only once—he might as well have been looking at a mote of dust—and he withdrew the Pearl of the Dead from the lobe of his ear, where it had spoken to him with the voice of my own dead god for as long as I had been alive.

The wires vanished first. If I had had enough warning or coherence to expect anything, I might have expected them to withdraw, slither down out from his skull and back into the pearl from which they had emerged. I would have been wrong. They crumbled into dust instantly, as if they were sand. A few of them left rough pale trails down my father's plump cheek, where a beard might have been. Except for that, it was as if they had never been at all.

There was a hole in my father's head, and it was bleeding.

My recollection is blurry after that, grown soft with time and shame. I remember wailing. I remember the arms of my father's guards, as tight as an ill-fitting dress. I remember how hot I felt, with humiliation and fury and something that it would take me twelve more years to begin to name—I was blind with that heat, deaf with it. I remember the soldier girl, her sharp handsome features, and how she eyed me with the amusement of an Alectelan watching pigeons fight in the street. For many years, I wondered whether she had ever forgotten me.

What I remember most of all, though, is how bare my father's head looked. How naked. He patted the trickle of blood from his temple, and our soldiers looked away.

"If she won't stay quiet, take her back to the ship," he said at last. I shrieked louder at that, sobbing denials, promises—but it was too late, and it had always been too late, and all I could think, buried in my blankets on our ship that night with the Szayeti carvings flat and unmoving above me, was that at least when Arcelia knew, she would not hate me for being chosen anymore.

CHAPTER

FOUR

CEIRRAN

Sir, with all respect," said the civilian, "I think you ought to just land at Alectelo Harbor?"

We hadn't expected to need a Szayeti expert. Strictly speaking, we hadn't gotten one. Joaquim Nequeiron—who, according to Galvão's report blinking on my tablet, had served his seven years without promotion, slipped immediately into a failed jewel trade entirely on the strength of a loan from his wealthy father, and spent my war quailing in that father's run-down villa on one of our local satellites—was a wide-eyed stick insect of a man, with a voice like a broken zipper. But all of his years trading before the war had been whiled away counting waves in Alectelo, and to my great annoyance, no one in my own squadron could claim the same experience. It made sense, of course: Quinha had handpicked her soldiers many years ago, as had I. If she had fled toward Madinabia, we would have known what we were walking into as well as we knew our names. I suppose she had a little sense left in her.

I had known the last king myself, of course, though no one had known him as well as Quinha. But I had not ever been to Szayet, nor to Kutayet, nor Itsaryet nor Belkayet nor any of the other planets of the Swordbelt Arm. I had spoken out in the Merchants' Council once in support of a resolution naming the Szayeti king a friend of Ceiao, and been paid three thousand dekar for it, but I had needed no special knowledge of the planet to do *that*. All my victories in Ceiao's wars gave me only a Ceian eye to the quarter of the galaxy that had once been the ancient Sintian Empire.

Even if Madinabia's subjugation, completed in the spiral arm of the Shieldmirror light-millennia from here, had not taken so many long and terrible years, I do not know if I would have ever returned to the Swordbelt Arm. I had once known a planet near here very well. I had never seen virtue in revisiting the past.

"Citizen, with all *respect*," I said, "the queen of Szayet is not our generous hostess. I understand the local tradition. Tell me what to do once we have made contact."

"It's not just the local tradition, sir?" said the civilian. He was in fact still on his father's run-down villa, and the holo of his face was blurred heavily with the distance. "*Dom* Caviro has been on the throne for three centuries, sir, and the Szayeti have history for millennia before that. The family's had to put down more than a few rebellions on the outlying islands before. It's no disrespect meant to you, sir, but this is her territory, and she needs to show she's strong in it. If it were you on the planet, sir, and her in the ship, she'd come to you and bend the knee without a thought."

"If her position were so precarious," I said patiently, ignoring how Galvão's face pinched at *bend the knee*, "how would her family have kept the throne through any rebellion at all? The Szayeti may have long memories, but three centuries is no eyeblink."

"They're not all Szayeti, sir?" Nequeiron said. "The population's a mess—it's like a Nevede harbor on market day. Natives for the most part, of course, but it's *full* of Sintians. Alekso left half a city's worth behind him, and when Caviro carted the corpse there he brought even more. And besides that there's the modern Sintians who come for the Library, and the Diajundot who come for the treasure-hunting, and there's even a Cherekku quarter—of course, there's always a Cherekku quarter—"

"Diverse," I said. "I understand."

"Diverse, sir," Nequeiron agreed.

"But they *are* governable," I prodded. Getting useful information from my own men was difficult enough, but getting it out of a civilian was like pulling teeth. "They are governed. Even Faifisto managed it. They have the Aleksan cult"—Galvão's wince was palpable—"they have fine enough farming on what little land is left, they have the treasure—"

"The treasure is sunken, sir," said Nequeiron, more confidently.

"Of course," I said, "but it washes up every morning. Every good name in Ceiao has a few Twentieth Dynasty diamonds lying around her house. *When I came, gold flowed like a river; all rivers flow into the sea.*" Nequeiron looked blank. "It is what Alekso of Sintia said about the place," I said, "very famously. Was he wrong?"

"Yes, sir," said Nequeiron, "or—no, sir, but—it doesn't wash up reliably, sir? And not in any real quantity. There's all sorts of adventurers diving into the ruins of the old cities—I lost thousands of dekar to smugglers!—but digging up a whole planet of tablets and temples and ship fleets and gold without damage needs *fleets* of undersea drones, steel spiders, lifters and ladders and submarine cranes—equipment that they'd need half a continent of mines to build, anyway, sir, and they haven't got continents to spare. What scrap metal they can get has to go toward the fleet they've got. Or if they wanted ore, they'd need the spare cash to buy it from us, and they can't get the cash without digging up the treasure. It's why merchants haven't overrun the place already, sir. I hardly made a living on the resale. They're sitting on top of a fortune, but they're poorer than a shoeless man in Little Muntiru."

"It seems to me," I said, "that if a queen wanted to relieve herself of some debt, she could lift the ban on selling Ceians the diving rights."

"*Religion!*" wailed Nequeiron. His voice jumped to such an extent that the feedback in the holo squealed. "Holy *ground*—they say *Alekso put the old world in the water*, and *Alekso's people must take it out again*—but we *know* it's because *they* know we'll pay centonos on the dekar for it, and make a *fortune*, and they'd rather no one make the money at all!" He coughed. "Sir," he added.

"What about that pearl?" I said.

"They finished diving for the last of that in the Oracle's great-aunt's time," said Nequeiron resentfully, and then, understanding my meaning: "Oh! It's a treasure to them, sir—but not to us? Besides, they'd never let go of it."

I drummed my fingers on the desk. "There's no way to seize it, I suppose."

"You could try, sir," said Nequeiron, "but you'd be in the middle of a riot before you got past opening negotiations. It's a cult unto itself, sir? It would be like—" He rolled his eyes to the heavens, visibly struggling for the Ceian equivalent.

"It would create a lot of trouble," I said hastily.

"A lot of trouble, sir," Nequeiron agreed. "More trouble than money."

I caught Ana's eye over his shoulder. "Over a computer?" I said.

"A computer that can mimic Alekso of Sintia pretty well, to be fair, sir," said Nequeiron. "So they say, anyway. You know how fast quicksilver pearl is. All you'd need to do is let it rummage around in your skull."

"Is that what they say?" I said. "That it can mimic Alekso *pretty well*?"

Nequeiron closed his eyes and sighed with true Ceian unhappiness. "They say, sir," he said at last, "that at the moment of his death, Alekso of Sintia uploaded his soul."

Nearly the whole bridge flinched at that. Only Ana was still. Her fingers were tapping on her mouth, and she kept trying to catch my eye. "And despite the power of this cult," I said, ignoring her, "it remains so important that the queen should preserve her dignity that she is terrified of the prospect of my landing anywhere but her front door?"

"Well," said Nequeiron, "I mean, the sister?"

"Ah," I said, pleased at last. "Tell me about the sister."

Nequeiron shrugged. "There isn't much to tell, sir. About twelve minutes older, I think. They say her father favored her. I wager that's why she took the name when she declared herself queen? More or less popular in the city, before the war. Bad luck the real queen got hold of the Pearl."

"Friend to the people," I said. It had been the first thing I had noticed in Galvão's report.

Nequeiron's mouth pinched. "The people don't have high *standards*," he said to my raised eyebrow. "She learned their horrible little language. That's *friend*, to them. My sister—Izabel who took over the shop, not Marcela who—anyway, she told me she said she would lower taxes. She said she would give them holidays. They're a backwater mob, sir. It's not like it's hard to buy them."

I knew a little more of mobs than Nequeiron, both in backwaters and in the heart of Ceiao itself, but I kept that well to myself. "And would she?" I said. "Lower taxes?"

"None of them would, sir," said Nequeiron. "None of them will ever pay off the debt. The queen is the same as her father—she lives on cactus fruit and bathes in mare's milk. It's only that her father spent the money that was left on the dole, and *she* spends it on new guardsmen, and new ships, and new walls to build around the palace. And it's money she doesn't have, sir. None of them will ever have it, not until Alekso can conjure divers out of thin air."

I understood then, and I nodded to Galvão. "Send the holo," I said. "Find an island not far from the city. Somewhere small. We'll meet her there."

Galvão saluted. Nequeiron said, unhappily, "Sir," but I dismissed the holo with a wave of my hand. Ceiao had its own dignities to preserve, and I would not abandon them by acting entirely as the Oracle's guest. But I knew, now: Even a civilian had seen how desperate the queen was to preserve her pride. In the face of that, my empire might be magnanimous.

Laureathan had been drifting down the tide swell for the last hour, and was beginning to list toward the sun. I barked the petty officers into action and watched their flurry of salutes with a ripple of the first real satisfaction I had felt that morning.

In my quarters my tablet was waiting for me, blinking with today's data packet from Ceiao: four holos from my informants in the city on the doings of local gangs I supported, two from my husband on domestic matters, one public commendation from the Merchants' Council for absolutely nothing whatsoever, and forty private messages from individual councillors who had supported Quinha in the war, each of which offered me gifts or invited me to dinners or praised my war on Madinabia or, from the slowest or most naive members, bluntly pleaded with me to spare their careers. I dismissed them all, though I made a note to have Ana make a list of the councillors who had begged.

Then I pulled up a map of Szayet, flicked it to its largest size, and called up projections of everywhere the Szayeti ocean had washed up treasure worth over five hundred dekar in the last five years.

I had thought I was being sensibly limited in my search. Immediately I discovered I was not. The holo sprouted like a porcupine. I groped for the tablet and pulled the globe down to what I hoped was a reasonable size, blinking furiously against the glare and somewhat disappointed Ana was not there to laugh at me.

What a forest of light I now held in my hands! The tablet had called up cameos of the most costly items, and they winked at me from every square inch of space: a curved knife with red diamonds at its hilt, a gleaming jade hippopotamus the size of my head, a funerary figurine of pure silver, a blue-glazed amulet of a man with a lion's head. Even that which was not art was of value: aluminum and steel in astonishing quantities, petrified wood floating up from underwater forests, ivory and obsidian and marble, even palladium and uranium, though only a team of the very strongest divers could bring up the latter. Billions of tablets had gone under the sea, but hundreds of thousands had survived, preserved in metal boxes by a stroke of luck or by what the Szayeti might have called a miracle. Whole ships lay under Szayet's oceans, with molecules of antimatter still bubbling at their cores.

And there was the pearl—always the pearl. The oysters might have gone extinct everywhere but Ceiao, but the stuff itself remained, lining markets and temples and rooftops. The computing capacity in quicksilver pearl! With the quantities of it that had once been on the planet, *Dom* Caviro might have developed navigation computers for a fleet of ships that could have been laid end to end across the galaxy—and they used it to *decorate*. Some of it was degraded now, of course, after years under the unkind ministrations of harbor exhaust and human activity seeping into the waters, but so much was salvageable, so much remained. At home, our scholars said the sacred was poison to the mind. I didn't know whether I believed it true, but the world would have been very different had different things been sacred to the Szayeti kings.

"Ceirran," said Ana at the door, "they've found—ah." She strolled to the projection and flicked at one of the cameos, a thin chain of diamonds, which might have been a bracelet or necklace. "I like this one."

"Then you will need to ask Quinha for it," I said. "I recall she bought it four years ago for her collection."

Ana looked at the chain for a moment, her face unreadable. At last she said, "What's the world coming to? A year now we've been fighting, and nobody's gotten rich yet."

"Civil war makes for poorer plunder than pillage, Anita," I said.

"Don't I know it," Ana said. "But I'll pick up one of these pretty war trophies, sooner or later. You watch."

CHAPTER FIVE

GRACIA

There was not much room on the satellite, but I was used to that. It was larger than prison.

It was difficult to tell whether the smuggler was glad to have us, those first six days after our escape. She liked to talk, as I had found, but her conversation went no further than her business and herself. She appeared to run a very minor trading hub on the satellite, where other smugglers stopped every few days for tea and highly profane discussion—or so Zorione told me, at any rate, and I had no choice but to rely on her recollections. Every visitor that arrived sent me running to a storage closet, with Zorione guarding the door.

I would not have had much interest in talking to the other smugglers, even if I had been able to trust them. Zorione reported that their subjects of conversation, too, were limited: their prices, their troubles in the ether, the profligacy of my sister, the Ceian war.

Everyone knew about the Ceian war. You needed to, otherwise

the Ceians would tell you about it. Even I, who had followed Ceiao's doings with great interest these last ten years and Quinha Semfontan's with an eye like an eagle's, grew weary of finding and re-finding its root.

It was so difficult, in any case, to trace what was enmity and what was friendship among the Ceians. I knew that at one time some years ago, just before Admiral Ceirran's rapid and total conquest of Ceiao's neighbor Madinabia and its thirteen moons, Admiral Semfontan and Ceirran had sat at a Ceian table and divided the galaxy between themselves as if we were a peeled orange. And then Ceirran had turned from Madinabia to Far Madinabia and to the rest of the Shieldmirror, and then Admiral Semfontan had begun to complain that Ceirran was covering himself in a great deal of gold and glory and sending Ceiao not a great deal of money, and when Ceirran had ignored this, she had said that in addition to this he was promoting within his portion of the army men of no lineage and little talent whose only redeeming quality was their loyalty to his person, and when he had ignored this, too, she had said that what was more, he was advocating for laws in Ceiao that would favor cultists and their habits over free-thinking Ceians, all so that he might build them into a power base for himself, and rule the city by gang warfare and bribery. And then Ceirran had said that Admiral Semfontan had spent years deliberately corralling the city into a place that might be ruled by gang warfare and bribery, and that rather than principled she was only jealous; then Admiral Semfontan had said that Ceirran governed Madinabia as a cult and had made himself its high priest, and had him declared a criminal; then Ceirran had come back to the city with a conquering army and driven Admiral Semfontan away, and he had been declared commander of all the fleet. But this was all for political reasons, having to do with the balance of power and a conspiracy that had been put down several years back and another civil war decades before that, and land reform on Ceiao itself, and immigration, and imperial expansion, and in this era of Ceian's council politics, all of this had great consequences for Ceian views of the Ceian military, and for Ceian identity now that Ceiao's territory had grown to such an extent, and for all sorts of Ceian ideas about what Ceiao was and how Ceiao should be and why Ceiao did anything and, most importantly, how Ceians felt about it. There were so many of these arguments in the marketplace between visiting Ceians that I began to worry another broken friendship would plunge the empire for the fifth time into civil war. In a real sense, being cut off from talk had been something of a relief.

Yes, all right. That was a lie.

On days when the satellite had no guests, I paced it like a caged animal, settling only when Zorione attempted to placate me with tea or conversation. I was unused to needing to receive information through data packet—it had been common enough when I was at court and my father still lived, and every piece of news from the empire came in floods every morning—but when I had been fighting in the streets of Alectelo, everything I wanted to know was on the surface of the planet, and no delay was necessary. Here, on the edge of the Szayeti atmosphere, even an hour's waiting was interminable.

What news I did receive made me no happier. Arcelia was cleaning up the last remnants of our war. Some of my few remaining soldiers had been able to make it off-planet, as I had, but many had not. My sister was not a merciful woman. Neither was I.

The smuggler watched me the morning of the sixth day, as I strode back and forth along the perimeter of the satellite's central room, flicking through a tablet with the latest lists of executions. "It makes me dizzy to look at you," she said at last. "Is there any use to this?"

Zorione started—she did not like how the smuggler spoke to me. I shook my head at her. "It doesn't matter whether there's use," I said. "I do still have *some* duty."

The smuggler snorted gently at this, which I ignored. Zorione did not. "Was it funny when she was driven to exile by the false prophet?" she demanded. "Was it funny when she was attacked at the gate of her own home?"

"It depends on how you look at things," said the smuggler implacably.

"If you wanted to be a respectable trader," Zorione snapped, "you would learn courtesy to your betters."

The smuggler grinned unpleasantly. "I've been a respectable trader. I've had enough of courtesy."

"You never were," said Zorione. "Otherwise—"

"—why would I be smuggling?" said the smuggler, and curled her lip. "You have had little misfortune in your life, merchant."

Zorione said, quite quietly, "You don't know what my life has had."

I looked sharply at her, afraid she would drop her cover, but the smuggler shrugged. "Perhaps I don't," she said. "Nevertheless. I used to import quicksilver pearl. This was in *her* father's time." She jerked her head at me. "Twenty years back, maybe. People remembered when there were the quicksilver oysters living on Szayet then. They were desperate—so. I bought pearl from Ceiao, where they were wise enough to breed them. I paid good Szayeti men to ship it for me. I sold it in the Summer Market, and I made more gold than you can imagine. Staked all I had on each shipment, and why not? It's common sense, yes? To bet big on a sure thing?"

She paused to toss back her liquor. "So," she said, and shrugged again. "The Oracle wants dozens of crates of good Ceian wine, very urgent, top priority. He's holding a feast for some Ceian general. He wants to show her she's such a friend to the Szayeti people. What the Oracle wants, the Oracle gets. The quickest ship from Ceiao was the one with my shipments of pearl on it..."

I exhaled softly. The smuggler grinned without humor.

"It's not all his fault, I think," she said. "Any dockworker with half a brain in her would know every cargo jostles a little. All it takes is one bottle to break."

Every native-born Alectelan knows what alcohol does to quicksilver pearl. My father had loved his feasts, but he savored his liquor slowly, and I had never seen him truly drunk. It was too dangerous to be clumsy with a full cup around the Pearl of the Dead. In a cargo hold full of pearls, I could only imagine the chain reaction.

"I'm sorry," I said.

"I think you are even telling the truth," said the smuggler, and laughed a little, sounding surprised at herself. "What does it matter? What's done is done. You know that as well as anyone, princess."

I did, but reminding her would have been the sort of thing my father would have done. "Still," I said.

"Still," said the smuggler, "the general from Ceiao thanks him, leaves the feast, and goes to plant her flag on Belkayet. Thirty days later, the Ceian governor installs himself." She busied herself with her tablet, where a series of numbers was scrolling down. "I hope it was expensive wine."

Belkayet was the planet nearest Szayet. It had been one of the last independent worlds in the Swordbelt Arm to fall under Ceiao's control. There were not many of us left.

That night, in the little room where our two cots lay, I once again called up the list of executions from my tablet and stared at the glimmering litany, chin propped on my hands. Not all of the names were names I knew. My rebellion had not been small, and my sister's vengeance did not discriminate. But each of them,

I knew, was a face I had at the very least seen, a hand I had clasped, a head I had touched in blessing. There were so many who had died. There were still so many left for my sister to kill.

"Belkayet," I said.

"Princess?" said Zorione.

"They were Szayet's colony once," I said. "Only for a generation, and then they rose up and installed their own lords and ladies again—but the Belkayeti throne has always remembered. Even under the Ceian governor, the barons have kept their funds, their reserve guard. If I went to those barons, and declared myself a rebel against the Szayeti throne—"

"Princess," said Zorione, looking alarmed. "When you say *rebel*—"

"They would never send troops to fight for the rightful heir of the Pearl," I said. "Not that they even take the word of the Pearl for the Undying's true word." Szayet was the only planet in the Swordbelt Arm where Alekso's soul, through the medium of the Oracles, ruled as king. Very few of Alekso's sworn companions had held Caviro as a friend, and none had wanted to accept that Alekso, after His death, had chosen my ancestor as sole disciple. The Swordbelt Arm, parceled out among them over a decade of war, was divided likewise in its faith. The Belkayeti claimed Alekso's spirit had gone to reside in the void between worlds, the Itsaryeti and Medveyeti that He had gone into the afterlife and struck down its demons and become its king. The Kutayeti went so far as to say Caviro had lied about bringing His corpse to Alectelo, and the body in the tomb was not His body at all, and He had instead been burned in His palace in the capital city of Kutayet and now dwelled for eternity in every temple flame. No two Sintians had ever been able to agree on what happened to Alekso's spirit at all, but it hardly mattered now; they had been under Ceiao's dominion for a century.

"Still," I said, "they have neither any reason to strengthen the

Szayeti throne nor any reason to uphold Szayeti justice. But if I said that I was *not* the heir, but rather a would-be usurper—if I begged them to send reinforcements to the rebels, to stop the executions, to help me go to war against the true, the rightful queen—"

Zorione's face had gone gaunt and pale. "But what about the trial?" she said. "Your rights, madam? If you gave up your legal standing, abandoned your claim, you could not bring a suit to the priests; they could never name you Holiest before the people."

"Perhaps it would not matter whether the people thought I was the Holiest," I said, "if I held the palace." My hand drifted up to the list of the dead, flotsam in the air. "If I brought reinforcements to the rebel troops. If I stopped their dying—for even a day."

"Princess," said Zorione softly, "they fought in your name, for the truth of your cause. They do not go before the firing squad because they want to be heretics. They do it because—because they believe."

I stared at the list of names again, flickering gold around my hand. Then I clenched my fist, and they vanished.

"No matter what they are dying for," I said, "they are dying."

I was slow getting up that seventh morning, when the imaginary Kutayeti ship was due to arrive with its pearls that did not exist, and did not look at my tablet for nearly an hour. When I did pull it into my lap, it was not to look at my data packets, or at any of the maps of Alectelo that had taken my attention over the last weeks and months, but to slowly, painstakingly compose a letter. I could hardly look at the words as I typed them.

When at last that afternoon I emerged from the little room where our cots lay, Zorione and the smuggler were standing by the window in the central room overlooking the planet, conferring in hushed tones. When they saw me enter, Zorione stood to attention at once.

"Princess," she said. "Do you have orders? Do you have a plan?"

"Ah," I said, "the Kutayeti ship hasn't yet arrived? Madam Buquista, you'll need to arrange a call. We must delay a few days longer while we wait for a reply. Perhaps further payments to the consortium—"

She opened her mouth to reply, but the smuggler beat her to it: She laughed aloud.

"You haven't heard?" she said. "Worse luck for you. Matheus Ceirran has come to the City of Endless Pearl."

CHAPTER SIX

CEIRRAN

I had been thirteen years old when Quinha Semfontan sent me to Medveyet.

Not that I knew it was her then, of course. She became careless in her old age, and obvious, and bold; but in those young days of the empire there was a value placed on subtlety, higher than the one placed on ships and steel. It made you seem clever, to be a name unspoken. It made you seem quick, and graceful, and safe. People said that Ceiao had grown violent, those next fifteen years, but it showed their ignorance to say it. It had only grown crass.

I say young—of course the empire was hardly young. Of course I was hardly young, a soldier trained and grown. I had only felt very young at the time.

I had been born into the merchant class, but my father was dead, caught fever on an outpost near Sintia, and my mother disgraced and imprisoned in some interminable scandal regarding customs and tax. I was alone in the world, and knew it. Ceiao has always been proudly, noisily free of any desire to pass on the sins of the father—but in practice, there had been no one to buy my commission, no one to bribe and persuade my way into a station or planet that would launch me into glory. If Quinha hadn't been watching the cadet lists, she liked to say afterward, I likely would have died a foot soldier in some muddy trench in Kutayet. I let her. It made her happy to say it. Besides, at that time it afforded me much, and cost me nothing, to pretend myself as grateful as she wished me to be.

And in any case, I had not understood until my first posting how entirely boredom had taken hold of me in Ceiao. In cadet school I had run up the scores on each game the petty officers could provide until the sandboxes ended and the leaderboards broke. In Medveyet's hills and its snowy forests, though, there was at last no end to the world. I chased rebels into their caves and out of them. I met with fanatics and warlords, and learned to speak to them with a harsh tongue and a silver tongue and a flurry of gifts and a hand on my gun. I flew in a squadron, and then directed one, in quick, sharp battle-blasts across Medveyeti sky. I was stationed in young Prince Stanislau's honor guard for a year, and I learned how to speak to him, too, and the other lieutenants called me a Medveyeti princess and I let them, because the number of Ceians in the queen's honor guard doubled the first spring I was there and tripled the summer after.

When I returned, I was twenty, wiser, stronger, newly appointed inspector of one of the more lucrative river harbors, and filled with a nearly unbearable curiosity. It didn't take long to follow the trail of Quinha's hand in my posting—I thought myself very clever, and realized only years afterward how badly she had wanted to be followed—and met with her in her home, a sprawling penthouse just down the street from the Libeiracópolan, overflowing with imported carpets and jewels and decades-old medals. It became apparent that I remained in need of a patron. It became apparent that Quinha would one day be in need of an ally. Fine. I liked the thought of being the sort of man whose alliance was a valuable commodity. Quinha had guessed that much about me, too.

How do I remember her best? She was a difficult woman to pin down, Admiral Semfontan. She was deceptively great, deceptively opulent, like a sleeping dragon. I remember her at her dinner parties, grinning with cup in hand, how we in her entourage would swirl and flirt and snarl and laugh at all of her awful jokes. I remember her on the Merchants' Council, when she would watch the guild leaders haggle through half-lidded eyes. I remember the gifts she would give to her friends at the New Year in autumn, gold and paintings, rare animals from Diajunda and elaborate mosaics, new engines for their old ships, always beautiful, always costly, always a little more than the recipient could afford, and they would thank her profusely, and kiss her hand.

She asked me often for advice on these gifts: Would a certain banker prefer this ruby necklace or that one? Would the governor of Cherekku rather have a rare book of little-known Sintian philosophy, or this shipment of wine from the vineyard where he grew up? In this way she taught me to navigate like star charts those who made up what she called the quality of our city: how to distinguish between money and power, how to foment a grudge or end one, how to appease or to leave hungry. She was an unerring judge of character, my friend. I should say, rather, she was an unerring judge of taste: She knew precisely what any person wanted, and how dearly they wanted it, and how grateful they would be if she gave it to them.

Or perhaps I distort my memory. Perhaps character is what she knew, after all, and I lie to comfort myself, and to make her into a spider in my heart. I loved her once, and in the absence of love, all its old belongings become excess freight.

This, then, is how I remember her best. I was eight months besieging Madinabia before anyone realized I was actually going to win the war. Once they did, they flooded down in torrents to kiss my hand, setting up tent after tent on the grim grey craters of Madinabia K where I'd made base camp and causing enough distraction I nearly considered asking the Merchants' Council to ban them from the system. Quinha was neither the first nor the last, but she was the only one I was glad to see, and she had brought a case of good Ceian wine, and that night we drank until the planet rose and turned the iced-over canyons outside my tent door into waterfalls of gold.

Anita had been with us, of course, but begged off before long to go find some petty officer she'd been eyeing. Quinha watched her consideringly as she disappeared into the hazy planetlight, and said, "She wasn't worth the effort, you know. Amusing, I'll grant you, but hardly reliable."

"Are you still jealous," I said, "after all this time? She can't be the first captain you've had poached away."

"Oh, you'd be shocked," said Quinha, and swilled the dregs around the bottom of her glass. "Very few people manage to steal from me. I am difficult to fool, and rarely surprised."

"Now that *is* shocking," I said. "Here I was planning to ask you for advice on getting my ships through Madinabia G's atmosphere without losing half of them."

"And so you should!" said Quinha. "Why in the world not? Have you forgotten all I did in the Swordbelt Campaigns? And Belkayet was ringed round with warships as thick as your skull! I tell you, I climbed in my fighter and took two good men—"

"You wouldn't let me forget if I wanted to," I said, and laughed at her affronted face. "I only mean to say, I think an old officer ought to be used to being surprised. Should I be worried you won't know what to do when your plans make contact with the enemy?"

"Perhaps I'm not so old," she said peevishly, and then laughed herself, unwillingly, at my expression. "Top up my cup again. If I'm in this sort of mood, it needs filling."

I leaned over my table to pour. She had given that to me, too, a sturdy old wooden thing, which folded into quarters when we needed to transport it, and whose legs and edges were carved in an intricate Madinabic pattern of running wolves. I treasured it dearly, and she knew it. As I bent over it with the bottle, though, she caught my chin between her fingers, her eyes glinting.

"Straighten your back, Matheus," she said. "You've been abroad too long, I think. Have you already forgotten? A Ceian bows to no one."

I thought of that, as we climbed down from the ladder and into our rubber lifeboats. Ahead of us, through the spray, Alectelo was wavering like a mirage. They said it was the loveliest city in all its spiral arm. Under the high morning sun, though, it threw so much light on the water that my men squinted and murmured with irritation. Whether or not it was as splendid as the stories, we would have been hard-pressed to describe one tower.

Alectelo is an island city. It's had to be. Alekso sank half the planet underwater when he smashed through on his way to Cherekku, and when he lent the place to Caviro a month before he died, the man never bothered to build back more than the land needed for farming. On Ceiao we might've drawn the shoreline out into the water, spiderwebbed bridges from island to island, thrown soil onto steel beams, made the sunken world into a new one of iron and glass—but even if the Szayeti wanted to, they couldn't. All their mines and metal are twenty fathoms deep. Besides, they take it as a great blessing.

Nearly all these Aleksan planets think it a great blessing, the things that dead emperor did to their homes and their lives. Even Ceiao used to, once.

The island the queen's spokeswoman had agreed to was a humped little thing, without much more on it than huddled poplars and a lanky, teetering comms tower that flickered a red greeting as we approached. Nequeiron had named it as the highest point of some old Fourteenth Dynasty capital, which had been in disrepair long before the Sintians had drowned it. As its shores swelled up before us, I saw Anita in the lifeboat in front of me lean over and squint down into the water. A moment later she sat up again, a quizzical set to her mouth.

"What can you see?" I asked her, once the currents had pushed our boats close enough together that I would not have to shout.

"Oh," she said in an odd tone, "nothing you could sell."

I looked down. Running flat on the seabed, many fathoms below, were the wavering edges of a railway. It had been covered almost entirely by the sand, and what wasn't sand was grey concrete without feature or crack, but there was a tram on it, a few yards behind us. Its roof was speckled with silver studs, and its walls were a line of gleaming black windows. When I squinted, I could see the shadow of a curving steel wire, flung out along its side. This had been a cable car.

There was a sudden swell in current, and my oarsmen fought to steady the boat. When we were upright again, I looked back at the tram. The angle of the sun had changed. The front window of the car was not entirely black now: There was something white in it, just visible where the light slanted through the water. It was strangely shaped, almost like a fan, and it was pressed up against the glass, where it had been clawing—

I jerked my eyes away. The swell had carried Anita farther from me. I could hear her distantly, laughing at some dirty joke her oarsman had told. We were nearly at the shoreline, and my own rowers were beginning to unstrap their life vests, and to tighten their gun belts across their torsos. I curled my hand over my own gun where it sat at my hip, warm with sun, and felt how it fit neatly into my hand, just as it had been made to. I inhaled—the heat of the morning, the smell of brine—and exhaled again.

The Szayeti faction were arranged on the beach in front of a row of wooden boats, looking like a bouquet of bulky carnations. In their midst stood a small woman in a robe and a gauze veil that entirely covered her face. Nequeiron had warned us that the queen would likely be surrounded by priests—Faifisto always had been, when he rode through Alectelo's streets—but to my eye, the delegation was military in its entirety. It was as well not to deal with the cultists, of course, but it also made me uneasy. It was early for false intelligence.

We clambered from our boats, drawing into a ragged line. I was at its head, Galvão at my side—I had no intention of letting Anita attempt diplomacy—and set in a forward march along the pebbles and dried curls of seaweed. As we drew closer, I saw that the veiled queen was holding something in her hands: a wooden box, about the length and width of a tablet and a handspan high.

"Oracle Arcelia Caviro Diomata," said Galvão, and saluted with great propriety. The queen's veil fluttered with her exhale. "On behalf of Ceiao and the commander, may I express what a pleasure it is to arrive in your historic homeland."

"And what an honor to receive such distinguished guests," said one of the Szayeti soldiers, and bowed deeply in return. It made my back hurt to watch her. "On your arrival from beyond the sky, we welcome you home to the earth"—she proffered a silver tray—"and the sea."

The bread was stale and the salt refined well out of savor, but that was no worse than I'd expected. I made as if I enjoyed it, and looked hard at Anita, who was pulling appalling faces to the amusement of a blushing lieutenant. She caught my eye and subsided.

"We're moved by your generosity," said Galvão. "Unfortunately, the commander is here on a matter of some delicacy and haste. A terrible enemy of the people of Ceiao is arrived on your shores, and likely planning to do you great violence. As we hope you remember, Oracle, your father considered the commander not only a protector, but a friend. In the name—"

The queen held up a red-gloved hand, which so startled me I nearly laughed. Galvão's jaw flexed.

"We know the matter on which you arrive, Commander," she said in Ceian. Her voice was sweet and surprisingly clear, with only a flicker of an accent on the sibilants. "Those of us in the Empty Grave of the Ever-Living God are already familiar with Admiral Semfontan's movements."

"What good fortune," I said pleasantly. "That will save us some time. May I ask whether you and the admiral have already met?"

That got a reaction from the Szayeti faction I had not anticipated: A half dozen of the soldiers burst into snickering. Galvão, who had been beginning to recover from looking as if he were about to pop, drew himself up to his full height again at once, but I coughed a little.

"Shall I take it that you have not met with the admiral?" I said.

"I was hoping we might begin differently, Commander," said the queen. "In good faith."

Faith was not a word I liked to hear on Szayet, and *good faith* a phrase I liked to hear nowhere in the galaxy. It so rarely led to sincere negotiation. "My lady," I said.

"Holiest," said a soldier sharply to me.

"Madam Oracle," I said, without looking at him. "I understand that Admiral Semfontan was a great friend to your father. I confess that I hoped to begin, rather, with something akin to honesty. You have certainly spoken with the admiral, and there is no benefit in pretending otherwise. I suggest you make a clean breast of the matter. What did she offer you?"

The soldier sputtered. Behind me, so softly that I would not have heard it had I not been listening, Anita snorted. But the young queen did neither. Instead, she lifted one gloved hand and pulled aside the veil over her face, so that she was looking into my eyes.

I had been able to tell, even with the veil, that Arcelia Caviro Diomata was lovely. Without it, she was beautiful. She had a wide, heart-shaped face with high cheekbones, and a hooked nose and a full red mouth, and a warmth to her brown skin, so that when the sun from the ocean caught it, it flushed with gold. Her hair was loose, and it tumbled over her shoulders like ivy. She was looking up at me through kohl-darkened eyelashes, her eyes wide and innocent.

She said in that same low, sweet voice, "Commander Ceirran, do you think *I* was a great friend to my father?"

That promised trouble, too. "I would not presume, Madam Oracle," I said politely.

"You might presume," she said. "I could not stop you."

That startled me. I had understood the queen to be, as Anita had said, a woman of strategy. I had therefore assumed her to be a woman of delicacy. At the very least, I had expected tact.

She smiled a little at my face. "I confess," she said, "I intend to begin with honesty, too. I am hoping, Commander, that you and I will have much to give each other."

"To give each other," I said, very slowly.

The queen smiled wider, and then she opened the box in her arms and tipped it over. The thing that had been inside it thumped onto the shore, bounced, and rolled. When it stilled at last, in a tangle of grey hair and smeared red sand, it was facing toward the sky.

It was the first time in many years that I had seen Quinha look surprised.

CHAPTER

SEVEN

GRACIA

When I was very young, I thought everyone in the world must have a twin somewhere. How else would they know their reflections?

By the time I could read and write I had left this fantasy behind me. But Arcelia and I still stood by our bedsides in the mornings staring into each other's faces, she brushing an eyelash from my cheek, me threading a loose hair into her long black braid. We were never the sort of sisters who dressed alike—she was a rough-and-tumble child, who rarely spent a moment inside the palace walls that she could spend in its parks or gardens or, in our rare moments of escape from Zorione's loving clutches, the guards' barracks beside them. She would return with scraped knees and red knuckles, having dared the palace guards' children to fight her, and fought them regardless when they said no. Later, when she was grown, it was the treasure-divers that she loved, and their tight-braided hair and black gloves and tunics with billowing sleeves, and the swagger to their walk. It was in their fashions that she dressed herself, when she was allowed to dress as she liked.

But these things never appealed to me. What I loved was the palace itself. It went on forever in those days, a rambling maze of staircase and trapdoor and ladder and balcony, and behind every corner was a secret passage, and behind every archway a hoard of treasure. We found my three-times-great-grandfather Cipriano's library, an unnavigable labyrinth of barely balanced tablet stacks full of staticking holos and Sintian political essays, half of which Zorione confiscated at once as inappropriate for young girls; my great-aunt Azahara's armory, which Arcelia sprang upon like a lion so that she and I could play war in the garden until Zorione rushed down and wailed over the state of the swords; even, on one bitter grey afternoon while a storm lashed at the windows, my nine-times-great-grandparent Ciezo's wardrobe, stuffed with glittering morning robes and dresses and gowns. This I pillaged at once, though they had been twice my size when they had worn the things, and I made Arcelia watch me as I paraded up and down our hallways with their flopping gem-embroidered slippers on my feet and their silver organza robe fluttering behind me, declaiming in what little Malisintian I had.

Arcelia complained, of course—firstly, that she wanted to go out in the storm and find mud puddles and wished I would take those silly things off, and secondly, that she wanted to go out in the storm and she didn't *care* if I took those silly things off, and what did it matter, as long as I came with her? But I was stubborn—more stubborn than was my usual habit then, in the face of any of my sister's wants—and we stood our ground and screamed at each other, not realizing how loud our voices were growing or not caring, until Zorione burst through the door and shrieked louder than both of us put together.

But my father appeared in our rooms that night. This was

rarer than three full moons, and Arcelia and I clung to his legs as best we could, but he told us he was not there to stay. "Only to deliver this," he said, and handed me a small, flat box made of stiff paper. When I opened it, glittering up at me from the folded tissue were Ciezo's jeweled slippers.

They were still twice as large as my own feet, and I likely never would grow into them. I didn't care. I put them on top of my wardrobe and stared at them each morning until I thought my heart would burst.

Arcelia was not without presents of her own. When we were young, it was my great pleasure to comb the palace for trinkets I could present her with: a honey-soaked date stolen from the kitchen, a little falcon-shaped ship ornament begged off one of the engineers at the harbor, a map of Itsaryet's capital city sketched for me on a napkin by a visiting Ceian merchant at dinner, an arduously extracted promise from the drillmaster at the barracks to teach her how to throw knives. These first gifts Arcelia took with apparently enthusiastic gratitude but left in the feast hall by accident, tossed under her bed or trod underfoot, as she had with each toy or dress or holo she had owned for as long as I could remember. The lessons, though, occupied her for months. She demanded at first that I go with her, and I did my best for a day or two to endure the aching muscles, and the frustration of missing even the beginner's targets, and the omnipresent smell of sweat, but soon enough I begged off and left her to her own entertainment.

I was to find myself glad for that in later years. The camaraderie in the barracks appealed to my sister—it seemed to be one of the few things in the world that, unlike our education or our father's governance or our periodic sacramental duties, really held her interest—and when she and I would fight, it was no small relief to watch her throw herself out of the palace to mix with the cadets below us. If nothing else, it left the palace as my sole possession. It was not only palace guards who trained at the barracks, but young people hoping for commissions in the Szayeti fleet, treasure-divers angling for a license from the crown, even travelers from far-flung islands across the planet who hoped to hire themselves out as mercenaries. At first Arcelia was an object of curiosity among them because she was a child, begging the recruits to teach her to spar or shoot; later, she was an object of curiosity because she was a princess with torn trousers and a habit of coming to their mess hall for breakfast, and it shocked them to learn she was only sixteen. I remember her strong-arming the drillmaster into measuring her for a private's uniform, and hanging it in her wardrobe beside her crown and her formal clothes, and the very next day losing the jacket somewhere in one of the practice fields. I had long since given up looking for gifts to give her.

We grew more clever, Arcelia and I, and Zorione grew older, and slower. In the evenings we took to climbing the palace walls in our shoddiest cloaks and making our way through the streets of the City of Endless Pearl. Arcelia would always claim, later, that these excursions were her idea; I was certain then that they were mine; now I cannot say which of us was in the right. What is true is that by that time, it was one of the few matters on which we agreed. The closest I came to argument was protest that, even in our best disguises, we might be robbed or hurt by some desperate Szayeti in the seedier districts, and I hardly even meant it. Alectelo had never harmed me before, and I did not think it ever would—after all, was not every tower and street of it the work of the god who loved us? But Arcelia bared her teeth, and cracked her knuckles, and said, "Then let some desperate Szayeti try."

At this I could not help but laugh, less from disbelief than surprise, and after a moment, she laughed, too.

"Just watch me," she said.

She always longed to go to the gambling halls and boat races; I always longed to go to the old Szayeti temples and markets and musicians' alleys. Between us, I think, we must have walked every block in Alectelo by the time we were seventeen. It was at this time that I first bent to study Szayeti in earnest. The shopkeepers and entertainers of the marketplaces haggled easily in the same rough Sintian that merchants traded in across the Swordbelt Arm, and the Szayeti language itself, in accordance with the habitual disorder of Alectelo, had become rife with Sintian technical terms and idioms and curses and army slang. Even visiting Ceian ambassadors and merchants spoke easily in our native tongue to the two of us, and to my father, smilingly asking in Sintian for concessions and compromises and exceptions to our Sintian laws. Arcelia and I both watched these conversations closely, though I cannot recall us ever speaking about them to each other, afterward.

Perhaps we might have been happier if we had. Instead, after a long string of Ceian visits, she began refusing altogether to attend our Ceian language classes, and her Sintian lost a good deal of the frequent oaths and poor grammar that the soldiers made a habit, and she developed overnight an exacting insistence on the small formalities that our language possessed. I half expected this would hurt her friendships in the barracks, but if it did, she gave no sign of it, and the guards who paused to greet her by name in the hallways seemed to have lost none of their usual warmth, and indeed to my increasingly trained eye might have even gained a new respect.

For my own part, after those same Ceian visits, I began to ask our tutors for books on the native language of our own planet. It was a curious urge, and one I did not at first understand. I knew that by all good reason what I should want was a better command of Ceian itself—a stronger fluency in bargaining, in diplomacy, in catching and comprehending the smooth flatteries and subtle insults that the Ceians leveled on us in the belief that we would not understand them. But what I sought out instead were those few surviving scraps of narrative from the Szayeti who had been Alekso's own followers. Our palace kept some diaries from the early days of Caviro's reign, but it took me months in the Library of Alectelo to find those few firsthand accounts that remained from before the flood. At my desk, surrounded by dictionaries and patchwork grammar charts, I tried to piece together my own careful translations of the appearance of a conquering empire in Szayet's sky.

Before long the books had no more to tell me. But by then the comfortable strangeness of my people's language, its suffixes and harmonies, had begun to compel me as deeply as the palace itself once had, and on our nightly excursions I would attempt conversation with the temple-keepers, speaking haltingly of old kings and older poems, while Arcelia waited impatiently in the doorway. When at last my accent and my grammar improved, it became less a matter of historical interest than the sort of game of dress-up that I had always enjoyed, pretending myself to be a visiting scholar at the shrines, a gawking tourist in the markets, a wealthy ship owner from a nearby island at Arcelia's beloved gambling halls as she shoved increasing stacks of dekar toward the bookmaker. It was intoxicating in more ways than one: Were it not for our disguised expeditions, I think Arcelia and I might have gone years without ever traveling farther than half a mile from the palace grounds. Certainly my father never did, except on feast days. We would accompany him in these rituals—me marching behind his right shoulder, Arcelia at his left—singing in harmony with the psalms of the priests and sworn devotees behind us, waving to the kneeling multitude who called out to us *spaschoyety* in their own tongue, which was *heirs* in our own, until it was time for the ceremony to end and the guards to accompany us back to the palace and shut the clamoring crowd out at the doors. It was this way that my family knew and had always known the people we ruled: caught in the midst of worship. But the Szayeti in the streets, the Szayeti of ordinary time, were not like the Szayeti of the barracks, or the Szayeti who swept our floors or dressed me in the morning. Those early conversations in their language were some of the first I had ever had with Alectelans who were not oath-sworn to my service. I cajoled Arcelia, too, to apply herself to that task with which our father and his father and his mother and hers, reaching back and back to Caviro himself, had never bothered. But she refused. "Why should I," she said, "if you've gotten there first?"

I should have known then that she intended to steal my throne.

I thought, naive though it was, that Arcelia did not want to be queen at all. She seemed so uninterested in the prospect. When we marched on those feast days, Arcelia always complained in whispers to me of her aching feet, and tapped her fingers and rolled her eyes while the priests chanted benedictions upon us and while they begged our father to bestow Alekso's blessings on the people, and she tore her ceremonial headdress off as soon as we crossed through the palace gates. She forgot the words to any hymn longer than four lines. She never paid attention in royal lessons. We had had a long succession of tutors, who had guided us from our unpromising beginnings in Ceian toward a comprehensive understanding of theology, medicine, local and galactic history, strategy and tactics, and even some rudimentary engineering, and in addition to Szayeti, Ceian, and my native Sintian, I had picked up Kutayeti, Cherekku, and, of course, the Malisintian I needed to read Alekso's writings and to pray. But Arcelia hated the history fiercely, the theology more, the philosophy most of all. Medicine interested her, but only for a little while. This was well enough, as far as I was concerned. I was ahead of her in every subject.

Before long I left the tutors behind entirely. In the afternoons I began to order crab-litters down to the Library of Alectelo. I was accompanied only by a young bodyguard, who had once been one of the guards' pimple-faced children that Arcelia liked to fight, and whose stolid earnestness I rather enjoyed. In these litter rides, crawling up Alectelo's broad avenue on six jointed steel legs operated by a pearl computer designed by Alekso himself, I saw a new perspective of the city entirely. I was used to the way that the Szayeti servants bowed and scraped to my father, and how even Zorione's loving reproaches had been tempered with deference as Arcelia and I grew. Now I saw how Szayeti stared at my litter, how they whispered and pointed—how, on occasion, the bravest of them would come to the curtains of the litter itself, and whisper to my bodyguard some small token of praise or blessing, or on occasion, a wish.

My bodyguard blushed when he recounted the praise, and blushed further when he told me their blessings. The wishes he refused to share entirely. "Raimundo," I said cajolingly, "what disrespect could there be in it? I am not queen. It is no burden to hear what small things my people need. I only wish I could speak to Alekso on their behalf."

"They know you can't, madam," he said. "They only want to say their prayers near to the holy presence. The king—" He cut himself off abruptly.

"Please don't be afraid," I said. "I know my father prefers the palace to the street. All the more reason I wish you would tell *me* what they say." He murmured something inaudible. I considered making it an order, looked sidelong at the deep red his ears had turned, smiled to myself, and said instead, "Please."

"They wish for—for a larger portion of the dole, madam," he said. "Or for their children to be healthy, or for their businesses to prosper, or—or smaller things. That last asked for his, um. For his sweetheart to notice him."

"Thank you," I said. "Was it so difficult?" He ducked his head. I added, a little mischievously, "And I wish you would call me Gracia."

"Madam," he said, ears gone as dark as plums, and I smiled to myself and tucked the wishes into my memory, and for the moment let the matter go.

At the Library I met with flocks of shaven-headed priests, whose role it was to guide me among the treasures kept there. Above and under the city ran walls and walls of stacked tablets, old Aleksan relics under panes of glass, battle plans and daily officer's reports from all the years of His campaigns, holo-portraits and biographies of every one of His soldiers from His nearest bodyguards to the most minor of His infantry, books in a hundred tongues gathered from as far away as Muntiru, new star charts and ancient ship computers, dictionaries for languages and alphabets otherwise long dead in every part of the galaxy, wood and soil and insect samples from old Ostrayet and from Szayet before its drowning, the bones and dried skins of animals from across the Swordbelt Arm, recordings of the first performances of the earliest Aleksan hymns, holo fragments of Sintian theater performed six hundred years ago—even carefully preserved paper under the dim light of the basements, on which I could see pencil sketches of the city plans that would become Alectelo, and the Ever-Living God's faintly scribbled notes to Himself beside its towers and roads. In that cool marble temple I poured myself into philosophy, anatomy, astronomy, the Itsaryeti tongue and the Belkayeti, economics, poetry, playwriting, mathematics—though I learned later that its collection had shrunk since the days of my ancestors, and people no longer flocked from every part of the galaxy in the numbers they once had to study beneath its red-painted roofs, it seemed then that there was no end to what the Library could offer me, and no end to the time I could spend drinking its knowledge down. Never had my curiosity been given so free a rein.

As a child, I had loved to tell Zorione over again all of the lessons of our tutors, to ask her how she liked the poetry and beg her for help drawing the maps, not realizing how lacking a nursemaid's education was—even a princess's nursemaid—in comparison to mine. Traveling back from the Library, though I knew now that a bodyguard was taught even less, I took pleasure in repeating to Raimundo the history of my god as I had learned it just hours before. I asked him all the famed Malisintian questions—is a pious act pious because the god loves it, or does He love it because it is pious? Is justice the restoration of happiness or obedience to the law? Did the apotheosis remove Alekso's mortal inclination, or did it add a divine one? I do not think Raimundo liked to hear these. He was as orthodox as I, but to him religion was a matter of hymn and chapel, a love content to remain in the bent knee and not in the mind. Nevertheless he answered as best he could, and when he could not, he did something that I always remembered him for: He listened to me. He never forgot a word I told him, my bodyguard; he would repeat them to me weeks later, even months. It was for this reason that I could not help telling him, too, the history I had learned of my family, all the Oracles to whom Alekso had ever spoken, their marriages and prophecies, their wars and diplomacy, the neighborhoods in Alectelo and the palace towers they had built, the roads they had laid down, the ships they had christened, the priests who now were descended from their favorite ministers—the work that my father was doing at that very moment, somewhere silently in the palace ahead of us. My sister, I heard, had ceased to appear at her tutoring sessions at all.

And it was not long after her education came to a halt that my father—

I don't think I'm going to tell you about that right now.

It was not as if there was no precedent. No matter how poor Szayet becomes in land or in resources, precedent is the one thing in which it will never find itself lacking. Oracles had died on the battlefield, for example. Oracles had even died on other planets. There was, as with all other things, ceremony.

Even now it is difficult for me to distinguish any one of those days from another in my memory. I recall them as empty, but when I think back on what I did, the truth is that they were filled to the brim with petty tasks—I remember sorting possessions, opening rooms and closing them, drawing back curtains and covering mirrors, signing papers left unsigned, paying bills left unpaid, and yet I remember neither eating nor drinking, nor distinguishing between morning and night. I know that that time cannot have lasted longer than two weeks. Without the relentless fact of the calendar, I would not know whether they lasted two years.

It might have been on any one of those days that Arcelia came into the Yellow Room, where my father had been accustomed to conduct most of his business that did not need to be done publicly. I do not think I would remember that, either, if it were not for what happened later. It is not a memory I would have had cause to tell to myself over again—like every other occupation of those days, it seemed so empty of meaning. It is not a memory I would have cared to tell you.

At first I hardly realized she was in the doorway. When I looked up, it took me a moment to recognize her: She was dressed, for once, like royalty, in a shirt of red silk, her hair tied back with a wide white ribbon rather than loose to her shoulders, no tatty borrowed boots on her feet and no gun belt on her waist. She was watching me silently, and looked to have been doing it for some time.

"What do you need?" I said. "I'm busy."

Her mouth pursed. "I wanted to talk to you," she said.

"About what?" I said.

She came a little ways into the room, to the edge of my desk, and rested a fist on the wood. There was a look on her face that I could not parse, or did not recognize as hers; the irritation in her mouth had bled away, leaving only tension and thought.

"Did he—ever talk to you?" she said.

"Talk to me?" I said, bewildered. "Who?"

"Your—Faifisto," she said. "About what it was like for him, when—"

She gestured, impatient and juddering. It took me a moment to think through what she meant, and then I looked away, down at my tablet, overcome by a rush in my lungs and my throat, heat and bitter salt.

"I expect it was the same," I said shortly. "The—going to the island. I think her husbands helped him with—" I could not say *burial*; I gestured, as gracelessly as Arcelia had, trying to indicate it. "He didn't—Just because he sometimes spoke with me about—" I wanted to say, sudden and furious, *Did you know him at all? No matter what you believe about me, can you possibly think he and I ever spoke about how he* felt*?*

"Not that part," she said. "I mean after. When he was—chosen." She mistook my hesitation for confusion. "The first time he spoke to Him," she said, more loudly. "When he knew that the Undying wanted him. Did he ever tell you what it was like?"

"You might have studied theology, if you had wanted," I said. "The Library has royal diaries stretching back to the earliest days after Caviro. You would find more in the palace—if you cared to look for them."

Her nostrils flared. "If I looked for them alone, I suppose," she said.

"You can have what adventures you like," I said coldly. "Someone else will have to pay attention to the practicals."

"Is that what you call them?" she said, just as coldly, and then shut her eyes and shook her head. "I'm only asking—" She exhaled through her nose. "Do you remember him saying anything about the days before the coronation? About whether he heard—whether he knew?"

"No," I said, fast and hard, and looked down; and then I said, "Actually—" It was a distant memory, and I might have been half imagining it. I closed my eyes, trying to call it up: lamplight, high marble ceilings, the burnt smell of incense, the clear chimes of bells. "I was very young," I said. "We were at the Library. A ceremony, it must have been, you were—you were next to me. I was watching him. And I remember him saying something to the priests... about dreams."

"What are you doing?" said Arcelia, in quite a different tone.

"Oh, for—" I said, and opened my eyes. She was staring down at my hands, and her face was a thundercloud. "Were you even listening?"

"What are you *doing*?" she said again.

"Settling accounts," I said, "if you care. The feast, just before the—" As before, I could not say *illness*. "The musicians? The dancers? The fruits from Medveyet, the Sintian lamb? Do you think none of them require payment, just because he's—"

Again, I could not manage the last word, but Arcelia didn't need me to. She said, "You're signing his name."

I could feel my knuckles go white around my stylus. After a moment, I said, "The treasury is in the name of the throne. He must pay his debts."

"You're signing his name," she said again, flatly. "His—as if it were your own."

"You haven't been listening to a word I've been saying," I said, and clapped the stylus down on the desk. "Why did you come in here—just to fight me?" I could hear my voice growing sour. "Lord Undying, Celia, can't you rest for even a week?

If you must act like a child, can't you go to the barracks and shout and spar with *your* kind of people, and at least get out of my way?"

Her face went very blank. She lifted her fist from the table, careful and deliberate, and turned and walked from the room, and did not look back.

I picked up the stylus and signed the next bill, a furious scribble of pixelated light. It would only occur to me much later, lying in my little room on the satellite as the night wore on and on into the small thin hours, that it was the last conversation we would ever have before the war.

I liked the priests of Alectelo, and they liked me. Arcelia they did not dislike, but it would have been difficult, as they hardly knew her. They spent nearly all of their time indoors, doing the rapid, desperate, and doomed work of archiving centuries-old artifacts in a seaside climate, and argued rapidly among themselves in Malisintian too obscure even for an educated Sintian to understand, and when summoned into the palace occasionally found the time to timidly explain in small voices the revealed nature of the Ever-Living God. Arcelia, though she of course attended services with both me and our—with me, had hardly ventured through the Library doors at all. This was for the best; she would certainly have knocked over a tablet display. But it meant that when the priests trooped into the palace chapel, a week after Arcelia and I returned from the Island of the Dead, it was me that they came to, and my hand they clasped, and me who they called princess while Arcelia watched beside me, her eyes blank and dark.

"The choosing is simple," said the head priest, a bulbous-nosed Szayeti by the name of Teodozia Intsulaya. "It will happen within two weeks. Any candidate for the Pearl will sleep in the royal palace, where the spirit of the Undying resides. Each night she will pray, and each morning she will come to this chapel and meditate on the Undying's will. Within fourteen days He will tell her she is His voice—sometimes less, sometimes only ten days, or only seven. It is only that she must remain within the palace, and she must return to the chapel daily. Nothing difficult at all."

"Pray—orisons?" I said. The chapel was a small, dusty room, made of white stone with a ceiling carved with faded Szayeti reliefs. I had always liked it, the way one likes a good dress that does not quite fit anymore. For years I had been thinking of the paintings I would commission for its walls. "Hymns? How will she know? Will He speak to her? Will He appear in the room?"

"What excellent questions you ask, princess," said Teodozia, and conferred with her fellow priests in rapid Malisintian, of which I could make out only a little. "The physical manifestation is an effect only of the true Pearl. But Brother Waldemar advises that he has, after many nights spent in meditation with the aid of laserwort tinctures, occasionally been able to access some small part of a mystery, which we advise should be researched—"

"Excuse me," said my sister.

The priest looked as startled as a rabbit under a hawk. "Princess Arcelia," she said, "what an honor—yes?"

"Yes," said Arcelia, "only I was wondering. Is this all necessary?"

"My apologies?" said Teodozia, and looked around at her robes and priests and the basalt pillars of the chapel, as if one of them would turn out to be a holo if she stared hard enough. Eventually she said timorously, "The vision, madam?"

"Mm," said Arcelia. "Yes. I was just wondering. Is it really necessary to spend all this time trying to see which of us is going to have visions, if Alekso Undying's already given the throne to me?"

There was a brief silence. Then there was a good deal of shouting, pierced through after five or so minutes by Arcelia calling out, "Silence, please."

The priests quieted. Teodozia quavered, "Madam, what do you mean?"

"Oh, He came to me in a dream," Arcelia said. "He said, *Good news: You're the heir.* That was a week or so ago. Do you think it might have been important?"

This started up the shouting again, louder than ever. At last Teodozia cut through her fellow priests and said to my sister, nearly begging, "Madam, are you sure?"

"Of course she isn't sure," I snapped.

The priests turned to stare at me. My sister turned, too, as coolly as if we were discussing the weather. "Of course she isn't sure," I said again, this time directly to her. "She's lying."

Arcelia's expression did not change at all. "Princess," said Teodozia apprehensively, "it is a great thing, to accuse someone of blasphemy against the Undying. His justice is eternal, and His wrath endures from generation to generation—"

"She hasn't had a *dream*," I said. My face had gone hot. "She hasn't had anything. She's afraid of waiting for His voice. She doesn't want to go through with it, because she's afraid of what's going to happen. She *asked* me how our father knew it was him—she *asked* me how to lie, she's afraid of—of having to watch Alekso choose *me*—Celia, you're *jealous*—"

"Jealous!" Arcelia said, and laughed, brittle. "As if there were any need!"

"Madam," said Teodozia, and quailed at her look. "Madam—the princess is right. You *must* perform the weeks of waiting. Three hundred years of royal precedent demands—"

"Does it?" said Arcelia. "What a pity for it. I don't see what that has to do with me."

"*Madam*," said Teodozia.

And Arcelia said, "If you fail to call me princess again, I will have you shot in the street."

The silence then was thick and terrible. At last I said, "The people would tear you apart."

"Do you really think so? Well, perhaps they would try," said Arcelia. "Do you know, as a matter of fact, I've been discussing that possibility with Captain Mateno of the palace guard all morning? How convenient, isn't it, Gracia, that I have some friendships with *my* kind of people!" She smiled at me, a joyless smile, with all her teeth. "He thinks it's very dangerous for me," she said, "all of this royal succession business. *He* thinks the barracks ought to keep the streets full of soldiers until the coronation. It seems like a sensible precaution for everyone."

It was then that I understood, and had to sit down abruptly on one of the long stone benches. The priests did not, and the one Teodozia had called Brother Waldemar said, "Mada—Princess, why would the palace guard need to be involved in the coronation at all?"

"You know, you can call it paranoia," said Arcelia, "but I just can't stop worrying about someone else trying to claim my throne."

She turned then, and walked through the door of the chapel. I sprang up at once to follow her. "You can't," I said, my voice rising. "You are committing the worst heresy. You are making yourself a liar, and a thief, and a false prophet. You'll bring the wrath of the god down on every island of the planet—" I was shouting by now. It did not matter. She never turned back.

And it was a week later, in the small hours of the morning, that her guards arrived at my bedroom door.

Prison was more of a shock than anything else, the first week. I was too surprised to be bored, and too furious to be hungry. They had put me in a solitary cell, of course, deep beneath the palace, and there I paced from one corner to another, whispering in rage to an Arcelia who was not with me, staring longingly at the sunlit window in the high far corner of my cell. By the second week the boredom had come at last, and I curled up against the wall and eyed that square of light, listening for any movement, any sign, any omen of what might have been done to my city without me.

On the third week Arcelia came, and the Pearl was in her ear.

I neither moved nor looked at her. I only stared up at the window as she strolled behind me, down along the border of the glimmering force field that separated me from freedom.

"I don't want to keep you in here forever," she said at last.

"Then give up your heresy," I said.

"I was afraid you would say that," she said, and crouched down. I turned and wished at once that I hadn't: The sight of the Pearl of the Dead disappearing into her skull, my father's Pearl, made me want to be sick. "I *will* have to keep you in here awhile, though," she went on tranquilly. "Do you know how much trouble the people are making?"

"Good," I said, turning away again.

"Only rabble-rousers," said Arcelia. "And soldiers, too, of course, veterans, our father's men. It irritates me, Gracia. It's not necessary. I've had to let half the palace staff go, and then I see them in the riots—or after the riots, among the bodies..." She paused. "And I just can't figure out how they got the idea you ought to be queen at all."

"I don't know," I said to the wall.

"The priests must have told them," Arcelia said thoughtfully. "That has to be it, yes? Unless it was one of the palace staff. In which case I have to wonder—" She paused. "How many of them have you told our father's little lie?"

I spun back then, heedless of my nausea. "You knew," I said.

"Of course I knew," said Arcelia. "He told *me*, a week before he fell sick. How I cried! And how I laughed, later, to discover the truth! I wonder what Alekso said to him, after he passed on so blatant a false prophecy?"

"You don't have to wonder," I said. "You can ask Alekso what He has to say now."

Arcelia smiled with great tolerance. "Gracia," she said gently, "I *don't* want to keep you in here forever. The sooner you say I have the right to be queen, the sooner all of this will go away. And I would like it to go away, Gracia... I have plans for you."

I had been hungry for two weeks, and lonely for three, and mourning for longer. And the Pearl was winking in her ear, Szayet's Pearl, which, no matter who carried it, held my god's voice within—and she was smiling at me, Arcelia, and I knew her smile like I knew the smell of seawater or the sight of the moons, and it had been so many years since my sister had smiled at me.

I shuffled a little closer to the force field. "What plans?" I said.

Arcelia smiled wider. What a thing it was, always: to see another's feeling on my own face. "Listen," she said. "How would you like to go to war?"

I stared. "War? Why?"

"Why?" said Arcelia. She clasped her hands behind her back and began to walk again along the length of my force field. Her eyes were fixed on some distant point on the far wall. "Because Ceiao does," she said. "Because Ceiao does, and they hold half the Shieldmirror, and Arquera, and they have eyes on the whole Swordbelt Arm. Because they are rich, and their people are happy, and the galaxy respects them." At once she stopped in her tracks. "Because Szayet is a laughingstock!" she said. "Because *Dom* Caviro are laughingstocks. We, the children of the beloved of Alekso Undying!" She smiled again, but now it was not a smile I recognized at all. "Because I *want* to. The better question is, why not?"

I sat very slowly, and unfolded myself, and lay back down on the cold stone floor of the cell.

"I see," I said. "Blasphemy has made you insane."

"Oh, *Gracia*," said Arcelia. Her voice was far away and terribly pitying. "Are you afraid of dying? Not all generals need be pilots, you know. We could keep you on the planet for the battles, if you're weak of heart. You're wasted in a prison cell."

"You are out of your mind," I said tonelessly. "Szayet cannot become the Ceian Empire. Szayet has not been able to make war beyond the edges of her system for eight generations."

"Antono Caviro Donacanto conquered Belkayet," said Arcelia.

"And Calixta Caviro Diketa lost it," I said, "a generation later, and it lived under its own king for a whole century until the Ceians came. We don't have the *ships*, Arcelia. Expending half our fleet would get us a toehold on one planet—if we were very, very clever—and that would leave our own planet undefended."

"Then bring the whole fleet," said Arcelia. "Cleverness I'm not worried about. I have you."

But I was beyond empty flattery now. "They would retaliate," I said. "They would come to Szayet. Arcelia, do you understand what I'm saying? They would destroy Alectelo."

"Alectelo!" said Arcelia, and scoffed. "Gracia, there are a hundred Alectelos up and down the Swordbelt Arm. If I lose it, I'll get another."

I sat up and said, trying to make sense of it by repetition. "Get another."

"Of course," said Arcelia. "Why not, with the whole fleet under my command? Who do you think lives in my ear, and will tell me how to do it?"

"He'll never let you," I said. Arcelia laughed. This made me angrier, and I said, "Of course He might conquer anywhere in the galaxy. But He would never leave Alectelo behind. He'd never let Himself *lose* it. It's where His beloved is buried, Arcelia, be *sensible*. It's His home."

Arcelia smiled at me again, and she said, soft and very warm, "Gracino, this is why He loves me best."

It was then that I sprang at her, utterly unthinking for the first time since the chapel. But the force field caught me, and burned my hands, and I fell back onto the ground wailing, and by the time I could see again, my sister was already gone.

CHAPTER

EIGHT

CEIRRAN

This is barbaric," I said.

"Yes," said Anita.

"This is *barbaric*," I said, as though it would become less barbaric if I said it again.

"That's true," said Anita. "You should try the melon, though."

The Ceians had taken us to Alectelo after all. Then again, it was not as if it had been their idea. They had bundled us into their pearl-lined palace a little ways from the famous curving harbor-gate, all but a few. Nequeiron had not exaggerated its security: There were guards posted at nearly every door, bristling at every stone-faced Szayeti maid. Half my men were still behind, overseeing the burial of Quinha's head, in a sandy spot on the island beneath that staring red comms tower. In an airy, sunlit room on the highest floors of the Oracle's palace, my lieutenants had been given an enormous feast, and told that the queen would return soon to discuss matters of great importance. Neither of these seemed a particularly promising sign.

"Here's the thing," said Anita, and gently extracted a mackerel bone from between her teeth. She was sitting on one of the beautifully embroidered Szayeti chairs, with her boots up, and I was pacing the room from corner to corner. "Of course it's barbaric, I don't deny that. She was a councillor of Ceiao, not some blue-painted chieftain from Madinabia. She should've had a proper funeral, with weeping women and the city painted black and a pyre the size of a tree. And then you and I could have gone along afterward and spat on the ashes and had a good laugh. But as it is, so it is, that's how Fortune turns. And as I recall, you were the one who let the cultists have the head start on her in the first place. So what exactly were you expecting?"

"I wasn't expecting them to *kill* her," I bit out.

"That much I got," said Anita.

"I expected to negotiate," I said. "I expected to blackmail them for custody with their own debt. I expected to halve it, Anita, in exchange for *treasure-diving rights*—and now all I have to bring to the Merchants' Council is a cranium and a couple of inches of spinal cord!"

"How in the world could you have promised the Szayeti to halve their debt?" said Anita, startled. "Quinha never had any children, did she? The property passes to the council, debts too—they'd never have agreed to a plan like that. The only way you'd have gotten more than a handful of votes is if she was standing in the chamber, telling them—" Then she stopped.

All of the anger drained away at once. "Yes," I said, and sighed, and sat down beside her. "I know."

Anita shut her eyes. Then she said, very calmly, "You and your *fucking* pardons."

"It's not only—" I began.

"Don't," said Anita.

"It's not only the Szayeti debt at stake," I said anyway. "Domestic land reforms. The officer pipeline, too. After two months—"

"Don't," Anita said, "don't, *don't* tell me a lot of bullshit about the council and Veguion's faction and Cachoeiran's. Don't do that to me. Don't make me listen to you talk nonsense about diplomacy and reconciliation and the peace and—*why not just kill her!* Kill her quickly and kill her well and drag her body along the Rouan Valquíria for the people to jeer at! Tell me this wasn't out of *sentiment*!"

"No," I said, looking her steadily in the eyes. "There was no sentiment at all."

Anita put her hand over her face. Her shoulders rose, then fell.

"She tried to kill my sister," she said. "You know that, don't you."

"I know," I said. "She tried to kill me, too."

"I like my sister better," said Anita darkly, but she lowered her hands again and sighed.

"She would've voted with you," she said sourly, "in the end. She would have, is the thing. And I would've had to watch all of your nonsense start over *again*."

"I know," I said again, though I was not at all sure that she was right.

"One day," she said, "one day, you *will* meet someone who you can't talk rings around. And what will you do then?"

But before I could answer this there was a knock at the door, and Galvão came in, carrying a stack of bags so high they obscured his face. I sprang up to help him, and when all the bags were on the ground, unfastened one. It appeared, bewilderingly, to be full of clothes. So was the next. The third was soaps, and the fourth, cementing my increasingly grim suspicion, was packages of bread and fruit.

"You can't be serious," I said.

"The queen of Szayet," said Galvão exhaustedly, "invites us to remain her guests in the palace at Alectelo, until such a time as the matter of Quinha Semfontan's death and the continued exile of her sister, Altagracia, are resolved."

"The queen of Szayet," I said, "is my *client.* Ceiao's client, in any case, and as far as she is concerned, there is no difference. Am I at her beck and call? Is Szayet a child, that the empire should sort out its squabbles? Have I nothing better to do than to remain in the Swordbelt Arm while my enemies on the Merchants' Council whisper behind my back?"

Galvão waited until he was quite sure I was done, then said, "Sir, she says she wants to negotiate."

"What in the world could she possibly have to negotiate about?" I said. "The only thing I ever wanted here is already buried in the sand."

"The debt, sir," said Galvão.

That gave me pause, though I wished it didn't. "The debt passes to the council," I said slowly.

"She says," said Galvão, sounding very unhappy, "that she would rather negotiate with you than the Merchants' Council. She says Alekso Undying commands her to negotiate with you and not the council, sir. She says Alekso says he doesn't see a difference, in any case."

I looked at the ceiling. "Those were her words?" I said.

Galvão nodded. "Well," said Anita, sounding much more cheerful than she had a moment ago, "she can flatter, in any event."

"She certainly can," I said, "in front of her men and my own. Fortune and misfortune! *Alekso says?*"

Galvão was looking bewildered. I rubbed a hand over my eyes. "We'll stay," I said. "But if she demands we act as her guests, we'll impose on her hospitality as much as we are able. Have the Szayeti fetch luxuries—the best of everything. Sweets from Kutayet, tapestries from Itsaryet, eiderdown beds for the men, curtains, Madinabic carpets, rare tropical birds, I don't care, just tell her we need it and ensure it is expensive. I want her to want us gone by market day. I want us to eat her out of house and home."

"Sir," said Galvão, and saluted.

When he was gone, I drummed my fingers on my desk and looked out the window to the three jagged moons.

"Tell me, Anita," I said. "Do you believe a man can live forever?"

"What, you mean Alekso?" said Anita, and shrugged. "Why not? Narcisa Cipon lives in her cups. Semfontan's friends live in disgrace. I'm sure a man can cramp himself to fit into an earring."

"You are no great adherent to skepticism," I observed.

"I'm the truest nonbeliever Ceiao has ever produced," said Anita, "for I believe in nothing at all. Believing in disbelief is far beyond my talents. What is it you want to know?"

"Do you think, then," I said, "that the Caviros have lied about hearing the voice of Alekso for all these years? Or rather that it is a hallucination, and Szayet is ruled by the insane?"

That called up a flicker of interest in Anita's face, for the first time since she had said *my sister.* "That's a classic," she said, and considered it. At last she said: "If it were me, I'd be lying, but it's not me, to my good fortune. The queen's about as solid as a rotten apple, but if she's mad, I'll give you forty dekar and won't complain. Like as not they're telling the truth. I don't see that it's much of a question. Anyone can write a computer program."

"Anyone can write a computer program," I said. "The question is whether, should that program be an identical replica of a human mind, that mind can be said to remain alive and well."

"If a man happened to be alive," said Anita, "I wouldn't put him in a grave. Seems ill-planned."

"You are refreshingly straightforward," I said. "Approach it in this way. Say I were to write a message on a tablet and send it to you. Say I then smashed my own tablet. Would the message be destroyed?"

"Of course not," said Anita. "Difficult to get any paperwork done if it were."

"All right," I said. "Say now that my message is a book—a very long and complex book, which I have written and of which I possess the only copy. I send this book from my tablet to yours, and then smash my tablet. Does the book remain in existence?"

"You're going through tablets quickly," said Anita, and when I raised my eyebrow at her, "Same book, isn't it? Why shouldn't it?"

"You have come to the heart of the matter," I said. "Say that, rather than a book, I send an extremely complex set of information and protocols—many petabytes' worth of information and protocols. Rather than send this information from tablet to tablet, I send it from one highly complex computing instrument—my own brain—into an equally complex computing instrument. Then I leap into the sea."

"What a nasty game you play," said Anita lightly.

"Do you believe a man can live forever?" I said. "Or, to the point: that he does?"

Anita thought this over, deliberately now. The ever-present amused curve of her mouth had flattened. "The message on my tablet isn't the message on yours, though," she said, at last. "It's a copy of it. An identical copy, I grant you. But *identical* isn't *the same*."

"Why not?" I said.

"Why not?" said Anita. "Well—because it's not, is why. You could see that they showed up on the tablets at different times, for one thing—yours when you wrote it, mine when I received it. They record that information."

"Then answer this," I said. "Imagine I sent you out of the room. Imagine then that I sent the message from one tablet to another, and after doing so erased all the data in each tablet regarding its sending and receipt, leaving only the message's contents. If I then summoned you back into the room, and smashed one tablet, and did not tell you whether that tablet was the one that had sent the message—would you know whether the remaining tablet was, so to speak, the living man?"

"What would it matter if I knew which sent it?" said Anita. "*You'd* know."

"And if I died?" I said. Anita's mouth curled down at that, and I said, "Well, take this. If I told you I had been replaced with an identical copy of myself, retaining all of my memories, would you still consider yourself oath-sworn to me?"

"Have you been?" said Anita, interested.

"If I said no," I said, "would you be able to tell whether I lied?"

Anita propped her chin on her hands and looked at me through her eyelashes. "Have you been?" she said again.

"No," I said, "but how would you—"

"Right," said Anita. "So I know."

I held her gaze a little while. "I think, Anita," I said, "you may be a woman of faith."

"Oh, I knew that much," she said. "But I wondered if you'd catch me out in it."

CHAPTER

NINE

GRACIA

It was the sixth week since my father had died, and the fourth week since my sister had made me her prisoner, and three months before I would board a ship to a little satellite hanging far above the home I loved, on the day the dungeon wall shattered.

If it had not been on the other side of the force field, I might have been badly hurt. As it was, I watched it collapse with a kind of awe: The stone wall flung itself in shards to each side of the hallway with such abandon that those fragments that did not immediately rebound stuck several inches in, and those that did rebound were smoking. Behind the hole in the wall was a wash of yellow moonslight, and then there was a silhouette, six feet tall and impossible to make out the features of, except that it was carrying a gun.

"Princess," it said, and moved closer. A moment later I recognized the face: Raimundo, as clear-eyed and earnest-faced as if he were about to welcome me into a crab-litter to the Library. Behind him appeared two more people, who saluted at once.

"Lord of the Grave," I said to myself, and then, to him, "What are you doing? How have you gotten here? What in the world have you done to the guards?"

"Honor and long life to you, Holy Princess," said Raimundo. "This is a rescue mission. We don't have very much time."

As this was one of the longest speeches I had ever heard him make, I was very cooperative while they blew up the rest of my cell. This took eleven or twelve patches of resin, carefully placed while I stood as far back as the narrowness of the space would allow, and even then the heat of the field's implosion curled the hairs on my arms. But by that time the soldiers were through, helping me out toward the hole in the wall and into the night.

It was apparent at once how little hold Arcelia had kept of her city. The streets were nearly empty, but emptiness made the sight starker: the boarded-up shops and taverns, the cracks running up the pearl of every roof and cathedral, the fragments of glass glittering along the streets like stars. There was graffiti, too—Szayeti, mostly, and difficult to make out in the light of the moons' crescents and spindles above me, but it was with a dull jolt that I recognized my own name. She had said *bodies*, and every time we turned a corner, I flinched, but I saw none. Only much later did I suspect that my rescuers might have led me away from the areas of greatest casualty, out of their fear of my inexperience, and the thought that I might become hysterical at the sight of death.

It was a sensible precaution. All that long walk from the palace I was indeed on the edge of hysteria. It was the first time I had breathed fresh air in a month, and the first time I had seen my city since Arcelia's coronation, and I was becoming aware, slowly, that it would be the first night I had spent outside the palace in ten years. At last we arrived in a neighborhood that I had rarely visited with my sister in our wanderings and where hardly any Sintians lived at all: poor and residential, full of narrow, looming, red-painted houses jostling for space with their neighbors. From here Raimundo and his fellow soldiers led me up a spindly staircase and into one such house, a Szayeti amulet hanging from its doorjamb and its paint faded with wind and salt spray. It was very dark within, and I had to grope to find my way down another set of stairs after their footsteps. After some time the steps began to echo, and I knew we had come into a much larger space.

"Hello?" I said softly.

"Someone turn the lights on," said a voice.

There was a click, and the room was flooded with brightness. I was in the midst of an enormous hall, crowded with Alectelans, Szayeti and Sintian, dressed in red. For a moment they only stared; and then, in a great movement, which began nearest me and rippled back and back toward the walls, they saluted, hands to their hearts.

"Princess?" said another voice, and I turned, and was embraced at once by a pair of familiar arms. "Princess—oh, your sister is going to be in *such* trouble!" She looked thinner, Zorione, and she was weeping, but her eyes were like stars.

I had never led a war before. It was not as easy as the Sintian writers had made it out to be. This was not precisely surprising, but my ability to predict the difficulty did not at all decrease it, and my only comfort was in knowing that Arcelia had not read the Sintian books at all.

In the most part—I suspect you will not like to hear this, but even I cannot lie well enough to deny it—I found war very boring, and the boredom not alleviated at all by the enormity of my terror. Everything I did and said, whether I set men on guard on the first floor of a house or the second, whether I sent a scouting party out at midnight or at five minutes past, whether I looked out one window or another, might result in my death, or the death of Raimundo or Zorione, or of all the loyal soldiers I held dear. It was not safe to eat or to sleep through the night—every clatter in the street, whether at dinner or at one o'clock in the morning, might be the enemy coming to seize our position. There was hardly any food, and what little of it we had was likely to be stale or cheap. There were barely any spare clothes, and none fit for a queen, and I found myself wearing dresses and robes and mantles borrowed from the poorest of my people, with no way to repay them. There was great difficulty in sanitation, a topic better left undiscussed altogether. There were no books at all. Worst of all was that it was not safe to hold conversation: Any raised voice or suspicious noise might alert an unfriendly neighbor who could give me away.

The most extensive speech we ever risked was prayer, and this we attempted weekly at most. I was a woman of ritual faith, and to me, prayer was something belonging to the palace chapel, the way brine-smell belonged to the sea. My faith, too, was a particularly Sintian faith, passed down from Caviro to Caviro from the time of the making of the Pearl. I had taken an interest in the popular forms of worship when Arcelia and I had been young, and in our wanderings through the city the temples had been where I had felt most at home, but it was a different thing entirely to stand beside my soldiers in the basements of safe houses on market day evenings, listening to a square-jawed elderly woman with her mantle drawn over her head stumble awkwardly through the Malisintian orisons I knew by heart—and what was stranger, listening to my soldiers chant those orisons back to her in the Szayeti language.

The Alectelans had their own Szayeti prayers, too, prayers that were not translations from Sintian at all. This was a fact of which I had been entirely ignorant, and of all the things I had to acclimate to in exile, that ignorance was perhaps what I hated most. There was one prayer in particular, which the soldiers always asked me to read rather than one of their own doing it: the prayer for the dead. I had never heard that we in Alectelo knew what became of the souls of the dead—our god was alive—but He had power over all things, the dead no less, and to recite this prayer in the palace chapel at the weekly service had always been thought a great honor. I hoped my soldiers meant it in the same spirit. But I soon learned that there was a Szayeti prayer for the dead, too—a prayer that, Zorione told me afterward, was older even than Ostrayeti rule—and this I could not say for my soldiers if I had wanted to, because no adolescent language mastery, however prodigious, could have taught it to me. I could only stand there, listening to them mourn their own fallen in their own way. I could only listen as silently as if I felt no grief at all.

But despite war's tediousness, despite its misery, despite my ignorance, to my surprise I found myself good at it—or, at the very least, good enough to survive for a month, which turned into two, which turned into the remainder of the spring. It did not hurt that war seemed to be mainly a matter of logistics. Violence I never quite grew used to, and terror was no more bearable for the constancy of its companionship, but hunger I could address, and hunger was often a greater danger than any of Arcelia's guns. It was her great advantage that my object was to seize the whole city, and her only object was to seize me. Still, this also gave me a sort of freedom of imagination, which she did not seem to grasp. She made attacks on the Szayeti neighborhoods where I was staying, and in their gutters and alleyways she set fires that spread to whole blocks. But she also left the Summer and Winter Markets utterly undefended, and so too the sea harbor where the grain came in, and my sparse spies reported that it seemed a great shock to her when I first besieged and then took hold of them entirely. Similarly, my spies told me she was bewildered when I made an attack on the theater district. I was deeply surprised by that piece of intelligence, as she knew very well it was where the palace kept all of the pearl computers that allowed them to project images across the sky.

More than that: It concerned me that she did not anticipate these things, because in her ear lived the greatest tactician the galaxy had ever known. Raimundo and his soldiers said nothing to this when I voiced my worries, but I knew they felt that it had to do with Alekso's favor—it was disconcerting, sometimes, to live amid such piety. I could not walk by day in the Alectelan streets, of course, but when I crept out with my men on the rare occasion of a mission safe enough for me to risk my own body, the graffiti was alarmingly passionate: I saw murals of myself hand in hand with Alekso, murals of my head crowned like the old pre-Ostrayeti kings—even some very nasty murals of me hacking Arcelia to death with a sword. There seemed to be more of these the more streets she set fire to, and it made me even more suspicious that this seemed to affect her behavior not at all. Had I been in her place, I would never have let such sentiment grow. Zorione, meanwhile, said it was silly to worry about Arcelia's tactics, because the important thing was that she *hadn't* won the war yet, and wasn't that enough?

It was coming on summer when we began to draw close to the palace itself. It was difficult to say at any given time how much of Alectelo either I or my sister held—the fighting was often house to house—but as the days grew longer, my safe houses began to move out of those poor Szayeti districts, and night after night I slept nearer and nearer the familiar curves of the harbor.

I remember a warm night when the moons were as full as the moons ever grew, and I dared against all prudence and reason to climb to the top floor of our safe house and open up its roof hatch and look for a few seconds into the sky. Raimundo accompanied me, of course, his face a silent protest, and did not let me even raise my head above the level of the rain gutters where it might be seen from the street. But across the glimmering roofs of the city were the gates and towers of home, and it was enough: Inside my chest, my heart turned and caught the light.

We had had, recently, a string of small and bloody victories. My spies in the marketplaces reported with delight: That fickle and self-interested thing, the favor of the Alectelan crowd, was more firmly settled in my corner than it had ever been. My battles swallowed my sister's attention, took the eyes of the throne from citywide crime, from construction and repairs, from the dole. It was an advantage of which I had always been conscious: Had I been in her position, forced to divide my time between the extraordinary business of war and the ordinary business of peace, the inhabitants of the city would likely just as well have hated me. They were a people of long memory, but they were not patient. They wanted the world restored to its ordinary turnings again. They wanted, without delay, for the true Oracle to reclaim her throne.

Perhaps it was this that I hated most about war: that it had become impossible to tell the difference between what I was trying to convince others to believe, and what I desperately wanted to believe myself.

But it was not as if Zorione discouraged me. It was not as if Raimundo discouraged me, and he was the strategist I trusted most after myself, for all that he was hardly older than me. It was more than half the force of our rebellion, eyes shining, who crowded in next to me around a map of the city in the basement of that same safe house. A decisive push, I said. A show of force. Arcelia was on her last legs, and she knew it. The city knew it. Our god knew it. The reports from the marketplaces were full of nothing but hope. We were so close to coming home.

I took the reconnaissance guard, along with Raimundo and two of his lieutenants, whose names I have since forgotten. It was a warm night, and we circled the palace for nearly half an hour before we crept in for our investigation. The palace's defenses had multiplied in the past few months, from numbers of guards to force fields that sprang up when alarms were tripped to very ordinary electric fences, and even now they grew from day to day. I was unused to moving with so large a group—stealth had been our watchword—and though we intended to travel as quietly as possible, it was impossible for dozens of rebels to go even a short distance in total silence, and so the night felt, as I crept from house to house, more than a little unreal, and no more real when we were close enough to the palace to see the gleam of the pearl and the glitter on the windows. The palace has always been a strange hodgepodge of a building: Caviro after Caviro has added to it, swallowing up more and more of the land on our little island, with the result that one white-friezed tower in the Malisintian style may nudge up against a statue in a later Szayeti design, which itself may blunder against a gate built by a hired Cherekku. I recall thinking that night that it was not dissimilar from my people themselves.

My hundreds of soldiers spread out, as silently as they could, to each side of me—they were few of them trained, and it was extremely difficult to practice maneuvers in the cramped quarters in which we had to work, and what I remember most from that last moment, I think, is pride. I could think of very little except the sight of my own house; but if I could think anything, I was proud that they had chosen me. I was proud to be at their head.

One of the nearby lieutenants coughed, and whispered: "Why are none of her people watching the gate?"

I was turning to her in surprise when the eastern wing exploded.

Instinct took over before thought. I ducked, hands over the back of my neck, and curled into a ball on the ground.

My ears were ringing, my vision black. There was a weight on my chest, unbearably heavy, unbearably hot, pressing me into the earth. I shoved at it, unthinking, and felt it roll away. My skin was sparking with pain—hands, ankles, anywhere that had been uncovered—and I cursed as I rose to my feet, unable to hear my own voice through the noise, and I looked down.

It was Raimundo. He had been the weight. He must have thrown himself over me. When I had shoved at him, his body had fallen faceup.

I said something. I do not know what. I could not hear. I still could not hear. My hands were burned, I thought, burned on the knuckles. The palms were uninjured. I could use them still. I pressed them to his chest, I pulled at his shirt. He came up easily, so easily. His head flopped to the side—what was left of his head—

"My lady," said someone. "Lady—" It was some minutes later. I did not know how many. I was a little ways down the street, shaking another body. I did not know her. I did not know its name. "Lady," said the voice, and pulled at my shoulder. It was the lieutenant who had asked the question earlier. She was burned badly on her forehead, and her voice was thick with smoke or overuse.

"We were betrayed," she said fiercely. I lied: I do know her name. She was called Estera, Estera Vertaya, and she was a year younger than me, and two days later she would be shot in the head, and her body would be thrown into the harbor for the gulls and the flies. "They *knew* we would be here! There must be a spy, my lady. We'll need to investigate—we can start with the ordinary guards—"

She went on speaking, but I wasn't listening any longer: I had seen something glittering in the ash, among the bodies. I knelt and brushed the ash aside, until I could lift it away and hold it up to the moonslight. It was a tiny ruby, no bigger than my pinkie nail. A few pale threads were still dangling from its base. I pinched one: silk. It had once been woven into something beautiful.

I knew that ruby. It came from the tip of Ciezo Caviro's embroidered shoes.

"We are going to flee the city," I said.

"Princess," said the lieutenant, but I did not look at her.

"We are going to flee the city," I repeated. "Find Zorione. Clear the safe houses. Tell the soldiers to consider their oaths ended. Tell them, if there are any of them left. I am done with burning the City of Endless Pearl. This is the last day of the war."

Now, weeks later and five thousand miles above Alectelo, I sat down hard on the smuggler's couch and put my head in my hands.

"Damn her," I said, and then, fervently, "Damn Ceiao. Damn their soldiers, and damn their empire, and *damn* their civil war. May they rot in cold and darkness and never wake. May their air turn to carbon and their rain to sulfur. May they learn for one day of their lives to mind their own *business*! Is there anywhere they are capable of leaving well enough alone?"

"He may not stand with her," said Zorione hopefully.

"He will," I said. "She is queen of Szayet, and besides this, she wants him to. Every particle of persuasion in her will go toward doing it."

"He may not be persuaded," said Zorione.

I knew that her faith had led her to this satellite with me, and I loved her for it. But there was no way to tell her what I knew as deeply as instinct: that Matheus Ceirran had been a conqueror these eight years, and he was Ceian, and he thought so little of her and of Oracles that there was no possible defense he could have against my sister in fullest passion. "It's what I would do, if I were in her place," I said at last. I knew no better way to explain it. "If I *were* in her place—if I were in the palace, if I could only speak to him—"

"You'd get him on your side, and accept the throne of Szayet from a Ceian's hand?" said the smuggler coolly.

I had nearly forgotten she was in the room. "I don't want the throne from a Ceian's hand," I said to her. "The priests *would* name me heir, if I claimed the right, and if there were anyone to let them. If it came to a trial—but it won't come to a trial; you can't try a case when the plaintiff can't enter the atmosphere. I thought to let Alectelo recover, and build up my army—"

"You can," said Zorione. "Lady, you have the favor of the god. And even if you said you were not—even if all you had was Belkayet—"

"Belkayeti barons will not fight against Ceiao," I said to my hands. "Not against their conquerors, not against the fleet that has taken the world—if I were only on the planet! If I only hadn't left—"

"If you hadn't left, you would be dead," said Zorione, who believed it, "and that's no question. You *can* get an army, princess, and force her to trial; all you need is time—"

"There is no time," I said. Arcelia thought herself a master planner, impossible to augur, but she never had been. Cruelty was never unforeseeable. It was only capricious. It had always been her error to mistake one for the other.

Zorione was looking bewildered. I shut my eyes. "She will offer him the right to dig treasure from our oceans," I said. "She will offer him our only holy thing remaining. And once she has done it, she will turn his guns on me."

The smuggler cleared her throat. "What will you do?" she said, in a tone that was not quite detached.

I thought of Alekso Undying, then. He had been in my place, once, hovering outside of this planet, waiting for her to open her arms to Him. Ostrayet had opposed Him. The people had not known Him. Nevertheless, He had overcome.

It was, I thought, a different prospect to overcome difficulty when not accompanied by thirty million destroyer-class warships. "What can I do?" I said bitterly. "The planet is barricaded, and the city is a prison cell. Her guards are wing to wing over every inch of atmosphere. My people are as trapped within the city as I am without. The only thing that moves through Szayet's borders now is money."

And then I went still.

CHAPTER

TEN

CEIRRAN

"What a dump!" said Anita in Ceian. This was unhelpful, as in Sintian the word was the same.

She was not entirely wrong. Civil war is a grim business at the best of times, and on Alectelo it had been devastating. The market through which we were strolling had once been a clear, ordered square of neat terra-cotta, hemmed on each side by two lines of tall marble pillars and curving pearl roofs beyond. I could see scuffed chalk on the ground where, in the usual Sintian style, merchants had marked the city-designated locations where they might set up their stalls at the beginning of the day and collapse them at sunset. Some particularly insistent merchants had even scratched their names on the tile, though these were beginning to fade with wind and time.

The rest of the market was empty. No stalls stood by their chalk marks, though a few canvas roofs lay crumpled on the tile, metal poles scattered at odd ends and angles beside them. A curly-headed man and his children were collecting scattered coins and bits and bobs of trash, murmuring to one another in their hushing, fluid language. Otherwise, every Alectelan passing through the square moved quickly and kept their heads down, avoiding our gaze. The pillars themselves were nearly black with graffiti. It was difficult to read through its own density, and what little I could make out was almost entirely Szayeti, but the remainder of the invective was both visual and imaginative. Around and above the marketplace, the pearl of the roofs was cracked, and in places had broken off entirely to reveal the clay below.

"If you were given governorship of this city tomorrow, Anita," I said, "what would you do about all of this?"

"Two weeks of games," said Anita instantly. Behind us, one of the minor officers audibly scoffed—on their return from the island they had begun to follow me around like dogs, taking advantage of Galvão's insistence that I have a bodyguard and hoping desperately for a word of approval—but Anita went on, unruffled, "Find a festival and celebrate it—any festival, Feast of Alekso's Left Toe, I don't care. Parades down every street, free dinner for everyone, racing, dog-fighting, wrestling. Then draft a squad of repairmen, all called into service for a year, civic duty, no occupation allowed but rebuilding—paid in very fancy officer posts, not money. Announce that in the festival's second week, and announce another festival in a month's time." She paused. "And increase the dole."

"That sounds expensive," I said.

"They're already in debt up to their ears, who cares?" said Anita. "It's their money, I may as well spend it."

"What about the sister?" I said. "She might attack at any time."

"Not with the queen off-planet," said Anita at once. The Oracle of Szayet had boarded a dinghy to one of the ships hovering at the edge of Szayet's atmosphere, purportedly to aid her soldiers in the endless search for smugglers. We suspected a different motivation. "Do you think the sister's raised an army already, then? Wherever she's gone?"

"It depends where she *has* gone," I said. "Belkayet, perhaps. They'd like to destabilize the Szayeti if they can—they've never forgotten the sting of that old conflict. Kutayet has been eyeing the outer planets in this system for years, and might give the sister ships with which to take them, if only to put Szayet in their debt. If I hadn't already arrived here, she might even have gone to Ceiao like her father."

"But as you are here—" said Anita.

"As I am," I said, "I expect Kutayet is eyeing this system even more closely than before. We'll need to deal with them, once we've dealt with matters here."

"Well, what *about* the sister?" said Anita, though that last had made her eyes glint. "We might as well deal with matters here, if that's what's waiting on the other side of it. Shall I take a few ships and go hunting?"

"Even if we had any idea where she was, I wouldn't bother," I said. "*The deer wears herself out with running; the spider grows fat...*" Anita looked blank. "Sintian philosophy," I said, and waved it aside. "I think she'll come to us. The Oracle offers us the greatest store of wealth in half the galaxy. I can't turn down such an offer without being drummed out of the Merchants' Council—"

"They'd find that difficult, at this point," said Anita.

"Control of the fleet is not control of the council itself," I said, not for the first time. "And I cannot run an empire on my own, Anita, however charmed you might be at the prospect."

"Yet," said Anita, very cheerfully.

"As I say," I pressed on, "I can't turn down the Oracle's offer without being drummed out of the council—or at the very least rousing their ire, a cost hardly worth the benefit. Which means you and I *will* need to do battle with the sister sooner or later—but the sister wants, above all other things, Alectelo, and for that she, too, needs to do battle with us."

"You think she'll attack?" said Anita.

"Doubtless she'll make an attempt," I said. "Perhaps try to bombard Alectelo, perhaps try to invade the palace itself. She may threaten me, if she reaches us. If she has neither weapons nor manpower, she may even try to charm me."

"I'd let her charm me," said Anita, looking altogether too pleased at the prospect.

"I wish I could feel the same," I said. Medveyet was long forgotten among the Ceian Empire's possessions, but my reputation had lingered among every prince or chieftain I had met since. It was not the attentions I disliked—far from it—but it rankled to be seen as an easy mark. "The most likely outcome, in any case, is that she will make a frontal assault and be shot down from the air. And then, with any fortune, we will negotiate a diving treaty, collect our soldiers, and arrive home in a hail of glory. Then, Captain, you may begin to think of leisure time—on Ceiao, where our business is."

"Business," said Anita, and sighed, and stretched. "Worship regulations. *Land reforms.* I should have known Kutayet was just sweet talk."

I smiled, though I didn't let her see it. Behind us, the officer was making another disgusted face. "I've seen enough of the market," I said, carefully not looking at him. "If we're going to discuss business, perhaps we ought to do it away from prying ears?"

"None of these people speak—" said Anita, and then caught on and grinned wider. "Why not? Lead the way."

The little room where the queen had stationed us was filling up increasingly with nonsense. Galvão had passed on all of our requests for luxuries, and to my great irritation, the Oracle had turned down none of them. She seemed entirely unconscious of money, and what was worse, entirely unconscious of host etiquette. Today, apparently from her distant ship and without being asked, she had ordered the servants to lay out a full feast on our desk, all Ceian foods: pottage with ground meat and fennel, flatbread with soft cheese, currants and pears.

"In the name of all fortune," I said. "She must have had the cheese shipped twenty-four thousand light-years."

Anita made a face at the pottage. "If I wanted to eat like a soldier, I'd be on campaign," she said, and popped a handful of currants into her mouth. "Maybe she's trying to give us a hint."

"I don't give her credit for that kind of subtlety," I said.

"Speaking of subtlety," said Anita, picking up a sharp little knife from beside the pears. "Do you not trust Paulo?"

"Who?" I said. "Oh—the lieutenant. How do you know his name?" She grinned wolfishly, and I raised an eyebrow at her, not entirely amused. "Perhaps you have too much leisure time already. I'm afraid I don't trust anyone with our business before it's concluded. You don't think he'll take offense?"

"Doubt it," said Anita. "*Two* nights with him and it's still you he thinks hung the moon. They all do."

"And you?" I said, for the pleasure of hearing the answer.

"I only think you shattered it into pieces, personally," she said. "Get it over with: What did you want to discuss? Belkayeti in officer school again?"

"No," I said. "It's gods I would like to speak of, in fact. You are from a family of no real power, Anita—"

"Thanks *very* much," she said.

"Don't take insult," I said. "I am not Thiago Veguion—you know how little I care for lineage. If you or your sister had any real loyalties to other families, I would find you intolerable to deal with. You are from a family of no real power—well and good. None of these Szayeti in the city are from what the Sintian leadership here would consider *quality*, but many of them have become priests, and have risen in wealth and status from there. A few are even now in government. Clearly there is something the Oracles have done that preserves not only the city's stability but the popularity of *Dom* Caviro, and what I want to know is, were we to attempt such an integration, how would we go about it?"

"You *do* like making enemies, don't you," said Anita.

"Not at all," I said, surprised. "You know how hard I worked at—"

"Not what I mean," she said. "Am I meant to understand you see me as one of these priests? Can't say I like the haircuts." She sliced deeply into the pear, withdrew the dripping knife, and ran a finger along the flat of the blade. "I suppose at the end of the day you're talking about having foreigners on the council."

"I might not put it quite so bluntly," I said.

"You don't need to," she said, and licked thoughtfully at her knuckle. "It'd solve the problem of Veguion, at any rate. Glad to hear you're finally tiring of allowing your detractors a voice in policy."

"I am not *tiring* of every old family on the council," I said. "Though if I did want more loyalists present, I suppose the first step would be expanding officer recruitment off-planet—but that would be extraordinarily radical, even for me."

"Can't do it with the empire's borders unstable, anyway," said Anita.

"Certainly not with Kutayet eyeing our provinces to the extent she is," I said.

"You *have* been meaning to go on campaign again," she said, and grinned.

"So *if* I wanted it," I said, "perhaps our first step would, necessarily— What is it *now*?"

There was an Alectelan at the door, wheeling an enormous box. "Delivery, sir," he said. "Imported carpets."

"Did you order them?" I said to Anita.

"I might have," she said. I stared at her, and she said, "I toss them off as they come to my mind. It's like being a poet. Was I supposed to write it all down?"

"You had to deliver them to *our* room?" I said to the Alectelan.

"Says on the package they had to be delivered to your room specially," he said stubbornly. "Says right here it's a personal gift."

He tried to show me, but I waved him away. "No, never mind, dismiss yourself." And then, to Anita once he had retreated: "Let the queen trip over them, next time she stops in to deliver us *pottage*. She can get a good look at the price of trying to charm us."

In retrospect, I expect that was rather funny.

CHAPTER

ELEVEN

GRACIA

It was after four hours in the carpet that I began to have difficulty breathing.

We had accounted for the claustrophobia, of course. I had hidden in more cramped spaces, and Zorione and I had crawled through tunnels half our height when fleeing Alectelo. Panic I could handle.

We had not entirely accounted for the heat. By the third hour I was desperately glad that the smuggler's station hadn't carried any kohl for me to put on my eyes. After another I was wondering if I could take off my robe altogether. This was a remarkably silly idea, as I had no idea when I would be deposited at my destination, but by this time the oxygen in the box had begun to grow thin.

Coming down from the satellite had been nearly painless. Being carried from the harbor was less so: I jolted across the carriage floor every time it stepped over a bump in the road, up and down and rattling against the crate's walls until my head ached. I began to wish that I had had Zorione accompany me, and damn security. Were we still by the shoreline? Were we passing by the boat races, or the dance halls? Was this the Winter Market, or surely it was the Summer Market? I could hear people talking distantly, in Szayeti and Sintian and Cherekku and a sprinkling of Ceian, but I could barely make out the words. My city came into focus, and then faded again. I shut my eyes and tried to count the bumps—one hundred, two hundred, three—until that too grew hypnotic, and then I tried only to remember every prayer I knew.

It was after a series of particularly heavy jolts that I realized I was going up a flight of stairs—many flights of stairs. Someone was carrying me. I tried to pull my swimming mind together, to push myself upright within the tightly wrapped cloth. Whoever it was that was carrying me was saying something, and then came the hardest thump of all, and I was at last blessedly still.

Retreating footsteps, then a welcome rush of cool air. I rolled out of the carpet and onto my palace floor, and lay there flat as a dying fish, gasping for breath.

The ceiling was familiar. Why was the ceiling familiar? I propped myself up on one elbow, with as much poise as I could muster, and looked around.

I was in the Yellow Room again. It had been cleaned since I had used it last, but I could still see the dust high on the walls and the windows. Someone had brought in stacks of new books. Someone had taken away my father's favorite tapestries.

There were two other people in the room with me. One was the woman who had opened up my crate. She was young and very pretty, with a cropped head of straight dark hair and a deep blue cloak pinned with gold, in all aspects an officer from a propaganda holo. Only her eyes ruined the picture: a disconcertingly flat black, a shark's eyes. The other person was sitting behind my father's desk, his hand half-lifted over a tablet, looking straight at me.

The first man of Ceiao was not very tall, nor was he very broad. He was much darker than me, with a long, narrow face and hooded eyes, and he wore his hair shaved very close to his head. His nose was long and crooked and his mouth full, and there was a sheen of faint stubble on his chin. Underneath it, running parallel to his jaw where a dimple might otherwise have been, was the forked and wavering line of an old, deep scar.

He stared at me where I lay on the floor. "Ah," he said at last.

"I am Altagracia Caviro Patramata," I said, "father-beloved lady of Alectelo, heir to the throne, and rightful Oracle of Szayet. To the governor of Madinabia and commander of Ceiao, hail."

There was a brief silence. Then the woman in the soldier's cloak began to laugh.

"Captain," said Commander Ceirran reprovingly, without turning away from me. His eyes went from me to the box, and back to me again. "Well," he said, after a moment, "I hope none of the men have lost too much money betting on the frontal assault."

I struggled to my feet. The dizziness from the carpet was passing, and I was beginning to realize how very fortunate I had been that the journey down had been quick. "I have come," I said, "despite great personal danger and through the massed forces of the false prophet's illegal war, to beg your mediation in negotiating a peace for the lasting prosperity of Szayet and her allies."

"Yes," said Ceirran. "You know, I rather imagined you did. Altagracia Caviro—Patramata, was it? I see. Patramata, I must admit that this doesn't come at a convenient time."

This seemed so inane that I was not sure how to reply.

"Not that I don't appreciate you, ah, taking the trouble," he added, and looked me up and down. I drew myself up to my full height at once. My robe was blue organza, and patterned with lilies, and my hair, though doubtless mussed, fell over my shoulders as artfully as I could arrange it. I tilted my chin up and angled myself so that the light from the windows shone on my body directly: mouth, hips, chest, lowered lashes, bare throat.

He sighed. "Ana will find a convenient room for you to stay in until I have time for your suit," he said. His Ceian accent gave him a very slight drawl, shading his sentences gently into boredom. "Please entertain yourself until then. You're dismissed." And he picked up his pen again.

For a moment I could neither see nor hear, so hot was I with rage. In the next I felt the officer's cool hand on my shoulder, and I jerked away at once. She was smirking. I ignored her. This was the great man of Ceiao? This was the man who held half the galaxy in his fist?

"Crude," I said.

Ceirran's hand paused in its movement. Beside me, the officer raised an eyebrow.

"I'm sorry?" he said.

"Crude," I said, "and graceless. And obvious. Was that meant to make me feel small? *You are dismissed*, you say, as if I were your servant. Why should I care? I am the rightful queen and sovereign lady of the palace in which you sit. If you want to injure me, tell me *I have no further need of you*, as if I am worthless except that you may need me—*that* might strike home. Or tell me *Try not to get in the way*, as if I were a child. Or pretend at concern for my health in the carpet, so that I should feel myself to be weak, and feel that you knew it. Or compare me to my sister—or to my father—or to the Undying—anything that would acquit you better than this paltry dig, this half insult, which any of my city's tavern-keepers could manage at closing time."

Ceirran put down his pen.

"Does it really matter so little to you what I call you?" he said. I could not read his face. His drawl had vanished entirely. "Certainly you believe yourself to be a queen. I don't doubt it. But I rather think you already know that your army disagrees. Why else smuggle yourself into my presence like a thief?"

"Should I rather have sent you a message by tablet to beg for an audience?" I said. "Will you pretend you would have granted it? Only a fool would have allowed you any choice in whether or not to see me."

"And you are no fool," he said, tone still entirely unreadable, and leaned forward. "Tell me this: What would happen if I brought you before your sister's army, and let *them* see you, and do with you whatever your sister willed?"

"Then you would make yourself into a villain," I said, "and me into a martyr."

"A martyr is not a queen," he said.

"Perhaps not," I said. "But a martyr *will* be seen. She will become a display that no one watching her will soon forget."

He blinked at that, a slow, dark sweep of eyelashes. "Make myself a villain," he said. "So now both your reputation and my own are entirely dependent upon your good opinion. Forgive me if I doubt that. It's a Ceian habit, I'm afraid."

"I forgive you," I said. "It's a queen's habit to be generous to her guests."

At that I saw his mouth twitch upward, though he stifled the movement almost at once. "Your guests," he said. "Your palace, and your good opinion. No one could ever accuse you of not being possessive. I might even be forgiven for forgetting that you came here to ask for my help."

"To negotiate your mediation, Commander," I said, a little more sharply than I intended to. I was having some difficulty keeping control over my own mouth, which wanted to curl in reply.

"To negotiate my mediation, Patramata," said Ceirran. "My deepest apologies. I'll watch my words more carefully in your presence."

I almost thought I was being condescended to again—there was an edge in his tone that suggested mockery—but his face made me uncertain: His body was as unmoving as a stone, his gaze intent. I met it unblinkingly, and saw some minute muscle at the corners of his eyes relax.

"You guard your words with so much care already," I said. "I think if you had guarded your presence as closely, Commander, I might never have managed to arrive here to ask for help at all."

His face broke open: a real smile, broad and unhidden. "Now that was very nearly a compliment," he said.

"Does that mean you care for my opinion after all?" I said. Something funny was happening in the area just under my rib cage, a warm and peculiar adrenaline, sharper and stronger than wine. I thought briefly of the hard, terrible spikes of fear, which had stolen my breath every morning of these past months as soon as I opened my eyes, and dismissed the thought at once. What made me breathless now was clearer than fear, and had neither its sense nor its wisdom.

"What an interesting question," Ceirran said. "Perhaps a better one would be whether you care for mine? You have burst in upon my conversation, put yourself entirely in my power, demanded my judgment in your favor, and insulted me openly. You know my reputation. How do you suppose I might answer that?"

Did he mean it? Was he threatening me? His smile had vanished. The silence was stretching, and he made no move to fill it. I was conscious of the weight of his anticipation, of his fierce and steady stare. I met it as I had done before, but this time he looked away abruptly, down toward his tablet, and my heart jumped.

"Might," I said. "You *might* take me to my sister's guards, and have me thrown in prison, as you have already threatened to do. You might shoot me where I stand. You might take me to Ceiao and parade me as a captured enemy. You might cut off my head and present it to my sister as a gift."

At that last he looked back up at me, eyes narrowed. "I might," he said.

"But you haven't," I said.

His head tilted. "And why shouldn't I?"

I swallowed. My heart was singing in my ears, as high and thin as a piper.

"Because if you and I are at all the same," I said, "I think I am the first person in a long while who has managed to surprise you."

The commander leaned forward, his hands splayed on the desk and his face as blank as stone, and I nearly was afraid of him. Then he closed his eyes, and sat back again, and smiled a smaller smile.

"Do you know," he said, "perhaps you're right."

Then he turned to the captain, who was staring. "Please leave us," he said. "The princess of Szayet and I have much to discuss."

"Ceirran," said the woman.

"Captain," said Ceirran. "You may stay outside the door, if it pleases you. Nevertheless I assure you that I do feel capable of defending myself against open attack by a weaponless refugee."

The captain gave Ceirran a look, which had a great deal too much in it for me to read. "*Sir*," she said, and strode from the room in a swirl of blue cloak. A moment later I heard her bootheels clacking down the corridor.

Ceirran pushed his chair away from the desk and stood. "I thought you might prefer not to be outnumbered," he said.

"How generous," I said.

He laughed. "I call that fair. You *have* risked it all, haven't you? There's five hundred of your sister's sworn men between you and the door. If I opened it and shouted for Captain Ana to fetch any one of them, you'd be dead within a minute."

"I would," I said. "But you haven't."

"I haven't," he agreed, and circled slowly round the desk. He was not a thickset man, but even without the scars, it would have been plain he was a fighter: There was a presence to his body, a consciousness to how he moved and leaned and crossed his arms, that made him seem larger than he really was. "I suppose you've guessed what the queen has offered me."

So she had already tried to cut her deal. "Arcelia is a fool," I said.

"A rich fool," said Ceirran, "if she can deliver."

I had known Ceians at my father's court. There had been nothing they loved better than a rich fool. Ceirran was watching me closely, now. I tried to picture him among them, tried to picture that sharp stare following me across my father's crowded banquet hall, and my mind shied away.

"No one could deliver on that promise," I said. "Not a single ingot of the cheapest iron will come onto any Szayeti beach without half the populace rioting. What you'd buy wouldn't be treasure, but a bloody and expensive war. You'd lose the whole system for the sake of a plunder that would last three weeks."

He inclined his head. "A fair answer," he said.

"I should think so," I said.

"Fair," he said, "but too quick. Too confident. I would linger over it a little—I might even look sorry to deliver the bad news, if I felt I could manage it." His mouth softened, though his eyes did not. "And another tell, Patramata," he said, almost gently. "You avoid saying *she*. If discussing your usurper is so painful you cannot do it without wincing, you had better not let me know so soon."

"I hadn't—" I said, and then stopped when my voice caught.

"No," he said, "I didn't think you had realized." He turned away and busied himself deliberately with his tablet.

The sudden absence of that gaze was like surfacing from water. Awareness surged back into my body, like blood returning to a limb. "Do not offer me pity," I said harshly.

He stopped, though he did not turn. "I don't pity you," he said.

There was none of that terrible gentleness in his voice. There was no generosity in it at all. But still I said: "Then look at me."

His hands on the tablet curled briefly into fists.

"I have been looking at you," he said roughly.

I was conscious at first of a great heat in my face. Following it almost at once, so strong my ears nearly rang, was a fierce rush of deep and brilliant feeling, too unfamiliar and too savage for me to name as triumph. "Commander," I began, and then, blindly, impulsively, "Ceirran—"

He winced. I was sorry for that, abruptly, in a way I did not entirely understand. Every inch of me felt a tender place, and I was still conscious of the tightness of the carpet, its heat and airlessness, its constriction of my lungs and hands. "Ceirran," I went on, my heart still skipping with that brutish electricity, unable to see any other path forward except to strike home, "isn't there anything I might say? Isn't there any bargain you'd strike with me—isn't there anything I could offer you—anything I can do for you, to convince you to help me—"

"What an absolutely merciless person you are," he said softly.

I was very nearly sorry for that, too. It was not the question, which had hung between us since the moment I had rolled out of the carpet. Rather it was the fact that I had said it aloud at last, and there was no taking it back now.

"Ceirran," I said again, and stepped forward, meaning to set a hand on his arm, but he turned then, and came toward me.

There was a startling grace to the way Matheus Ceirran

moved. It was not at all like the grace I had learned, carefully and diligently, in the ballrooms of this very palace. Rather it was of a piece with that consciousness that made him seem greater than his actual size: the certainty that he could move with great speed, or great violence, and what was notable was not his potential for savagery but his restraint over it. A hairsbreadth before his nearness might have been called crowding, he stopped before my face.

"Tell me to believe you," he said. "About your sister—about your treasure. Tell me to believe you."

I wet my lips, almost more nervousness than show, and watched his eyes flicker. "Believe me," I said.

"Tell me to trust you," he murmured.

"Trust me," I said.

"Tell me to give you the Szayeti throne," he said.

"Ceirran," I said, more breath than sound, "give me whatever I want."

His mouth parted a little. Then he said, "Tell me something. Tell me the truth."

"What do you want me to say?" I said.

He said, "Did you come here to try to seduce me?"

I looked him in the eye. Then I let my gaze travel, very slowly, down the length of his body: the glitter in his eyes, the breadth of his shoulders, the faint stubble peppering his jaw. Ceirran held very still. When my eyes drew back up to his face, he exhaled silently.

I said, "Will you let me?"

He said, a little roughly: "I haven't decided yet."

"Oh," I said. "All right," and I reached behind myself, and undid the little knot that held my robe together, and let it slither to the floor.

Ceirran's face went absolutely blank. I said, "Let me know when you do."

He looked up at the ceiling and mouthed something. If he had not been Ceian, I would have thought it was a prayer. "'Crude,'" he said despairingly, and lifted his fingers to the edge of my jaw.

"Oh, please, Commander," I said, my eyes wide, "tell me how you would have done it differently," and he was laughing as his mouth met my throat.

CHAPTER TWELVE

CEIRRAN

She lay boneless on the floor, afterward, with one knee hitched up and her breaths slowing minute by minute. I watched her from the corner of my eye, and after only a few seconds of my observation the faint line between her eyebrows disappeared, and she tilted her chin a little, and the soft curve of her jaw caught the light. I leaned over and cupped her cheek in my hand.

"It's a lovely picture," I said.

I would not have seen her mouth twitch if I had not been looking. "I thought it might be too much to hope for a moment's truce," she said.

"I could say the same," I said. "Another man might be insulted by it, princess—how relentlessly you press at my borders."

"*Your* borders," she said, laughed disbelievingly, and opened her eyes. The sun was a cool living white on the walls and the desk and on the planes of her face, and it hollowed her irises into metal where the light struck them through. "And would you like me to stop?"

That was pressing, too, but she knew it—she knew I knew it—she was smiling again, and I bent to kiss her mouth, helpless not to and more than a little amused by it. When I withdrew, she stood, and picked up my cloak where I had discarded it beside the desk and drew it around herself, and went to the high window and twitched aside the curtain there. Her mouth worked, either in thought or disappointment. I wondered which.

"It doesn't escape me that you have made me no promises," she said.

I stood and went to her, and peered over her shoulder at the sea of milling soldiers. The fabric of my cloak was rough, and thin enough that I could feel beneath it her warm shoulder blades, pressing into my chest. I curved a hand round her waist, and let it slip forward and down, along the swell of her stomach.

She let the curtain fall, and I could feel the edge of her smile. "I might have known a general would never really rest," she said. "Why? Is it too like being unprotected?"

"On the contrary," I said. "What protection do I have left? You caught me out of my armor, and now you have stolen my cloak. I don't doubt that if I had a crown, you would lift it from my head."

At that she went still, and shrugged the cloak off so it slipped between our bodies to the tiled floor. "Is that what Ceiao expects of me?" she said, without turning her head.

"No," I said, and bent, enjoying the pleasant tiredness in my muscles, and lifted the cloak and tucked it around her bare shoulders again. "Take me lightly. I haven't even given you a Szayeti crown yet."

She did turn to face me then, and she was smiling. "So it is *yet*," she said.

It had been some time since I had walked into so plain a trap. I looked away, but it was too late: She had seen me smiling, too. "It doesn't escape me that I have made you no promises," I said, and spread my fingers out over the warmth of her arms beneath the cloth.

"Haven't you?" she said. "Let me see if I can find them," and stood up on her toes, and fit her mouth to mine. Behind her, the cloak crumpled to the floor again, forgotten.

Before, we had been on my desk, her legs spread and her head thrown back, her long black hair brushing the surface of my tablet as it swayed back and forth. Now I pushed her gently against the wall beside the window, one hand on her shoulder and the other on her hip. Her mouth was curved again, but there was a curious distance to how she looked at me. I felt as if I were being watched through a pane of glass.

"So ask, princess," I said, and let go of her hip and slid my hand across her belly, my palm broad and rough against her soft skin. "Demand a promise from me."

She said nothing, still, but her breath gave her away, hitching and irregular. I could feel her hiccuping pulse under my hands. Her mouth was a little parted.

"Say, *Promise me soldiers*," I said, and moved my hand down and down. Her pulse, beneath it, beat harder. "Say, *Promise me a crown*," and I curled my fingers, and began to move them.

"And what then?" she said roughly. I bent to kiss the sensitive spot on her neck, so that she would not see me smile, and felt her shudder against my body. "Do you mean to tell me this is an exchange?"

"An exchange?" I murmured against her jaw. "Of course. What else would it be?"

Then her hand was between us, covering mine. I stilled, but she only laughed breathlessly and pushed it down harder; after a moment I understood and began to move my hand to the rhythm she set me, slow and steady.

"A collusion," she said into my ear, and spread her legs, and it was not thought but instinct that fit me between them.

The next morning Anita sulked for six hours, a new record, and then sauntered up behind me while I was locking the door of the Yellow Room. "All right," she said. "What are you going to do with her now? I don't suppose you can keep her locked in a spare office forever."

"I wasn't planning on it," I said. "In fact, I was imagining I would put the matter of her queenship to the priests."

If I had been hoping to surprise her, I failed. She smirked and fell in beside me as I turned toward the staircase down to the lower levels of the palace. "They might drum you out of the Merchants' Council," she said.

"They won't, I think," I said. "A rather unstable woman, the current queen. Not precisely the kind of partner Ceiao would like to have in the region, especially not if Kutayet appears threatening. She may have made attractive promises, but can she deliver, et cetera, et cetera? Does that sound convincing to you?"

"If it doesn't, I can think of something that will," she said, and then, when my stride stumbled, "Don't give me that look. You *know* what I mean."

I looked straight ahead at an elaborate tapestry of what appeared to be a Szayeti king wrestling a lion. At last I said, "I would prefer not to use her death for this."

She was quiet as we passed through the door at the end of the hallway and made our way down the spiral staircase. The whole palace seemed to be nothing but staircases and hallways: Three centuries of limited space had led *Dom* Caviro to build its house up, rather than out, and it made my legs ache. "Ceirran," she said, "how much of this is about sentiment? You don't have to lie this time."

"Sentiment for Quinha," I said, "or sentiment for Gracia?"

"Oh, she's *Gracia* now?" said Anita.

"I'm afraid she will remain *Gracia*," I said. "At least for the foreseeable future. If the priests perform as she expects, I think she will be a better friend to us than her sister would have been—no matter the sister's promises. She is at least a reasonable woman."

"I don't doubt she is," said Anita. "But that's not what this is about, is it? You *like* her."

I shot her a hard look, but she only smiled.

"I like her, too," she said.

"You hardly know her," I said, surprised. We had at last reached the bottom of the staircase, which turned outward into a long entrance hall, nearly all marble floors and walls and pillars. Only the ceiling was ordinary limestone, painted with stylized scenes of Sintian soldiers marching over mountains and rivers. At the end were a wide pair of double doors, beside which four Szayeti soldiers stood, faces impassive.

When I pushed the doors open, I looked down the long expanse of the Bolvardo del Tombo, which stretched before me through hundreds of cross streets until it came to a point at the thin silver hem of the sea. Along it, Alectelans drifted by in groups, ducked into shops, sat on steps nibbling on bread from street carts. There were plenty of my soldiers, too, sitting on the sidewalk out of the way of the scampering crab-litters and drinking beer. Those few near enough to see me jumped to attention and saluted guiltily. At the end of the road nearest us, standing at the base of the palace steps with the hood of her robe over her head and her arms crossed, was an elderly Szayeti woman half my height.

"I could say the same for you," said Anita. And then, before I could reply, "Who's our new friend?"

I led her down the steps, and held out a hand to the little woman. "Zorione Buquista? I'm glad you were able to catch the ship. Your mistress is waiting for you upstairs."

She didn't shake my hand, though. Instead she stood on

tiptoes, poked her finger directly into my face, and demanded, "Who did you tell?"

"Tell?" I said, startled.

"Who did you tell!" she snapped again. "Which of your soldiers did you give the coordinates?"

"You're talking to the commander of Ceiao," said Anita, and reached out a hand to pull the little woman's arm down, but I caught her wrist.

"None, madam," I said. "Only the pilot sent to fetch you."

She stared at me. "You're not lying," she said.

"I dislike the habit," I said. "What is this about?"

"Our satellite exploded," she said. "It was hit by a royal missile. Your pilot and I were the only ones who made it out alive."

I swore and spun round. "Anita," I said, but she was already halfway up the steps, gun drawn. When she pushed open the doors, there was a shout in the Szayeti tongue, and the guards' hands went to their gun belts. Anita fired several times in rapid succession. There was a series of thumps.

"*Damn* that woman," I said, and then cupped my hands around my mouth and shouted, "*Ceiao!*"

It was like watching the river rise in a thunderstorm. My soldiers sprang up all down the boulevard, hands flying to their guns, dropping pocket breads and glasses of beer. Those who weren't already running were shouting across the street, waving to their comrades on cross streets and at the ends of alleys. The Alectelans were scattering like flies. They moved like hunting dogs, my men, and we would have the advantage of the charge, but the palace guard had the advantage of holding the damned building, and I had no time to watch them. "Do you know a safe place you can get to?" I said to the nursemaid Zorione and, when she nodded, spun and followed my captain up the steps at a sprint.

My men within the palace had heard the shout, too. The

entrance hall was already the scene of a firefight, pulses of green light ricocheting off pillars and walls. I got off one lucky shot at a red-cloaked soldier before I was forced to throw myself down behind one of the enormous statues. From there, at least, I was able to aim more carefully, picking off Szayeti one by one as they clattered in from one adjoining hallway after another. When my men arrived at the doors in a great wave, I shouted, "Cover me!" and, as they surged in, I took off up the spiral staircase.

There was no sign of Anita, but there were signs that she had been there: corpses, sprawled at all angles across the stairs. There must have been five or six of them—it was a relief to see so few, for it meant that the palace guards did not know which room Gracia was being kept in. There was time.

What *did* the guards know? I had only told the pilot sent to fetch the nursemaid the coordinates of the satellite where she was staying, and I had only heard them once, from Gracia in the Yellow Room. The pilot was the only one who could have leaked them to the queen's people, and that made no sense. Why would she have done that and still brought Zorione safely home?

There were more corpses in the hallway, staring sightlessly up at tapestries. Anita was crouched before Gracia's door, her gun raised. When I strode forward, she swung the barrel toward me at once, and then relaxed.

"They only came because of the noise," she said to me, jerking her chin at the bodies. "I'm sure of it."

"Good," I said, and bent at the door to unlock it while she stood cover. When I slipped inside, Gracia was standing behind my desk. Her robe was thrown over her shoulders again, and her eyes were bright with terror.

"Is it her?" she said. "Has she come for me?"

"Not yet," I said, "but she's going to. Is the palace bugged?"

Gracia's face froze, then she cursed.

"Not by ordinary means, no," she said. "But the Pearl of the Dead has powers beyond ordinary means."

I wanted to kick through the wall. It did not surprise me at all that a quicksilver pearl computer built by Alekso of Sintia was capable of extreme surveillance, but— "You didn't think to mention this?" I said.

"He has never helped her against me before," she said.

The tone in which she said it made me pause. I had known many of the devout over the course of my career: There were worshippers of Alekso on Medveyet and Madinabia alike, and the dregs of them on Sintia and its outlying systems. There were even a few in secret on the outskirts of Ceiao, among the refugees I knew so well. Gracia did not sound like one of these faithful. It was rather the opposite: She sounded as if she had been betrayed.

"We'll have the palace soon," I said, and indeed below us the noise of gunfire was already beginning to die down, and I could hear shouting in muffled Ceian. "Then we'll mobilize our ships. Your sister is in the atmosphere—"

"She isn't," said Gracia. "Not if she knows I'm in the palace. If she hasn't already landed on Szayet, it will be a matter of hours." Her face changed abruptly. "Zorione. If Alekso Undying told Arcelia I was here—"

"She is safe," I said. "Nearly safe—she is the reason the fighting began. She arrived here, and told us that your sister had blown up the satellite."

Gracia took that like a blow. She sat down in my chair, hard, and rubbed a hand over her eyes.

"The smuggler?" she said. "The woman who helped me?"

"Your nursemaid said she and my pilot were the only ones left," I said. "I'm sorry. Was she close to you?"

Gracia exhaled, and made no reply. A moment later she opened her eyes again, and they were clear.

"Fine," she said. "I am in my palace, and I am among my people. I have saved all of these that I can save. I can ask for no more."

"You do have a little more than those, I should think," I said.

At that her mouth curled at the edge, satisfied. She held my gaze.

"So I do," she said. "Let her come."

CHAPTER THIRTEEN

GRACIA

I lied about the war.

The siege of the palace lasted for three and a half days. Few new lovers have ever had such a honeymoon. Ceirran had, of course, the full use of his fleet. When his enemy Semfontan had died, he had not sent it back to Ceiao. This had been Arcelia's demand, and now it was her great disadvantage. We were given almost complete cover from bombing and other attacks from the air, and those parts of the Szayeti fleet who remained loyal to Arcelia—many did not—were entirely unable to reach the planet. Dozens of Ceirran's officers, Captain Ana among them, boarded fighters and leapt in them from the harbor to the sea to the wide black sky, where they engaged in endless skirmishes over our small part of the atmosphere. For three nights, we could see their fighting with the unaided eye, as bursts of green and red light stuttered and burst between the moons, and streaks fell through the stars down into the sea.

Among those stars: an absence. A satellite, which had once held a woman I had asked to help me.

I lied about the war. I lied about how it began.

I said, *A week later, the guards came for me.* I told you that the people rose up to break me out of prison, Raimundo at their head with his red cloak and his eyes full of fire, as cleanly and beautifully as if it were an act of God. I told you that they rose into a host of rebels for me, rallied to my side while I lay in captivity, staring at the window like a caged bird.

The part about prison is true, of course. But the worst mistake Arcelia ever made was waiting even a minute to have me arrested. It gave me a great deal too much time.

I gathered my army. Raimundo was first: He had been my bodyguard, and he knew me, and I knew that he was strong and careful, and that he could keep his head amid danger. I chose him for these reasons, and because though he was young, he was well respected among the other soldiers, and because he spoke fluent Szayeti. Most of all, I chose him because he was loyal to a fault, and he blushed when he looked at me, and I knew I could use that, when the time came.

Then, when I was sure of him, I did what I had never done on my own, and put on my shoddiest cloak, and wiped the kohl from my face and the paint from my mouth, and climbed over the palace wall. I went to each of the taverns in the plazas, where I knew I would find the wealthiest of Alectelo's merchants and landowners, the ones who thought they were clever, and night after night, I began to ask questions. I asked them what they knew of Arcelia Caviro, the army's pet. I asked them whether they had seen her shifting her feet and rolling her eyes at ceremonies, whether they had heard the rumors that she was as impious as a child. I asked a merchant if it was true that she was reckless with money, a landowner if it was true that she had fled all her lessons on soil management to practice wrestling. I asked if it was true that she was planning to double taxes, and draft their sons and daughters to be sent halfway around the planet to work the farms. I asked them how much Szayet understood her—how much she understood of Alectelo, of its people. I asked them if she spoke Szayeti. I asked them whether, if they were the Lord Undying—if they were the god of Szayet, who so loved Szayet's people—they might not have chosen another heir entirely. And when they told me that the god had already named her heir instead, that she was the Oracle, I asked them whether they really believed it.

Perhaps they would have risen up on their own. Perhaps they might have just as easily come to their own conclusions about Arcelia's heresy. Perhaps Zorione's word would have done it—Zorione, and some sense among my people of resentment at the thought of a bad monarch, or a passion for righteousness, or love for justice, if in Alectelo there has ever been such a thing. Perhaps, rather than sowing doubt, I should have had faith. It was only that, when I handed the bartender eighty centonos to buy another round of drinks, I thought of my father's face.

On the evening of the fourth day, I opened the tap for my bath and seawater ran out.

There was no mistaking it for fresh. It was brown as bread, and the smell was undeniable: thick, briny, sharp, and wild, the wide untamable planet come running into this little room. I cursed and went out into the bedroom, where Ceirran was half-dressed on the bed, peering on his tablet at a map of the atmosphere.

"Are you sure you have her location?" I said.

"Nearly," he said. "In a few days' time—"

"We may not have a few days," I said. "Come and see."

When he saw the salt water pooling against the marble, he cursed, too. "It'll be the whole palace," he said. "I never took her for a poisoner. Where are the wells? You people can't possibly have fresh water shipped in from off-planet."

"There's fresh water all under the island. Alectelo is almost hollow beneath," I said. "Our god did leave us the means to live on. And the recycling plants—but no, it's the wells she'll have ruined. The pipes for the palace begin just north, along the Bolvardo del Tombo. Some traitor in Alectelo has redirected them—dug a tunnel to the sea, if I had to guess. She's always had loyalists—"

"She won't for long," he said grimly. "Order your men to have new wells dug. Fresh water under the *whole* island?" I nodded, and he said, "Behind the palace, then—near your harbor-gate. Lay pipes. I'll pay your workmen's wages. Bring me my cloak, and give notice to the harbor; Anita can't have gone far. The ships can be prepared in an hour's time. The men have had less notice for worse missions."

I stood at the door of my bedroom, when he had his cloak on, and pressed his hand in my own. "You'll come back soon," I said.

His mouth curled. "Do you really find your own victory so tedious?" he said.

I had not liked fighting a war. I liked *not* fighting a war still less. "Come back with your shield or on it," I said dryly, and drew his face down. "You are *sure* of her location?"

He let himself be kissed, then drew away. "With my shield or on it," he said. The daylight was draining down outside the windows behind me, and the long shadow of our bedposts bent at sharp angles over his face and shoulders. "Captain Orcadan has the palace detail. Ask him if you should need anything." He hesitated and then said, far more gently than I liked, "I'll be back in only a day or two."

"I don't doubt it," I said, and nearly didn't.

My view of the sea and the harbor sky was as white-striped as a tiger pelt, and had been for three days. My book could not hold my attention. The men digging the wells behind the palace were insects, the shadow of the palace sliding over them long and slow, blurring their faces into invisibility. I watched the ship plumes cool into purple and then brown and at last into an ashy grey, and tried to pick out one among their number.

It was hours before sleep came for me, and even then it was a threadbare thing that left me hot and restless under the bedsheets, drifting into darkness and out again. Perhaps that was why, when I snapped into wakefulness at some small hour, it was without violence and almost without surprise that I realized someone else was in the room with me.

Senses came second, after certainty. The figure was a shadow in the corner. It was not sight that had alerted me, but the slow drip of water, and the gentle sound of her breath.

"How did you get past the guards?" I said.

"He built the city," said Arcelia. "Do you really think any barbarian can keep the palace against Him? Scream and I'll shoot."

I sat up slowly. She was carrying a gun, the barrel of which I could see glinting in the moonslight, and she was holding it loosely at her side, pointed at the carpet.

"You'll shoot anyway," I said.

"Probably," she said, and her shadow moved closer, up toward the foot of the bed. She was dressed like a treasure-diver, in tight pants and a loose white shirt, and her hair was in a long braid, hanging over her shoulder. It was this that I had heard dripping. She smelled like salt, I thought, and then I understood: the pipes, the new wells at the harbor, the doors thrown open to her by my own order, not twelve hours before. "Hello, Gracia."

I looked at her: her pointed chin, the hook of her nose, the dark hollows where I could not see her eyes. It had been a long time since I had last seen her face.

"Hello, Celia," I said, and watched that shadowed mouth curve into a smile. "What did the Ceians find," I added, "when they reached wherever it was you were supposed to be?"

"The *Ceians*," she said scornfully. "An ambush, of course, what do you think? Can't you talk about anything else? Though I suppose I shouldn't be surprised." She stepped closer again. "Do you know—I didn't expect this of you. I thought, *There must be something left even she wouldn't do.* Even after all you've said and done, I thought you had a little shame left. I should have known better, shouldn't I?" She laughed a little, under her breath. "I only thought I might finally have gotten *one* thing you wouldn't take away."

"I'm sorry to disappoint," I said. There was a light behind her through the windows, which I carefully did not turn my head to see.

She said, almost fondly: "You wouldn't know how to be sorry if you tried."

"*I* wouldn't?" I said. "You called Ceiao into the royal palace, Celia! You thrust yourself into their war! You meddled in their affairs as if the empire was a toy our father had lent you—Celia, how could you promise them the oceans? You sell them Szayet!—and you tell *me* to be sorry! And you accuse *me* of shamelessness! How can you? What gives you the right?"

Her mouth moved again, but it was not really a smile this time. She said, "Well, this, for a start," and she lifted the gun toward my head—but I had been waiting for her to do it, and I brought my fist down on her thumb to knock the weapon from her hand, and leapt out of bed toward her face.

As teenagers we had rarely fought. Despised each other, yes—insulted each other, yes—but touched each other, hardly ever. It was only as children that we had come to blows, and when we did we fought like animals, tearing at each other's faces, kicking at the soft places on each other's bodies, wrestling on the ground like a pair of dogs over a scrap of meat.

Arcelia, now, fought me like we were children. She was on top of me at once, pinning me to the ground with her knees, hitting anywhere she could reach—I scrabbled at her, at any piece of skin I could see, her neck, her arms, the flush of her cheeks—and one of her hands came to my throat, not strong enough to choke, but her nails were digging into the soft skin under my ear. I screamed and pushed up, rolled over her, slapped her hard across the face, slapped her again, at which she bared her teeth like a tiger and shoved me off so forcefully that my head smacked into the floor and rang like a bell. I was reaching for her before I could see again—

—and found nothing but empty air.

"Hold her," said Ceirran needlessly. Ana had already snatched Arcelia up, and was pinning her arms to her sides. In the shadows of my room there was nothing in the captain at all of the propaganda-holo soldier: I could see the way her arms flexed while Arcelia struggled, and the gleam of her black eyes.

My sister threw such a look of hatred at Ceirran that I wondered it did not burn him. She said to me: "I had forty warships."

"I had Ceian soldiers, Madam Oracle," said Ceirran. He was a silhouette framed in the doorway, black against the gold of the hallway, and his voice was as I had heard it when I had first met him, distant and utterly without warmth.

I sat up. My head was still ringing, and I could taste blood in my mouth. "You were a fool," I said to Arcelia. "You were a fool to let me come here, and a fool to come back. You were a fool to play with fire in the first place. What did you *think* was going to happen?"

Arcelia spat onto the carpet by Ana's boots. "I may be a fool," she said, "but I am the Oracle of Szayet, and the queen," and smiled.

I stood and crossed toward her, where Ana held Arcelia's wrists in one hand and pressed the other arm across her throat. I leaned in close, and took hold of the Pearl in my pinched fingers, and yanked it out of her ear.

She cried aloud. The web of wires dissolved at once, so much rust on her cheek. From the hole in her head, a drop of blood bubbled up, and began to work its way through the golden dust toward her jawline.

"You were a fool," I said, "and a heretic, and a usurper, and what I don't understand is—*how*, Celia? How could you think *you* had the right? How could you be so jealous?"

"Jealous?" she said. "Jealous—of *you*?"

"You stole my throne," I said. "You stole my crown! You stole my Pearl—"

"*Jealous!*" she said. She was smiling—smiling, though the blood was a long black line from her temple to her neck—it made me want to hit her again. It made me want to tear her skin open. I was a princess. I curled my fingers around the cool hard grain of the Pearl in my hand.

"You've hated me," I whispered. "You've hated me—you've wanted to destroy me—since our father took *me* to Ceiao, instead of you. You've hated me for taking him away from you, you've hated me for being the one he loved, and don't deny it—"

My sister laughed, high and hard.

"Oh, Gracia!" she said. "As if it were *him* I missed in the first place!"

For the first time since I had rolled out of the carpet, I found myself wordless. All I could do was watch as Ceirran nodded and Ana tugged Arcelia upward, as they led her out of the room with her arms pinned to her sides, and she turned at the very last moment and smiled, wide and white, into my face.

They left me alone, then, for a little while. Behind the palace, beyond the harbor-gate, a deep and nearly invisible blue was rolling into the sky. I sat on the carpet, my arms around my knees. Then I got up, and went through the stairs and trapdoors of the palace until I came to the end of a hallway, and opened a door onto empty air.

It was a sheer drop. When I looked down, I could see where the whole wall had been sheared away neatly, like Alekso had taken a knife to the roof. The ash had long since scattered. All that was left was a great pile of brick and charred stone. In the low light of dawn I could see the pale sprouts of new grass, as small as my fingernail, and some little fox or rabbit moving among the ruins.

Yes, I lied to you about the war. I lied about its ending, too.

I wanted you to believe that Arcelia was no strategist. I wanted you to believe that she was only a child, wanton and destructive, and when I had called off the burning of Alectelo I had acted the grown woman, who knew when it was time for wars to end.

And indeed my sister understood nothing of war, in the craft and the art of it. But she had never needed to. All she had needed to understand was me.

I had mistaken it for hatred, the white-hot and endless fire of her attention. Perhaps it was hatred, a little, by end. Perhaps things might have been different if I had ever hated her enough to understand her in return.

When she had set the explosion in the palace, she had understood me better than anyone else alive. She had understood me, and she had been careless with something beautiful.

I told Ceirran this, just as I am telling you. I told him all of it, cross-legged on his bed, while behind the balcony at his back the sun rose and spread like oil over the ocean. He listened carefully, sometimes thoughtful, sometimes amused, sometimes surprised. He asked me about the hunger, the fear, the dead. I expected him then to tell me about the planets he had conquered—I knew how many planets he had conquered. I expected him to tell me about the things he had done in those wars, brave and cowardly, evil and something less than evil.

He said none of this. He only said: "Did you love him? The boy who died in the explosion?"

There was neither suspicion nor rancor in it. I might have said yes, if it had been the truth.

"No," I said. "No, I didn't love him. But he was Szayeti. I was responsible for him."

He nodded. I watched his face awhile, and said, "Do you believe me?"

"Patramata," he said, "I understand you. Is that close to the same thing?"

I knelt up on the bed, and took his face in my hands, and kissed him. After a moment, I felt his hand come to rest on my cheek, calloused and warm.

He left, then, to attend to his army, and to find Arcelia's tunnel and shut it against further invaders. I watched him shut the door. Then I unlocked our balcony door, and stepped out into the morning air. It was the first time I had been outside in Alectelo since the day I had fled.

The sea was dazzling, at first. The sea always was. They were a city in their own right, those lights on the ocean, how they leapt and shuddered, how they clustered and broke against the blue. They moved like spirits, or moths, faster than ships, faster than thought. They put the sight of Alectelo from the satellite to shame.

But the sight of Alectelo from my own palace, from my city and home, was a different thing entirely. I could see the Library domes, gleaming like fire under the noonday sun. I could see the curves of the harbor-gate looping along the shoreline, from this distance as lustrous as the day they had been made. I could see the market squares' low silver roofs, wavering in the heat, and the curving shadow of the train tracks, and the towers, and the iridescent theater lights, and the distant plumes of smoke at the horizon where the ships rose and fell over the sea. I could even see the narrow white strip of the beach and the faint figures moving along it in insect trails, stooping at rare intervals to see where the ocean had relented to wash up our history for us.

There was a wind coming up from the water. I shut my eyes and blindly turned my face into it, and it swelled, rushed harder, against my chest, into my arms. It knew me, too.

CHAPTER

FOURTEEN

CEIRRAN

I was amused by the priests. They were an owlish bunch, shaven-headed and splotch-faced, blinking in the sunlight as they shuffled out of the Library. I nearly wanted to bark at them to fall in, to see the fright it would cause.

Their head was a pouch-faced scholar, who looked much too young for the job. "Commander," he said to me, and bowed, which made Anita laugh softly. "What a very unexpected honor to speak with you—"

"Tell me about how you choose new kings," I said, and pretended to be listening very hard for the next ten minutes while he did.

The fact was that Ceian soldiers had made an assault on the Szayeti palace, killed a great number of Szayeti soldiers, and arrested the Szayeti queen. This was diplomatically awkward.

Szayeti sovereignty was not what it had been when Gracia's ancestor had made the pact with Ceiao's long-overthrown cabal of priests, centuries ago. Szayet was no longer an empire, for one thing, and had lost not only Belkayet to us, but several of the greener moons at the edges of their system to Kutayet's ever-reaching hands.

Nevertheless, they had been Ceiao's dedicated ally these two hundred years, and its client kingdom for the last seventy, and besides this there was a deep unease in the Merchants' Council at the prospect of violating or being seen to violate Szayeti sovereignty. It was the home of the body of Alekso of Sintia. It was, some said, the home of his living soul. It would disrupt the feeling of the populace in our provinces—only in the provinces, of course!—to disrespect his legacy.

Consequently, the priests. It had been difficult to locate men willing to accompany me to them, which irritated me. I understood their discomfort, but the fact remained that we needed both Ceian and Szayeti witnesses. Anita was the only soldier who had volunteered with any enthusiasm, and it was very difficult to distinguish Anita's enthusiasm from her mirth.

The priests had brought a small mountain of tablets. Within these, they explained to us, lay three centuries of precedent in Szayeti law. From this assemblage an excitingly justifiable narrative of the last several days swam into view. Rather than having performed a coup d'état in the center of the Szayeti government, it became apparent, the Ceian fleet had arrived to restore order to an anarchic planet. It was in fact Arcelia Caviro—the head priest clipped off the *Diomata*, with an audible clack of teeth—who had seized power, unlawfully and blasphemously, and Arcelia Caviro who had monstrously attacked not only the priests of Alekso—the priests of Alekso!—but her sister, the very heir, whose innocence and whose martyrdom—

"All right," I said. "Thank you very much. And this—ceremony? The two weeks of waiting, and the back and forth to the chapel?"

The priests exchanged a look. "Strictly speaking," said the

head priest, "we advise—we strongly advise—that the princess meditate for the two weeks. But regarding potential signs or omens sent by the Undying Lord of Szayet, er. We also feel—respecting your sensibilities, of course, and the sensibilities of the Empire of Ceiao, and the presence in the Swordbelt Arm of a disestablishmentarian faction, whose long-held respect of our differing—"

"You mean to say that you think Alekso *made* the commander do it?" said Anita.

The head priest went blotchy. "Theologically," he said, "only theologically—it must be understood, of course, that the *nature* of the Undying, as distinguished from the *person* of the Undying, which operates through the mechanisms granted by the Pearl, or rather the *soul* of the Undying whose residence—"

Anita tipped her chair back on two legs and shrieked with laughter. "Thank you," I said to the priest. "I think we've heard enough. As for the current Oracle of Szayet—"

The priests exchanged another look. "She no longer holds the Pearl," said the head priest. "It is a simple fact that she no longer hears the voice of the god. She may be queen—but as to whether she is still Oracle, well, the precedent—"

We strolled through the streets, back toward the looming melted-cake outline of the palace. Alectelo was a patchwork city, built over centuries, and only the pearl roofs and steeples made it seem any kind of whole—that, and the fact that no matter where you stood, you could always see the gleam of the sea. In this neighborhood, the houses were low and flat, and their walls were grey-painted stucco, and all had square gardens of rock and caper bush and beach-weed. In the little alleys between, the sourgrass grew electric yellow from the gaps in the cobblestones. On Ceiao, land within the city limits became more and more of a precious commodity as our power grew. The larger one's house was, the more ostentatiously one showed off one's influence. It was funny to think that here, too, not for political but for natural reasons, every square inch was an extravagance.

Or unnatural reasons, as the case might be. "I'm no expert," said Anita, "but it seems a weak sort of government that can be exploded by someone grabbing a rock. *Is* a pearl a rock? Is it a kind of crystal? Is it one of those things like a horn or fingernail?"

"The philosopher Lorenza Albina said that all governments are exploded, in the end, by someone grabbing at one thing or another," I said. "Not quite in those words, of course."

Anita considered this. "Well," she said, "I suppose we proved her right."

"Rather Gracia did, I should think," I said.

"Oh," said Anita, "were we talking about the war on Szayet?"

There was no possible response to this except to ignore it, which I did through the rows of stucco houses and down the sprawl of the Bolvardo del Tombo toward the palace where it lay framed against the silver sea. Our soldiers jumped to attention as we approached. "Commander," said one. "The princess said she wanted to speak to you upstairs, in the council room."

Gracia had, in the weeks since the end of the siege, begun to gather some ministers and councillors around her, whose histories were entirely unknown to me. As far as I could tell they were intelligent enough, but it was plain that their wisdom came second to their loyalty. It was not a qualifier I blamed her for invoking. In her situation, I would have done the same, and it was more by misfortune than by policy that I could not on Ceiao.

No Ceian had held the title of commander since Valquíria Barran had laid it down a hundred and fifty years ago to return to her gardens. Rather than being divided among the many admirals and their own mercantile interests, as things had been before the civil war and as they were in ordinary times, the army was at this time a single organism, which had ears for only my voice and which moved at only my hand. The soldiers seemed content enough with this arrangement. Their commanding officers tended to feel a certain amount of discomfort, though, for which I could hardly blame them. I had only taken the title in order to pursue Quinha across the galaxy and end the civil war—and Quinha had been the friend of nearly every person on the Merchants' Council. I would have called the Szayeti arrangement charmingly simple, if I had not spent the last weeks walking through the ruins of Alectelo.

The princess was sitting at the far end of the table when we came in, speaking in low and urgent tones with a shaven-headed man who she had told me she intended to make minister of war, once she had the legal ability to do so. "Just who I wanted to see," she said, looking up. "I want your advice on Arcelia's soldiers."

"Gone," I said. "You can find them waiting under the palace in the dungeons, if you need them."

"That's precisely what I want your advice on," she said. "Iker"—her minister—"thinks we ought to wait for the executions until we've addressed those ships still in the atmosphere. I think we ought to hold them now. What's your opinion?"

"You ought to consider the expense, first," I said. "Do you intend to carry them out publicly? If not, you might spread them out over weeks or even months—though if you do, you should carefully consider the public's response."

"I don't intend to carry them out publicly," said Gracia. "Frankly, I would prefer to do them quietly. Even if I wanted to make a popular entertainment out of them, it would be near impossible. Most of the city knew soldiers on both sides of the war, I'm afraid."

Anita coughed, and Gracia looked at her, surprised. "Princess," she said, "a word about the prisoners, if you don't mind."

"Have several, if you wish," Gracia said. "What about them?"

Anita ran her tongue over her lip. "I was wondering," she said, "if you might think about letting them live."

I twisted abruptly to look at her, but she didn't meet my eyes. "You want to spare them?" said Gracia, surprised. "Captain, you must have killed a dozen in the palace assault alone."

"I did," Anita said. "Now I'm not killing them anymore. Why should that be strange? It's only common courtesy."

Gracia hesitated. "Captain," she said at last, "I'm afraid courtesy is the luxury of those who live without war, or those at truce within it. I am neither."

"Soldiers aren't known for courtesy," said Anita.

"I know that, thank you," said Gracia shortly, and then paused, and cleared her throat. "I'm surprised at you, Captain," she went on. "You strike me—with no insult intended—as a woman with very little time for etiquette."

Anita's eyes narrowed a little, but all she said was, "Why would I be insulted?" in cheerful tones. "I'm a fighting woman, and proud enough of it. The airs and graces must be left to my betters, and luckily enough, they so often are. I'm as unhappy as you to find myself saying the poor fools ought not to die."

"But you do think they deserve not to die," said Gracia, "and even that they deserve to make trouble for me in the future. What sort of example should I send to my enemies if I give them their lives?"

"Who said they should make trouble for you?" said Anita at once. "Give them to me and the commander, and let us take them back to Ceiao, and show them off in the streets at the triumph. Benefit us both, eh? That's politics."

There was a strange note in her voice. But Gracia looked at once satisfied and utterly contemptuous.

"I see," she said. "Very well. I suppose you agree, Commander?"

I smiled apologetically at her, which she fortunately took as an opinion. I did not like to lie to that woman aloud.

That evening it took me nearly forty minutes to track Anita down to the soldiers' quarters within the palace, already deep in drink and laughter with a group of ensigns. They all leapt to their feet when they saw me. Anita climbed to hers, and saluted with great propriety.

"Thank you, Captain," I said. "Are you quite finished? I'd like to speak to you."

She followed me without complaint down the hallways and through the back door of the entrance hall, where we crossed down the grass and shrub that covered the ground between the palace and the sea. After some time, she said, "You can't be angry, can you?"

"I'm not angry with you," I said.

"Delighted to hear it," she said. "So why are you about to walk me to the sea and throw me into the harbor?"

I stopped, not very far from the edge of the grass, and turned to face her. Her hair was tousled, her cloak half slipped from her shoulders. The days after a lengthy battle were often the worst with her, but they were the days when I least had time to rein in her excesses. Now was a rare exception.

"Why would you rather Arcelia's soldiers walk in my processional as my prisoners," I said, "but Quinha be burned on a funeral pyre?"

"More prisoners, more glory," she said at once. "Simple mathematics."

"What an inveterate liar you are," I said.

"I'm wounded," she said. "All right. Perhaps I respect them. What would you say to that?"

"*Respect* them?" I said. "And why the Szayeti more than the Madinabic chiefs? Each of them is waiting in our hold to be paraded before the laughing mob when we return home."

"Fortune knows we might stay on Szayet a long while," said Anita. "Seems sensible enough to buy ourselves a little goodwill."

I turned, and walked across the wet grass, toward the sea. After a moment I could hear her footsteps rustling behind me.

"Well," she said, "it's plain enough you think you know why, so tell me."

I said, "You wanted to see what she would say."

Just behind my ear I heard her low, rough laugh. "And what if I did?" she said. "Would that surprise you?"

"Why?" I said. "What is it you need to know about her that you don't know already?"

"About *her*?" said Anita, sounding surprised. "About the woman who threw away a kingdom over a pair of shoes? About the throne won or lost on the strength of who holds a rock the size of my thumb?—about the largest treasury in the Swordbelt Arm?"

I had never, in all the years I had known her, regretted sharing my secrets with Anita, nor did I regret sharing Gracia's secret now. Still, when we reached the harbor and stopped at the edge of the sea where the concrete fell into darkness, I sat down rather than look at her, and let my legs dangle over the edge as if I were a child.

I heard her sigh, and she settled down beside me. "Do you know?" she said, and her silhouette jerked its chin toward the sky. "Which one's Ceiao?"

I let my eyes trace across the great wash of light, falling from one horizon to the other. "This planet faces the Black Maw at night in summers," I said eventually, "and if the Swordbelt Arm lies counterclockwise..." I pointed up toward the starry river. "There."

"You're lying, aren't you," she said. "I don't think even Alekso of Sintia would know where it was just by looking."

"He might," I said. "They think here that he could do many strange things. I suspect you and I will grow tired of hearing about that, in the coming days."

"And you'd rather I didn't *undermine* you," said Anita, and heaved a sigh. "If you had told me, when you poached me from

Quinha's staff, that this is where you and I would end up—I'd have sent you packing."

"Would you have?" I said.

I could hear her breathing for a little while. "About telling me which star's Ceiao," she said, at last. "Don't worry. Only tell me when you want me to invade it again. I'll be there by morning."

CHAPTER FIFTEEN

GRACIA

In the lean grey hour before the sunrise, as the night had begun to drain away from the tapestries and the carpets and the scattered tablets, I slid out from between the sheets I shared with Ceirran, and put on my skirt and my shoes and my violet mantle, and quietly and carefully eased open the bedroom door, and went out into the world to look at the mist on the ocean.

It wasn't a warm morning. It would be; there was a heaviness in the air, settling on the back of my neck, licking at my forearms. But for now the sky was dense and cool, and the plum-blue of the dawn was spilling up the hem of the horizon, and it swelled upward as I drew closer to the shoreline. I could hear my breathing, in my own ears, and the distant crying of a gull, and nothing more.

Where the grass ended and the wide heavy stones began I eased off my sandals and left them there. My skirt I rolled up to my thighs. Even in the low light of the dawn, the sand glittered. I crossed the stones, which clacked beneath me, and stepped onto the damp white smoothness, and felt the crust break gently beneath my weight. When I knelt and pressed the edge of my palm into the beach, my hand came up heavy. The shore was filled with silver and gold.

I let the wealth trickle out of my fingers, and wiped what was left on my calf. Then I rose to my feet and walked on, toward the soft heap of shadows that had collected in an uncertain tower down the beach. At my shoulder, red at the horizon and berry-dark beside me, the ocean sighed and hushed.

The pile was covered with kelp, great ropes of it, which knotted around bits of lumber and smelled of salt. I peeled one strand away, still damp, and closed my hand around the little limestone figure that had been hiding below. It must have belonged to a statue just the right size to stand on a bedside table. Here, on this silent beach, it fit in the palm of my hand. It was the head of a lioness.

Her eyes were wide, and her mouth opened in a snarl. Though time and seawater had worn away the finer detail, the sculptor's skill was plain: the edge of her nose, the curve of her ear, her teeth, her tongue, her fury. She might have protected a noblewoman once against violence, or great disaster.

I knelt again, and set her carefully on the sand. Then I crossed away to the stretch of wide stones and wiped my feet on them, fastidious, and I stepped back into my sandals and let my skirt down around my calves, and I walked up through the pale stucco houses to my own palace, where my maidservants waited for me.

The Island of the Dead is not far from Alectelo itself. Standing at the southern tip of the city, on a clear and cloudless day, a woman of five or so feet in height can almost see it against the unbroken horizon: a dip in the sea line, a faint grey mark where Alekso might have caught His thumbnail against the green. Upon setting off from that pier, it almost at once begins to resolve into shape and form. What was haze becomes peaks and angles, and what was the sea's absence becomes waves, soaring and savage, lashing against the Island's stones with all the fury of a winter storm. Any sensible sailor would quail.

My people did. They clustered around the Island in dinghies and fishing boats, skiffs and kayaks and canoes, at such a distance that the roughness of the sea at the rocks could not upset their little vessels. There were thousands of them—sweethearts with hands clasped, elderly men leaning on husbands and wives, fathers with children on their shoulders, old women and men in faded army cloaks, girls holding gold figurines up to the sunlight that might have been human or bestial or both, teachers gathered with children, musicians with pipes in their hands, on and on as far as the eye could reach, so that every mile from Alectelo to the Island of the Dead was filled with them, face over face, rising and falling with the tide.

There was a great noise, at first, of music and chatter and laughter and trumpet. As my ship drew near, though, they fell silent. Those whose boats were large enough for them to stand did so, and those who could not safely rise lifted their heads to stare at my face. No one knelt. My prow was white, and narrow as a knife, and murmured softly through the dark water. I stood as near its end as I could without danger, and the wind lifted my loose hair from my neck. My robe was very heavy—plain, but woven with gold—and I longed for my sandals, instead of the tall and intricately patterned ceremonial leather boots. Still, I held my head as high as I could. I could feel the people's stares, hot on my skin. Near me, abruptly, an infant cried.

Where the shore curved in and dimpled and the rocks faded to pebbles and gravel, there was a moderation in the waves. My ship bore me in, and two attendants helped me into the coracle and lowered me by rope gently into the water. I hardly needed to set hands on the oars before the currents had already brought me to the shore.

No one but Caviro and his children had set foot on this island in three hundred years. It was nearly bare, except for a collection of pines just brushing the sky. Where the shoreline ended and the boulders began, someone had carved a path, which wound upward for a few yards and then hooked abruptly to the left and out of sight. I stepped across the gravel, at last glad of the boots, and lifted my robes around my ankles to climb.

The way was steep, and I was out of breath before I reached the first gravestone. I might have tripped over it had I not already known it so well. The last time I had stood here, it had been a cool and misty day on the island, and I had been wearing black robes that had felt far heavier than these.

The grave was not large. It was only a block of marble, about half the length of a human body. Its side was carved with a relief in the old Szayeti style, which showed Alekso feasting with the freed slaves, and its lid bore a human face. This, too, was in the old Szayeti style, symmetrical and fine, with no features that were particularly distinct. Its eyes were painted a cool brown, and its red lips were upturned slightly. On its chin was a small, curled beard, which the body within had never worn in life. Neither was it wearing his glasses. Along the rim of the monument were neat Sintian letters, which read *Casimiro Caviro Faifisto, 9544–9601 33D.*

Arcelia had wept over this grave, had sunk to her knees amid the rocks and covered her face with her hands. I had stared at her, dry-eyed. My arms were aching from dragging the marble. It had felt, at the time, as if I had more in common with the tombs than I had with my sister. It had felt as if she were the only thing on the island not made of stone.

The next grave was much the same, if a little more worn, and read *Azahara Caviro Fratramata, 9529–9573 33D.* The relief was of the fleet of Sintian ships above Szayet, but the portrait was nearly identical: fine features, slight smile, painted eyes. I had never met my great-aunt. She had died at my grandfather's side putting down a minor rebellion, many years before I was born. My father had become king young, too. Then there was her mother, Casandra Caviro Savanta, and my great-great-grandfather Alvaro Caviro Kikero, whose paint had already begun to fleck away so that his eyes were a patchwork of staring black and rain-greyed white, and Cipriano Caviro Bonfaranto, and Ariel Caviro Guste, and Cayetana Caviro Merkura who had reigned from another planet, and Amaia Caviro Nova who had never reigned at all, onward and upward through the island, face after smiling face. I knew their names, each of their names, as well as my own. I had read their journals, and worn their cloaks, and walked through their bedrooms. But their faces were strangers to me.

The last grave was not far. It was not a grave at all. If the island had been a little less rocky, I might have seen it from the beach: a flat-roofed marble tomb, almost twice my height. There was a door set into it, sitting slightly ajar. Above the door was engraved in shaky Malisintian:

HERE LIES HE WHO RULES THE WORLD

And below it, more neatly:

BELOVED DISCIPLE CAVIRO ORAKOLO
9264–9343 33D

The door was difficult to shift. I could see where my predecessors had scraped a hard line of white along the stone below. When I had budged it far enough that I could fit my body inside, I hesitated. Light was slanting in through the gap. I could see dust, floating gently upward in the haze, and two low, narrow shapes.

I had expected Him to be larger. It was absurd for it to be my first thought, standing before the little limestone coffin, but it was: I had expected Alekso's body to dominate the room, to be itself like a statue, and instead it was an ordinary size, not quite as long as a bed. My ancestor's was larger, but only by a few inches. It lay at the south edge of Alekso's coffin, crossways, to form an inverted T. In the shadowed, dusty marble room they seemed almost swallowed up in the silence.

I attempted to brush off the dust on the floor before Caviro's coffin—it did not do much good—and knelt awkwardly with my ancestor at Alekso's feet. Were they His feet? Alekso lived, that much I knew, and had known since I was a child. Alekso lived in the Pearl, and in the hearts of the people. Did that mean Alekso lived in this coffin, too?

If He did, I could not hear Him. My own breathing, and the low thrum of my heartbeat, were the only things audible. Not even the birds disturbed this tomb.

"Undying," I said, or tried to say, but the word caught in my throat with the dust. I cleared it, and tried again: "Undying God, who is lord of all stars and commander of all armies. God of Casimiro, and god of Azahara, and god of Casandra. Open my ears, that I may hear You; make me Your advocate, that I may speak for You. He who is king over kings, make me king of Szayet, that in Your living name Your nation may live. Humbly I pray."

It was a short orison, and not an embroidered one. It had been the same for three hundred years. I was close enough to touch the coffin of the man who had written it.

I knew what to do next. The ceremony was not elaborate, either. But I waited, listening to the whistle of my breath, for—I did not know what I waited for. For the light to shift; for the wind to change. For something to rise up from the bones of the dead.

After some time, I sat back on my heels and shut my eyes. Then I shook the Pearl out of my sleeve, squeezed it briefly between my fingers, and pressed it to my earlobe.

There was a short, sharp pop, which I would not have heard had it not been so close to my eardrum. As it was, it made it ring for a moment—and then the pain came, less hurt than heat, and a sudden dizziness: all the blood in my body rushing to my skull.

I caught myself with one hand on Caviro's grave, just before I fell. Something very cold was happening to my ear, a slow, tickling sensation curling up from my earlobe. There was a little weight in it—I had never felt a weight in my ear before, impossible to describe, like an itch, an uncomfortable awareness, something crawling to the top of the shell, and then questing, prying, across the line of my hair, and—

I think I screamed. I know I swore, with a crudity I had not known I possessed. I also know that I did not weep, though every inch of my head was at once on fire, though my vision swam and my ears rang and my right eye throbbed, though my skull pulsed with the pain so that I thought I would vomit on my own ancestor's grave, and could only feel the horror of the act distantly, like a dream. Then I realized I could not do so, as my left cheek was pressed flat against the floor.

I had fallen after all. I pushed myself up with one hand, wobbling. The pain was retreating, and I could hear again, though my vision was blurry. When it had cleared enough that I could see the cold crossbar of the coffins, I rolled onto my knees, and from there carefully upward to my feet. All that was left was that strange discomfort in my ear, that heaviness.

I lifted two fingers and touched them, very gently, to the Pearl.

There was a man sitting on the far coffin.

Man was not quite right. He was hardly older than me. He

looked like me, a little: the amused arch to His brows, His fish-hook nose. But His hair was straight and thin, and His eyes were lighter, almost copper, and the sun shone in them—shone *through* them—with a hard, mocking gleam. He was dressed in a pair of plain black trousers and a fair, almost colorless tunic, and there was a loose leather belt around His waist, with an empty holster, which might once have held a gun. On His head sat a plain golden circlet.

He looked up at me. Then He said: "I might have known."

"Lord?" I said. "Known what?"

Some time later, I left the tomb. The way to the other end of the Island was quicker than the path through the gravestones, downhill nearly all the way, and the rocks were smaller than they had been at the northern end of the island, more worn, better footholds for the sharp shaggy pines. It was easy enough to pick my way down toward the crash of the sea.

I hesitated before I rounded the last bend. It seemed such a great thing to do it. And my father was here on this island, besides, and in the warm sunlight and the smell of pine sap, I was alone at last.

Except that I was not alone anymore, and I never would be again.

A still small voice inside me, which sounded nothing at all like the voice in the tomb, said: *If you don't start moving now, you'll stay here forever.*

I stepped forward.

The boats were spread in front of me, wood and rubber and cloth, large and small, face over staring brown face. Those with larger boats were standing again. This time, not even a child cried. My people were silent.

Then, in a little dinghy near the shore, a white-haired man in a soldier's cloak fell to his knees.

It was as if the ocean had taken hold of them. They crumpled, one by one and then in hundreds and thousands, waves and waves, reaching back and back toward the horizon, and from them came a noise I had heard only once before in my life, and then from a great distance away. They were praying, my people, no single prayer but a rising, moaning mass of them, devotions and hymns and wordless sound from the heart, and I stepped down the beach and lifted my hands toward them, and they reached back though they could not touch me, as if even longing for me would bring them all they were praying for. And the sound resolved into a word, over and over between and among them: *Oracle, Oracle, Oracle! Oracle!* And when I stepped into the coracle again, when I passed through them in my narrow white ship along the gleaming water, I saw their faces were streaked with tears.

There was very little ceremony afterward. All the ritual that meant anything had been done already: the authority of protocol had passed from the weight of tradition back into a human mouth. There was the presentation of a crown, gold and gleaming with rubies. There was a short procession by the Library, up the Bolvardo del Tombo. And then there were the open palace gates, and the receding noise of my people when the gates shut behind me.

They were in the Yellow Room, both of them, seated next to each other at the table and murmuring softly over a holo of a young Ceian with a great cloud of hair. When I entered, my guards behind me, they looked up, and stood at once. The holo vanished.

Ceirran's eyes were a narrow glitter of satisfaction. "Welcome," he said, and then his gaze flicked to my ear. I turned my face a little and let him look his fill. He exhaled at last and pressed his lips together. Then he leaned in and took my hands, and carefully kissed each cheek: first left, then right.

"Welcome," he said again, "Oracle and queen," and sat across from me and set his hands flat on the table. “We have much to discuss.”

Ana was still standing. When I met her eyes, she smiled slightly. Then she tucked her hands behind her back and bowed, formally, from the waist.

“Szayet,” she said. “What an honor it is.”

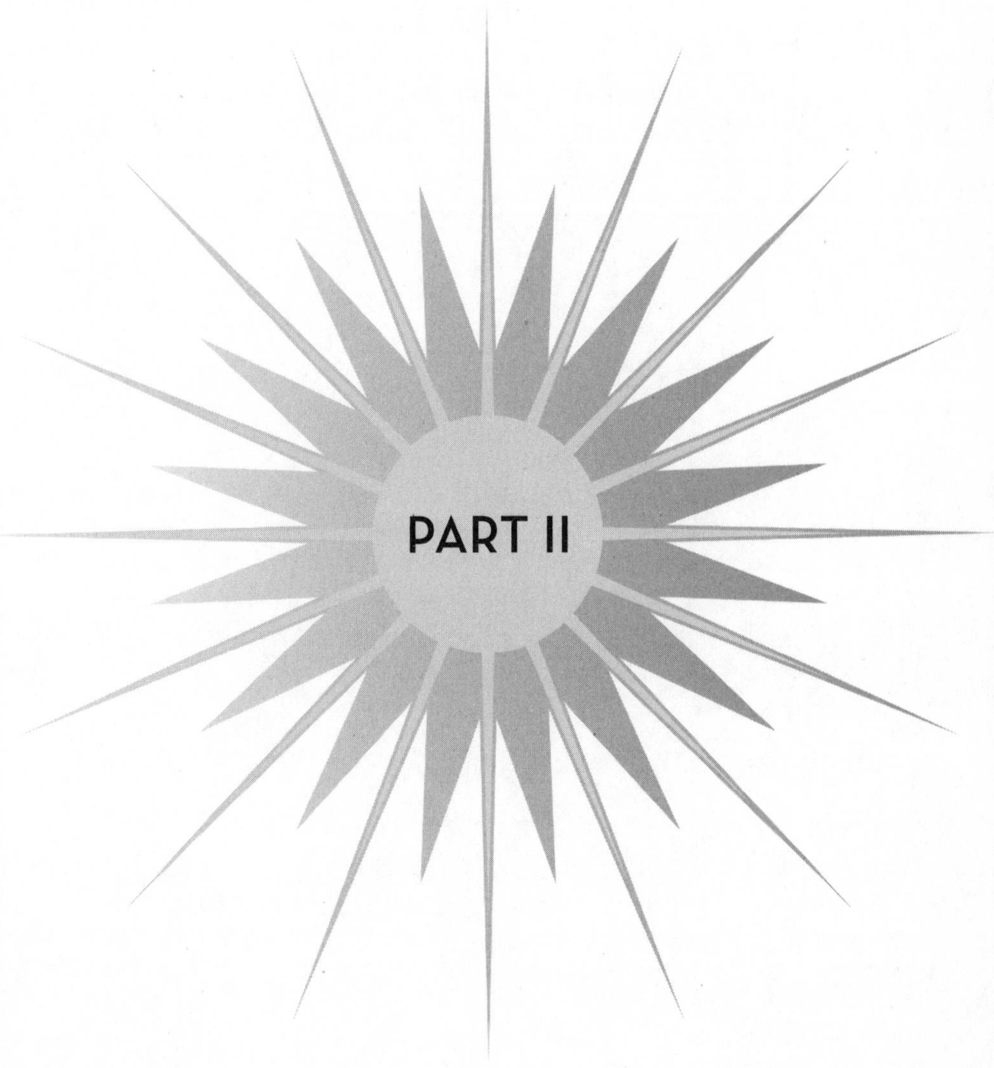

PART II

In a little village in a little valley in a little part of the world called Pruskory, three hundred years before any of this happened to any of us, just outside a house that will later be two thousand fathoms beneath the surface of the ocean, a man is falling in love.

He isn't expecting to. It would be difficult for him to expect much of anything. It's been three days of hard fighting, with nothing to do against the enemy but grit his teeth and keep up his shield and bellow at his men to hold formation till his throat is sore, and then his lungs, and then his chest, and by that time his eyes are coals and his feet are screaming hounds and his whole body is nothing but acid and bruise, and the enemy is rushing over the hilltops whooping as if in their minds they've already begun the pillage, and he says very quietly, to a god whose name will later be banished from even the most venerated libraries in the galaxy, *Lord, if I die here, let him think—*

Now he sits outside the house his men have seized as a base and watches his king move among the battle plans with a kind of warm incomprehension of reality. Between him and the world seems to be a pane of glass, which makes the king look at once very distant and very clear. He fancies he could count every hair on his head. The valley is full up with a low golden sunlight, like honey, and under that light the king's face is very soft, and very young. Earlier that day, he rounded up forty-nine prisoners of war and shot them one by one in the head.

"Where's my right hand? Ah!" says the king suddenly, looking up. "Come here. I want your opinion on crossing the river."

Getting up is a slow process. He's forgotten how his legs usually operate, and has to guess. When he's by the king's battle maps he leans against them, trying to look as if it's only because he wants to look the king in the eyes.

"Dagila of Ostrayet sent Hildimer to secure the far bank," his king says. "When we get across, the little shits won't know what's hit them—the question is *how* we get across. They've burned the bridge, which is a shame. I don't suppose you can find a place to ford?"

He shakes his head. "The supply trains won't make it," he says. "If we let the cars idle at the banks while the men carry the food across, that's days wasted. And then we've left the cars behind."

"Oh, damn the cars," says his king, irritated. "All we do is wait on the lazy things. If I could halve the supply trains and double the men, I'd have an army to rival legends."

"You are a legend," he says.

His king steps back from the map, and looks away. He tries to follow that gaze, but it's difficult through the evening light and his own exhaustion, and all he can see is the curved horizon, full up with flowers.

"Not yet," says his king.

He watches his king a moment longer. Then he says, "What if we built a bridge?"

The king's attention turns to him with the force of a floodlight. "But that would waste time, too," he says. "You'd be exposed for days."

He hesitates. "I remember Hildimer," he says, at last. "He's—an ambitious man. We spoke at Rezedny."

"Write the letter and send it," says his king, at once. "Sign my name. I'll fetch you my seal when we're done." He smiles then—it's like lightning, the king's smile, cutting across the shadows beneath his eyes and gone just as quickly. "But be careful when you build the bridge."

"I'm always careful," he says.

The king hesitates uncharacteristically. "Be more careful than usual," he says. "I can't afford to lose you right now."

When could I ever afford to lose you? he thinks, and doesn't say. The king has turned back to his maps. "Once you've built the bridge," he says, "once we've crossed, we'll need to push on to the mountain. When we've finally killed Dagila I want to build something, it's been months—are you all right?"

He's slipped against the battle maps and nearly stumbled. "Nothing, lord," he says. "Only tired, is all."

His king gives him a long, hard look. Then he says, "This can wait. Come to my tent."

They move through the evening slowly, like ghosts. When he looks up, the sky is speckled with clustered ships as thickly as a locust cloud. For the last thirteen years this plague has followed him. It has been the only sky he has ever seen, no matter what planet, no matter what day. It's grown to be a kind of comfort, this unnatural weather, these unnatural stars.

In the town are hundreds of soldiers, ducking their heads to the king as they pass, and among them are thousands of people, ordinary people, come from the cities and the villages. They began to follow the king when he first landed here, as soon as they were freed from their chains. A few of them have picked up guns and force-shields, but many more have not. They don't seem to want to go to war. They seem only to want to be by the side of the king. To look at him. There has always been some unspeakable quality, he thinks, to the king's face. He is no longer certain how he would live under an empty sky.

In the king's tent he sinks into a pile of cushions and watches the king move among the dishes of food his servants have left. The king is speaking, softly enough that he knows he is not expected to reply: the bridge, the enemy, the weather, the new weapon the king is building, the weapon with which the king will end this war. When the king comes to him with a plate of grapes and cheese and kneels at his feet with it, he puts out a hand weakly.

"Not to me," he says.

"Don't be absurd," says the king. "You too are Alekso of Sintia," and raises the fruit to his lips.

CHAPTER

SIXTEEN

CEIRRAN

I came into Anita's room early in the evening, just after supper. Her eyes flicked to me in the mirror, but she didn't greet me, only proceeded with the tying of her boots, the loading of her gun, the slow and careful fixing of her officers' pins to the blue cloak hanging over her shoulders.

After some time, she said pleasantly, "Are you enjoying the view?"

I said, "The accretion-tide's strong today. I'm giving you Bruno, Casa, and Daniel Strike Groups. The others are on rest. Secure the troposphere. Don't kill any more of them than you have to."

"Hark what a slave driver he is," said Anita. "You could come, you know."

"To the harbor?" I said. "I intend to. There are at least forty Szayeti ships still entirely uninspected."

Anita fixed her captain's pin onto her cloak, the last one, and turned to me in a swirl of cloth. There was always an ease to her in uniform, a grace to her shoulders and frame, which I never saw from her even at her most abandoned, laughing or dancing or deep in her cups. "As a matter of fact, I don't mean looking over ships like a dockworker," she said.

I opened my mouth to speak, but Anita waved my objection away at once. "Don't come with me to mop up the *Szayeti*," she said. "I'd be laughed out of the fleet. I only thought I ought to mention: This past month is the longest you've been planetside in about six years."

"You're mistaken," I said automatically. It was a safe bet; she so often was.

"I'm not," said Anita. "I've counted—don't give me that look, I have. Think back: How long was the Madinabia B campaign, even after the sandstorms? And you were on *Laureathan* for more than half the plunder after, and Fortune knows you haven't spent more than three weeks together in Ceiao since the council gave you the fleet in the first place. When you took the governorship—"

"You've been speaking to Flavia," I said.

"I should hope so," said Anita. "Be unsisterly not to." Her face was a picture of innocence.

"I'm sure," I said. "Show me the holo, please."

She gave me a cool look, but she fetched her tablet from the writing desk and woke it. Rotating gently, mouth half-open, was the head of Flavia, who on this particular day of the week was sporting green-painted eyelids and elaborate braids woven through with silver thread. After a moment, her image jumped and began to speak: *—and another search this morning. Not that we don't love a good scandal! And he* is *twelve thousand light-years away, of course—it's only that people have begun to ask questions, and you should hear the way Thiago Veguion—*

"What scandal?" I said.

She gave me a look so blank that I felt my heart skip, and

then said very lightly, "You *have* been distracted, haven't you? You recall Kostya Arzhenty?"

"The Kutayeti boy?" I said. "Teo Pulcron's pet thug?"

"Hasn't been Teo's since we buried the man," said Anita, ignoring my wince. "And not a boy any longer, either—very nearly managed to make himself into a respectable businessman. *Nearly*, of course. He had the bad fortune to be caught in stolen tablet trade or some nonsense—something only a prig like Veguion would care about, at any rate—and when the guard came by to raid his house, what should they turn up under the stairs but a shrine. He pulled a gun, and ended up dead in his own front parlor." She shrugged. "Careless, honestly. He should have opened fire when the guard were still in the street. Higher ground."

"One dead smuggler—why a scandal?" I said.

"Oh, half the council owed him money," said Anita. "Fortune knows I did. You ought to talk to your bookkeepers yourself... Guess what Veguion's done with the story, go on."

"Cultist infiltration," I said. "Evidence of deep corruption. A threat to the city's venerable character. An insult to its finest traditions."

"I think you didn't even work very hard at that," said Anita. "And he'd like us to know, besides all this, that we wouldn't be hiding on Szayet if you didn't know he was right."

"So Flavia says," I said.

Anita's mouth twitched. "So Flavia says," she said.

"You ought to know she loves to stir up trouble," I said resignedly.

"Of course she does," said Anita. "So do I, only I've got a couple of first-class warships to do it in."

"And Flavia has you," I said, "which is not significantly less dangerous."

Anita startled at that, and went irritatingly wide-eyed.

"It isn't a compliment, Captain," I said.

"Is it not?" said Anita, busying herself with the cloak pin she'd already fixed. "In any event, I feel well inspected. Shall we go to the harbor?"

On our path down the palace staircases we crossed paths with four or five of the Szayeti palace guard. One of them skittered out of our way in that frightened manner the locals had, but the others nodded at Anita and smiled with an alarming familiarity, and one of them stopped so Anita could whisper something in her ear that made her cheeks go red. I gave a dubious look to her back and said to Anita, "Flavia says nothing about *your* going native, I suppose."

"Since when have I got any reputation to ruin?" said Anita cheerfully. "Maybe once they hear I'm doing your dirty work in Szayet's atmosphere."

"You did my dirty work planetside in Ceiao, once," I said, "the year I was on Madinabia F, and made you magistrate. You might recall Túlio Cachoeiran has since said a great deal about your reputation."

"What—*me*?" said Anita, clapping a hand to her chest. "What was I ever accused of? Formally, I mean. Besides—there's about a hundred square miles of the Outer City where you and I can't walk without twenty men buying us drinks, so if I were you, I wouldn't complain. Though if I were you, I wouldn't have left me at home in the first place." Her mouth twitched. "Nice neighborhoods, too," she said. "Clean water, very well-kept roads. Charming places, in my opinion."

"There are a hundred square miles of the Outer City where the rest of Teo Pulcron's former pet gangsters are a few hundred dekar poorer in bribe money than they otherwise would have been," I said dryly.

"And who besides Túlio Cachoeiran would find a way to call that a tragedy," said Anita. "In any case, it's Veguion who's talking about *going native* in the first place, him and the rest of

Quinha's old henchmen—when they aren't clustering round her house hoping for a word with the executors. Flavia's only passing on the message. *She* says you can stay in the Swordbelt Arm until Fortune throws her wheel down, for all she cares."

"Uncharacteristic of her," I said, "to let me keep you from her for so long."

"Oh, don't worry," said Anita, "she'd come to Szayet."

"Ah," I said. "In a two-mile-long silver cruiser, no doubt, with a dozen tugboats ahead of her blasting hymns into the ether."

Anita smiled often, but it tended to be a disconcerting thing, as blunt as her wit and often as offensive. This smile spread over her face like a candle flame, slow and warm. If I hadn't known her so well I might have said she looked softer for it. "She wouldn't," she said.

"Three years ago she dragged her husband's corpse through the streets of Ceiao wailing until an angry mob rose from the streets to force the council to give him a decent funeral in the middle of a meeting," I said.

"Oh, *well*," said Anita. "That was just good politics."

I did not dislike Flavia, though I counted myself very fortunate that she had spent her required years in our army behind a desk and left at once when her time was up. It was no use arguing with Anita about her, in any case, and never had been. "You may tell her," I said, "or you may tell her to tell Thiago Veguion, if she likes to put it that way, that I will happily leave Szayet when my business here is concluded, and it is the right of neither councillors nor gossips to tell the commander of Ceiao how he conducts his business."

Anita was grinning. "If she meets any gossips," she said, "I'll tell her to let them know."

It was a beautiful day at the harbor. Szayet seemed sometimes to be nothing but a long string of beautiful days, like gems in a necklace. Gracia said we were in the height of summer, but you would never have known it from the air, which was as clear and clean as snowmelt and through which we could see for miles to where the ships roared over the ocean. I had grown up with thick, muggy summers, summers that broiled the city and stole its sleep and fanned its headaches and dried the river to a trickle, broken only by those few thunderstorms that managed to rumble over Mauntan Bau—and even then, only for an hour or two before the humidity settled in again, as close as the breath of a lion. But here there was such a thing as the *heat of the day*, which drained away again into the sea at nighttime, and left the mornings empty and waiting for the sun.

I had sent the strike groups their commands earlier, and now they were waiting for Anita in tight rows, looking like a neater, bluer pocket of sea. Anita checked the charge on her gun, tucked it back into her belt, and jogged down the wide flight of palace steps toward them.

"Good morning, boys and girls," she said. "Any of you ever been duck hunting?"

Laughter rippled up from the group. Anita grinned at them.

"This is going to be dangerous and difficult, and I won't pretend otherwise," she said. "Fortunately, dangerous and difficult are our specialty. More fortunately, it'll be quick. Keep an eye on the rest of your squadron—the cultists might be pirates by law, but in practice they're trained soldiers. Don't try to get under their bellies on your own or they'll circle up on you, and don't show them your flank or you'll be rammed. The better we hold formation, the easier it'll be to pick them off."

She cast a lingering glance over the group. "Soldiers they might be," she said, "but Ceians they aren't. We have the advantage of discipline, and more to the point, we have the advantage of backbone. I want a nice harvest of prisoners for the commander's victory parade when we're home. Clear?"

The pilots saluted as one, and roared *Captain!* in a voice that sent seagulls tumbling up from the concrete. "All right," said Anita. "Get in your ships, the lot of you. I don't want to see your ugly faces again till you've killed something."

They went, laughing. I fell in beside Anita again on the way to her fighter, a blue-painted little thing with four scratched silver wings and *Loba* carved in blocky letters under the nose. "How sophisticated a speaker you are," I said.

"They ought to put me in the council," Anita said, scrabbled up the ladder, and swung herself into the ship. A moment later she was dropping down in the pilot's seat on the other side of the viewscreen, and in another she had reached up to pull her helmet down over her head. "Well?" she said into its microphone. It came out as a tinny rattle from just under one of the wings. "You don't want to fly out with us after all?"

Her elbow was on the dashboard, her chin propped on her fist. Through the glass and the helmet's goggles her eyes were like coins. Never, in all my years leading the fleet, had I managed to send my men laughing into battle.

"Good luck, Captain," I said. "I'll be watching."

"You had better," she said, and grinned.

CHAPTER SEVENTEEN

GRACIA

"You look like shit," said Alekso Undying.

"Good morning, Lord," I said. "I was hoping I might talk to you about some financial matters today."

"You can try," he said. "Your circles are dark enough you look as if someone's hit you. *Very* royal. Don't you ever sleep? Forget I asked—I know what you're doing." He yawned and stretched elaborately, so that his right hand passed through my bedside mirror. "Must we talk about money problems? I'm sick to death of money problems. I want to talk about my palace guard."

It was difficult for two reasons to hold a conversation with the god. The first was practical: I brushed my hair in the mornings, fifty strokes each side with what had been my sister's golden brush, and when I pressed two fingers to the Pearl in order to call up his image, I had only one hand to do it with. The second was that, even though Ana's recent string of victories had rid our atmosphere of nearly all my sister's stragglers, he had no interest in discussing anything else.

"I'm afraid money problems cannot wait, Lord," I said. "When my father devalued the currency—"

"Anything can wait," said Alekso, "if you're powerful enough to force it. You aren't—that's your problem. I want to talk about the palace guard because it's full of barbarians."

This was a test. "That's true," I said, shook out my hair, and began to brush the other side. "Regrettably, the barbarians were a great aid in enacting the priests' decree to crown me."

"It *is* regrettable," said Alekso. "Forget the priests. I don't care about them, and neither do the heathen hordes. You called on a foreign military to interfere in Szayeti government—"

"I called on them for nothing," I said, stung. "It was Arcelia who—"

"You *used* a foreign military to interfere in Szayeti government," Alekso said over me. "Fine—there's nothing we can do about that now. But to station them by our front door is idiotic. It makes you look weak, and worse, it makes them feel strong. Either you can rule on your own or you can't, and if you can't, you might as well give me to your pet general and let him douse me in beer."

"I *will* rule on my own," I said. It came out sounding childish, which annoyed me further. "Those guards who died in the war, or who defected to Kutayet, must be replaced—and the replacements must be trained—none of this means that the situation is *permanent*. If I were to rid the palace of Ceians now, I would be left undefended entirely."

"You don't need to rid the palace of Ceians," said Alekso, "but if you insist on having them, you need to keep them out of the eye of the public. The people of this city people fought for you, and died, some of them. Do you think they like it when you throw their failure in their face?"

"They didn't—" I snapped, and then took a deep breath in, set down my hairbrush, and picked up a little clay kohl jar and paintbrush. "They won't like it if they starve once autumn comes, either," I said, beginning to apply it to my lids. "Which is why we *do* need to discuss my father's devaluation of the currency, Lord. Military power is not the only sort of power at hand here."

"Maybe it isn't," said Alekso, "but if you have to make anyone angry, I wouldn't pick the people who carry the guns." He waved away my objection. "Fine, Caviro's daughter. Tell me about your money problems. I'm listening."

"Caviro was not my father," I said, not for the first time.

"You think I can be expected to tell you all apart?" said Alekso. "Talk to me about coinage, if you're going to. Quickly, before I get bored."

I went down to the harbor-gate after to discuss some problems of ships with my war minister. The harbor was full of Ceians again—it always was lately, repairing their fighters or running in panting packs like dogs or just sitting by the pearl gate, smoking sílfion and watching the sea. They saluted me as I went by. I nodded to them, more uneasily than I meant to. Alekso's words were niggling at the back of my mind. They had an unpleasant habit of doing that.

Once I had met with my minister, I crossed back from the harbor and along the great lawn behind the palace. That was busy, too. The Ceians had dug pits in it, and were sparring in them, cloaks scattered carelessly on the grass. Some were clattering at each other with wooden practice swords, while others were fighting hand-to-hand, some mix of Sintian wrestling and unsophisticated brawl that I didn't know. I stopped in my tracks to watch them. It was a fine warm morning at the harbor, and the sun was gleaming on their backs and their chests, on their muscled forearms and thighs.

One pair of hand-to-hand fighters in particular had a small crowd gathered, a man and a square-shouldered, straight-haired woman whose back was to me. The woman was holding her own very well, especially for her size. I picked up my skirts and made my way closer to them, and then the woman turned and grinned. "Szayet!" she said, saluted me sloppily, and dodged a jab from her opponent, who I saw now was one of my own lieutenants.

"Good morning," I said. "Is all of this new?"

Ana feinted, feinted again, and shoved up against her opponent, knocking him back a few steps. They both retreated, circling with fists up. "Started it up today," said Ana to me, without taking her eyes off my lieutenant. "Thought your boys could use a little exercise."

"You surprise me, Captain," I said.

Ana turned to look at me, and paid for it a moment later when my lieutenant grabbed her and tried to pull her into a headlock. She twisted with surprising dexterity, landed a hard punch on his side, and wriggled out of his arms, circling him from a few feet's distance with her fists raised. "Why?" she said to me.

"I suppose I thought we had dispensed with—all this," I said, waving at the spectacle of it: the sweating soldiers, the practice swords, the pits dug in the grass. "Even discounting ranged weaponry, surely advances in naval warfare—"

"Navy doesn't dispense with the need for hand-fighting," said Ana, sounding out of breath. "Has the crèche dispensed with the need for sex?"

Did she hope to shock me? "They're not at all the same," I said. "Sex is not a need for all, and when it is, it is not only a need but a pleasure. Whereas all of this bloody stuff—"

The lieutenant shoved, ducked, and kicked Ana hard across the back of her knees. She tumbled and rolled onto her back at once, chest heaving.

"Are they not?" she said, and grinned up at me. "My mistake."

It was in a foul mood that I went up to the palace and dressed myself for the council meeting. There, at least, there were more Szayeti than Ceians, and they knelt to me when I passed through the hallways, murmuring greetings. I had Zorione bring me one of my most formal robes, a heavy teal silk thing that wrapped in elaborate folds around my shoulders and waist, embroidered in pearl thread with exotic Muntiru birds. It was only when she brought me the accompanying Sintian headdress, which was made of brocade and silver, set with imported sapphires, and weighed five pounds, that I sighed and dismissed her and the headdress so that I could manage to collect my composure.

My council consisted of Ceirran, Ana, and seven of my ministers, hardly any of whom had experience: Three of the previous set had been loyal to Arcelia, two had been disloyal to her and had to flee Szayet, and one more had been loyal to none but himself, but he had advised the beheading of Quinha Semfontan. The remaining was the minister for religion, a wispy-haired old man named Severo Santo, who had escaped my sister's wrath by nodding off in meetings rather than espousing opinions.

Fortunately for him, we needed his input on the new coins I was issuing not at all. Unfortunately, we seemed to need the opinion of nearly everyone else: The minister of justice thought it was far too soon to issue new currency, the minister of the interior thought it was far too late, the minister of agriculture thought the main thing was to put out a great deal of them, with which the minister of the treasury disagreed vehemently, and the foreign minister said she thought we ought not to be having this conversation at all in *mixed company*, throwing a pointed look at Ceirran, who looked on the verge of laughter.

"Can we at least agree that they ought to have my face on them?" I said, pained.

"Ah, the same as the last ones," said Ana. "That's convenient."

This very nearly broke up the meeting. It was only Ceirran who rescued it, rapping on the table until my ministers quieted. "As a matter of fact, Oracle," he said, "I was hoping to discuss your sister. May we?"

That was unexpected. "Please," I said.

Ceirran nodded to Ana, who produced a tablet from beneath the table and woke it. From its surface rose a holo of Szayet, surrounded by blinking red dots.

"These are the sites where, at the beginning of this month, we suspected the former queen's loyalists remained," he said. "These"—Ana tapped a stylus on the screen, and all but a few of the dots dwindled into sparks and died—"are the sites remaining we haven't yet wiped out. We expect that within a short time, these too will disappear, either due to our military action or lack of supplies."

My eyes flicked toward the minister of war, farther down the table. He was sitting with his back ramrod-straight and his jaw set tight, staring at the gently rotating globe. I thought of Alekso, and cursed myself.

"We're all doubtless grateful for your support, Commander Ceirran," I said. "Is this a report on your military progress?"

"Not quite," said Ceirran, and reached over to tap the tablet himself. Around the planet, dozens of green dots bloomed. "These," he said, "are the smugglers, pirates, and common criminals who have declared loyalty to Arcelia since."

I leaned in to inspect the globe. "Tell me," I said to my minister of the interior, "to your eye, how radically does this differ from the ordinary crime rate in Szayet?"

She watched it rotate, eyes narrowed in thought. "Hardly at all, Holiest," she said, "at a first glance. I would need to run reports, but—"

"I don't doubt that," said Ceirran. "In fact, Oracle, I wouldn't be surprised if the number of overall smugglers and pirates has gone down since your reign began. I am not suggesting that any real resistance to your rule is alive in Szayet, especially after the last month of fighting. I am, however, suggesting that the former queen may—or already does—act as a banner for those who otherwise oppose you. If she is ever able to communicate with her supporters outside prison—within the realm of possibility, as you yourself well know—she is increasingly a liability to the stability of your rule."

I raised an eyebrow at Ceirran. I was beginning to suspect that I was being ambushed, and I disliked the feeling. "And your solution?" I said.

Ceirran nodded at Ana, who clapped her palms together over the holographic Szayet with a flourish. When she pulled them apart, the planet was a blinking blue dot marked within a wide white curve. Farther along that curve was another dot, this one blinking red.

"There is a mountain on Itsaryet," said Ceirran, "which once, they say, housed the grandest temple in the Swordbelt Arm. It has since, alas, been burned, but the ruins are now inhabited by an order of Sintian priests, vetted and appointed by the Ceian governor in Sintielo, and considered the most responsible and secretive jailers in all the Ceian Empire."

"No," I said.

Ceirran, who had been in the middle of nodding to Ana again, stopped. Ana looked put out. "No?" he said to me.

"The offer is—generous," I said. "The point regarding the smugglers was well-made, and I thank you for it. I count Arcelia safer here than anywhere else in the world."

"With respect, Oracle," said Ceirran, "recall that you yourself were broken out of that very prison not so very long ago."

"Believe me," I said, "the memory remains fresh. I think it best she remain in Szayeti custody."

Ceirran flicked a glance to Ana, which I could not read. "Are you sure?" he said. "She could stir up more than a little trouble among your people. We are offering you our help, if you are inclined to accept any generosity."

I dearly wished I were not in front of my ministers so I could tell him what I thought of *that*, but by now even Severo Santo had awoken and was watching me. "Your offer is appreciated," I said. "I regret that I must deny it."

"Patramata," said Ceirran, "I am afraid that she is very dangerous to you."

"Ceirran," I said, "I am afraid that she is very dangerous anywhere. Do you think she couldn't stir up trouble among the Ceians? Safer to have her on Szayet than Ceiao—safer to have her on Szayet than anywhere! No matter where she is, she will draw chaos, and where she finds chaos already, she will try to get to its heart. If you think she isn't a danger to you, too, you're mistaken."

"So kill her," said Ana.

I didn't turn. "If you have a serious suggestion, Captain," I said, "I'd be glad to hear it. Otherwise, I wonder why you remain at my meeting table."

"I am serious," said Ana, and my eyes snapped to her face. Those shark eyes were amused, but they always seemed to be amused; that meant little. "She's in the third cell from the door, is she? Send me to her. I'm your knife hand. Only say the word and it's done."

I was briefly and unpleasantly struck dumb. Ceirran rescued me after a moment, without looking up from the tablet: "When I wish you to be a brute killer, Anita," he said coolly, "I'll tell you."

I heard it as I would have had my sister said it, and my eyes went to Ana's face, in anticipation of her anger. But she only smiled.

"I look forward to it," she said.

"I agree with the barbarian," said Alekso, later that night.

I did not look up from what I was doing, which was scanning the latest draft of the debt-relief plan Ceirran had sent me, and writing *I must be confused?* in the margins where he was lying about the numbers. "You will have to specify, Lord," I said, "as they are all barbarians to me."

"You know who I mean," said Alekso, unfazed. "She's right, you know. She'd very much like to do it, besides."

"If you were alive," I said to my paperwork, "would you allow a member of the royal family to be either captured or executed by the empire that already plans to drag her soldiers through the streets as entertainment?"

"I am alive," said Alekso, "and I would *be* the empire—something you and all your family take great pleasure in forgetting, Caviro's daughter. In any event, that's not why you won't let her do it."

The Pearl could not read minds. It had no need to. Though I could only myself see him when I touched the Pearl, Alekso possessed at all times, according to the best priests and philosophers, the power of omniscience. "Please enlighten me, Lord," I said.

"You're a soft touch," said the god of Szayet, "and you don't like to kill. It's a flaw in your makeup. You'll leave it behind one of these days."

I stopped writing and exhaled. "You may remember," I said, "I have already been to war once."

"Oh, I remember," said Alekso. "You lost."

"Is that what this is about?" I said sharply. I had wanted to speak to someone, anyone. Now I regretted it. "Would you like me better if I had let Arcelia destroy the palace? If I had seized the Pearl from her at any cost?"

"Of course," Alekso said. He sounded surprised that I had asked the question.

I set the pen down beside my crown where it lay on the desk and rubbed my free hand over the bridge of my nose. It had been a long series of late nights, with only the light of my tablets for company, and the way the ocean whispered beyond the palace walls.

"Tell me," I said, "why did you break Ostrayet?"

"Ah," said Alekso Undying.

I did not like the way he said it. "Is this a conversation you have had before, Lord?" I said. "Should we skip to the parts you find interesting?"

He looked at me awhile with his head cocked. When he stood beside me, most of the time, he seemed very ordinary: a plain Sintian boy who Arcelia might have fought with at the Summer Market. But there were moments when he showed something—a peculiar concentration, a peculiar stillness—and I was reminded very suddenly and unhappily that he was not a boy at the market, and had never been, even when his body had been flesh and bone.

"Why do you think I broke Ostrayet?" he said.

I took my time answering. I liked games, but I did not like losing, and less still did I like being set up to fail. "My father once told me," I said at last, "that you came to Szayet and saw the people had been made slaves."

"That much is true," he said. "The Ostrayeti were doing far more with their little moon than Szayet ever managed, even when it was half continent. If quicksilver pearl had originated on Sintia, I'd have blasted all the way to Muntiru in the space of a month. Do you know they were already making ventures into extra-system space? It was no wonder they made these people call them gods. I can't imagine it was difficult to convince them of it."

"And you freed us," I said. "The Szayeti." I did not like to say it—I did not like to be backed into a corner, either. But there seemed very little else to say.

I had known Alekso was going to laugh, but it made it no more pleasant when he did, jarringly cheerful. "Free!" he said. "Why not? Yes, I freed them. I drowned half of them, when I brought up the oceans. That was a type of freedom, I suppose. And half a population still living is a better deal than the Ostrayeti got."

"And they gave you the apotheosis," I said. "They worshipped you, and called you God. And it was with their pearl that you built the Pearl of the Dead. That was part of the deal, too."

His smirk soured a little at this speech. "Yes," he said. "I suppose that's true. One god replaces another...the Sintian gods certainly cleared out of the way soon enough, and I didn't even have to destroy their planet to make them do it—only a few books and statues, and who noticed those? You ought to think, Caviro's daughter, not of the people who called me a god, but of the people who didn't."

"Is that your answer?" I said. "The Ostrayeti refused to worship you? Is that why you shattered their world into pieces in the sky?"

"How much do you know about Szayet's religion, before Ostrayet took over?" said Alekso.

"A faith of prophecy," I said at once. "Ordinary people could speak with the voices of animals—lions, ibis, jackals—"

"And still do, no doubt," said Alekso, "but they never worshipped them." He smiled again when I raised my eyebrows. "No one likes a messenger, I'm afraid. They did want to hear what the animals had to say. They wanted it because animals were so close to nature, so close to its blood and simplicity. Above all, its shortness of life span. If anything, Caviro's daughter, what the Szayeti worshipped was death. Or not *worshipped*, perhaps, but *feared*, if there's any point in noting a difference. There was nothing in their lives that did not prepare for a life after the corpse was in the ground. All of their books were about it, all of their carvings. Most are deep underwater, but I'm sure you've seen a few."

He laced his fingers together and looked out into nothing. "I thought that they were obsessed with dying," he said thoughtfully. "They seemed to talk about nothing else in the world. And there was so *much* else in the world, then—there were empires, there were star charts, there were my officers, there were my friends. There were so many worlds to conquer. But now I believe they weren't obsessed in the least. They were perfectly logical. They only thought: A man is dead for far longer than he is alive."

He smiled, more to himself than to me. "And after all," he said, "they were right."

I pressed my lips together. I was beginning to suspect something, something I could not quite name, or was not sure that I wanted to. "Lord," I said, when I at last felt able, "when I smuggled myself into the palace in the carpet, you told Arcelia at once. So why did you deny her your counsel during the civil war?"

He looked deeply irritated, and I knew at once that my instinct had been right. "She could have had it at any time," he said, "if she had only been sensible."

It took me a moment to understand. I said nothing when I did, but I must have narrowed my eyes, or flinched, or otherwise given myself away. The Undying laughed aloud.

"Yes," he said. "I wouldn't advise her until she agreed that you should be executed, rather than merely taken prisoner." He shrugged. "She was a coward, too."

I exhaled.

"Good night, Lord," I said. "I'll ask your counsel in the morning."

Alekso gave me a skeptical look. But all he said was: "I look forward to it."

I went to bed alone. When I had left him last, Ceirran was caught up in adjudicating a pair of petty lieutenants' disputes, and I did not doubt he had returned to his own rooms after a lengthy arbitration, expecting that, given the late hour, I would be asleep, with no interest in being woken.

It ought to have been true. Instead, I lay with my face turned into my pillow, listening to the sigh and hush of the sea, counting the hours as they dwindled down. At long last I closed my eyes, and when I did, Arcelia was smiling at me, and the barrel of her gun was pointing straight at my heart.

I sat bolt upright.

The room was silent. When I climbed out of bed and went from the window to the wardrobe to the door, the train of my nightgown dragging behind me like a snake, I could not see so much as a twitch from the shadows. The only motion was my own body in the mirror on my bedside table.

"But she did try to kill me," I said aloud.

I was not touching the Pearl. Alekso, if he had anything to say, did not say it to me.

"Liar," I said.

There was no reply to that, either. My own voice sounded distant, like a recorded holo.

I went back to my wardrobe, wrapped a silk robe around my shoulders, and pushed open my bedroom door. The lights in the hallway had been extinguished. In the pale moonslight the colors of the wall paintings were faded whites and greys, and my shadow rippled over the outlines of warriors, ships.

The staircase to the dungeons was not far from the conference room. But there, too, I saw a blur of shadow, slumped in front of the door. I was very close indeed before I could make it out: the figure of a soldier, sleeping, cloak wrapped round its knees.

"Are you drunk?" I said.

I had only been startled, but it came out harshly. Captain Ana's head lifted. Only the flat slash of her mouth was visible in this dimness, hardly even that, and as I watched, it twitched into a smile.

"Szayet," she said. "It's late."

I meant to say, *Get out of my way*, and was surprised to hear myself say, instead: "You always call me that."

She had pushed herself to her feet as I spoke, and been in the process of dusting off her cloak and her tunic, but her hands stilled. She said, "So I do."

It was not quite a question. I said, "What are you doing in front of this door?"

"Standing guard," she said, as if it were obvious.

"On whose orders?" I said sharply. I was sure that Ceirran would not have sent her, or any of his men, to stand at the door of the dungeons without telling me. I was almost sure. "Does Szayet have no guards of its own?" Alekso's voice from that morning rose up once again in my memory, unwelcome. "Who are you guarding against? *Are* you drunk? Who in the world did you think would come tonight?"

She gave me a long look from under her eyelashes.

"You came," she said.

"You cannot be guarding my sister against *me*," I said. "You offered to slit her throat in my name not twelve hours ago." A thought occurred to me, and I drew back, shoulders stiffening. "You can't be waiting here to—"

Ana did not relax, exactly. It was a motion altogether less visible and altogether more rapid: She shifted her weight onto the balls of her feet, leaned forward, and without warning the tension in her lean muscle was not that of a soldier on edge but of a great cat, coiled, prepared to spring. Her eyes were glittering.

"But, Szayet," she said, very softly, "you told me not to."

"Captain, do you always take orders from me?" I murmured back.

It came out both lower and rougher than I had intended. Her eyes widened in shock, and then narrowed, satisfied.

I took another step back, involuntary. My face was growing hot. "Why are you here?" I said sharply again.

At once the thin smile vanished.

"I couldn't sleep," she said.

It was so unexpected an answer that my temper drained. I

blinked at her, feeling stupid. "You were sleeping just there," I said. "In front of the door."

"Something wrong with the bed your people gave me," said Anita. "Too small."

This was ridiculous—she had bulk, of course, but she was only a few inches taller than me. I ought to have been insulted. Better yet, I ought to have laughed at her. But there was no humor at all in her face.

She held my gaze a few moments longer, then smiled again. This time it did not reach her eyes. "And why are *you* here, Szayet?" she said.

It should have sounded like a challenge. Perhaps she had meant it as one. I wonder now whether, under that strange colorless moonslight, she was in any better control of herself than I.

She had pulled Arcelia off me, that night. When I had ripped the Pearl from Arcelia's ear, I had been able to do it because Captain Ana held my sister in her arms.

"I wanted to talk to—" I began, and swallowed the end of the sentence. "Someone," I said, at last. "Anyone."

It was a meaningless pretense; there was only one person in the dungeons behind this particular door. But Ana was only quiet a moment, and then she said, "When I call you Szayet, does it make you angry?"

"Angry?" I said. "No, I—" It occurred to me that perhaps it should have. The other Ceian soldiers called me *majesty*, or *madam*, or even *Oracle*. "You might call me by my title," I said, "if you're worried about disrespect."

"You can't expect me to call you Holiest," she said. The smile had reappeared, or a ghost of it, hovering at the curve of her dark mouth.

"I don't expect you to name me holy, or even say *my lady*, or bend to kiss my hand," I said, and then I had to break my gaze from hers. My cheeks were warming again; I was glad it was dark. "But you might call me Patramata."

I had heard her breath hitch when I had begun the sentence, but as soon as I said the last word, a door slammed down behind her eyes. "No," she said.

"Why not?" I said, bewildered. "Your commander manages it."

Her breath hissed out, a long, harsh rattle, and at once I wanted to step forward and peer into her eyes, to see in her narrow handsome face what it was that she was not telling me, whether she willed it or no. The urge that had driven me here—to speak with Arcelia, to ask her when she had grown desperate enough to kill me, just to see her face—was hard and heavy in my throat, a swallowed bone. But a bitter swell of feeling had joined it, though I did not know when. It was something too swift and hard to be called tenderness.

When it became apparent she did not intend to reply, I took another step back. "Sleep here," I said, "if you can't sleep anywhere else," and turned to go.

She said nothing. It would only occur to me later that she had obeyed my order, after all.

CHAPTER
EIGHTEEN

CEIRRAN

The matter of the sister was dropped, to my annoyance, but the matter of the smugglers remained. The fact was that Szayet's atmosphere was far too lightly policed to allow for any real enforcement. It was much too easy for small ships to evade its network, and now that the war had ended and ordinary trade had resumed, there were far too many great cargo ships for the Szayeti military to effectively search them all. Still, the foreign minister flatly refused to allow our aid.

"Try to understand her point of view," said Gracia, not for the first time. "She has no reason to expect that your soldiers will be honest. As far as she knows, you might have already ordered them to pocket every antiquity they find."

"So she chooses to do nothing at all?" I retorted. "She imagines that because my men *may* be thieves, she should entrust the wealth of Szayet to hundreds of Szayeti whom she *knows* to be?"

"Many Alectelans would rather the treasure go to Szayeti thieves than Ceian soldiers," said Gracia, "and not even I could convince them otherwise. You must understand the situation your men are in. The heavier your touch in any affair of state, the closer you are to being seen as an occupying army."

I looked sidelong at her along the desk in the Yellow Room. The trouble, of course, was that we *were* an occupying army, though I was not at all sure that she knew well enough to think of us that way.

"Szayet's been liberated by foreign soldiers before," Anita said. She was sitting on a corner of the desk at my right side, hand splayed by my tablet for balance. In the last week or so, it had been her habit to put herself between me and Gracia in meetings, for no reason at all that I could see. The last time she had behaved like this, the Madinabic chieftain with whom we had been negotiating had tried to kill me two days later. "Your ancestor, as a matter of fact."

"Yes," Gracia said to her. "That's a problem, too. If you were devout, they might like you a great deal better."

I could feel my mouth pinch. It was very rare for Gracia to raise my and Anita's lack of faith to our faces, and it was rarer still that she discussed her own religion. I assumed that she, like me, had no intention of letting it come between us. The issue was that it *did* lie between us, as clearly as the twelve thousand light-years between here and Ceiao, and I wished that Anita had not brought it up.

"What do you suggest, then?" I said.

Gracia leaned back in her chair and folded her hands on the desk.

"I want more Szayeti in the palace guard," she said.

Anita gave me a look that spoke volumes. I gave her a look that said to be quiet. "Are you sure?" I said to Gracia. "You trust them?"

"Not all," she said. "But enough to increase the staff, I think. More to the point—and I hope you won't take this the wrong way—I am not entirely sure that I can trust them if I keep them *out* of the guard. I am only recently made queen—"

"And by whom?" said Anita, sounding offended.

"Yes," said Gracia. "I'm afraid that's the heart of the matter."

I gave Anita a look that said, *You might have kept your mouth closed.* Anita gave me a look back that said, *You might have expected we would offend her eventually, and why not now?* It was an expression I was well familiar with on her face. "I'm not sure I see the issue," I said.

Gracia looked deeply skeptical of the both of us. "You may not," she said, "but the Szayeti do. It's not a matter of the skill of your men—of course I have the utmost confidence in *them.*" Anita scoffed, and Gracia sighed. "Look at it this way, Captain," she said. "My people feel that, as long as the majority of the palace guard is made up of your fleet, they are denied opportunities for employment. Is that sufficient motive to appeal to the Ceian mind?"

"And what are my men meant to do when *they're* put out of jobs?" said Anita. "Wander around the city getting into trouble?"

"Captain," I said reprovingly. "Patramata—if more Alectelans in the guard is what you want, then more Alectelans in the guard is what you shall have, of course. Your judgment is law. I am only asking whether you are entirely sure."

Gracia hesitated. Her hand, which had been lingering on the table, drifted up to her earlobe.

"You'll forgive me, Commander," she said, after a moment, "if, when you question my judgment, I wonder at your reasoning."

On Medveyet once, many years ago, I had been creeping through the thick red fur of fallen leaves in the woods on my way back from scouting an enemy camp. I had been moving quietly—this was early in our campaign, and the woods were mottled with fanatics—but I was not nearly so well trained as they, and had already frightened away a rabbit and a few lash-tailed grey lizards. This had disappointed me. It was rare to see any such animal on Ceiao, where civilization or winter had long ago banished anything that might have been called wild, with the exception of scavengers and parasites.

So it was a shock when I stepped around a tree and found myself face-to-face with a hawk, perched on a branch directly in front of me. It had smooth brown wings, and a white chest flecked down to its legs, and a long, cruelly curved beak, pointed toward my eyes. It was astonishingly still. Being larger than a pigeon, it was the largest bird I had ever seen.

I came to a dead stop. The hawk looked at me. I looked back. Some part of my mind said that I ought to get closer—and indeed I did want to see it better, if only for the sake of novelty. Another, greater part of me, though, was experiencing a different sort of novelty. It was the knowledge that I was in the presence of something that could hurt me very badly, and had no particular reason not to do so.

The hawk swiveled its head and stared at me from first one eye, then the other. Then it unfolded itself and rose into the canopy, its great wings beating unconcernedly. A few moments later, it caught a wind, and I watched it sail upward until the sun winked it away.

There was a manner about Gracia—a particular set to her mouth, a particular way she held her head—whenever she touched her hand to the pearl in her ear. It was easy to forget, when she was alive and glittering in our private conversation, that the little machine living in her ear had extended its wires into her brain.

"Very well," I said. "We'll begin to take our men out of rotation in the next week. Is that acceptable to you?"

Anita had seen it, too. She came to my room after dinner that night and said, "Are you planning to keep troops here forever?"

"I think Gracia might take issue with that," I said.

"Then I wouldn't mind hearing when you're planning on reassuring her," she said. "Flavia says Veguion's stopped speaking to half the council over the cultist gangster scandal. She's going to Cláudia Pulcron's sea house for the summer to get away from it all."

"Fortune, I hadn't thought she had liked Cláudia well enough for that even when she *was* married to her brother," I said.

She ignored this. "And even your best friends on the council will want approval for a Kutayeti campaign," she said. "Yes, I know they can't demand it from the commander, but if you'll insist on pardons and reconciliation and keeping order and smoothing over friendships, that's your own fault, as far as I'm concerned. So how soon do you mean to start convincing them?"

"I've told you I have business here," I said. "Are you homesick, Captain?"

"Homesick?" she said, face expressionless. "No."

"Then I will begin convincing our friends on the council when I am ready to do so," I said. "What is this about?"

"When *will* you be ready?" said Anita. "When the Oracle is surrounded by enough troops to conquer the Swordbelt Arm, and manages it before we do? When she's ended smuggling forever and the planet is empty of crime? When she's gone to the crèche to make herself an heir?"

"I thought you liked her," I said.

"I never said I didn't," said Anita. "I like half of her, at any rate."

I sat in the chair at my desk, and she went and sat down on my bed, hands in her lap, looking uncharacteristically solemn. "Are you having a theological revelation, Captain?" I said lightly. "Do you believe the Pearl of the Dead to be a human soul now?"

"Do you?" she said.

"No," I said, startled. "Of course not."

"You keep looking at it, though," she said.

I didn't doubt her, but I hadn't known I was doing it, and I disliked that. "I expect I do," I said. "I look at the queen often."

At that she turned her head away. "All right," she said. "If that's how you want to play it. Is that what I should tell Flavia, next time she calls to say Veguion's trying to double the guard in the Outer City, and staff it with his own paid men? That you won't come home because you can't stop looking at Altagracia's face?"

It was an unpleasant shock to hear the queen's real name in her mouth. "You can tell your sister the truth," I said. "I am the commander of Ceiao, and I come and go as I please. And when I am ready to come home, Captain, you and I will have a great deal of work to do."

Anita's eyes were dark. "Do you promise?" she said.

"Of course," I said easily.

"All right," she said, and stood, and went to the door. "I hope you know I'll hold you to it."

She was nearly out the door when I said, "Captain?" and she swung back in.

"I think you should stay away from the meetings," I said.

"What?" said Anita blankly.

"Stay away from the meetings," I repeated. "Go out in the city. Train with your men. I don't blame you for being restless. If you're unhappy spending all of your days with the queen's ministers, spend them with someone else. If you are afraid of the Pearl of the Dead, you certainly don't have any obligation to act as my bodyguard against it. I don't want you to be miserable here. Find something you like better to do."

She stared at me for a moment, her face unreadable.

"Yes, *sir*," she said at last, and was gone.

CHAPTER

NINETEEN

GRACIA

With fewer foreigners in the guard Alekso's ire quieted, and I was even able to draw out of him some conversation about the more urgent matters of the treasury and the city's repairs. This latter was a project which, to my relief, proceeded with not only alacrity but Ceian support. There was no alternative for buying the steel and stone needed besides borrowing against our debt, unfortunately, but the labor situation was easier: Ceirran was more than willing to press his men into labor on the reconstruction alongside mine. This was sorely needed, as their presence in the city was otherwise nearly as great an irritation upon the populace as my own rebellion had been.

Ana's point about soldiers wandering around getting into trouble had proved to be less of a warning than a threat. She herself was the worst offender—every day I received new reports of her drinking, of her gambling, once of her using the pillars in the Summer Market for target practice. For some time she had been very popular among the Alectelans—the news had spread of how she had argued to spare the prisoners—but Szayeti had long memories, and too little faith to let one Ceian's generosity mark Ceiao for them forever.

"Just ask the barbarian why he hasn't punished her," Alekso said to me. "Have the matter over and done with."

"I can't," I said. I was taking my luncheon in my rooms that afternoon, and he was sitting on my desk, his hand planted halfway through a platter of fava beans. "She is his soldier, and it would make him out to be an object of contempt in my eyes. I have no authority to tell him how to conduct Ceian affairs."

"You have every authority," said Alekso. "She does it on Szayet, doesn't she? It's the businesses and property of Szayeti she does it to, isn't it? It's your obligation to tell him how to conduct her affairs, as far as I can see."

"Since when is your central objective the welfare of Alectelans?" I said.

"Since their welfare made you seem weak," said Alekso.

The truth was that I was deeply reluctant to speak to Ceirran about his closest captain, and had been since that night we had met at the door to the dungeons. It would have been easier if Ana had only been his right hand, who did all that Ceirran asked her and followed him like a dog and slipped into bad habits when he was away; then I might simply have hinted to Ceirran that his officers' poor behavior reflected poorly on him, and let him follow that thread to its conclusion. But I heard Ceirran speak ill of Ana nearly as often as my people did, frequently to her face, at which she only grinned. Whatever passed between them, there was no ignorance in it.

The other Ceian soldiers loved her dearly, but there was no mystery in that—she ate with them, fought with them in the sand pits behind the palace, talked their coarse talk, came down to the harbor when it was time to dig into the guts of her ship and came out covered in oil up to the elbows, laughing. I had no respect for that love, and no curiosity whatsoever about its workings. It was precisely the kind of love Arcelia had managed to cultivate.

"Your own guard don't love her, though," Alekso said. I startled, and he rolled his eyes. "Your face," he said, "not your mind. It's the *I'm-only-a-crude-soldier* routine. *They* know she isn't. And the tavern-keepers of Alectelo are their friends."

"That's an advantage, then," I said.

"Is it?" he said, but before I could ask why, his head snapped up like a hunting dog's. "She's coming down the hallway."

He would do this, sometimes—tell me where people were in the palace, what they were doing. This behavior was sporadic and utterly arbitrary. If I ever openly asked for information, he would refuse to give it. He was only ever able to tell me what was occurring in the palace, but no matter how far I was from the palace, he was able to tell me what was happening there. Much as when he told me my own thoughts, it was impossible to determine what was the sensitivity of the quicksilver pearl computer and what was his fortunate guess.

On this occasion, I only just had time to settle my crown on my head before the door opened. Alekso's face, already skeptical—he had not liked this plan—dissolved into flecks of color as soon as I let the Pearl go. "Captain," I said, without looking round.

"Impressive," said Ana. Her footsteps came closer. I turned at the last moment, and found her bending to reach over my shoulder, her cheek brushing past my own. I was struck temporarily mute; by the time I had recovered, she had lifted a piece of flatbread from my table and laid it on her tongue.

Her mouth closed, and her throat worked. She licked her lips and smiled. "What can I do for the Oracle of Szayet?"

"I want to talk to you about Lieutenant Dessouthan," I said, when I was able. "I received a report from my captain Vuszaya of his—damaging public property."

"Damaging public property!" said Ana. "We can't allow that. I'll have him whipped at once."

I had had an entire speech planned—the lieutenant had vandalized one of the walls of the Library, scrawling a word in Ceian that very few Alectelans comprehended and a picture that absolutely all of them understood instantly—but I came up short. "He's sixteen," I said, highly annoyed. Not many of Ceirran's soldiers were what we Szayeti would call children, and in fact most had been with him since the early days of the Madinabic campaign, but those who were shocked me each time I saw them, like missing a step in the dark.

"But a lieutenant," said Ana, "and a representative of Ceiao! And one of my own men. What on earth was he thinking? Szayet, if you like, I'll throw him out of the air lock."

I inhaled, exhaled, and curled my hands into the folds of my robe. Those days after the coronation, I had thought of nothing else, had even once dreamed of it: that moment after I had returned from the Island of the Dead, when Captain Ana had bowed to me. When she spoke now, though, it was impossible to understand how she was one with the woman who had made that obeisance. She seemed to have entirely forgotten both it and our conversation in the darkness at the dungeon door.

"Perhaps you ought to spend more time modeling good behavior," I said shortly, "and less time in Karadzaty's, Jedmaya's, and Berolla's taverns in Cabero Plaza, losing thirty dekar a night."

She looked up sharply. "How do you know about that?"

They had come to my ministers on four separate occasions, complaining that she would not pay her bills. "Prophecy," I said.

She smiled, but it had no humor in it.

"You'll forgive me, Szayet," she said, "if I do as I please. The city may be yours, but you'll find my time is my own, and neither you nor your god can reform me into the kind of woman the Sintians like."

"I don't want to reform you," I said, startled. Then, recovering myself: "Is it your own time? Aren't you an oath-sworn soldier?"

"You know, you're right," said Ana. "My mistake. My time is Matheus Ceirran's, and I do as he pleases, and neither you nor the god can gainsay *that*."

"I don't *want* to," I said again. Eternal God, did she have to make everything so difficult? "But I don't think it's unreasonable to ask if you're capable of more than this."

She looked at me a moment, then she tipped her head back and laughed, loud and long. When she had finished laughing, she wiped her eyes ostentatiously. "Am I capable of more than this?" she said, and smiled into my eyes. "What, exactly, is it you want me to be capable of?"

To my immediate horror, I felt my ears grow warm, and forced myself to stare back without flinching. "If you could make Lieutenant Dessouthan scrub his artwork from the Library walls," I said, "that would be something."

To my relief, she glanced away, and her lip curled in a sneer. "Something," she said. "Very well, Szayet. Perhaps I can be *something*—for you."

"Good," I said. "And—Captain?" She raised an eyebrow, and I said: "Don't ever eat from my table again."

"My deepest apologies," she said. Her eyes were glittering. "Consider it sacrosanct."

And when she left the room I felt a great deal more discomfited than I had before.

It was a warm night, and Ceirran and I took dinner in the palace gardens, under a triplet of full yellow moons. Alekso had, after Ana left, made his feelings on what I should say quite clear, but I sat with my chin propped in my hand and listened to Ceirran explain to me how he had outflanked a certain war chief on Madinabia C, demonstrating with dried fruit as the Ceian formations and fried onions as enemy ships, as the moonslight crept higher and the lights in the city around us began to wink out one by one.

I nodded along as best I could, but midway through wrapping one onion string around a cluster of ten or twenty raisins, Ceirran paused. “Why haven’t you said you’re bored yet?” he said. “I expected you to interrupt me nearly twenty minutes ago.”

“I’m not bored,” I said. He raised an eyebrow, and I amended: “As an intellectual exercise—I find it very interesting. I do! Only—”

“Only?” he said, amused.

“It’s very different,” I said, “seeing it drawn out on a table on a fine night in a garden, with your belly full and your clothes clean and in the midst of pleasant company, and seeing it from the middle of a battle with your heart going like mad, and a hundred thousand lights and noises bombarding your senses, and every wrong movement being your death.”

“Of course it’s different,” he said.

“But you discuss it as if it *were* the same,” I said, “as if it had all happened behind a tablet’s glass, and you were watching from a long way away. I don’t understand how you do it.”

Ceirran pushed one of the raisins to the edge of his plate, the one that had been about to destroy the enemy, and tapped his fingers on the table. “Will you promise not to take what I say next as an insult?” he said.

“I won’t promise,” I said, “but say it, please.”

He smiled, then his expression grew serious again. “You waged war against Arcelia well enough,” he said, “but Arcelia was, I suspect, one of the only enemies against whom you would be able to wage war with any real success.”

“It’s not an insult at all,” I said. “I have heard it said before.”

“I wonder at the nerve of whoever it was who said it to you,” he said and, when I only smiled at him, shrugged. “Very well. I suppose that, between myself and the world, I impose a sort of distance. It's not that the danger must be ignored, it's that it must be—absent, perhaps, or forgotten. It's like the way that, when you walk over a high and very narrow bridge, you must forget for a little while that you are capable of falling. I'm sure you can achieve the same. I have seen you do it already, when you argue policy that might result in poverty for your people or in wealth."

"But that's not the same at all," I said. "Yes, they might live or die from policy, and I want them very much to live, but I am in the towers of my palaces, and however much I care about their poverty, I will never live it again. It would be absurd for me to try. I must reach out in my own mind through the glass of a tablet to know their fears—I must choose to feel. I *do* choose to feel. Suffering does not come to me and scream to be felt."

"It might, if you refused to feel it long enough," he said. "It happened to the rulers of Ceiao, once."

I frowned at that.

"I'd like to make a tour of the planet," I said. "It's been a long time since any member of *Dom* Caviro visited the outlying islands. After the war, I think it's best I should see something of the Szayeti across the globe."

"I think that's very wise," said Ceirran, though for reasons I could not fathom he looked a little melancholy. "You'll go soon, I expect?"

"Soon enough," I said. "There would be so much to prepare—I don't know if any of the seaships are even fit to sail, and of course I will need to chart out a course, and alert the islands I am coming. But I don't intend that any of this should take very long. I would like to see Szayet. I would like to make several tours, if I have the time, and if Szayet ever finds the money."

"Ah," said Ceirran, eyes crinkling at the corners. "About the money," and we were drawn into another fencing match about the debt-relief plan, in which he suggested a great deal that Szayet could not agree to and I suggested a great deal that Ceiao could not afford. By the time the servants brought out the cakes, the moons were high in the sky, and the reflected gleam off of Alectelo's pearl roofs had brightened to a spotlit glare.

"Who did say it to you?" said Ceirran, as I was licking honey from my fingers, and when I raised an eyebrow, "That you would lose a war against any enemy but your sister. Who said it to you, before me?"

"Why do you want to know?" I said.

"Oh," he said, "perhaps I'm interested in knowing the name of any person who likes to insult you. Who was it? You can tell me."

But I didn't tell him, any more than I intend to tell you.

At least, not for now.

CHAPTER
TWENTY

CEIRRAN

Summer was running steadily out of Szayet like water, and the poplars were bursting into gold along the avenues. Gracia's servants rowed us to an outlying island one cool night, in a little red boat filled with soft quilts and bottles of rich Ceian wine, and she pointed out where the autumn constellations were beginning to peer over the horizon, and named them for me in the language of her ancestors: la Drako, la Kolĉeno, la Okulo del Sinmorto. Alectelo lay at nearer latitudes to its planet's equator than Ceiao, and the sunsets came on more gently here, but they slipped closer nevertheless, like water toward high tide.

There was no good reason for me to stay with Gracia now that she was established enough to tour her own planet, of course. Each day I woke to messages from friends, or enemies, or flatterers who meant to be both: Might I bribe this inspector, might I tax that one? Might I advise them on how they should vote in council, might I give a speech on their pet subject? Thiago Veguion had said this or that; was it acceptable to invite him to a party? This man had stolen from them, but they suspected him to be my particular friend; should they prosecute? Was my leave in Szayet expected to last very much longer? Was my leave in Szayet something they should expect to be permanent?

My absence was yet more noteworthy to those local gang leaders and neglected neighborhoods where I was known and loved. Kostya Arzhenty, the gangster who had been shot, had been important to more than just the council members to whom he had lent money; his death left a gap in the poorer Kutayeti or Medveyeti neighborhoods that more than a few of his lieutenants longed to fill, and even the councillors who were most loyal to me wrote nervously of shootings in the Outer City. His house still lay empty. So did Quinha's. It was this last, above all else, that made me miss Ceiao deeply: the memory of Quinha Semfontan's house as I had known it once, its feasts and its laughter, the glow spilling from its front door. I had no appetite for the city, but I longed to see Quinha's house again. It would—it *would*—be good to go home, to greet my husband, to greet my friends, to begin the work I had meant to begin for over a year now. It would mean the end of the war.

Anita, as the autumn crept at the edges of our vision, made herself increasingly absent from my company. This was for the best—I had no desire for her to follow me into Gracia's quarters as she had, on *Laureathan* and Madinabia, followed me into my own whenever she felt entitled to my conversation or my dinner—but it was also unsettling. I kept looking over my shoulder for her, as one prods at a missing tooth. If she had missed a rotation on palace guard duty, I might have summoned her for upbraiding—but she never did, which was perhaps most uncharacteristic of all.

"Why do you keep her with you?" Gracia said when I told her this. We were lying in her bed, sweaty and sated, and her face was propped idly in her hand. "It seems to me she has very little use."

I smiled into the darkness, where she could not see it. "I'm glad of that," I said. "I greatly prefer it when she is misjudged."

"Ah," said Gracia dubiously. "Obfuscation. She enjoys being underestimated, of course."

"Not at all," I said. "Expects it, perhaps, but I suspect that in fact she would prefer error in the opposite direction. But, to her great fortune, I remain her commanding officer, and to my great fortune, she remains my captain. And as long as that state of affairs continues, I am afraid she will be estimated no more highly than my arm or my hand."

"Hmm," said Gracia, turned over my arm, and drew a finger from the wrist down along the palm. "You do have lovely hands."

I looked at her from the corner of my eye. "Patramata," I said, "that was crudely done."

She looked startled, and then her face smoothed over and she laughed. "You wouldn't just let me distract you."

I caught her hand where it lingered in mine and ran a thumb over her knuckles. "Later," I said, "I assure you. What are you distracting me from?"

She had a curious look on her face, almost uncertain. I leaned forward. "Yes?" I said.

"When I was young," she began, "my father—"

But what had happened with her father when she was young I never found out, for at that moment there were two short, sharp pops below our window, and the sound of a scream.

We looked at each other and rose as one, Gracia throwing one of her robes over her shoulders and hovering at the bedroom door for me to finish pinning my cloak. By the time we made it downstairs and into the great hallway, the crowd there had already grown to an unmanageable crush, Szayeti guards and Ceian soldiers jostling at one another's shoulders, every man pressing in to get a better look. The crowding was getting violent. Some of my men were beginning to shove.

"*Attention*," I barked. The blue-cloaked soldiers sprang apart at once. The soldiers in red stared at me mutinously, but snapped to attention when they saw their queen.

That was a bad sign. "What's happened?" I said. "Who's been hurt?"

"Me," said a familiar voice.

Anita was leaning against the palace doorframe. Her face was splotchy and grey as sand, and her cloak was torn. A length of blue cloth had been tied tightly around her upper arm.

"And someone else," she said. "Well. He isn't hurting anymore."

I strode through the crowd, Gracia behind me, and lifted Anita's arm from her side. There was a dark patch spreading on the makeshift tourniquet, and she hissed when I ran my thumb gently over it.

"It looks worse than it is," she said. "It's only a scrape—I got him before he got me. Matheus—"

"Fetch a doctor," I said to the nearest Ceian soldier. "Do it now. I can't think why—" and that was when Gracia, who had pushed past me to the front steps of the palace, shouted a word I hadn't thought the Sintian language had.

She appeared beside me again a moment later—Anita went, if possible, paler—and seized my captain by the shoulders. I let go of her arm, startled. "Captain," she said. "What the *hell* have you done?"

The boy was sprawled at the foot of the steps. The burnt hole through his chest was neat and, for a gunshot wound at close range, remarkably clean. He was not a boy, not really—on Ceiao he would have been five or six years into his mandatory service. He was certainly old enough to be a killer. The gun, lying on the concrete a few inches from his open hand, said that well enough.

But we were not on Ceiao.

Crouching a few feet from his body, eyeing my men at the

top of the steps with a palpable mixture of fear and hate, were another boy and a girl. He had come with friends. And behind them, scattered down the whole Bolvardo del Tombo, gathered in twos and threes by lampposts and doors of buildings, made into shadows by the gleam of the lamps and the moons off the pearl, were the Szayeti, a few whispering to one another, more silent. All were staring fixedly toward the corpse.

When I climbed the steps again, Anita was gone. "The doctor," said one of my men, and "*Our* doctor," said one of Gracia's, and the murmuring among them rose, but I held up a hand.

"Enough," I said. "Tell me what she's done." The Ceians hesitated. The Szayeti were staring daggers. "*Now*," I added, with force.

The story came out, bit by bit, from those soldiers who had been on guard with her, or in the hall, or on the street itself. Anita had been in front of the palace, speaking to the two officers on duty there. Both were Ceian, and both good friends of hers. The conversation had lasted for some time. The boy had come up to the bottom of the steps and offered her invective, followed by his friends.

"He was drunk," said the lieutenant who was telling this part of story, "and he said—"

"He was not drunk," said an Alectelan. "He was angry, but he was sober as I am."

"He was drunk," said another. "Sorry, Stefek. He always was."

"Not tonight," said the first. "I saw him with my own eyes."

"He *was* drunk," my lieutenant insisted, "and his friends, too. Commander—" He quailed at my look. "As I say. They came up to the bottom of the steps—"

No matter the boy's state of sobriety, Anita had ignored him for five or so minutes. Then, apparently provoked beyond patience, she had begun to return his insults with a certain colorful verve. The boy had demanded she come down the steps and repeat herself to his face. Anita had refused. The boy had demanded it again, at which Anita had apparently laughed at him and stood to go. It was then that the boy had pulled his gun, and raised it to fire—

I stopped the petty officer who was speaking. "Did he?" I said to the Alectelan who had called the boy sober before.

He hesitated. "Yes," he said at last, without meeting my eyes.

"He was a merchant's son," said another of the Szayeti. "He liked to hunt on the outlying islands. Thought he was a crack shot."

He had pulled his gun, they said, and raised it to fire. Anita, to his misfortune, had moved faster.

"But what was this *about*?" I said. "Was he an Arcelian sympathizer? Was he a rebel against Ceiao? How did the argument begin?"

The Ceians looked at one another with deep reluctance. "*Tell me*," I said.

"Gambling debts, sir," said my lieutenant. "She'd spent the whole night previous cheating him at cards."

I went out of the palace again in a white rage, and stopped dead. The crowd had grown. What had been dozens of Alectelans had become at least a hundred, and I could see more, drifting in farther down the boulevard. They were all of them whispering to each other, now, a low susurration like snakes, staring down the street. All were staring at me.

"Ceirran," said Gracia softly.

I had nearly forgotten she was there. She was leaning against the frame of the palace door, just where Anita had been. Her face was still and unreadable, like a Szayeti moon.

"Patramata," I began, not knowing how the sentence would end.

"Don't," she said. "Don't bother."

"I'll speak to the people," I said. "I'll—" What could I say?

"Don't," she said again. "Let me."

"Let you?" I echoed, bewildered.

She looked away from me, toward the growing crowd. Then she stood upright and began to walk down the palace steps. She seemed very small there, suddenly, her robe too thin for the chill of the night, her eyes bare of kohl. When we had run downstairs, she had not even waited to put on shoes. I moved to follow, but without turning, she shook her head.

When she reached the bottom of the steps, she bent toward the boy's friends. "What was his name?" she said to them. Her voice was gentle, but it carried. After a moment, the girl offered it. Gracia nodded, and said, "And his father's?" The girl said it. "Thank you," said Gracia. "May I?"

I did not know what she meant, but they must have. They hesitated, wide-eyed, but nodded in the end. "Thank you," said Gracia again, and then she knelt down by the body of the boy, and folded her hands together, and began to chant in Malisintian.

I didn't speak Malisintian, but there was enough of both Ceian and modern Sintian in it that I could understand a little. Gracia spoke to Alekso; she asked him for something; she hoped; she blessed him, again and again. The crowd was watching her, now, not me. The murmuring had stopped entirely. In the low gold of the streetlamps it was impossible to make out their faces clearly, but what little I could see made me no calmer.

After some time, Gracia stopped, and opened her eyes, and offered her hands to the boy's friends. I started at this, and so did they. But they took them, uncertainly, and Gracia said, "Thank you," and began to speak in Szayeti.

Speak was the wrong word, but it took me a minute to understand why. Her voice rose and fell, gentle and rhythmic. I thought of Szayeti as a harsh language, but in her mouth it sang and hushed, rushed up and fell back. The way she spoke, it sounded like the sea. I knew then that she was praying again.

She spoke for a little while, then she looked up, at the boy's friends. She said something to them in Szayeti, to which they responded in unison, that same rhythm, and her voice grew louder, and she stood, a barefoot girl in a nightgown, and called to the crowd, and listened to them call back. I had thought she was only translating what she had said before. I had been wrong. This was something they knew—all of them knew. They were rocking back and forth, the people along the street, their hands clasped in front of them or raised. Some of them were embracing each other. I could hear others weeping.

I turned away. My fury had gone. All that was left was a cold, silent drumbeat in my throat, deeper and more unhappy than shame.

It was not difficult to find the room where the doctor had gone. "She's fine," she said to me, "or will be. She's lost blood, but there's not even a chance at infection, I don't think. She's a lucky woman."

"Thank you," I said. Behind her in the room, Anita was a silhouette against the starry window. "Please leave us. I'll call you back if she needs any help."

When I went in, Anita's head was ducked down, her face hardly visible. I bent and gripped her chin between my thumb and forefinger quite hard, and tilted her face up toward mine.

I said, very low, "Captain, I expected better from you."

Anita's expression had been a parody of penitence, perfunctory and disdainful. It was only typical of her. But now that face cracked like paint, and beneath it was a real and animal anger.

"From *me*?" she said.

I let go of her chin, but she kept staring. Her eyes were dark with fury. "Go on," she said. "Lock me in the brig until landfall. Berate me before the men. Kill me, if it pleases you. You have the right."

"It has become apparent," I said softly, "that you have not the least idea what pleases me."

I could see it strike home—perhaps the first thing I had said to her that really did. If she had not been a soldier, she might have curled over her knees. As it was, it was as if a sudden wind had entered the room, and I could see every part of her tense against the force of it.

"Kill me," she said, again, but now it was desperate. "You have the right."

I put my hands on her shoulders, and I leaned in—she flinched—and I kissed her, just as gently, on the temple, and I said softly into her ear, "Do I look as if I can afford to lose a soldier?"

She exhaled as hard as if I had dealt her a physical blow.

"Commander," she said.

I pulled away. "I am sending you to Ceiao," I said.

Her eyes went wide. "*Commander*," she said, and, "Matheus—"

"I am sending you to Ceiao," I repeated, "where you will be my voice in the Merchants' Council these next several months. You will find, I expect, our council unusually persuadable so soon after Quinha's death. It is too great a missed opportunity not to have those in my inner circle among their number."

She looked as if I had slapped her across the face. "What the *fuck* am I meant to do with Ceiao?" she whispered.

"A good deal," I said. "You asked me when I meant to begin persuading the council toward a Kutayeti campaign. Do so in my name. Flavia asks when I will address Thiago Veguion's acts against immigrants he suspects to be cultists. Gather the votes of those councillors sympathetic to me, and block him from speaking entirely. Appoint magistrates who would act as generously toward neighborhoods in the Outer City as you once did in their place. Recruit those foreigners and colonials you can who are loyal to me into the Ceian army, and recommend them for whatever promotions the law will allow. Argue, Captain, for land reforms. Túlio Cachoeiran wishes for the admirals to take back the power to conduct campaigns without my say-so. Convince him otherwise. Veguion wishes for me to lose the fleet altogether. Let him lose his lines of credit across the galaxy. Am I making myself clear?"

Throughout this speech her face had been drawing into itself, emptier and emptier, until by the end it seemed a block of sandstone. "But where will you be?" she said at last, in a voice I hardly recognized.

"On Szayet, of course," I said. "The queen wishes to make a tour of the planet. I intend to accompany her."

"A tour?" said Anita, as if she had never heard the word before.

"Her staff will keep you apprised of where I am," I said, "if you should need to know. There is no need to report regularly. I trust you."

I left her like that, standing at attention, as still as if she were one of the statues washed up on the beach. The only part of her moving was her eyes, which followed me wordlessly out of the room. It had been the cruelest thing I could possibly have said to her.

CHAPTER TWENTY-ONE

GRACIA

I was afraid of leaving so soon after the shooting, of course, but Alectelo calmed far more quickly than I had expected, and we made the necessary arrangements with speed. A third of Ceirran's soldiers were going to Ceiao with the captain. The rest were entirely on internal palace duty, with no interactions permitted with the populace. Captain Orcadan had been given charge over all who remained, and my minister of the interior given charge over Captain Orcadan. What surprised me most was how little of a difference this made in how the people treated me. If anything, when I went out among them, they pressed against my litter more closely, called to me with increasing fervency, for blessings and for protection from evil.

I felt like a liar. I had done nothing at all. I had prayed their orison with them—neither my father nor my sister would have done that, and could not have if they wanted to—but what was an orison? Why should they care if I chanted with them to a god who, if I had listened to him earlier, might have prevented this altogether? But I was given no time to find an answer. We left on a market day, waving to the crowds who had come to the harbor to cheer our ship, and Alectelo disappeared over the horizon with the same implacability as the sun.

No Caviro had made a tour of Szayet in many years. Cipriano had done it, but that had been almost entirely a scientific endeavor, and he had spent the better part of his time taking notes on the shapes of leaves on islands barely an arm-span across. Azahara had begun one, but she had been called away by the war almost immediately, and she had never returned.

It was not precisely a tradition. There was a kind of sentiment on Alectelo, I was aware, that the Bride of Szayet contained so much of what Szayet was—the people both Szayeti and Sintian, the immigrants, the Library, the tomb on the Island of the Dead, the Oracle herself—that there was very little need for a monarch to leave its shores. Perhaps, had Ceirran not been my companion, I might have agreed with them.

The first week of the journey was spent nearly entirely without sight of land. Alectelo lay midway between Szayet's tropics and its frigid zones, and the sea captain took us southwest for some time, away from the equator. We would not circumnavigate the globe, of course—by sea that journey would have taken close to nine months—but before Alekso had come to drown the world, the majority of Szayet's landmass had been in its western hemisphere, and still this was the part of our planet that held the bulk of that little of old Szayet remaining on dry land. We intended to visit those islands where the oldest and the strangest and the most unique of Szayet's animals and artifacts could be found, to greet those of my people who we could greet, and to return with no particular haste to Alectelo at the beginning of winter.

The ship itself was a great steel thing called *Cesta de Higos*, which had sat nearly unused in the sea harbor since Casandra Caviro Savanta's time. It required forty sailors to man it, most of whom Ceirran and I never saw, and another fifteen attendants and staff from the palace itself, who brought us breakfast on the deck each morning and supper in our rooms each night, prepared our baths and clothing, fanned us when we were hot and warmed the braziers when we were cold, and sang to us when we were in need of entertainment. This was rarely. Though it was difficult to get any clear holo connection at sea, and the data packets were few and far between, we found ourselves almost entirely occupied by our own company, for what I think was the first time all my life.

The sea changed as we drew farther south. I was used to Alectelo's white beaches, and to the mirror-brightness of its water. I knew my city as a circle of stillness, where in summer it rarely rained and in winter it rarely snowed. Farther from human civilization, though, the water grew rougher and darker. The sea life, which at home tended to be goatfish and prawns and silvery schools of anchovies glittering in the harbor, grew larger and more wild: On those few small islands that we did pass, we saw snapping blue crabs, urchins, even once a green lumbering sea turtle. A few days later, on a greyed-over afternoon when there seemed no use going out on the deck except to shiver and come back in, one of the sailors exclaimed and knocked frantically at our door. By the time Ceirran and I had gotten our robes on and rushed out to the railing, all we could see was the distant splash where the dolphins had disappeared.

He was never still, Ceirran. This is what I remember most about him now. He moved like one of the stray dogs in Alectelo's alleys. Even when he was hesitating, some part of him was always in motion: his feet, his hands, his eyes. When he walked along the deck with me, I would press close to his side, and we would talk of theater, and history, and birds, and dressmaking, and Sintian mathematics, and any other subject that happened to catch our fancy, and he would be clever and thoughtful and attentive and everything a queen could ask for in a partner in conversation. But I would catch him, whenever he thought I wasn't looking, and it was never me he was staring at. It was the sky, always. It was the distant fingernail marks of our ruined moons.

I would not have called him vain, but living in such close quarters with him, I found him more careful about his appearance than I would have guessed—or perhaps this was only my new and acute intimacy with his body, the fine details of which even our months of affection had allowed me to overlook. He would dictate letters into his tablet from before the mirror over the course of an hour, while my barbers coaxed his hair with a bristled brush into fine, narrow waves. His jaw stubble, which I had thought a symptom of his perpetual busyness, turned out to be an affectation: He would stare at it for ages, turning his head from one angle to another, and then at last set his pearl-handled razor to his jaw and shave a fraction so slender it was hardly noticeable. He was sensitive about his scar. Even during sex, he did not like for me to touch it or kiss it, no matter how gently. His elbows and knees were sensitive, too, and went bone-dry in the slightest cold. It was almost as a joke that I offered him the scented cream I used on my hands, expecting him to reply with some soldierly nonsense about enduring hardship and showing one's travails—but to my surprise, he took to it immediately, and my attendants were kept twice as busy ordering more to each new port.

After the second week we caught a warm current and were borne north toward a city called Zhivatselo, which had been the capital of Szayet at one point during the Eighteenth Dynasty. Here we stopped for supplies, and to look briefly around the new buildings and old ruins. The people here, to my great relief, seemed to like me as well as the Alectelans had. I had worried that they might think me a brainless girl or a lawless rebel or, worst of all, a stranger, but when they saw me they pointed at the Pearl and whispered and crowded forward to kneel at my feet and call me Oracle and Alekso's Voice and Queen. I spoke to them in Szayeti a little, at which they pressed closer and exclaimed, and I asked if their harvest had been good and if their governor was fair, and if any of them would be willing to show me around the old temple.

One elderly man agreed, and Ceirran and I climbed across great flights of stone steps and peered at neat carvings where the paint was flaking off, and I translated into Sintian as best I could what the man was saying about the Eighteenth Dynasty king and his god and his queen and their odd theology. Much of the place was smashed—Ostrayet's work—but Alekso's priests had spent the last three hundred years restoring what little was left. When we had circled the whole building, Ceirran and I settled ourselves against one of the pillars and drank wine in near silence. The sky was a flat stone above us, and the tall gold pillars of the temple made the sea entirely invisible. I found myself thinking that I could come back to this spot in another three hundred years, and sit against this same pillar, and the island would look entirely the same.

It was in a strange mood that I departed Zhivatselo and set north toward warmer climes. The days, though hot and lazy with false summer, were beginning to grow shorter in slow minutes. I found myself waking up later, increasingly to an empty bed—Ceirran had a soldier's habits, and liked to take his exercise on the deck around dawn. This did not trouble me, but it made me thoughtful. It was, except for a few mornings between my return and coronation, the first time I had woken up alone since I had left prison. I would linger in our bedroom for an hour or more on those days, conscious of the sway of the sea underneath me, trying to feel out the edges of my solitude.

On one such morning, after I had at last come to breakfast—at the previous port we had picked up fresh fruit and vegetables, and today Zorione had corralled the cook into spreading out pomegranates and warm bread, cucumbers and newly baked date cake, duck's eggs with spiced honey—my thoughtful mood lingered. Ceirran spoke to me about a message he had received in a data packet earlier that morning, a party some politicians he knew were arranging, and I listened with half an ear, looking out over the sea.

The water was smooth and clear that day. I could see below the roofs and steeples of a crumbling town, where a very young kelp forest was beginning to spring up. At the beginning of our voyage every new building had been a cause for discussion, but now they were so common that it would have been like remarking on gulls. Our journey had taken us above villages and hamlets, through fields of floating logs from old forests, around the little steel peaks of radio towers that broke through the sea's surface like nails, down the paths of highways long since grown over with weeds. This collection of buildings in particular sat very shallowly on the seabed, nearly high enough to be a danger to the ship. At one time it must have been a city on a hill.

"Let's dive in," I said.

Ceirran looked at me, startled. "What?"

"Dive in," I repeated. "Zorione—have the maidservants bring up swimming costumes. There ought to be something in the commander's size, oughtn't there? If the ship has any masks, we might even be able to see the ruins up close."

"I don't think so," said Ceirran.

"Why not?" I said.

"Well, for one thing," said Ceirran, with not a little amusement, "I can't swim."

I stared. "You're joking."

"Not at all," said Ceirran. "When would I have learned?"

This brought me up short. Every child in Szayet learned to

swim nearly at the same time she learned to walk, as not only a pleasure but a necessity. An Alectelan who had no hope of survival off dry land was an Alectelan who had confined herself to a very small world.

"You couldn't have learned in your river?" I said.

"Anyone who puts their head underwater in the Nevede is asking to grow another eye," said Ceirran. "And I'm afraid no moon of Madinabia is known for its beachfronts. There's the ocean at home, of course, two hundred miles or so from the city, where the highest quality of the merchant class keep their summer homes. But everyone I know who has seen that beach grew up with parents very well established among that quality, with no need to worry about promotion or turns of the market."

"And the commander of Ceiao isn't listed among that number?" I said, laughing, and was surprised when his face drew at once into unsmiling preoccupation. "But of course you weren't always the commander of Ceiao," I said quickly, a little bewildered at the suddenness of the change. "I should have thought."

"Well, I might have visited the seaside as a child," said Ceirran, so pleasantly that I wondered if I had mistaken that flash of seriousness, "if things had gone differently. My mother's mother lived there year-round."

"Your mother's mother!" I said. "What an extraordinary thing to have."

"Not so extraordinary," he said, "if you aren't royalty, made only from a single monarch and the workings of the crèche."

I seemed to have offended him again, without knowing how, and was a little irritated by it. "Plenty of people are drawn from the crèche on Ceiao," I said, "unless its technological advancements are even more removed from civilization than I understood them to be."

If I had been hoping to provoke him, I failed; any remaining sharpness in his face vanished at once, and he laughed as if I had told a good joke. I had been serious, but I smiled anyway. "I suppose I'm only jealous of your having living family that you might visit," I said.

But at that he frowned again. "I don't," he said. "My mother's mother invited me to come to the sea and meet her grandchildren once I returned from campaign, but there always seemed to be some delay, and then she died not long after I was married. The children are gone away to the army." He stirred, and laughed. "Listen to me, Patramata! You must wish you had never asked me to swim in the first place."

"Not at all," I said. This was the first time he had ever spoken of his family. In all our far-ranging conversation over the last weeks and months, he had told me about his time in the army, his education in Sintielo, even a little about his husband. He had managed, though, to entirely avoid so much as a mention of his parents. I had thought they must not be important to him. "I could teach you, if you'd let me."

He smiled. "Maybe later," he said. "Not now, I think. You've seen more than enough of unpleasantness from me for one day—let's not add my coughing up salt water onto your beautiful deck."

It took me a few moments to realize that *unpleasantness* must mean what he had said about his family, and I smiled, a little uneasy. "Not at all," I said again. "If you change your mind..."

"Enjoy yourself," he said, and gestured to where the servants were coming up with towels and swimming costumes. "Bring me treasure, if you find any."

Kicking down toward the city was as easy as flying. The water was warm and very still. My bathing costume left my legs and arms bare, and I felt almost naked beneath the surface, as much a part of the sea as the foam and weeds. With the mask over my face I could see the city plainly: The kelp tumbled up from the streets and the boulevards, only small stalks now, already tangling with one another. In another few years this part of the ocean would be impassable. My only companions this near to the surface were fish, moving in darting yellow-black clouds like wasps. High above, the sun was a rippling circle of green gold, more halo than light.

I surfaced, inhaled deeply, and dove again. The city was not as close as it had seemed from the ship. If I wanted to walk the streets I would need real weights, and oxygen. Even the roofs were difficult to reach: If they had been our Sintian-style peaks I could have touched them, but they were flat and made of clay. Everything was made of clay—this was why the city was crumbling so badly. Most of the buildings were less than half of what they had once been, eroded or fallen down or burrowed through by seaweed. Many looked hollowed-out, like lightning-struck trees.

There was a steeple very high above the seabed, though, and there was something on it, greened over but gleaming. I swam toward it, though my ears were beginning to ache, and reached out deliberately through the thick current. It broke off in my hand with ease—three hundred years of rust at work. It was not heavy, and it took barely a thought to kick downward and let the great weight of the water below push me up toward the sun.

"Look," I said to Ceirran, when I had climbed back on deck and left a trail of seawater from the railings to our breakfast table.

"I'm looking," he said.

"At my hand," I said, laughing, and looked myself. It was a carved copper head of an elderly man. The rust had worn away nearly all of the detail—there had been two eyes, which were now only sockets, and an ear and part of the mouth had fallen away, leaving jagged holes behind—but what remained was fine work: a carefully carved nose, a delicately engraved curl over an ear.

He took it from my palm and turned it over. "It's lovely," he said.

"It's Sintian," I said. "Do you see, the hair—the way the cheeks are sagging a little, the wrinkles—how he purses his mouth a little, and the muscles of the mouth are pulled in? The Szayeti and the Ostrayeti would never have commissioned a head like this. They would have thought it informal, disrespectful."

"From one of Alekso's soldiers?" he said. "Before he raised the oceans?"

"I don't think so," I said, sitting down beside him on the towel the servants had laid over my chair. "It was attached to a building. Sintian visitors, maybe, or their children. I'm sure there's an answer in the Library."

He lifted it up to his eyes. "It reminds me of the Strato Akademio," he said at last. "The end of it, where the theaters are. That cathedral with the carved masks."

"I'm sorry?" I said.

"In Eksteregula," he said. "Well—you might not have been to the neighborhood. I'll admit they're against the idea of queens there. But if you had cut down from Kolumnino, and taken an escort—"

"I presume this is on Sintia?" I said.

He stared open-mouthed. "You've never been to Sintia?"

"When would I have?" I said, a little more acerbically than I meant to.

Ceirran's mouth pursed. "I don't know," he said. "Only I forget sometimes, that you're not—"

"—in the merchant class of Ceiao?" I said.

"That you haven't traveled the galaxy," he said. "That you haven't been educated in Sintielo, and spoken to philosophers there. Yes, all right—that you aren't a member of the Merchants' Council." He glanced out to the flat colorlessness of the ocean. "If you were a merchant of Ceiao," he said, "you likely would have done all of these. You would have been in the army seven years, and you might have gone anywhere."

"But I am not a merchant of Ceiao," I said.

"Of course," he said. "But I am astonished at how easy it is to forget."

"Well," I said shortly, "remember."

He had still been turning the little head over in his hands, and at that he looked up and tried to hand it back to me, but I pushed it away.

"It's yours," I said. "Take it back to Ceiao, if you like."

He set it on the table, next to the date cake. "Thank you," he said.

There was a solemnity in his tone that pierced my mood. I took his warm hand, where a few streaks of rust were smeared along the knuckles, and applied a napkin to it. On the linen napkin they showed up as green as grass.

"What is it like?" I said. "The cathedral."

He was smiling down at my hands. "Very large," he said. "Marble, mostly. A great wooden dome. There are no services there anymore—they've given up more than half of the Aleksan worship in Sintia in the last few decades, though they'd never admit it."

I set his hand back on the table and waved to a maid, who bustled over to collect the napkin. "Do you expect that to happen everywhere in the empire?" I said idly.

He gave me a sidelong look. "Patramata," he said, very gently, "would you like me to make you promises?"

"No," I said at once. And then, unable to help myself: "But you are trying to change laws on Ceiao. I know that much. A relaxation of the disestablishment. I understand"—he had begun to speak—"I understand that has very little to do with Szayet, in practice."

"I'm afraid it has very little to do with Alekso altogether," he said. "Ah—please tell him to take no offense."

"I will," I said dryly. He did not mean it.

"I want to relax the worship ban," he went on, "and I'll admit that freely—but that has less to do with any fondness for your god and more to do with how astonishingly popular the idea is. Among immigrants, naturally, but even my own people have some very strange desires. Worshipping Alekso is anathema, of course—even were it not for their memory of the theomachy, I think they would resent kneeling to a Sintian—but they seem to be very fond of the idea of worship in general. I suspect that if they wanted to—" But he shut his mouth at once, and would not tell me what he suspected they wanted, no matter how I cajoled.

"Fine," I said at last. "*Why* won't they worship Alekso? What was the theomachy, that its fury has lasted so long?"

"Don't you know this?" he said, laughing at me. "Haven't you had tutors?"

"I have heard a story from my tutors," I said. "I want to hear it from you, though. I want to hear the truth."

Ceirran sat back in his chair and pursed his lips.

"Do you think," he said, "that the truth is something I am likely to tell you?"

"What an interesting question," I said.

That made him smile. He shut his eyes, then, and steepled his hands. When he spoke again, his voice was quieter, singsong.

"The high priest of Alekso Undying," he said, "was a man by the name of Luĉjo la Senkompata."

"Malisintian," I said, surprised.

"Just so," said Ceirran, opening his eyes. "What did you expect?"

"Nothing at all," I said. "Go on."

"For a hundred and fifty years," Ceirran said, closing his eyes again, "the priests of Alekso had ruled in Ceiao. It was a strong city, under their rule, if not a great city. There was law, but no invention; there was piety, but no greatness. And this was so"—his voice took on an arch, lecturing tone, and I was sure at once of the ghost of some distant teacher in his mouth, a petty officer many years dead—"this was so, because every piece of wealth, every moment of study, went toward the temples. Every thing in the city that was good or great went into the mouths of the priests within the Wall. Every Ceian in the city who was wise or strong was made exhausted in serving them. And it was so for this reason: Though the priests sent Ceians out to seize other planets, they ruled from the Inner City, and the Inner City was set aside from the rest of Ceiao by a great wall. And what crossed the Wall never left, least of all the priests, who, though they declared war after war, feared fighting, and were the only ones in Ceiao who did not go out to the stars. And so Ceiao was never able to conquer beyond the edge of her system. The priests never wanted us to. Why would they, when they had so many obedient sheep at their feet?"

"That doesn't seem true," I said.

Ceirran's eyes opened again, looking not a little irritated. "Oracle," he said, very politely, "I assure you it is."

"Of course I believe they ruled as tyrants," I said. "I am Szayeti. I believe well enough in tyrannous gods. I only say this: I have never met a wealthy man who was not hungry for more gold in his pockets, let alone one who worshipped Alekso the Conqueror. Especially if they had a taste for empire-building already."

That startled him. After a moment he smiled thoughtfully, and his face was his own again, the phantom of that long-gone teacher vanished.

"Perhaps they wanted to conquer further," he said, "but were afraid that, if they failed, the people would believe they were out of Alekso's favor and overthrow them."

"Perhaps they wanted to conquer further," I said, "but it took many years after Alekso's conquest for Ceiao to build up the resources. Perhaps they were stymied by infighting."

"Perhaps all three," said Ceirran. His eyes narrowed thoughtfully. "The scholars would like you," he murmured, "on Ceiao."

"I very much doubt that," I said.

"That doesn't surprise me," he said. "You have a talent for doubt, Patramata." He smiled to himself, as if enjoying a private joke. "I wonder if anyone else has caught you out in it."

"You can catch me out in what you like later," I said. "Will you continue?"

"If the Oracle will allow me," he said, smiling. "For a hundred and fifty years, as I say, every good thing in Ceiao crossed the Wall and did not return. They went as tithes, for the most part, and the more tithes one gave, the closer one came to the right hand of Alekso Undying, in the world to come. Food crossed, and books, and ships. People, sometimes, too, if they were strong and good builders, or if they were clever and good servants, or if they had spoken blasphemy against Alekso Undying, or if they had been late in their tithes, or if they had spoken ill of the priests, or if their parents or friends had spoken ill of the priests . . . or, eventually, if they had not bowed low enough, if they had hesitated when a priest had asked for a tithe of something very dear to them, if they had thought in their hearts that there was something—anything—which was not right or good about the priests or the Wall."

"Slavery, then," I said. "It is like Szayet, after all."

"Like and unlike," he said. "I understand that the tyrants from your moon—what was your moon—used your people only as builders and farmers and domestics. On Ceiao, someone had to fight the wars. And someone had to maintain the lines of trade that sprang up when they were won, and so those admirals who did became very rich indeed—became, unto themselves, a merchant class."

"So not all of the wealth in your world was handed over the Wall," I said. "Ordinary men kept at least a little. Unless your admirals were all embezzlers?"

"Oh, I'm sure they were," he said, "and I expect plenty took bribes, too, if the officers I know now are any guide. Governing a province has of late become an unfortunately lucrative business. I intended to send an officer home to clear out the less useful corruption, but—"

He trailed off, his mouth curling down. "So what was it that these admirals really lacked under the priests?" I said hastily, uncomfortably certain that he was thinking of Captain Ana again. "Not profit, but power?"

"And the freedom of the city, I should say," he said, his eyes clearing. "And the right to question their betters. And above all, dignity. Yes, I think you're right—they did have a real share in Ceiao's profits. Perhaps it's because they had a little of the priests' privileges that they grew tired of being denied the rest. Valquíria Barran was among the wealthiest admirals of all."

"Ah," I said.

"Yes," said Ceirran. "I expect her name you have heard already. Barran had fought wars for the priests for over twenty years, on the rings of the planet we now call Ceiao Quinhorze, and besides making herself a wealthy woman, she had become a powerful one, with many friends among her fellow officers. And then, as it always does, winter came."

Even a thousand years ago, Ceian winters had been famous. After Alekso had come, and knocked the planet's axis nearly a whole degree away from its sun, they had become historic. "Not a mild one," I said.

"Not mild," said Ceirran, "no. The harvests failed, one by one. The people suffered, and then they died. And the priests called for more tithes, and more. People were entering the world to come in great numbers, they said, and Alekso's right hand was growing crowded."

"All of this you say about his *right hand*," I said, "I've never heard it before. Here we only speak of his voice, or his mind, or his endless life. We have no *world to come*, on Szayet—we hope Alekso is kind to the dead, but if he knows where they go, he has never told us. Was the next world to the Ceian priests a kind of crowded dinner table?"

He laughed, sounding a little shocked. "I don't believe the priests ever spoke of his living soul," he said, "if that makes any difference to you. Though of course even they could not deny that Alekso's body rests here in Alectelo."

"They might have," I said. "Don't you know that that is the Kutayeti heresy?"

"Is it?" he said. "Well, perhaps you would have considered these priests heretics, too. I believe the world to come was a sort of endless throne room, a great celestial Kupolo do Dio—that would be the domed marble temple where the head priest had lived for a hundred and fifty years, which we now call the Libeiracópolan. Is that heresy enough to offend you?"

"It makes no difference to me," I said. "Well—I expect it would make no difference to *him*. I guess that he would call them all barbarians and dismiss the matter. What happened in this harsh winter?"

"People starved, as I said," said Ceirran, settling back in his chair again, "and even the admirals were growing short of food. At the beginning of the very last month of winter was the Feast of Alekso's Crown."

"We celebrate that here, too," I said. It had been one of my father's favorite holidays: three days of dancing and drinking, parades through the streets and raucous singing, bells shaken to summon the blessed dead to celebrate the coronation with us.

"It isn't celebrated on Ceiao anymore," said Ceirran. "None of the old feasts—not his apotheosis, not his birth, not his victory at Kutayet."

"Don't you celebrate the New Year in the early days of autumn, though?" I said.

"Yes," he said. "On Ceiao that was almost a month ago."

"Ah," I said, "and how fortunate that it should happen to be at the same time as the Feast of His Name."

Ceirran smiled a little. "In any event," he said, "Valquíria Barran had to herself a little piece of garden within Ceiao's limits, not far from the Wall, which her mother had owned, and her grandfather before her."

He shrugged. "The high priest of Alekso, as I say, was a man by the name of Luĉjo la Senkompata, and he had been high priest for around a year. The priests were desperate for money with which to put on the festival. He felt he ought to prove himself."

"He seized the land," I said.

"Not precisely," said Ceirran. "He tried to seize the land. And when Valquíria refused him, he took her only grandchild."

My first instinct was to call him a liar. I hesitated, though, and Ceirran saw what I was thinking, and he closed his eyes and looked away. "She was not the first child to disappear," he said. "She was not even the first child to disappear from one of the great admirals' families. You must understand: They didn't do it to be cruel—they did it because it worked. Whatever had been denied the priests would be granted at once, or if it wasn't, more children would disappear, and there would be no word, no sign. And then at last the defiant worshipper would acquiesce, and the priests would tell them: What an honor, what good news. Your child is sitting at Alekso's right hand."

I thought at first, without knowing why, of Arcelia: Arcelia as she had been in the streets of Alectelo with me, bright-eyed and laughing. Then I remembered that the Ceians would not have thought her a child. They sent their children into the army the day they turned thirteen.

"Did they—keep them?" I said. "Did they have them become priests?" I did not sound, even to myself, as if I believed it, and Ceirran shook his head.

"The priesthood was a birthright," he said. "It was not like your Library, where anyone might come to study. They did not keep the children." He paused. "We were told, in school, that when it was all over, Barran discovered a furnace. Around its door there were prayers inscribed—for Alekso to purify what was burned there of the sins of the fathers."

"Undying God," I said reflexively, and wished at once I had not, but Ceirran did not seem to be paying attention. He was looking past me, over the endless sea, where the light winked on the water like stars.

"But even I doubted that," he said distantly, "when they said so in school. Perhaps they kept the children in the dungeons until they starved. Perhaps they did use them as slaves. But as for burning…I have been where bodies were burned in great numbers. Some of the battles on Madinabia—" He shook his head and sighed, and still wrestling with my nausea at the thought, I did not press him. "There is no record of the people of Ceiao knowing what happened to their children," he said, "and I think they would have known, long before Barran crossed the Wall. Not the details. But they would have known there was a smell."

I was not superstitious, but I wanted to make the sign against evil, which I saw among Alectelans daily. I kept my hands still in my lap. "You cannot think that Alekso asked for this," I said. "No matter what you think of me—of my people—of my faith—you have seen my city. You cannot think it is the city built by a god who would ask for this to be done to children."

"No," he said. "No, Patramata, and nor does anyone else." He still was not looking at me. "The staunchest Ceian skeptic does not think Alekso ordered any of this done. The staunchest Ceian skeptic thinks that Alekso has ordered nothing at all since he was laid in the ground, three hundred years ago. But I was taught that whatever was done to children—it was not done by

Alekso of Sintia. But because of the power of his name, no one did anything to stop it."

"But Barran—" I said.

"But Barran," Ceirran said, "took a full complement of her soldiers and went to hammer on the gates of the Wall for seven days and seven nights."

"That long?" I said. "She didn't sleep?"

"She might have," said Ceirran, "but after the third day, she was joined by another of the admirals, who had been her dear friend, and with whom she had been speaking quietly of unrest for many months."

"Many months!" I said. "Long before they took her grandchild, then?" His eyebrows went up, and I said, "Are you sure it was about her family's garden? If she had been fomenting rebellion before winter had even come—"

"Perhaps it wasn't about the garden," said Ceirran, "but as all the priests are long dead, I'm afraid we would need quite a wonderful Oracle to ask them. You might also find it relevant that in Ceiao then, as now, it was very much the fashion to profess a passion for gardens. Your education is superb, Patramata. Nevertheless I don't think you've read very much Ceian poetry. Certainly a great deal less than Sintian."

His smile was growing a little tight. "Please go on," I said, subsiding.

"On the fourth day another of her fellow officers arrived," said Ceirran. "On the fifth day, more and more, until the soldiers filled the streets, until they surrounded the whole Wall. On the sixth, they proclaimed her commander at those gates, and gave her control over all the fleet, and the ships began to turn from their berths on the outskirts of the system and make their way home. And after the seventh, a priest emerged from within. *Are you here to negotiate?* said Barran, and the priest said: *I am here to give you a warning. Go home, Admiral. Do as you were ordered, as a soldier should. Kneel before the high priest, and beg his forgiveness. Or you will have no part in the world to come, and you will never see the right hand of Alekso Undying, though you walk through the darkness ten thousand years and more.*

"And Barran said, *My own hand works all right*, and shot the priest where he stood."

I looked at him a moment.

"Did she say that?" I said.

Ceirran smiled a little. "Every few years another troupe of actors pantomimes it all again, you know," he said. "Different words, different characters, except for that moment. Any educated person would be very startled if it were left out."

"I expect they would," I said, and let myself smile back at last. "You all treat priests with a great deal more suspicion than you treat historians. Next she burned the high priest, I suppose?"

"Next she invaded the Inner City and took the Avenuan Libeirguitan—it was the Avenuan Sanktan then, of course," said Ceirran, "and, yes, she and her soldiers burned Luĉjo la Senkompata on a pyre. But behind her the people had already begun to tear down the Wall, so it was less an army than a mob that broke into the Kupolo do Dio, and then they opened up its dungeons..."

His eyes had shut again.

"That's the end of it," he said, "more or less. Barran disbanded her army afterward, and went to live in that little piece of garden. She said she wanted to spend time with her family. What was left of it, I suppose. But she remained a merchant, and so did they all, all those old admirals, and—well, you can guess the rest. The end of the priestly class, but the merchant class remained. And the first law they laid down, the first law of the custom of Ceiao: disestablishment. No churches. No priests. No bended knees. No gods in the city, until the city falls." He opened his eyes. "Is it what you wanted to hear?"

What, exactly, had I wanted to hear? Something in the way he said it gave me pause. I said, "Was it the truth?"

"You seem better able and more willing than me to answer that," he said dryly.

More willing made me hesitate, too. At last I said, "I don't know that I believe it."

"I didn't expect you to," he said, and stood up. "Should we go and see about lunch?"

"But I think I understand it," I said.

He sat down again. "Do you?" he said. There was no accusation in it, but there was no affection, either, and its absence was more striking than I had expected.

"Not every part," I said, "and I think I might have had to be a child on Ceiao to understand it all—I think I would have to believe, in truth. But I understand her, I think. Barran."

"Your war was very different," he said. "She was fighting against a god, and you were fighting to gain hold of one."

I paused, and said, "But I think I understand how it felt to be that kind of afraid."

He gave me a long, thoughtful look. "You might," he said eventually.

"In any event," I said, "may she rest in peace."

"Don't," he said. "If you want to understand her, don't wish for that. It is the worst thing you can say to a Ceian—to *rest in peace*. Firstly, because upon death, the soul is gone forever—it rests in nothing at all. But also because no Ceian, given the opportunity of eternity, would choose to spend it peacefully. It would be the antithesis of the empire. It would be a decimation of her honor."

I said nothing to that, and we went to our lunch. But I thought to myself, lying beside him that night, that Alekso might have liked Valquíria Barran, and her faith in her good right hand, a great deal more than either Ceirran or I would have been entirely comfortable with.

CHAPTER

TWENTY-TWO

CEIRRAN

We came up the sea current along what had once been the coast of a continent. Under the sea we began to see pine forests, and tall steel towers, and once a heap of shining slag metal jutting out of a road of smooth black stone. "A volcano, Holiest," said a sailor when we asked. "In another hundred thousand years, that city will be buried in a new island." The dolphins returned and haunted our wake for nearly an hour before drifting away again. One day, passing along the boat in a great movement like a tide, we saw the mountainous swell of a whale.

Obedient to my command, Anita rarely contacted me. When she did, it was perfunctory: All was well on Ceiao, our friends and enemies continued in good health, this proposal had been passed and that vetoed, this party had been a success and that a failure, the mists had come and the new year had been welcomed and the cool rains had begun to fill up the river. I did not respond to any of these for nearly a month—then, relenting, wrote up a long list of Ceians of the merchant class but of no real quality who I wished raised to positions as inspectors and judicial clerks, and sent it to her in a data packet, which took nearly six hours just to upload from my own tablet. Gracia thought this very strange—"You reward her by telling her to interview secretaries," she said, "and punish her by lending her Ceiao?"—but Anita responded with a rambling, effusive letter about Flavia and Cláudia Pulcron and Celestino and Jonata Barran and the plays showing this season and the latest absurd things Cachoeiran had said at council meetings, which surprised me by sparking a deep sense of relief.

I had thought of myself already well entangled with Gracia when it came to our mutual business of governance. In those days on the *Cesta de Higos*, though, I was unpleasantly surprised to find that where before I had been involving myself in her matters, the habit now had no choice but to become reciprocal. It was not that I had wished to hide the daily goings-on of Ceiao and its citizens from her, but it was disconcerting to feel her cool gaze as she read my letters over my shoulder, to answer her questions about why I supported this tax and opposed that one, and why I laughed to see a certain councillor flatter another, or a certain wealthy woman of quality snub a neighbor. Noticing the discomfort was a disturbance of its own, and I turned it over carefully in my mind, in those early silent hours on the deck while the black sea peeled away westward into dawn.

I could not be afraid that the queen of Szayet would use knowledge of the inner workings of Ceian politics against my city. She had neither the resources nor the inclination to do so. She depended on Ceiao entirely. More than this, I knew—though I did not say—that she depended entirely on *me*. I was no more threatened by Szayet or its queen than I had been on the last day of its civil war, when Gracia's sister had sent forty warships against me and thought, in her arrogance, that my own pilots would be inadequate to the task.

So what, I thought, was I afraid of?

It was on one such morning, after I had returned to bed and was flicking my way down through Anita's reports on the interminable cultist gangster scandal, that Gracia laid her hand on mine. "Hold there," she said. "Was that name Túlio Cachoeiran's?"

I waved the page back, startled. "So it was," I said. "Don't tell me he's made himself a nuisance to Szayet as well."

"A nuisance?" she said, eyebrows raised. "Do you mean another Cachoeiran? I was referring to the great writer."

"Ah," I said, and struggled for a moment to keep the grimace off my face before giving it up as a lost cause. "You have read his philosophy."

"You think so little of his writing?" she said, and propped herself up on one elbow. The shadow of the window curtain fell over her face. I could not see her eyes, but her mouth was a thoughtful curve, not entirely happy. "I had heard that on Sintia they called him the great defender of Ceian liberty."

"Of course I admire his *rhetoric*," I said, laughing a little. Again I had grown uncomfortable, and again it unsettled me that I did not know why. "But there's no need to admire the rest of him. You see here, from Anita, how he refuses to even meet with her about arguing in council meetings against the raids of Thiago Veguion? Thiago sends the guards to batter down the door of anyone he suspects to have the smallest scrap of a prayer scroll. Nearly all of this in the Outer City, you know, in the houses of immigrants from Madinabia and the Swordbelt Arm. Of course it's about me, really—me he hates, me he wishes to punish—and he harasses them only because of how well they love me. And Cachoeiran says nothing. Is this the so-called defender of Ceian liberty? And has the Oracle no opinion on that?"

The shadows shifted along her face. "Ceirran," she said abruptly, "may I ask you something?"

"Of course," I said, and very nearly followed with, *Anything*, and was startled enough by this that I nearly missed what she had said, which was:

"Do you enjoy having enemies?"

And then I was so shocked that it took me a long moment to reply.

"No," I said. "No. I despise it."

"I'm sorry," she said. She sounded sorry. I could not always tell when she was lying, but I believed her now. "I wanted to ask because—" She shook her head, and her hair shivered along her shoulders. "You were so unhappy that Arcelia had—you were so unhappy about your friend. I thought you must not have wanted to go to war with her at all."

"I didn't," I said.

"But you did go to war with her," she said. "And before that, when you and she were on the same side, you went to war against Madinabia—and now, when I thought Ceiao was finally at peace, another rival stirs himself, and another..."

I considered that and sighed.

"There was a conspiracy on Ceiao, several years ago," I said. "It was meant to overthrow the council—to overthrow Cachoeiran in particular, as a matter of fact. Only over money, nothing important, nothing real. I had a—" My voice caught, and I swallowed and exhaled carefully until I was sure it would not catch again. "Some who participated were my friends. I watched them go into exile, or—"

I had never gone to see Sílvio, when I had heard what happened. I had thought: I don't want to remember him looking like this.

Gracia shifted beside me, and I turned to look at her instead. She was beautiful, of course; there was no use denying that. But what struck me about her then, and what had struck me since the first moment she had rolled out of the carpet and insulted me to my face, was not her beauty but her gaze. The way she looked at me—the way she looked at anything she took notice of—was like standing under a bright light, like jumping into a deep well. I could not feel the smallest part of her attention without wanting its full weight.

"There will always be people," I said, "on Ceiao or elsewhere, who seek to be the cause of war. There are people now who seek out enmity with me, for no other reason than because it is their nature." I shook my head. "If I could end all dislike of me forever with a snap of my fingers, would I do it? Of course I would. I want nothing more. But I am only an ordinary man, and I cannot order Thiago Veguion to love me. All I can do is ask respected men to stop him from pursuing his refusal to love me to the point of tyranny—and to wish those respected men, however little *I* respect them, would agree to help."

Her free hand twitched up to her ear, then floated down without touching her Pearl. "I visited Ceiao when I was a child," she said. "Ten years ago. I was to have met with him—with Cachoeiran, I mean. My father, and me."

"I didn't know you had visited Ceiao," I said, surprised.

"I hardly did," she said. "I only saw the customs bay. All my time there I spent on the dock in your harbor." Her bare shoulder moved up, and dropped. "While I waited in the ship, I read his essays. I hardly understood the language then, of course. I only understood that it was beautiful." Her hand moved restlessly in the bedsheets, curling the linen under her fist and letting it go. "I imagine my father met him without me."

"Ten years ago? When he was newly made a councillor? He would have been still more insufferable than he is now," I said. "Patramata, you must realize he has never been an admirer of *me*—or of anyone besides himself, in my opinion. To him the city is a thing of dead texts and dying principles, without a thought paid to the real, living man to whom it belongs, or what that man might ask of him."

"What Captain Ana might ask of him, in this case, I see," said Gracia dryly, her eyes moving over the report.

I looked at her hard. She had not mentioned the shooting of the boy since we had left the harbor. But if there was any rancor in her face now, I could not see it, and I said, "As long as I stay away from the city, she is my voice. Ceiao knows that well enough." I turned the page forcefully, away from the sentence containing Cachoeiran's name. "Who disdains the pleasure of her company disdains mine."

Gracia gave me a long, unreadable look. "I wonder whether—" she said, and then stopped.

"Wonder what?" I said, but she shook her head.

"Put down the tablet," she said, and slid a hand under the blanket, along my hip. "I'd rather discuss the pleasure of your company."

When we were in bed, I was used to, and liked, the Gracia who made things difficult for me: who made me work with tongue and hands before she would spread her thighs for me to fit between them, who twisted and writhed under my touch, whose eyes went bright when I finally pinned her to the bed and only then said *Please* into her ear. Today, though, she was fervent, impatient, the warm weight of her surging forward in my lap. "Talk to me," she said raggedly, "I want to hear your voice," and moved steadily over me while I did, eyes fluttering shut, until my voice grew hoarse, and then caught, and then failed me entirely.

She rose after we were done, and dressed herself, and went to the deck to bring back fruit and fresh bread for our breakfast. I let her go, catching my breath and my wayward thoughts. My heart, I thought, had not slowed since I had asked her *And has the Oracle no opinion on that?* I had loved before, and lost before, but in the last twenty years of my life there had been only one person whose esteem I had both longed for and not already been certain of, and all that was left of that person was a head buried on a beach by Alectelo Harbor.

We did not discuss Cachoeiran again on the journey. Along our route now lay a long line of seaports on one island after another, a scale of rising musical notes. I followed Gracia onto crumbling wooden docks, onto great cement piers painted in flat yellows and blues, onto soaring orange bridges and jagged-rock beaches. Everywhere she went, the crowds ran to greet her, packed to overflowing along the roads and shorelines, hoisting children onto their shoulders, falling to their knees, stretching out their hands, eyes white and rolled up to catch a glimpse of her face.

On Alectelo she had been first a desperate and intelligent girl, then a thoughtful, recalcitrant queen. It was very odd to discover myself traveling with a God-bearer. The servants, of course, bowed whenever she passed, and called her Holiest, and came on rare occasions to ask her questions to do with the weather or their personal disputes, but this I had grown so used to that I hardly noticed it. The fervency of the crowds on the islands was entirely different. The strength of their feeling was like electricity: It curled off them in waves, it distorted the air, it so drew the eye that it was impossible to look at anything else, even the sea or the sky. Gracia seemed entirely unmoved by this, though I thought more and more often that I glimpsed barely half of what passed through her mind. In my case, it was a stronger compulsion, more magnetic. Her crowds were not gathering for my sake, of course, but they knew me as the Ceian who had brought her to the throne, and I heard them shouting my name, too, saw my face reflected in their eyes. What little I caught of their focus made me feel as if I had caught hold of a lightning bolt, like one of the old stories about Alekso's childhood, and it left me reeling with the sweet hot force of it.

"You might yourself be a goddess," I said to her as we left one of these islands, watching the parents and young women and elderly soldiers wave their handkerchiefs as we retreated from the docks.

She laughed at me. "Do you think I'm likely to knock Ceiao off its axis tomorrow?"

"Not at all," I said. "I only mean that if you asked them to call you one, like as not they would do it. It would be much the same thing, in any case. Isn't that what Alekso did?"

"You have a dangerous mind," she said, but she only sounded amused.

There was one town at the base of a surprisingly tall hill—it had once, of course, been an impossibly lofty mountain, and at the top of that mountain, an Ostrayeti man had built a mansion before the flood. His name was long forgotten, but he had been a collector of antiquities. Some of the best-preserved art of the old Szayeti kings stood on the steps of this little palace: intricately carved wooden coffins, linen dresses sewn with gold and jewels, long painted scrolls, hundreds of statues that had once stood as protectors in Szayeti children's graves. He had also, to the current priests' rage, cultivated a habit of hiring sculptors to create imitations, which had been so skilled that it was only by very slow and careful material analysis that one could tell which was which.

At the base of this town, Gracia declared her intention to teach me to swim at last. I protested greatly, and she had to bribe me with whispered promises of what might happen in our cabin that night before I agreed to strip down in our rooms and emerge, very reluctantly, in one of the Szayeti bathing costumes.

"Your face!" said Gracia, laughing. "You might think I'd painted hearts on your cheeks and asked you to do somersaults. You look perfectly ordinary, you know."

"I think I prefer you as a flatterer," I said. My arms were bare up to the shoulder, my legs to the thigh, and I was more than usually conscious of the faint scars and childhood pockmarks that peppered them. It was one thing for Gracia to touch my body when she was beneath me in bed; it was another entirely to have it bared under the light of the sun and the gazes of the servants lined up behind us on the beach.

Her eyebrows went up. "You look very handsome," she said. "Come into the sea."

A half hour later, she tugged my shoulders firmly up from the water and put her hands on her hips. "I wake up alone every morning because of your dedication to your exercises," she said tartly. "You cannot find *floating* difficult."

I spat salt water out, coughed, and struggled to my feet. The shore here was rockier than most were in this part of the world, and the stones dug sharply into my bare feet. "I didn't know it bothered you to wake up alone," I said. "Why don't you come out to the deck and take them with me?"

She sighed. "What is it, really?" she said. "I tell you, all you have to do is be still. Are you so afraid of drowning? I had thought you were enjoying the sea."

"I am," I said, and hesitated, and looked down through the rainbow spackle of my damp eyelashes. "Must your servants watch me struggle?"

It took her a moment to answer. Her hair was braided neatly back along her head, but a few sodden strands had escaped, and as I watched her, she pinched one between her fingers unconsciously, and curled it around her finger and tucked it behind her ear. "If you were to really begin to sink," she said at last, "I don't have the training to save your life."

"You're standing right here," I said, smiling at her. "With the rate I seem to be learning at, I can't imagine you and I will swim more than a few feet out from shore before nightfall. If you had to, how difficult could it be to save me?"

She smiled back, but it didn't reach her eyes. "Are you so afraid of looking undignified you're willing to drown over it?"

"That's easily solved," I said. "I don't plan to drown." She didn't smile, and I added, as patiently as I could: "Patramata—I trust you."

I was not expecting what happened in her face then: the sweetness that passed through, sudden and startled, all her habitual shrewdness vanishing as if cleared by wind. After a moment she turned away, and when she looked back, her eyes were full of laughter again.

"You must promise me that if you die, I won't have to explain it to the Merchants' Council," she said. "I have quite enough to worry about already."

"I've already been absent so long. I'm certain you could spend at least a few years pretending I was alive and simply didn't want to see them," I said, and when she didn't smile, "How's this? If I die, I promise you I'll explain the matter to them myself." At that she laughed and waved for the servants to return to the ship, and when they had gone, I found myself able to relax into the motion of the waves at last.

When we were climbing up the gangplank, hours later, both of us dripping and shivering, she caught my hand in hers. I glanced at her in surprise, but she only squeezed it.

"You did look very handsome," she said.

I could not tell whether she was lying.

There was another town on an island, one of the few that had actually been built out into the water for dozens of miles in the early postdiluvian days before Szayet's treasury had run quite so low. It was one of the only spots in the region where earthquakes were rare enough that it was possible to do this with any sense of safety. "Alectelo is another," Gracia said to me, "we hope." On this wide island were some of Szayet's only vineyards, where Gracia and I sipped wine in dark wooden rooms, and she gave the vintners effusive compliments while I wished desperately that Anita was there so we could share an amused look. Better were the huts of the beekeepers, who pressed upon us honey in every color from mahogany brown to watery sunlit gold to, bewilderingly, a bright and garish red the same color as a bar of soap. "Cherry dyes," Gracia explained incomprehensibly. This we sucked out of long steel straws under the bear oaks in the heat of the evening, watching the fireflies emerge from under their leaves and flowers and blink uncertainly into the nighttime.

Between the ports were glimpses of the Szayet that lay underwater, which fascinated and repulsed me in equal measure. Often, of course, we could not see them, as the sea was rarely both clear and calm enough that its seabed was wholly visible. These were the pleasant days when the world shrank to me and Gracia alone. Sometimes, though, the ruins of the world were impossible to dismiss. One afternoon as I was poring for the hundredth time over the Ceian calendar, Gracia called me to the railing. "Look down," she said.

Beneath the sea was a great face of green stone, which must have been at least sixty feet across. Its expression was smooth and without emotion, aside from its lips, which were turned up a little at the corners. On its head rested a vast golden crown, whose front half stretched from one ear to the other. The back half had broken off and was lost. The head was lying flat on the seabed, staring sightlessly toward the sky.

"That statue, if it were standing," said Gracia, "would have been head and shoulders above the surface of the ocean."

"Where did the rest of it go?" I said.

She pointed, and I saw: the seaweed that so choked the seabed was not even. Beneath it, if you squinted and waited patiently for the movement of the waves to show you, were dozens of enormous pieces of granite: I saw a finger, part of a chest, what had once been the edge of a golden necklace. Farther from the ship, standing upright from the seabed, were two enormous legs already crumbling at the knees.

"All of that gold," I said, staring down at it.

"They wanted him to have it in death," said Gracia. "They thought, if they built him tall enough and well enough, he would be able to keep it forever."

I could not stop staring at the sheer size of it, that broad golden crown. "I don't suppose," I said.

She ran a thumb over my knuckles, then leaned up and kissed me gently.

"Not even for you," she said.

It rained that next day. It was different, on Szayet, to live through rainstorms. For one thing, you could see them coming from a distance—never the case on Ceiao, where if Mauntan Bau or the harbor traffic did not obscure the weather, the height and breadth of the city itself did, so that only from the tip of the Libeiracópolan was it possible to glimpse the lightning over the river. On the Szayeti ocean, flat from horizon to horizon, storms began as haze and bruises far in the distance and moved toward us with all the leisurely predation of an owl. Gracia's soldiers always knew they were coming hours before I did, and would spring into action like a well-oiled machine, pulling at sails and fixing furniture and stretching canopies overhead, and we would press together as the rain clattered above us and shout to be heard over the drumming of the water. And then it would blow over, as quickly as it had come—I had always thought of rainstorms as opening up the sky from above, and even after years of piloting only now understood the sweep of their lateral movement, how they moved not *down* but *across*, and how they vanished into the distance without looking back. It made one feel startlingly small, to be a way-stop on that journey—startlingly irrelevant to the movement of the ocean, and of time.

I found Gracia under a tarp at the dining table near the stern, still in her morning robe. Traveling with the queen of Szayet seemed sometimes like a series of movements from sense to sense: rich color, soft sound, the slipperiness of silk, the pungency of brine. Today she was eating a peach with astonishing deliberation, closing her eyes with each bite and sitting in apparent thought after she had swallowed, mouth gleaming with the juice. She saw me on the deck a few bites after I arrived, and I saw her examine her shining fingers thoughtfully, glance at me, and then shrug and wipe them on a napkin.

"Did you see the sunrise?" she said.

"No," I said. I was waking up later and later the farther west we drew, as if the sunsets were pulling my mornings down toward the horizon. More often than not my exercises were taken well after dawn. In the flat blue shorelessness of Szayet there seemed to be a new breadth to the sun's motion, a magnification into months or seasons of every passing day. I did not know if Gracia felt this, too. She was looking away.

"The clouds colored up like berries," she said, "like if ripe berries went sour again, and the seagulls were falling toward the sky. I thought—" She shook her head. "I thought—if I could catch this in resin, like an insect, and keep it—"

I waited, and then prompted, "If?"

She stirred. "Oh," she said, "I don't know what I was saying. Have a peach. I tell you, they are *beautiful*."

I bit into one, and licked the juice from my lips. "Good," I said, and watched her as she finished her own. When she was done, she wrapped the pit in her white napkin and set it aside on the table.

"I've asked the captain to take a detour from our route," she said. "There's something I want you to see."

"Will you tell me what it is," I said, "or should I be afraid?"

I often forgot the nearly eight years that lay between us,

but when she smiled a true smile, I remembered: It made me think of myself, long before the civil war, when Quinha and I had given each other half the world and Madinabia had been a wild dusting of untouched moons in my radar screens. "Don't be afraid," she said. "Listen: The storm is fading. It's going to be a beautiful day."

Behind the storm were the moons, three spindly crescents faded in the light of day. We passed a long stretch of beach, along which lay a pod of sea lions who stared at us without shame, occasionally lifting their heads to grunt urgently at the sun; we passed another ship far in the distance, a Szayeti banner fluttering at its tip, whose people were small enough that they might have been insects but who waved frantically and saluted us through the magnified view of the ship's telescope; we passed a great hill of sunken crab-litters, legs broken off from their frames, rusting deep in the white sand.

At last we arrived at an island, so small that the ship could not have fit across it lengthwise. On it sat an enormous tree and very little else, besides a few yellowing patches of grass. It was here that the ship stopped. Gracia and I were let into the little boat, and I rowed her to the island, where she climbed onto the sand and reached out a hand to help me up.

"This," she said, "is the largest tree left on Szayet."

It must have been about a hundred feet tall. The bark was a bright reddish orange, pinstriped with deeper, darker veins, and you could see where the roots were growing out of the earth, great veiny things wide enough to seat two men each. The branches did not begin until I craned my head up, far up, and then I saw how they clustered and blossomed into a cone. It would have taken twenty or so people to fit around it, holding hands.

It loomed. Still, it looked strangely naked there in the sunlight. The patch of shadow at its roots, sprawling as it was, seemed small and uncertain beside the sand lying only a few feet from its edge.

"It'll fall," said Gracia, "in a few more decades. It can't stand on sand. There's nothing to be done."

I looked at her sharply, but to my surprise, she did not seem to be asking for anything. She was not even looking at me.

"The priests say," she said, "that there are parts of this world that Alekso spared. There are dry places in every flood. The land that would be Alectelo is one of these, of course. And there were thousands of Szayeti who prayed that they or their children might reach the boats in time, and because of the depth of their faith he heard them, and the waters parted. He was capable of many miracles."

I tilted my head back again. There was a quality to the great tree that I could not at first articulate, a peculiarity to the landscape around it. When I looked at the back of Gracia's dark head, I thought I understood some part of it: Though she had called it the *largest tree left on Szayet*, it did not seem large at all. It seemed as if it were the size that the world ought to be, and it was we who were unnaturally small, and the island, and the sea, and the sky.

I was not sure what Gracia wanted to hear. "It's beautiful," I said at last.

"Yes," she said. She still sounded as if she were far away. "It is, isn't it."

By the time we returned to the ship I could see another dark fingerprint on the horizon, and it was not long after its engines coughed into life again that the rain overtook us, thin and cold. The servants scrambled up to drag the tarps over the ship. In the warm lamplight of our cabin Gracia stretched herself over the bed. I settled beside her and began to comb my fingers through the waves of her long black hair.

"I remember," she said, "I remember that I once went with

Arcelia to the market square, and we saw a Diajundot couple there, who had a cage full of hoopoes. They had caught them on Cherekku, and they intended to sell them across the Swordbelt Arm. Do you know what the hoopoe means to the Szayeti?"

"Are they gods?" I guessed.

She curled on her side, so that I could better run my fingers along the back of her neck. "No," she said. "Nearly. They were the symbol of the heir to the throne. Szayeti writing is said to be their alphabet. On Sintia they are called kings of all birds, and among the Cherekku, they are thought to be holy messengers. In Alectelo, where all of these people speak and live together—not quite gods. Something approaching gods, maybe. It is said that one can find wisdom by learning the language of the birds." She hummed when I rubbed a thumb over her ear. "Arcelia wanted to buy one."

"But you didn't," I said.

"No," she said. "No, because—it was winter, and—they were scrawny, and their feathers were sparse. There was one with a great and bright crest. I remember him. I remember how he stared at me. I thought—I was afraid of keeping him in my home, when it was already so cold, and he was already so thin. I was afraid of trying to take care of something, some beautiful thing, and failing. I convinced Arcelia to come and find some other entertainment, and we returned when the sun had set. And he was lying on the floor of the cage."

I tucked a strand of hair behind her ear. From this angle I could not see where the wires disappeared into her skull, only where they gleamed at its helix.

"And you cried, I suppose," I said.

"No," she said.

My hand paused. "No?"

"I don't cry," she said. "Scream—shout—tantrums, yes, when I was young. But I never shed tears. Not even as a child."

"In Ceiao they would say that means you herald ill fortune," I said.

"How lucky that you and I aren't in Ceiao," she said, and I laughed against her back, and watched how she shivered at the sensation of it, without meaning to.

CHAPTER

TWENTY-THREE

GRACIA

We moved from islands into fog, and from fog along the blurred shores of distant islands, and watched them vanish into the fog again. For a whole week it was cold enough that Ceirran and I were unable to stay on the deck. We took our meals in our bedroom and sent the servants away, and lit stained-glass lamps so that the walls of our cabin moved in misty golds and greens. Perhaps it was the absence of sunlight that made Ceirran quieter that week, more subdued. I did not attempt to fill his silence, but spent long hours in bed beside him, reading and watching him from the corner of my eye.

"Listen to this," I said on one such evening, after the servants had cleared the plates from dinner and all that was left was the smell of roasted goose and a glass of wine on his bedside table. "Johano Delakruco, who writes four hundred years before Alekso of the last stand of Sintielo against its neighbor Crestona, says— Do you speak Malisintian?"

"Hm?" he said. He was staring at his tablet, where some dense chart filled with equations lay beneath a scattering of rotating planets. "Oh—a little. On Sintia the lessons were in the modern tongue. I was always told there was only a little poetry where the modern renditions aren't adequate, after all." He took hold of a holographic planet, lifted it from its orbit, and pinched it absently into darkness; the equations shivered and reconfigured themselves. "And the prayers, of course."

"I will translate," I said. "He writes of the death of his father, who might have fled the burning city but who turned back to save their household gods, and he says:

Silent the idol, and silent the gravestone, but swiftly he flew
through fire, through fortress; and never found I
his mantle or knucklebone. Nine days, now.
Silent or dead? Doubt creeps; did some traitor,
treading twist-paths—that's an idiom—*tasting liars' honey*—
  that's just bad poetry—*trap him;*
or will Fate speak fortune? He will find me; he is fallen.
Silent birds, silent companions. Six years gone. So.
I listen for him; I learn absent footsteps, new language.
I hesitate. Where now are the high towers? Where is the fire
  from the heavens?

. . . And from there the manuscript is burnt."

"Hm," he said again, without looking up, and I set my tablet down and hooked my chin over his shoulder.

"Tell me what's worrying you," I said.

"Oh," he said, "not worrying, only—frustrating. It is an imperial problem. I'm afraid you may find it tedious, after poetry."

"Tell me anyway," I said.

He flicked at the chart on his tablet, where the planets whirled round and round like a child's toy. "It's only policy matters," he said. "My empire grows, and the calendar's difficulty grows in tandem. Let me—ah, here: Madinabia K pays annual tax once every two and a half years. Not such a dilemma on its own, but the governor there becomes impoverished while the people grow rich, and she loses both resources and authority. Or here: On Belkayet they celebrate the New Year twice annually already, and within the decade will likely celebrate it thrice. Tllacatl has an orbit nearly the same length as Ceiao's, but rotates so slowly that Ceians hoping to do business on market day must wait nearly a month. Meanwhile, the Cherekku have their own system of calculating market days, adopted from Kutayet and based on the orbit length of the Kutayeti moon, though of course they claim Kutayet adopted it from them. They refuse to abandon it on religious principle, and no matter which planet they happen to be living on—you understand the gist." He sighed. "Commander of the greatest empire in the galaxy," he said, "and leader of the greatest city, and defeated by something as simple as time. It is an impossible calculation."

I set the tablet with the poetry on my bedside table. "Difficult," I said, "but not at all impossible. Haven't you ever been in a Szayeti ship?"

He looked up, abruptly interested. "What do Szayeti ships have to do with the calendar?" he said.

"I'm surprised you don't know that Alekso Undying was addressing this very problem at the time of his death," I said. "Caviro continued his work as well as he could with the Pearl's aid. Our map rooms have standardized time across most of the Swordbelt Arm, even up to the Great Maw—granted, a territory much smaller and less complex than the Ceian Empire, but the principles of Sintian mathematics apply and may be expanded. I studied them myself as a child. Quicksilver pearl has a capacity for thought that even the Library has not yet found the limits of."

Ceirran's mouth curled. "When you said Alekso Undying," he

said, "I was afraid at first that you would tell me he was making a tool that would pull all planets into the same orbit and rotation."

I laughed. "If that was what I had said, what would you have answered?"

"I would have said, *don't tempt me*," he said, smiling; and then the smile vanished, and he worked his lip between his teeth. "I wonder sometimes," he said eventually, "why your people use quicksilver pearl to decorate."

"It seems a great waste of resources," I said. "Is that right?" He tilted his head, apology or agreement, and I leaned back against the headboard and looked through our porthole. The ocean was an uneven field of grass today, olive green but for the tessellating white of the waves. Nothing was visible beneath.

"I said that quicksilver pearl has a capacity for thought that the Library has not found the limits of," I said. "If I'm honest—I don't think the limits of quicksilver pearl is what the Library is searching for. Or rather I think that, before they find that limit, they will find the limit of the human imagination. What did Alekso manage to do, in the short time he was able to touch the stuff and take it apart?"

"He broke a moon in three," said Ceirran at once. "He destroyed a whole world."

"And what did the Ostrayeti conquerors do before him?" I said. "Travel a twenty-millionth of a light-year and snatch power from those who could not fight back? And what have Alekso's heirs done, now that he has no hands to build with any longer—calculated the days of the week?"

"Is that nothing?" said Ceirran.

"I don't mean that it's nothing," I said. "I mean that you mistake the pearl's purpose. You speak as if it gave our god extraordinary powers—it did not. It allowed him to demonstrate that he was an extraordinary man. Why do we waste it on decoration? As well ask why Ceiao wastes human beings on factory labor or cannon fodder, when they might be sailing to new galaxies, or discovering cures for death—or writing poetry."

"That's a queen's answer," said Ceirran, smiling. "The Sintians *have* asked that question, some of them. They might tell you that any man could conquer the Swordbelt Arm, given the opportunity, and it is only the deliberate suppression of his opportunities that denies him such a conquest."

"Perhaps any could," I said. "But only one has. If there has been anyone since with his grandeur or clarity of vision, I am still waiting for him."

He looked at me for a while, then, and after a minute reached out for me, and his hand hesitated just before my face.

"May I see it?" he said, almost gently.

I began to tilt my head down and then understood what he meant, and stopped.

"What do you want with it?" I said.

He pressed his lips together. "I see the way the people look at it, on the islands," he said carefully. "I just want to—touch it. To see what it feels like. You don't have to."

Perhaps it was that last that changed my mind. In any case, I raised my hand to my ear. For a very brief moment, I thought I saw a face close to mine, its mouth open and eyes wild—and then it was gone.

"You're bleeding," said Ceirran, and reached up for me.

"It doesn't hurt," I said, but I let him wipe at my temple with his thumb. My right ear felt cool, as if there was a wind in it. I could feel the faint impression of dust on my cheek.

"Here," I said, and put the Pearl in Ceirran's open hand.

He rolled it gently along the furrow of his palm. Against his calluses it looked like ice. I almost feared it would dissolve.

"It's so small," he said.

"He wanted it to be small," I said. "He wanted it to be smaller. If he had had his way, it would have been small enough to pass into your lungs, it would have been seeded in the soil at every spring. There would have been a Pearl of the Dead in every fruit at harvest, in every summer rainstorm. If he had had his way, they would have passed into the body of every subject he conquered. An empire of Oracles, in every arm of the galaxy."

"I don't understand," said Ceirran. "Why should immortality need duplication? He had given himself a body that would never die. Why would he want thousands of them?"

I smiled a little. "Now that is a Ceian's question," I said.

"Is it?" he said. "What does a Ceian sound like?"

"Oh," I said, "trying to list out the rules. Trying to see how you could have done it more cleverly, were you in his place. You think of divinity as a list of set qualities, added together: infinite knowledge, infinite destruction, life everlasting. You might read his diaries. He was never trying to build immortality in the first place." Ceirran raised an eyebrow, and I amended, "He was—but not for its own sake. Before he came here, before he ever thought of drowning the world, he was conqueror, king. A god later, an emperor first. You put too much importance on how he reached apotheosis. You forget that what he wanted, above all, was worshippers."

In his hand, the little seed slowed and rattled into the crease between his palm and thumb. Ceirran said casually, "You speak of him in the past tense."

"Do I?" I said. "My mistake," and closed my hand over his. Between our fingers, the voice of Alekso Undying was a hard kernel, cool despite the warmth of our skin.

I bent to kiss Ceirran, and he made a pleased low noise and reached up for me, fingers strong around the back of my neck. When I lifted the Pearl from his hand, there was only a moment of resistance before he let it go.

I woke the next morning to a colorless, close-pressed mist at the windows, and the distant rumble of the ship's engines. Ceirran was gone to the deck, but the impression of his body beside me was still warm. I stretched out into the heat.

"Lord," I said.

Alekso was never shy, but he never seemed to like to come too close to me. Today he was sitting at the foot of the bed, cross-legged, chin propped in his hand. In the dim lamplight his face was round and soft, and his hair was falling into his eyes.

"We thought we would have more time," he said.

I sat up in bed. "We?" I said. "You mean you and Caviro?"

"He built Alectelo," he said. "He gave it my name. I thought I would find a way to use pearl as small as a molecule. I thought I would find a way for them to replicate themselves. I thought we would have more time."

He smiled then, a dreamy, distant smile. "It would have been a different galaxy," he said. "You shouldn't call it an empire of Oracles. There would have been so many that they wouldn't have been Oracles at all—there would have been no need to transmit my law to my people through this clumsy medium of kings, of human beings. There would have just been me; my voice, my name, in every atom, in every breath. Infants would have had me in their heads from the moment they cried. I would have been in the bones of the dead when they were laid in the ground. You wouldn't have needed to touch that thing in your ear in order to speak to me—there would have been no moment I was not present, there would have been no silence, there would have been nowhere else to go. Then—then I might have been a god... then I might truly have been able to rest in that tomb you put on the Island of the Dead. My body, my city. The endless Pearl of my soul."

"But instead you had prophets," I said.

"I had Caviro," said Alekso. "He built Alectelo, and he carried me. It was enough. It had to be enough."

He looked away. "But when he died," he said briskly, "yes. I had you."

"And your empire split into pieces among your generals, and that was all," I said. "You accepted defeat."

"I never accept defeat," he said. "Do you think I conquered half the galaxy without knowing how to bide my time? I learned a lesson, Caviro's daughter—you might try that, one of these days. I learned to watch. I learned to guide. I learned to give counsel. I learned to be careful with who I picked as my prophets—to seek out cunning, yes, courage, of course, but piety, above all piety. It is a very rare Oracle in whom I find all three."

"But you did find such an Oracle," I said.

He grinned up at me, a fox's grin. "I did."

I crossed my legs and leaned forward. "Lord," I said, "I am your Oracle. You say that you have learned to guide. You built a Pearl of the Dead once. If I acted as your eyes, as your hands, could you build one again?"

"No," he said at once.

I blinked, taken aback. "Am I unable?"

"No," he said. "You're more than able. You may be the first of Caviro's children with both the education and the talent—and the will." His mouth curled down. "What you are unable to do is build a Pearl for a soul that has already left its body. No one can do that. A soul can only be transferred into the computer from a body of flesh and bone. But you've already guessed that, haven't you?"

I said nothing. He said, "You can't imagine I would help you make a barbarian into a god."

"You wanted an empire without an ending," I said. "You might have built it—if you had had more time. Now such an empire has come to my doorstep. It slaughters my enemies, it shoots my citizens, it swallows my neighbors. For decades it has waited in the sky for Szayet to set a foot out of place—in our debt, in our army, in our succession—and now it sleeps in my bed at night."

"And you kiss it good morning," said Alekso.

"And I could be its Oracle," I said, "if you would help me."

He said tonelessly, "You would give me up so easily?"

To this I said nothing for a while, and then, "You know what lies between us, Lord." I swallowed. "You know what passed between us, long ago. You know where my loyalties lie, and I—I know the same of you."

He stood then and came toward me—it was disconcerting with the rocking of the ship to see how his feet did not quite touch the wood of the floor. "So what, Caviro's daughter," he said, "would you offer me in return?"

CHAPTER

TWENTY-FOUR

CEIRRAN

We came the next day to a green little isle lying in a long swathe of beach along a fallen old coastline. It was entirely uninhabited. Even the seagulls only swooped low over the white sand, and didn't roost. There was nothing very remarkable about it, except that it was the farthest the captain could sail with any certainty of seeing land afterward. Between us and the next western port lay thousands of miles of open ocean.

The barge docked on the beach and Gracia and I disembarked, followed by a flurry of servants with food and blankets. Gracia allowed them to fuss over us briefly before she dismissed them to the ship, and they went, grumbling.

I sat on a rock and watched her kneel on the sand. After a little while, she said, "You can never know, of course."

I stayed silent. It was often best. A few moments later, she continued distantly: "Nearly every island was once a continent, and nearly every continent inhabited. But the planet was already seventy percent water. Not everything is a drowned city. Some places were always islands. Empty, except for the trees."

She stood. "You can never know," she said, "of course," sounding more businesslike this time, and tucked her arm into mine, and guided me to the blanket where a feast of cakes and fruit and wine waited for us.

The servants stayed on the ship that afternoon. Gracia was uncharacteristically quiet, and had been since the day before; she seemed sometimes to be hardly aware she was with me at all. Nevertheless I fed her grapes, and laughed when she came to life enough to nip at my fingers. We went up into the greenery, and I watched her as she pushed through the tall grasses, her skirt hiked up around her legs, hair stuck to the back of her neck with sweat. At the highest point of the island grew a cluster of soft poppies with orange-silk petals. I plucked one, and she tucked it deep into her braid, and I watched it sway across her back all the way down.

Evening crept in, a soft grey like a cat's coat, and a coolness with it. We pulled the additional blankets over ourselves and sat on the slope above the beach, Gracia tucked into my side, and watched how the sun sank into the colorless page of the water, how the sky bloomed first deep blue around it and then indigo and then at last a flat, quiet black. The moons were scattered above it, tonight only thin slivers. In the water they multiplied into twelve, forty-eight, wavering in the dark.

At last Gracia said, a soft murmur below my ear: "What do you remember about your parents?"

"My parents?" I said.

"You weren't born by crèche," she said. "I know that well enough. How many did you have?"

"I—two," I said. "Two, a man and a woman. The man—my father, he died not long after I was born."

Gracia shifted a little against my side. She always ran very warm; tonight it was like a spark against my rib cage. "I'm sorry," she said softly.

"Don't feel sorry," I said. "I hardly remember him. I remember he was tall, I remember he dressed well. I remember his face was always scratchy, when he kissed my cheek—he wore a beard, I think. He wasn't killed in a war. Or he was killed *in* a war—some minor rebellion near Sintia—but he caught some disease from an insect, and died of fever instead of in battle."

"I thought they had cured all those sort of things by now," said Gracia.

"They have," I said. "They had. The war was going badly, and the medical staff were overstretched, and didn't catch it in time. Now there are half again as many doctors as there used to be, and the nurses are far better paid and better equipped. I have made sure of that. But it was a different time. The fleet was full of different men."

Gracia was silent for a while. Then she said, "And your mother?"

"Oh, she was brilliant," I said. "Sloppy, when it mattered, but brilliant. She lives in a house by the seaside now, and I have not seen her since she moved there. She was disgraced when I was a child, and I'm afraid if she ever returned to Ceiao she would find that the people there have long memories for scandal. But she was quicker with numbers than anyone else in the city. That was her trouble, as a matter of fact. And I remember—" I hadn't remembered, really, not until I spoke the words, but now I said to the night and the rush of waves, "I remember she used to make my father laugh."

"She sounds wonderful," Gracia murmured. Her voice was sleepy.

I looked out toward where the bulk of *Cesta de Higos* sat against the stars. Within it, the servants had lit their lamps, and I could see them moving on deck and through the portholes, leisurely mopping decks, stopping to talk, spreading tablecloths over the tables for their own supper.

"What about—your father?" I said. I called her *Patramata* so often that it was odd to make meaning of it: *Patra* for *father*, *Amata* for *love*. "What do you remember about him?"

I could feel Gracia's breath flutter out of her. It was funny how, in the dark, all other senses came to awareness like ghosts: the rustle of grass, the bite of the wind at your ears, the taste of wine at the back of your tongue.

"I remember when he was dying," she said.

I said nothing, but I rubbed my hand up and down her arm, until she went on:

"He never woke up, of course. But they thought for a little while that he might. And I remember they asked me to visit him in the royal suite...it was the first time I had been there. I had never come into his bedroom before. And all of his wardrobes were standing open, the door to his bathroom, anything the doctor might want to look at, and I could see all his clothes, his jewelry, his hair oil, his soaps, and—the doctor said I should sit by his side, and hold his hand, because he might feel it. But I was so ashamed to do it. I was ashamed to be in his bedroom. I was so ashamed to see him lying in his own bed.

"I did sit at his bedside, and I took hold of his hand. It was warm. And I could feel his pulse in it. But when I looked at his face—where his cheeks were starting to sink, and his stubble was coming in..." Her voice trailed off. Then she said: "He wasn't there. It wasn't his hand at all. All of the—wardrobes, the shoes, the robes—they were the only parts of him left."

On the shoreline, crickets were calling. The sea whispered and hushed on the sand.

"I'm sorry," I said.

"Don't feel sorry," she said. "I'm not sorry. There is nothing there to be sorry for."

I even thought she meant it. Still, I said: "Thank you for telling me."

"There is no one else I would tell," she said, and lay down.

The sky was wide and wild above us. We were so far from any city that each star was its own lantern light, and the satellites ran blinking red and blue over the dark curve of the horizon, as rapid as hounds. The whole pale streak of the galaxy was visible, poured from ocean to ocean, like the long loose river of a woman's hair.

I lay down beside Gracia, and let her shift until her head was resting on my chest. After a while, her breathing began to slow.

I woke with the dawn. Old soldiers' habits never properly break, however much you'd like them to. Gracia's eyes were already open. I could see, reflected in them, the scattered sliver-moons.

"Matheus," she said.

I sat upright at once. "What is it?" I said.

When she turned to look at me, I was nearly shocked. In the low light of the morning, every mark of wear on her face seemed magnified: the space under her eyes dark as fruit, crow's-feet flecking out beside her eyelashes, the unhappy edges of her mouth. And then I blinked, and they were gone again.

"Ceirran," she said. "When you asked to see the Pearl—when you held it. How long had you wanted to do that?"

I said nothing. She blinked, a slow sweep of eyelashes. Then she reached up and tugged, and I watched as once again, the wires that ran into her skull vanished into golden dust.

"Take it," she said, and set it in my palm. My fingers closed over it instantly, by instinct. It was quite cold.

"Do you know why our faith forbids us from allowing outsiders to raise the treasure from our oceans?" she said.

"Good sense," I said. My voice was still rough with sleep. "Otherwise every opportunist would plunder your waters bare, I imagine."

“Is that all?” she said. “Good sense?”

“No,” I said. “Because”—I closed my eyes, trying to recall—“Your god put the old world in the water, and your god’s people must take it out. Have I said it aright?”

She sat up and turned away from me, so that the light fell on her eyes. When I followed her gaze, I saw only the white motion of the morning sea, stretching forward and forward until it curved into horizon.

“I wonder, sometimes,” she said, “if the Ceians don’t see death as an ending. When a man dies, for you, he vanishes: into fire, into the ground, into forgetfulness. But for us, memory lingers. Even when consciousness vanishes—even when bodies become bones—we learn to live with the dead. We have no choice. They never leave us. That is why we allow no outsider to bring up the treasure: because it would be wrong to let anyone touch it who does not understand what *never* and *forever* mean.”

“But not all of your dead are in the water,” I said. “I know that on that little island near Alectelo, the one that the coronation—”

“Ceirran,” she said, and took my hand, and pressed her thumb over the Pearl, so that it dug hard into my skin. “What would you do to be given eternity?”

PART III

Imagine the city of Ceiao, as seen from above: an open eye.

Begin with the upper eyelid. This is the river: Nevede, called Old Icemelt or Mountainrun or, sometimes, the Cunning Lady, for the swift and devious current under the surface that snatches poles and oars and fishing boats and on occasion human beings—a long, deceptively gentle curve, sixty miles in length, in the winter a grey marble streaked with black, in the summer jewel-bright where it isn't choked with punts and ferries and long white houseboats rocking like sleeping cats. At the corners of the curve, where the city ends, are the Major and Minor Gates, and at the very apex the Gate of Shattered Chains, which one hundred and fifty years and no small amount of mandatory education have not broken the populace of calling God's Crown.

Then the lower eyelid, a smaller, shallower curve: the Rouan Valquíria Barran, marking both the city's southern border and the great artery of its land travel. Every mountain and canyon of the planet is Ceiao, of course, and has been since conquest long forgotten, but only the city itself is *truly* Ceiao, Ceiao in the brain and the heart of her, and from those mountains and canyons the travelers come to sell or to buy or to give tribute or to plead legalities or to leave the planet altogether—or, though neither they nor the city would ever dare to think it, to make pilgrimage: to see the center of their world, and how it becomes the center of *the* world more with each passing day. The road spills from the great tunnel under Mauntan Bau in the northwest, crosses south over the Nevede just below the Major Gate, reaches its nadir, and turns north to cross the river again below the Minor, and when that journey is done, flicks out into a hundred roads in the northeast like a whip. It is from these roads that travelers come to Ceiao, and along these which travelers go when Ceiao spits them out—if it has not swallowed them.

Along the road and the river, splayed out at every cross angle, are the harbors. They are named in the Sintian alphabet along the Nevede, where human travelers climb from their ships and dissolve into the great crowd, and in the plain Ceian alphabet along Rouan Valquíria where the traders deliver cargo to the city's doorstep. As the harbors mark the edge of Ceiao for the starships, they too mark the edge of Ceiao on the planet itself. The city can spill out from these fringes, of course, and does, and the factories and suburbs outlying the eye are thick and prosperous, and grow by the day. But Ceiao proper, Ceiao as the politicians dream it and the singers voice it, lies between the river and the road, and outside those twin curves, there is no world but barbarism.

But what is civilization if not a further drawing of borders? Ceiao, between the river and the road, is built atop a sloping and irregular hill, though in the shadow of Mauntan Bau the Ceians often forget this fact. Some miles within the border of the city the hill grows abruptly steeper, where millions of years ago some impulsive plate or piece of magma shoved up too eagerly against its neighbor. In the days of the priests, before the theomachy, this Step marked the border of the city. Now it only describes a wide, irregular circle within Ceiao, within which lie shops and schoolhouses, theaters and factories, markets and hospitals and museums and histories, the hundred thousand small things that keep a city alive and a planet living. Within it, too, sleep the millions of citizens, rich and poor, that by dint of their ancestry can call themselves Ceians. Without it, the Outer City: Tllacah mercenaries, Diajundot singers and jugglers and sword-swallowers, Sintian scholars and businessmen, Madinabic prisoners and refugees, Itsaryeti and Belkayeti and Medveyeti competing for the few factory jobs remaining that might offer the chance at an employment visa, the tight-knit and secretive Cherekku quarter by the Major Gate from which the occasional trader ventures with carefully silver-painted lips. Even the Szayeti take lodgings there, when their pride will let them come to Ceiao at all. The whole of the galaxy lives on the outskirts of that steep circle, and the whole of the galaxy jostles there for pride of place, hoping to be allowed to set foot on that Step.

And at last, in the very center of the eye: a part of the city where once there stood a concrete Wall. Men were shot, at one time in Ceiao's history, for attempting to cross this Wall. Women were tortured. A child attempted to climb it, long ago, and was thrown from the guard towers, and her mother watched while her body hit the concrete below. On a cold winter's day, one hundred and fifty years ago, the people of the city tore it down with their own hands. Now all that is left is a long, gleaming brass line running along the path where the Wall once stood, down streets and through alleys and up into itself in a circle within the great circle, separating house from house, market from market. The line is there—so says the council—so that Ceiao should remember.

Perhaps Ceiao would remember regardless. What once stood within the wall were, of course, temples—but alongside the temples, and in greater number, were palaces, where the priests who the people so feared once lived. When the Wall came down, the temples were burned. No one ever burned the palaces. No one has ever wanted to. There is something about those great mansions, their sweeping wings and tall white pillars and sloping blue roofs. They are by a wide margin the oldest buildings in a very new city. It is difficult to look at them and not think of the many who have lived there: not only priests, now dead and gone for many years, but merchants, and generals, and all those in Ceiao with the wealth or birth or fame to be considered *people of quality*. It is difficult to look at those palaces and not dream of sleeping within one of them.

It has been ten years since I first saw you in your city, and I still do not know whether you have ever managed it.

But one palace alone stands uninhabited. No one since the last high priest has ever slept in the Libeiracópolan.

The line which was once the Wall is visible from above the city. Call that brass circle a sort of pupil. If it is, then the Libeiracópolan is the gleam inside. It crouches in the center of what was once the Inner City, a marble welt swollen up from the earth. Its dome is the highest point in Ceiao, and its dungeons, which no one has been made to enter for one hundred and fifty years, spread like roots below. Once, the street where it sat was called in Malisintian the Road of Holies. Now, it is the Avenuan Libeirguitan in the Ceian tongue, and those who live in the mansions along it are the wealthiest Ceians in the city, and when they open their eyes each morning, the first thing they see is the Libeiracópolan's shadow as it falls across their bedspreads, and the knowledge of what it is they were once liberated from.

They like to distract themselves, those people of quality. They have become very good at managing it. Ceians are not a people of long memory.

Nevertheless, it lingers in the mind: the thought of that watchful eye.

CHAPTER

TWENTY-FIVE

GRACIA

You aren't thinking this through," said Alekso.

I hadn't even meant to wake him. I was reading at the captain's desk, a report of news from Cherekku on a crop of fanatics that had arisen recently, and my hand had slipped. Through his face I could see the star field of the Swordbelt Arm, drifting in great glittering clouds away from the ship.

It had been one month since we had left the little westward island, and one month since the last morning Ceirran and I had woken together. The ship waiting on the shoreline had brought us to a nearby harbor, and the journey that had taken us nearly two months by sea had lasted by air only two hours.

"I could stay," Ceirran had said, when we were again within the palace, tucked into a spare conference room on which the servants had laid bread and salt. Neither his men nor my own had been expecting us back so soon, and the hallway was a flurry of noise and activity: servants packing his possessions, soldiers packing their own, maids readying my rooms, my ministers knocking on the door with some piece of business or gossip for me. "I almost think I ought to."

"You forget that you've been reading your letters in bed with me," I said. "Captain Ana says that without you there to strike fear into their hearts, your political enemies will have half the city raided tomorrow."

He wrinkled his nose. "Anita is a liar," he said, "though perhaps not, I admit, about this."

"Perhaps you can also admit that by now she has undoubtedly spent twice the budget you gave her," I said, "and, if I have grown to know her at all, insulted the men you would most like her to respect. Best to discover what fires must be put out sooner rather than later."

"If I didn't know better, Patramata, I would think you wanted to get rid of me," said Ceirran. He was smiling, but only a little.

"You do know better," I said, "and so you know that if this works, I will never be rid of you again."

"I do know better," he said. "And I wonder whether you are afraid of my seeing the very process in which you intend me to put my trust."

I gave him a long look. He was leaning back against the table, arms crossed. The little smile had not faded, but his eyes were not amused.

"You know as well as I do that my god will never share the method for making a Pearl of the Dead while a foreigner watches," I said. "It is a wonder he has agreed to teach me at all."

"A wonder indeed," he said.

I shot him a sharp look, but he only shrugged and said nothing more. I crossed to the table, leaned against it beside him, and said, "Perhaps you should be worried, then. Perhaps I *will* work some strange and secret Szayeti sorcery—is that the sort of thing you think they'll say in Ceiao, when you name me your Oracle before the city? Perhaps I'll build a computer that seduces you to my faith. Perhaps it will make you forget all reason. Perhaps it will make you bark like a dog. Perhaps—"

"All right!" he said, laughing. "I understand. But if you were in my place, Patramata—wouldn't you, too, feel obligated to ask whether or not I could trust you?"

The warmth of him beside me felt abruptly overwhelming, the weight of gravity. I pressed into his arm, tipped my head onto his shoulder so that he could not meet my eyes, and said, "Haven't I trusted you?"

I felt him exhale. His arm shifted against my side, and he took one of the salt cellars and turned it round in his hands. "You understand, don't you," he said, "that it will not be as simple for me to present the Pearl as it was for your Alekso of Sintia. These are educated Ceians, brought up to question and doubt."

"And not the superstitious mystics of Szayet, who follow blindly wherever they are led," I said dryly.

"That's not what I mean," he said, and turned the cellar round in his hands again. "You understand as well as anyone, Patramata. Eternity will do me no good if I live it out in prison for attempting to overthrow the disestablishment. I have been declared a criminal by the council before, and even now that Quinha is only a memory, I have no desire to revisit the experience." I felt him huff a faint laugh. "If nothing else," he said, "I would prefer not to lose more friends."

"Then you should go to Ceiao as soon as possible," I said gently, "to prepare the way. You are already commander. Act the part now—go, to lay down your law and lead the city—and it will be easier for your people to accept it when you lay down the law that calls you commander in perpetuity."

"Commander Undying," he said, and smiled a little.

"And me, your Oracle," I said. "You must prepare the way for me, too."

"Yes," he said. "And you." I felt him shift. "But tell me one thing, Patramata," he said, setting the salt cellar back on the table, "if you won't let me stay." I looked inquiringly at him, and he said, mouth quirking upward: "Tell me you'll miss me."

I said, very easily, "I'll miss you."

I did not go to the harbor to watch his ship take off over the ocean. I did not even intend to watch the plume of smoke rise on the horizon. It felt too like that long evening in my own civil war, when the palace taps had run with salt water, and I had let him leave me alone, a princess without a crown or an army, not knowing if he would come back. But I could not help it: The thin white line of smoke split the sky in two, and it was a long while before it faded into the thick and distant blue of the afternoon.

"Holiest," said Zorione behind me.

I turned. She was alone in the doorway, her face drawn and worried, and a wooden box in her hands. I crossed to her, and opened it. It was full of quicksilver pearl, rough and pitted, gleaming like the sea.

"Thank you," I said. "You told no one what it was for?"

"No one," she said uncertainly. "Holiest—do you really mean to go through with it? The god—He agrees?"

"He agrees," I said firmly. "He will even show me how it is done." I lifted the box from her hands and set it on the desk. "Are the machines prepared?"

For each day of the next month, I worked harder and I slept less than I had even when I was at war. The pearl had to be ground down into dust—by specially prepared grinding discs that were also of quicksilver pearl, as nothing else was hard enough to break them—and then heated to the highest temperatures our forges could produce, and heated again, so that the impurities of sand and salt and the smallest specks of metal could bubble to the top, like foam on the sea. In the name of the humanity of the soul, work on the Pearl had to be done by hand, without the aid of any computer besides Alekso Undying. For this reason I had to remove the impurities from the pearl myself, clad in a thick heat-radiation suit designed for work on satellites that circled near stars, while I wielded tongs so thin and delicate I feared they would snap in the suit's clumsy fingers. Only then could I begin to form the material into the shapes Alekso instructed, and then the work I did was still more difficult—first bombarding the pearl with neutron radiation, then brushing it carefully with the sweet-smelling blue acids that could dissolve my skin in a moment if I were to knock over a bottle, and then finally, with the aid of an inch-long crab-litter controlled by tablet, exposing the pearl to one of the bubbling particles of antimatter that powered our ships. The crab-litter scampered through four doors constructed of foot-thick lead and gold, paused for three-quarters of a second in the same room as the antimatter, scampered back to me, and dissolved four seconds after the last lead-golden door closed behind it. Then, and only then, could I begin etching it as Alekso instructed me, one hand to my ear and the other scratching with a pearl stylus smaller than my pinkie nail, carefully inscribing each tissue-thin layer by hand before layering it on top of the next.

I was not even allowed to complain. "If you think this is difficult," said the god, peering down at an intricate whorl of patterning on one layer of pearl, "try doing it on a foreign planet, after having conquered half the galaxy. Try doing it while all your generals gabber in your ear about rebellions and marriages and sergeants who won't march. Try doing it for the first time it has been done, ever, in the whole history of the universe—*then* say you're tired, Caviro's daughter." He pointed. "This is wrong. Three-hundredths of a millimeter to the left."

"*Lord*," I said, scrubbing at my eyes with my free hand.

"This is why I told you to tell your maid to bring pearl to

spare," he said, merciless. "Do it over again. And be careful this time."

I bit my tongue, trying very hard not to blaspheme. When I had recovered my temper, I set the layer aside in the discard pile, lifted another and set it on the sheet of glass that made up my worktable, and bent over it once more.

"I suppose," I said, a few minutes later, pressing two fingers to the Pearl in my ear, "that it was also more difficult to do it alone."

I had been trying to be conciliatory. I hardly had time to read Ceirran's letters, and those long days, Alekso was close to my only company. But his voice, entirely disembodied, said: "I was not alone." And he refused to speak to me of anything but quantum geometry for the rest of the day.

"I can assure you," I said now on the bridge of the ship, watching the stars whirl away behind his face, "I have thought this through. I have thought about very little else."

"Don't be obtuse," said Alekso. "You are playing dice with the universe. And for what—*sentiment*?"

"Don't be absurd, Lord," I said. "You helped me. When Calixta Caviro Diketa came to Ceiao to bargain an alliance, is this what you said to her?"

"If I had known all of the ways you people would muck it up afterward, I would have," he said. "Likely I would have told her to bomb the whole place from orbit. You know why I helped you, and don't act as if it were generosity. But I'm beginning to doubt that you'll end up in a position to hold up your end of the bargain we've made."

"Perhaps you should already know whether I will or no," I said. "I understood you to be omniscient."

"Why should *I* have to see the future," he said peevishly, "when I have Oracles to do it for me? Don't change the subject. You do realize the whole endeavor isn't a one-way street? *Do* you realize that? I might as well ask, because in my case you act entirely ignorant of the concept."

"Believe me, I realize," I said.

"You are a very difficult person to believe," said the Undying. "I would be surprised if he feels any differently."

I looked down at the report from Cherekku for a few moments, trying to get my breathing under control. At last I said, "I suppose we're fortunate that you live not in his head, but in mine."

"*Fortunate*," he said. "You even sound like one of them."

"I doubt they would agree," I said.

He leaned against the glass of the window and crossed his arms. "I shouldn't be surprised," he said. "It's not as if this is the first time you've—"

But at that I let go of the Pearl as if I had been burned, and the god of Szayet vanished into the darkness.

I stepped out of the ship to the sight of a full complement of eighteen blue-cloaked soldiers, three rows deep. At their head was a lieutenant carrying two bowls, who went red at the sight of me and proffered them awkwardly.

"On your arrival on our—from the sky, we offer the—the earth, and water," he said in deeply nasal Sintian, and went redder immediately and saluted.

"How gallant you are!" I said to him in Ceian, and took a pinch of salt and a mouthful of dark bread. "What a courteous people Ceiao have become in my absence, and how well-mannered. Please give my regards to your commanding officer."

"He will take them gladly," said a voice behind me.

I had meant to look composed, but when I turned, I could feel myself smiling. "Did you expect I would think you couldn't hear me?" I said.

"I would never expect anything of you," said Ceirran, and kissed me on each cheek, swift and hard. "Patramata. What a pleasure to see you again."

"What a pleasure to see *you*," I said, taking in with a sweep of my hand the rows of soldiers and the bustle of the harbor. "Should I take it as a personal honor?"

He made a face, which I did not know how to interpret. "You may take it as your due," he said, "if you like. Shall we proceed to customs?"

I smiled and looped my arm through his, and he led me briskly across the concrete toward the little bay near the edge of the harbor. As we walked, I leaned up to murmur in his ear: "I don't know that I like you in your own territory, Commander."

"Why in the world not?" he said. "Have I done anything but pay you compliments?"

"That's what worries me," I said, and kissed him on his temple.

When I withdrew, he was smiling a thin, satisfied smile. "You may take them freely if you like, my dear," he said. "You aren't who I mean to worry today."

The soldiers marched in lockstep behind us as we crossed the customs bay. The floor was packed with people—well-dressed Ceians with bags over their shoulders flicking through their tablets, other Ceians with trays full of ragged scarves or greening copper knickknacks or meat skewers or steaming hand-pies shoving through crowds babbling practiced patter, silent Cherekku huddled in groups darting suspicious looks at passersby, a crowd of long-braided Diajundot pushing stacked tanks of brightly colored fish, a large number of people in ragged brown cloaks with children clinging to their legs, speaking rapidly to one another in what I realized in surprise must be Madinabic—but, as we passed, they parted like the sea, and every person from the little Madinabic children to the man selling the meat skewers turned to stare.

As a child, I had been so impressed by the simple facts of crowds and land that I had hardly noticed the harbor's other details. Now that I did, I found myself curiously disappointed.

The floor was a broad slab of grey concrete, interrupted by squat grey concrete pillars, broad grey concrete walls, and occasional white lines painted to mark where bags or passengers ought to line themselves up to board or to disembark from the ships. Below the pervasive smell of exhaust was a deeper smell of old dust. There was not a speck of dirt on the floor, but neither anywhere was there a carving, a mural, a mosaic, a cloth hanging, any speck of color except in the crowds passing by and in the wide, smoke-studded blue of the sky above.

Upon our docking I had been given directions to a private room in the customs bay, and memory flickered the closer we grew. When at last we entered, I was surprised by nothing in that little room except how unchanged it was. The dust smell was stronger here, and the official hardly looked up as my soldiers and I swept in. It might have been the very same woman I had seen there as a child.

"The ship from Szayet?" she said. "Ah—Oracle Altagracia Caviro Patramata." She raised her head to look behind me, and stilled. "And—what an—unexpected honor. Commander Ceirran, I wasn't informed—surely one of the junior magistrates—"

"There is nothing to inform," said Ceirran cheerfully. "This isn't a review, Inspector, I am here in a personal capacity. The Oracle is my guest."

The official ducked her head down and poked at her tablet, coughing. "Well—what an honor, as I say—regardless—Madam Oracle, have you or your party any food, plant material, animal products—"

I answered, paying considerably more attention than I had as a child. The list had changed since then, of course. Items were left off, items had been added on. The Ceians now wished to know if we had sílfion seed—controls were tightening, then, though Alekso knew why. The Ceians no longer cared if we had literature referencing maps—they must have been victorious in their dispute over the Janubi system.

"Last of all," said the woman. "The cult paraphernalia, please."

I had known it was coming. Still I exhaled hard. It did not matter, I told myself. I was not on Szayet, and I was still the Szayeti queen. It was not as if the Ceians respected Alekso's name in the first place. It was not as if I would not get it back. Still, when I reached for my ear, my hand quavered.

"Ah," said Ceirran, idly. "Must we?"

I stopped.

The official stopped, too. "Commander," she said. Her mouth worked. "Sir. Sir, with respect, the first law of the custom of Ceiao, sir, as written—"

"Such a small thing," said Ceirran, and smiled at her absently. "There are so *many* changes in the city lately. I'm sure Ceiao can overlook one little stone."

The customs official did not seem to be able to close her mouth. "Sir," she said again, and rallied bravely. "Sir, am I meant to rewrite policy, fifteen decades of policy, sir, for the sake of—"

"Rewrite nothing at all!" said Ceirran, sounding surprised. "Please, Inspector, I wouldn't dream of telling you your job. Is it *inspector*? What a surprise. I thought you would be magistrate by now."

"Sir," said the official. Her voice broke.

"I believe that's all," Ceirran said, and curved his hand around my waist. "Thank you for your service, Inspector. You *have* been serving here awhile. I'll need to send someone along to review your position," and with that he guided me away from the little room, toward the ship where my bags were waiting.

For a while, walking along that concrete strip, all I could do was breathe. When I had my Ceian back, I said softly into his ear: "What do I owe you now?"

"Owe me?" said Ceirran. "Why, nothing at all. Why in the world would two friends be in each other's debt?"

I caught his eye, or tried to. He would not look at me, but his lips curved a little. It reminded me of something, which I would realize only much later was the way the Szayeti carved statues of kings.

CHAPTER

TWENTY-SIX

CEIRRAN

It was a long time since I had been to the Outer City for any reason besides politics. They knew me there, of course, and as our spider-litter passed through the tall cinder-block towers, followed by the dozens of men with Gracia's possessions, I was stopped a half dozen times by various Medveyeti and Sintians who flattered me in low tones and then begged me for loans for their neighbors, visas for their friends, protection against raids, or a license to allow them to move closer to the center of the city or an allowance for some small tokens of worship. I agreed to the loans, promised what help I could, and dismissed them as soon as they would go, conscious of Gracia's gaze.

"Are they friends of yours?" she murmured.

"Yes and no," I said. "Leaders in their community, advocates for their people, some of them. Others are the heads of local gangs, who want to use my wealth or my status to gain power."

"And you give it to them?" said Gracia.

"Often," I said. "Whether righteously or unrighteously

minded, they are nearly all of them in my debt, and know it." There were faces, too, pressed to the windows of the towers, watching us go: women and men, tattooed and silver-lipped and braided and knit-capped, curious and solemn. "I would rather they consider me a friend than a scrupulous man," I said, and smiled through a window at one young girl, whose face lit up like a candle. "They have spent the better part of their lives grappling with Ceian scruple."

"Aren't some of them Madinabic?" said Gracia. "Do those consider you a friend, too?"

"You would be surprised," I said. "Or perhaps you wouldn't, considering the conqueror of whom you are Oracle. Most of the people who come to Ceiao from Madinabia were not rich before the war. Very few of them had any real power. Before the invasion, they spent their days trying to pull dead crops out of their fathers' dying land. After the war, things are much the same, except that now if they want to they can flee their fathers, and come to live cheek by jowl next to strangers with whom they share nothing but a language, in a strange country where they can be anyone they like. Do they love me? No. I doubt they ever will. But if you think all of Madinabia hates me, you would be much mistaken. And besides this—regardless of their feeling, for most, I am the only person with any power willing to help them."

Gracia thought this over. "And me?" she said. "Am I here seeking opportunity, or am I in your debt?"

We came to a stop before a tall sandstone house with a flight of brown steps leading up to the door. The top floors were set with stained glass windows, and there were brown stone pillars set around the base, framing a plain wooden door. It was neither a Sintian house nor a Szayeti one, but it was the finest house I had been able to buy in the Outer City, given the time available. "I would hope the opportunity is mine," I said. "Will you come to the party tonight?"

She gave me a searching look, which I returned blankly, and reached out for her maid to help her from the spider-litter. She stumbled a little—the spider-litters were not so different from the crab-litters of Alectelo, but their legs were thinner and more numerous, and one of them had caught her skirt—but recovered herself admirably. "I look forward to it," she said. "You'll give my men the address of this woman hosting?"

"I will," I said. "I'm afraid that you and she may like each other very much."

"Afraid!" she said, laughing. "You?"

"I'll see you soon," I said, kissed her when she stood on tiptoe for it, and bent out of the window to tell her men the address.

Flavia Decretan's house was visible from my own, and as darkness fell, its windows and open front door began to shine like a festival-day parade. The woman herself, when I found her by the drinks table, embraced me like a snake might have: as if she could devour me by doing it. "What a dreadful ordeal it was," she said, smacking a kiss on my cheek, "knowing you were back at last, and having to stay for weeks in that awful little seaside house, making conversation with Cláudia Pulcron's awful little gossiping friends! What a burden it is to have in-laws—and to keep having them even when you've been a widow for years! How on earth could *you* bear to stay away for so long? Was it very beautiful on Szayet? I shouldn't ask—I know the answer."

"It was beautiful," I said, "but what could be more beautiful than home?"

"Very politic," said Anita beside her, and grinned at me when I shot her a look.

"Isn't it?" said Flavia. "I'm *very* impressed. Look—" She stepped back and ducked her head. It was necessary to duck because in her new shoes she was taller than any of the rest of her guests, including me, which I was bearing with as much amusement as I was able. Her hair today had been sewn into dozens of elaborate braids, held together in a bun by three golden hairpins with emeralds at the tip. "I got your gift, once I'd *finally* come back to my own house. They're lovely—thank you. You'd never know they'd been underwater."

"Thank the Oracle, when she arrives," I said. "They were her idea in the first place."

Flavia's smooth hostess smile slid to the side and hooked upward, pleased. "Yes," she said, "I think I will. When will she be here?"

"I'm afraid I don't know," I said. "She is her own master."

"And yours, too, from what I hear," said Flavia, and laughed at the look on my face, though Anita didn't. "It's not me saying it!" she said. "You should really have kept a closer eye on your council friends, Matheus, it'll get you in trouble one of these days."

"It never *is* you saying it," I said, "and yet somehow it always seems to be said." She took that with good humor, and I added, "Which of these council friends are here tonight, might I ask?"

Flavia stood on her tiptoes and peered over the crowd. "I see Thiago Veguion," she said, "and Cipon, of course—what an awful snob that woman is!—and Emiliana Barboulethan, I know you like her but she strikes me as a bit of a crab, personally, she just *scuttles*."

"Wonderful," I said dryly. "Two people who have opposed my motion for cult contraband leniency without hearing it, and another who didn't understand what she heard."

Flavia laughed. "Jonata is here," she went on, "but I'm sure you knew that already. Cláudia never came back from the seaside with the rest of us, her lover's written another poem about her and she's staying in her summer house to sulk until spring. I didn't invite Cachoeiran—of course he's a genius and it's not his fault he's exhausting, but it's not my fault either, so there we are. And your husband, of course, but he isn't here yet, and oh, there's that other boy. He says he knows you."

"Other boy?" I said.

Flavia pointed. "That mouse of a man," she said. "*Does* he know you? I don't think I even invited him."

"Ah," I said. "Excuse me," and pushed forward into the crowd.

Joaquim Nequeiron was even thinner and younger-looking in person, and had an awful, fluttering kind of look about him. "Commander Ceirran," he said, and pressed my hand. "When I heard you were back in the city I came at once, sir. I was so glad to know that I might have helped you, in any small way, in your campaign on Szayet, and I was *so* glad to know, sir, that in future you might consider me, in *any* way, a friend to your cause—"

He wanted money, and it was going to take him half an hour to ask for it. "How flattering," I said. "What a pleasure to make friends." The trouble, of course, was that this was true.

"And can I just say how pleased I am to see you overcame your—misadventure—in the Swordbelt Arm," he said. "How—wonderful—to know that despite your struggles against the unfortunate Admiral Semfontan, sir, you were at last able to—to finish that terrible business—"

I could feel my knuckles go tight around my drink at once. "Indeed," I said.

Nequeiron quailed. He recovered a moment later, though, and coughed. "In any case," he said, "how wonderful, too, that you were able to develop—diplomacy—with the Szayeti queen. And on that note, sir, I was wondering—"

"Diplomacy?" said a voice behind me. Heart light at once with deliverance, I turned.

At the harbor by the river, climbing out of her ship with her eyes bruised with exhaustion and the Pearl winking at her temple and her bags scattered behind her, Gracia had looked to my eyes like the most beautiful woman in the world. Here, with her face painted and her hair gathered up behind her into a waterfall of curls, she looked like a goddess. She was dressed like a Ceian, in tall golden sandals and a narrow sleeveless white gown, which gathered at the waist and fell almost to her feet, and against which her skin appeared to glow. Her wrists were draped with gold, too, and she was wearing ruby rings and a little gilded leather bag, and someone had sewn a chain of rubies into her hair, which winked and glittered when she turned her head.

She stood still for a few seconds, smiling a little at my expression, before standing on her tiptoes to kiss my cheek. "Hello," she said. "I've met Flavia."

"Have you?" I said. "And did you like her?"

Without the kohl, her eyes looked smaller, softer. That smile was the same, though, even when she was trying to hide it. "Ought I to?" she said.

"Sir," said Nequeiron uncertainly.

I had entirely forgotten he was there. "Speak to my captain," I said to him, over my shoulder. "Tell her whatever it is you need," and I linked my arm with Gracia's. "Come with me, Patramata. There are so many people you must meet."

Most of the councillors smiled at her and murmured polite variations on the same few weak insults, of course, but that was only to be expected. Emiliana Barboulethan took ten minutes to say nothing at all, but that was to be expected, too. There were many others in the vein of Flavia, though, who had no official role in the city government but were married to people who did, or who were retired but still took an indecorous amount of unofficial interest, or who had no relations or position at all but had inherited a significant fortune. This second type took to her very well, and she received half a dozen invitations to teas and dinners in rapid succession.

"You don't need to go to all of those," I murmured to her, a little embarrassed. "Flavia can tell you who it might be dangerous to disappoint."

"But I would like to go to all of these," she said. "I want to know everything about your people."

To my surprise, she seemed to mean it. "That's very kind," I said. "They are not precisely my people—in fact, I can assure you that at least four of them are here specifically to impede passage of a motion I have been working on dedicatedly for all the month we have been apart."

"That isn't what I mean!" she said, laughing, but before I could ask her what she did mean, I spotted a familiar head of fawn-brown hair at the drinks table and turned at once.

"Jonata!" I said, and was gratified by their shock when they saw me, which collapsed at once into delight. "Patramata," I said, "this is my dear friend Jonata Barran."

It was always disconcerting for strangers to meet Jonata. They were quite young, with a square friendly face and a great cloud of soft hair that made it look smaller than it was, and a smile as wide and pleased as a child's. Tonight they were already a little bright-eyed with drink. They clasped Gracia's hand with great eagerness.

"What a pleasure to meet you!" they said. "You really came all the way from Szayet? I wanted to come visit, of course, but Matheus said no—I know why, but I *did* visit him in Madinabia, as a matter of fact, and I still don't see how one's very different from the other."

"And they were nearly killed in the shelling," I said, "for which Ceiao would never have forgiven me. Patramata, Jonata is the six-times-great-grandchild of Valquíria Barran, and her heir."

"And the city never lets me forget it," said Barran, but it made them blush further, which had been my intent. "Oh—I'm being awfully rude. Madam Oracle, Valquíria was the one who, ah—"

"—burned the high priest of Alekso on the Holy Road," said

Gracia, and smiled her smoothest smile. "There is no explanation needed, Councillor, I assure you. What a very fascinating woman your ancestor was."

"Oh," they said, "Jonata, please. You aren't offended?"

"Ought I to be?" Gracia said pleasantly.

"Well," said Jonata, and floundered. Gracia turned to me, one eyebrow raised and smiling—but I met her gaze without smiling back. I had told her on Szayet that I forgot on occasion she was not one of my fellow Ceians. She had taken it so ill, then, I had not mentioned it a second time. But still, sometimes, I let myself forget how little she knew of my past—how she alone among my circle had not been party to my struggles and triumphs, my grievances and my forgiveness, my hard-fought public griefs. I let myself forget that she did not know Sílvio's name.

Her eyes went wide at whatever she saw in my expression, and she turned back to Jonata at once. "Not in the least," she said to Jonata, her tone much warmer. "A Ceian priest is not at all the same as an Oracle of Szayet." She laughed a little. "Well—I understand they must seem much the same to you, here in the great city without gods. But there is no one on Szayet who would call them so, and so none have you offended. And you must call me Patramata, as our friend does."

"Patramata," they said, and clasped her hand again, with markedly less enthusiasm than before. It was the talk of religion that had done it. Jonata was, alas, a true patriot, in the way that most of us had only really managed as new recruits and spent the rest of our careers only striving toward on odd market days. That streak of headstrong idealism had always run in their family, and not always to the family's benefit. But Gracia was smiling at them, and I was satisfied.

"But you must have known the commander for such a long time," she said, "to have visited him in Madinabia, and you look so young, though you speak like someone with wisdom gained from many years—" I shot a look at Gracia, and if we were alone would have said *unsubtle*, but Jonata blushed and I stayed silent. "You cannot have fought with him, surely?" she added.

Their pleasant expression collapsed like cardboard. I suppressed a jolt of irritation—Gracia couldn't have known. "No," I said, not quite hastily, "Jonata has never managed to fight at my side, I am sorry to say. Perhaps in better times."

Jonata laughed. "Times would be much worse if you *did* bring me campaigning," they said, forcibly light. "From all I hear, you're doing more than well enough on your own."

"How charming you are," I said fondly, and squeezed their shoulder. "But you *will* need to campaign one of these days, Jonata. When your seven years are up—"

"Oh," said Jonata, "Cátia!" and slipped out of my grasp at once. "Commander—Oracle—I'm so sorry, again. My good friend is here—I haven't seen her in ages," and they squeezed my hand and were gone across the room toward a thin, light-skinned woman in an oversized black cloak.

I smiled after them. "They haven't seen her in ages," I said softly to Gracia, "because she has been in exile from Ceiao for years. She arrived here perhaps twelve hours before you."

"And at once you asked Flavia to invite her here," Gracia said. "How scandalous of you."

"Not very scandalous, I'm afraid," I said. "She was exiled for fighting beside Quinha Semfontan against me."

Gracia turned to look at me at once. "I suppose Jonata did as well," she said.

I should have known she would guess. "Not *fought*," I said. Across the room, Jonata was pumping Cátia's hand eagerly. Cátia looked equal parts amused and alarmed. "They really are young—and they know their ancestor's story so well, I'm afraid. They hate to spend any time out in the galaxy that they might spend between the river and the road. In love with the city, the

Barran family. They can't help it. It was only a month or so that they spent with Quinha on those rings near Sintia, and I think their heart was never really in it. It was only that she had told the city a very convincing story."

Gracia, watching the pair, did not appear convinced. "And their friend?" she said. "Is she a patriot, too?"

"Ah," I said, "Cátia Lançan. She comes from a manufacturing family, as a matter of fact, who own a number of factories just over the river. Ships, of course, but not just starships—seaships too, and underwater ships, construction equipment, things of that nature. I gather she employs a few of your subjects for their expertise, Patramata—or your former subjects, I suppose, now that they've moved here. I'm afraid she fought against me because she agreed with Quinha on a much less lofty point: that I owed the Merchants' Council rather a larger percentage of plunder from my Madinabic wars than I was inclined to send them."

"But you forgave her," said Gracia.

My eyes drifted away from Cátia, toward where a pair of dark heads were thrown back in laughter. Flavia was clutching Anita's forearm, tightly enough that her skin had gone white round Flavia's fingers, and Anita was wiping away tears.

"I have been at war most of my life," I said. "In the Swordbelt Arm or the Shieldmirror, foreign or domestic. Most of those wars I would like the city to remember—the glory I brought them, the gifts—and I have taken steps to ensure they do. But I don't love war for its own sake. And as for the civil war—I hope it is not remembered, either fondly or with rancor. I hope Quinha's life is called the life of a brave soldier and a good woman, and her death is forgotten with speed. I think the city agrees."

Gracia narrowed her eyes, but I turned away.

"I'm going to find drinks," I said. "You ought to go and talk to Jonata again—I'm sure that if they can be convinced civil war talk is over, they would love to converse with the queen of Szayet. I hope you two will be friends."

"Your hope is my command," she said, and I felt her eyes on the back of my neck as I pushed into the crowd.

CHAPTER TWENTY-SEVEN

GRACIA

Jonata Barran seemed a very ordinary sort of person to me, and I marked Ceirran's fondness for them as a mystery whose answer I would need to pursue later, but I disliked the look of the merchant Cátia. There was a sharp intelligence to her face, an animation to her eyes and in the way she moved her hands in conversation, which reminded me of the scholars in the Library back home. But when they were not debating philosophy, the scholars on Szayet were timid people, uncertain in crowds and eager to return to their posts when the conversation was done, and there was a keenness to Cátia's expression, a hunger, which made me at once certain that she was rarely satisfied with anything.

Still, I waited until Ana had disappeared in the same direction as Ceirran to drift through the crowd toward her sister. "How delightful this party is," I said.

Flavia looked genuinely pleased to see me, which was more than Barran had been. "Oracle!" she said. "I'm so pleased you're enjoying yourself. It's for your benefit, after all."

Ceirran had been right: Both at once and reluctantly I liked her very much. Flavia was taller than her sister, and her hair was curlier, but whatever genetics the crèche had lent the both of them were plain in their faces: that flicker of prettiness, in Ana a part of those clean good looks so unsettled by her eyes, in Flavia drawn out and molded into a real, striking beauty. The way she smiled at me was Ana's smile, too, though Flavia's had the gift of seeming to invite me in on the amusement.

I did not entirely trust this effect, but I could not help appreciating it. "Is it?" I said. "But I thought you had only just returned to Ceiao yourself. This seems a great deal of trouble to go to for one foreign guest."

"But you must be used to trouble by now," said Flavia. I narrowed my eyes, but she smiled again as if she meant nothing at all and sipped her wine.

"My sister has told me so much about you," she said.

"Oh, dear," I said, meaning it as the usual tired joke, but she only smiled wider.

"I'm sorry to tell you it was only good things," she said.

"Why should you be sorry?" I said, startled, but she was waving to someone behind me, her smile gone sweet and smooth.

"Commander!" she said.

Ceirran's hands were empty of drinks, but he had produced from the crowd, as if by magic, a pale stone-faced man with a modestly shaved head and a grim set to his mouth.

"Patramata," he said. "Allow me to introduce Celestino Xicaran—my husband."

I had heard from the Ceian gossips on Szayet that Celestino was no great beauty—that Ceirran had married him only for his wealthy and established family, and Celestino clung to their marriage like a dog with a bone. But looking at him, I did not know if it was true. Celestino's eyes were downcast, and his face was lined like a man twice his age. I did not think he often laughed. But there was a fineness to his features, a delicacy, that I did not wonder the quick Ceian eye had not observed. If I had met him under other circumstances, I would have been drawn to him immediately.

I leaned up to kiss the air by his cheek. "A pleasure," I said.

"Queen of Szayet," said Celestino, very coldly. "What an honor to meet you at last."

"The honor is all mine," I said, and I even meant it.

"Szayet," said another voice. I turned.

"Captain," I said. "How are you?"

Ana was out of her soldier's cloak tonight, but when I had first seen her across the room earlier that night, it had taken me a moment to realize it: The scuffed black boots, which reached to her knees, might well have been from her uniform, and she was wrapped in a deep blue stole. Up close, the difference was unmistakable—its collar sat low on her shoulders and skimmed over her chest, and I had to wrench my eyes upward from the clean naked lines of her clavicle to the sharp angle of her jaw, her cool black eyes. Her smile was as friendly and amused as if we were acquaintances from university in Sintia. "The better for seeing you," she said. "And how is the Bride of Szayet?"

"Better," I said. "It's better, too."

I thought her smile actually wavered at that, but Celestino coughed.

"I'm afraid I need to find Marcia before I go home," he said. "Husband, will you be taking our spider-litter?"

"Oh," said Ceirran, startled, and pulled him aside. Flavia watched them go, lips quirked in amusement.

"He never stays at a party past eight o'clock," she said. "As proper as a seamstress. Of course he's got no choice. It's a shame, though."

"No choice?" I said.

"What do you know about Celestino Xicaran, Madam

Oracle?" said Flavia, and smirked at Ana when she laughed softly. "His family?"

"An old family, aren't they?" I said. "Deep connections in the city."

"I should say they have deep connections," said Flavia. "They used to be priests."

I turned to stare at her. She smiled. "Did you think they all burned? I'm afraid not. Most of them even went into the army. No sins of the father in Ceiao, but *wealth* of the father, well, certainly. There's always room in the merchant class for people who are willing to marry well, or to pay. Plenty of these old families have priests in their lineage, though most of them manage to hide it. Poor Celestino never seems to have any luck."

"Poor Celestino," I echoed.

Flavia gave me a curious look at that. "Do you know," she said, "you aren't very Ceian at all."

"What do you mean by that?" I said.

But she only smiled and sipped at her wine. "The commander's gone onto the balcony," she said. "I think he might be waiting for you."

As I crossed the room the noise of the crowd battered at me like a flock of birds, but when I closed the balcony doors, it vanished instantly. Out on Flavia's balcony the air was crisp and cold. There was a peculiarity to the wind, a clean, metallic bite, which made my eyebrows go up. Ceirran was leaning against the railing, his eyes shut.

"Snow," he said.

Before us were the lights of the Inner City, scattered down the Avenuan Libeirguitan like fireflies. On Szayet they would have gleamed from the pearl roofs with such power as to turn the whole city into rivers of honey, but on Szayet winter smelled like salt. "It's beautiful," I said, to be polite.

Ceirran pointed. "Quinha's house," he said. "There, where it crosses the travessa Carenan."

At first I had no idea how he could tell one of the blue-topped mansions from another, but as I followed his finger I saw one a little taller than the others, a little narrower, with some kind of green tiling by its doors, which I could not see clearly in the distance and darkness. It was the only mansion on the avenue with no lights in the windows.

"The city's, now," said Ceirran distantly. "They'll auction it off soon enough. The councillors are already gathering in the evenings to have a word with the executors. Of course they're not meant to be able to be bribed. It's so difficult, though, to find anything that can't be sold."

On Szayet it had struck me how strange it was to live without him for a month; now it struck me how strange it was to see him again. His features in the low golden light—the crooked nose, the pucker of his scar—were difficult to pick out. Only his eyes gleamed.

"Ceirran," I said, but there was a clatter, and Ana blew in through the door a moment later, ruffle-haired and laughing.

"Admiring the view?" she said. "Szayet, look—do you see that roof, the one with the railing? Sonia Couron's. Killed in Madinabia, of course, but *what* a woman—I climbed down through that roof in the dead of night once when I was sixteen. Y'see, earlier that month, her father had caught us—"

"Anita, that's enough," said Ceirran softly.

Ana's mouth shut with a snap. She looked different, too, though in her case it was clear it was months of peacetime that had done it. She had let her hair grow until it fell over her eyes, and her arms were leaner, her curves under the stole softer. And besides this, there was an intensity to her expression at that moment, an utter and uncomplicated attention, which I had never seen on Szayet.

"Is it time?" she said.

Ceirran glanced back toward the party, his features briefly painted in gold.

"Yes," he said. "I think so. Come inside."

There was a little office adjacent to Flavia's ballroom, which she unlocked for the three of us, her eyebrows high. Ceirran smiled at her unreadably. Ana did not look at her at all.

When we were inside, Ceirran shut the door and gestured to the long couch, where I sat down, Ana on my far side. Ceirran locked the door and came to sit between us, his head bending toward mine.

"Show me," he said.

I took the black leather case from my handbag and clicked it open. It was not large. It might have fit a pair of glasses. On its left side, set lightly into the foam within, was the first item Alekso and I had finished together: a thin silver disc about the size of a circle made with the forefinger and thumb.

"That is the recorder," I said, pointing. "It stores the memories. Once every day—in the morning is best—you will need to rest a hand on it for at least ten minutes. As soon as you touch it, it will begin collecting your memories, beginning from the present and going back and back, and it will not stop until it reaches your very earliest moments. If you touch it daily, the memories recorded will be kept as current as possible."

"And I hold on to it with a fierce grip while I'm on my deathbed, I suppose," said Ceirran lightly.

"What deathbed?" I said. "Now, the recorder is a brute creature. It can store memories, and even thoughts, a little, and it can communicate them to a very limited extent, though there will be unreliabilities. But it does not have the capacity to store a—a program—which wishes to produce anything resembling an intelligence."

Ceirran's eyes flickered to mine. "For which—" he said softly.

"For which," I said, "you need this," and took out the second item in the case.

Ceirran reached out, then pulled his hand back. He said, more breath than sound, "Oracle."

"Commander," I said. "You can touch it, you know. It's yours."

He looked at me, and then turned his hand over. I laid in his palm the second Pearl of the Dead that had been made in the universe.

He had been right, on Szayet. It was very small. Alekso and I, marrying his experience to my intelligence, had managed a remarkable efficiency: Where the Pearl in my ear was the size of a thumbnail, his was half that, or smaller. It might have been an insect, if it were not for the way it shone.

"And this—" he said.

"Pinch it," I said.

He pinched it between his thumb and forefinger, and then hissed, his hand springing open. I caught the Pearl before it dropped. There was a drop of blood shining on his fingertip, which he rolled away against his thumb.

"You might have warned me," he said.

"And ruin the surprise?" I said, and set it back in his hand. There was a faint spiderweb of red on its surface, which shimmered for a moment and then vanished. "Fresh blood does the trick, if you'll forgive putting it so morbidly. It's coded to your genetic print, now, and will respond to no other's. If you were to lose it, I would have no choice but to go home, build another, and key it to your genetic print with another fresh sample—so unless you enjoy bleeding, I advise you to be very careful with it, and with the recorder. And when you are—when you have no more memories to add to the recorder, I will take the Pearl and link one with the other, and in this way, your soul will be transferred into the Pearl, and live as long as the Pearl lives."

I heard Ana's hissed exhale. Ceirran did not seem to be able to stop looking at the Pearl: He rolled it along the crease of his palm, just as he had done on the ship on Szayet, and pinched it between his finger and thumb again.

"You made this?" he said.

"Alekso made it," I said, conscious at once of the weight in my ear.

Ceirran looked up at last. "He let you?" he said. "He helped you?"

I nodded. It was true enough, and when it came to my god, it was not the worst lie I had ever told him.

Ana looked at him wordlessly, and he nodded to her and put the second Pearl in her hand. I watched as she raised it to her eye. Her face was, for once, utterly without amusement.

"Szayet," she said to me, "do you know what you've done?"

"I certainly hope so," I said.

She gave me a long, long look. Then she said, with a flicker of humor at last: "Bless you for it."

CHAPTER

TWENTY-EIGHT

CEIRRAN

The next morning brought a long, cheerful holo from Flavia, which, amid effusive thanks for coming to her party and introducing her to the queen of Szayet, contained a great deal of her thoughts on what exactly she thought of friends who kept secrets from their friends, and sisters who kept secrets from their sisters, and guests who held private conversations among themselves in the host's own rooms. None of it was serious—I had seen Flavia serious—and I sent her back an apology and an invitation for dinner with me and Celestino, which she would interpret correctly as a refusal to tell her anything that could not be said in front of him.

It was not, of course, that I considered my husband a liability. We had been married since the very early days of the Madinabic campaign, and his name and mine were one, and besides this he treated our marriage with the same kind of grave solemnity that he brought to his patriotism or his philosophy or his careful management of our household. It was for precisely this reason that I had no desire to tell him what the queen of Szayet had done. Were I anyone else in the world, he would have felt himself honor bound to report the second Pearl to the Merchants' Council, and watch its owner arrested. As I was his husband, he likely would have felt himself honor bound to retire to the country and stab himself through the gut. It seemed kinder all round to spare him my trust.

There was, of course, no way to spare him my business entirely. He was now sitting upright in bed, watching me with his morning robe wrapped tightly around himself.

"I don't like it," he said.

"I'm sorry to hear that," I said. While he was not looking, I had shut the Pearl in the cupboard behind the painting on our bedroom wall, where I kept all my precious things. The recorder I could not have hidden if I had wanted to. The little disc was slightly smaller than my palm and always warm to the touch, and it was quite easy to hold as I sat in bed in the morning, reading the fleet's reports on what had happened overnight in Ceiao and abroad. Abroad was, as usual, the more comprehensive and interesting set of problems. One general reported outbreaks of violence among the pilgrims on Far Madinabia, another the old puritanical rebellions stirring in Cherekku again. Kutayet was making advances toward its neighbors, but it always was.

"I don't like her," said Celestino quietly.

"I'm sorry to hear that, too," I said, flicking to the next part of the report.

"How long does she intend to stay?" he said.

The answer, of course, was *Until I declare her before the city to be the keeper of my immortal soul, and her descendants holy Oracles of all the Ceian Empire, and she returns to Szayet to tell her own people.* Or, alternately, it was *Until I declare myself before the city to be an ever-living god, and she returns to Szayet, her work done.* "I couldn't say," I said. "Until she has seen everything she wants to see, I expect."

He had not asked what the recorder was, nor what it did. I expect he was clever enough to understand how little he would like the answer, even if he had no guess as to what the answer was. But he reached for the disc, and flinched back when I brushed his fingers away with my free hand.

"What do you intend to show her?" he said.

"Whatever she would like," I said. "Do you have some objection to Ceiao cultivating a friendship with the sunken treasures of Szayet?" He looked blank at that, as I had known he would. In many ways he was the reverse of what annoyed me most about men like Cachoeiran; whenever I spoke of Ceiao as though she thought, or felt, or dreamed, he looked at me as though I had started reciting poetry in Cherekku. "Very well, then," I said, when he made no reply.

"She isn't Ceian," he said abruptly. "And she's very—" He curled his fingers into the bedsheet. "Matheus," he said, "she reminds me of you."

The recorder pulsed once and began to cool. I wondered how much memory it had dragged up from my past by now, in order to build this thing that would become my immortal self. Had it recorded my memory of my first landing on Szayet? My sleepless nights on Madinabia? Did it remember Flavia's husband Teo, or what Jonata had looked like in their mourning blacks at twelve years old?

And what if there was something I myself had forgotten, or something I only let myself think of rarely? Would it remember the faces of bygone classmates, or the words of old books? Would it remember how Sílvio had looked across Quinha's table at me, from his place beside his husband, the last night we had ever dined in the same?

I set it on my bedside table, put my tablet next to it, and

stretched. "Does she?" I said. "Good. Perhaps that means you might like her one day after all." To which he said nothing at all.

Gracia had wanted to tell everyone immediately. This was a problem.

Anita agreed with her, which was a bigger one. "Why in the world not?" she said. "You've been away for ages, and the people missed you to death. You ought to take advantage of their goodwill and make it clear you'll never leave again."

"That is precisely the problem," I said. "The people may have longed for me in my absence, but they also knew where I was. If I am to reveal the existence of the Pearl to the city, it must not seem a Szayeti object, gifted by a foreign queen. They must understand it as Ceiao's, Ceiao's to hold and to benefit from. Do you understand?"

"They'll benefit from it regardless," said Anita, "as it's yours."

"The captain is right," said Gracia. "Your people say that Matheus Ceirran is generous. They say he is gracious, and forgives his enemies, and rewards his friends. That's the kind of man they would like to follow. That man, they hope, will behave as Ceiao's friend, too."

"How do you know what the people are saying?" said Anita.

"Prophecy," said Gracia. I narrowed my eyes at her. It was certain that she had spies in Ceiao, as certain as it was that I had them in Szayet. But she only looked flatly back.

"It *is* a gift," she said. "You have taken it already. Let Ceiao take it, too."

"Ceiao is your host," I said, "and will resent being made the object of your generosity."

Her eyes flared. "So it may," she said. "What do you intend to call it, then? Tribute?"

I exhaled sharply. "No," I said.

"Then call it a benediction," said Anita. "Call *yourself* a benediction, if you like, once your memories are all in it. I will, if you won't."

"You won't," I said. "Neither of you will—I apologize, Patramata. I don't intend to give you orders. But I do intend to move forward cautiously, and with the love of the people, and I know them better than either of you."

Anita snorted, but Gracia leaned back on the couch, her mouth pursed.

"I would like to know them, too," she said.

She was quiet that afternoon as we approached the theater district. Anita was not, which was no surprise. She was no particular patron of the arts, of course, and would not have known how to be if she had wanted to, but she loved theater in the Sintian style. She loved the acting troupes, their cliques and petty wars; she loved the theater square, with its crowds and its multitude of screens, which reflected each actor in a hundred faces like the vision of an insect; above all else she loved the district, its odd rhythms and daringly superstitious habits. It seemed to fit her—not the way a battlefield fit her, but a different and stranger garment.

"Why don't you project them into the sky," Gracia said, "like we do with royal announcements on Szayet? It seems a great deal easier than looking at all of these banners. It makes me dizzy."

"If anyone could see theater in the sky from half a mile away, no one would pay for it," said Anita. "And then where would we be? Cultureless."

"Ah," said Gracia, "the end of all of Sintian civilization, brought about by poverty among Ceian actors in Ceiao's theater district. Fortune forbid *that*."

"All that's worth seeing of it, anyway," said Anita cheerfully.

Gracia ducked her head. "I wouldn't expect you to know better, Captain," she said, "for you have no talent for poetry."

Anita's eyes glinted. "Oh, Szayet," she said. "Your hair is like wine. Your eyes are also like wine. Your mouth is like a serpent's. What joy to die in your arms."

"As I said. Your scansion's off," said Gracia, and turned away. "And it doesn't suit you."

A low flute was playing a popular song, softly and not very well. When it ended at last, a man strolled on the stage before us, reflected a hundredfold in each direction. He was enormous, and wore a blue cloak and a gold helmet visibly too large for him, and he must have been nearly fifty.

"Six years my war has brought the city gold," he said. His voice was entirely incongruous with the rest of him, high-pitched and squeaking. "Across twelve moons I fought and conquered; then, when foes at home bestirred my eagle eye—"

"*Bestirred my eagle eye?*" whispered Anita, behind me.

"A soldier true and brave, without a flaw!" the actor was saying. "Each battle fought, for Ceiao's name alone, and yet alone *I* walk among the stars—"

He had snatched off his helmet and was pressing it to his chest in agony. "Oh *no*," I murmured, horrified. "He's *bald*."

A few minutes later the actor was interrupted: A broad-shouldered man in a blue cloak swaggered forward, a bottle of wine tucked under one arm. He was curly-headed but wearing a very bad wig of straight dark hair, which kept slipping onto his ear. "I'm bid to follow faithful to your will," he said, "for, oath-declared, your will is made my own, but had *I* firm will, here and in your hand—"

"What on earth is he talking about?" I said.

Anita snorted. So did Gracia, which confused me further. "You know," said Anita thoughtfully, "he's almost good-looking enough for the part."

"I'm not sure I agree," said Gracia, so quietly that I was nearly certain Anita didn't hear her, but I raised an eyebrow. She raised one back, unfazed, and said more loudly, "Might I ask where the chorus is?"

"There's no chorus," said Anita. "This is a comedy."

"That doesn't follow," said Gracia. "Why should a comedy preclude a chorus? In *On Spectacle* Artemio Santana argues—"

"But we're not on Sintia," said Anita, "and we do things differently here. Hush, they're bringing the next scene in."

"And where am I?" Gracia whispered to me. "I'm beginning to feel left out."

It took three more scenes, during which we learned that the two Ceians had landed on some sort of planet represented entirely by a cardboard palm tree and that the bald actor had covered himself in glory but was longing for love—Anita snorted—before a tall woman in an extremely tight red dress, very bright red lipstick, and enormous false eyelashes oozed onstage to a chorus of happy boos from the audience. "So!" she said to the audience in a beautiful, clear alto. "Here are heretics of noble worth; shall I, who strut before the kneeling crowd and poison ears and minds alike, fall? No! I know that on my shores an admiral made refugee is come, my honored guest. If I should claim our god commands it, I might any wickedness perform tonight. I'll seize a knife ere I should lose a crown, and Ceiao will reward my bloodstained hands."

"No!" shouted a few people in the audience.

"Yes!" said the woman, and went on to talk at great length about her bloodstained hands. At last, after several more scene changes, the two Ceians ended up in a great entrance hall. They were exchanging dialogue about the beauty of Ceiao and the righteousness of its values, but the effect was spoiled slightly by how often they kept glancing offstage. It became apparent why when, with a great deal of huffing and puffing, two people in cheap red cloaks wheeled in an enormous wooden box painted in elaborate designs. There was a door cut into its center. "Delivery

I bring, from unknown source," said one of the people, squeaking a little, and they both dashed offstage.

"What strange and foreign mysteries are here!" said the commander. "We'll open it, though no one tell us why," and rapped on the side of the box a few times.

The door popped open at once, and there was a brief cloud of fog—I could see a woman off the side of the stage frantically working a little pump—and then from its midst emerged a very thin girl with a white-painted face. She was wearing a great cardboard headdress, and a scrap of linen around her torso, which must have cost about ten centonos, and nothing else whatsoever.

"O!" she said. There was a brief pause. She added, "O!" A few more seconds stretched on. "O," she said, and then, a little desperately now, "O?"

Someone from offstage coughed something that might have been *carpet*. Her face brightened. "O from this rich carpet have I come to seek the aid of Ceiao's greatest lord," she said in an exaggerated Sintian accent, and plastered herself over the bald man's chest.

Gracia had buried her head in her hands. "I wish that I had not asked," she said, and then, a minute or so afterward: "Are you going to insist we stay for the whole thing?"

"What little stamina you have," said Anita, and winked at the girl in the headdress.

"I'll admit that freely, if it should grant me any dignity back," said Gracia. "Is there an intermission? If not, I might walk out through a set piece."

"I would advise against that," I said. "This production was fantastically expensive."

We did at last manage to shove ourselves back through the crowds, and as we strolled up the boulevard away from the hundred glittering screens, I bent to murmur in Gracia's ear: "Were you really insulted? I am sorry, Patramata."

"It's not yours to be sorry for," she said, and then shook her head. "Insulted—I don't know if this is what I would say. You understand such a thing would never happen on Szayet?"

"I do," I said. "I'm afraid there is significantly more autonomy among our acting troupes here, and significantly less respect for what you might call authority."

"It's not the disrespect," she said, and then reconsidered. "It is the disrespect, but not toward me—or not toward myself, not toward my *person*. It's—I suppose it's the crudity. It made people laugh. Very well. I like to laugh. But was there any beauty in it?"

"Were *you* the one expected to find it beautiful?" said Anita, from ahead of her.

Gracia said nothing to this, but her mouth was flat. I tucked my arm into hers. "Walk along the Nevede with me," I told her. "We'll talk of better poetry, and I'll show you the obsidian that washes up on the banks of the river. Would that clean the ugliness away?"

"Better poetry," Gracia echoed, and I could not read any tone in it, but a moment later she turned to me, smiling. "Very well," she said. "We'll go to the river, and you'll tell me about Ceian beauty. What could be lacking in that?"

The river was a dark, slow slate-grey ribbon along its rocky banks. We approached the Gate of Shattered Chains at a leisurely stroll, stopped to admire the gold on the apex, and proceeded westward toward the looming shape of Mauntan Bau above the towers. Before long the talk slipped from poetry to Sintia as a whole, and then to Ceian education there, and then to reminiscing, and Anita was left describing an adventure she had had in her academy days: "So naked as a jaybird I ran from the launderers' up three flights of stairs," she said, "my friends singing out their windows as I went, and when I stopped in front of Tibúrcio's door, what should I discover but—he had been behind me all the while with a tablet, and the holo of me had gone to the girl!"

Gracia snorted. Anita looked sidelong at her, her eyes glinting. "But perhaps this is too crude for the Oracle of Szayet," she said.

"I was told once that you were a rough soldier," said Gracia, "and the airs and graces ought to be left to—others."

I didn't recall this at all, but Anita grinned slowly, a true and delighted smile. "What a wise woman it must have been who said it," she said. "Does that mean you'll pretend to be amused if I go on telling soldier's stories?"

"If you pretend to be amusing," said Gracia, and her eyes crinkled at Anita's laugh.

Anita left as we approached the Major Gate. I hailed a spider-litter for Gracia, and looked at her from the corner of my eye as one skittered through the shuffling crowd toward us. She was watching the Ceians with a distant gaze.

"When you do tell them," she said at last, "will you only say that I am now your sworn Oracle? Or will you say I made it—that I made your godhood for you, with my own two hands?"

"Of course I'll say you made it," I said at once.

She hummed. Then she stood on tiptoes and kissed me. The little pinpricks of her fingernails dug hard into the back of my head.

"And will you come with me, and dine at my house tonight?" she said, when she drew away.

"If the queen commands it," I said, and her face reluctantly broke into a smile.

I returned home late that night, through a thin and frozen rain slanting outside the windows of my spider-litter that left the streets frozen and gleaming. My house was the only one on the Avenuan Libeirguitan whose windows were lit. Celestino was at the door, his eyes hooded and cool.

"Husband," he said, and let me lean in to kiss him, though he did not respond. We were undressed and in our bed before he spoke again, and then it was to say: "It's a long way to the Outer City."

"Not so long as it is to Szayet," I said.

I heard his exhale. Then he said flatly: "Do you want me to be angry with you?"

"Angry?" I said, and rolled over to look at him in the darkness, the sharp angles of his cheeks and the bow of his lip. "Have I insulted you?"

There was a long silence.

"When you fought on Madinabia," he said, "when you fought Quinha Semfontan, when you left my—my house—I never asked whether you would come back."

I said, quietly and calmly, "What are you asking now?"

"Now?" he said. His eyes were shut. "Now I am asking whether you intend to let that woman take your empire."

I smiled and rolled over on the pillow, away from him, and stared up into the shifting darkness.

"No," I said. "I don't think I will. But won't it be something to watch her try?"

CHAPTER TWENTY-NINE

GRACIA

It was impossibly loud in Ceiao, as I learned those early nights in my rooms, staring at the shadows shifting in their hundred colors on the ceiling. Every moment I could hear the wail of a train whistle, or some citizen arguing with another, or the barking of one of the dogs that ran everywhere in the streets. Ceirran must have lied to me when he told me this neighborhood was a fine one, I thought uncharitably—it was only later I would discover he had not, and the poorer neighborhoods were far worse—and turned over and put my pillow over my head. It did nothing to block the noise, but the light, at least, I could pretend away.

There was much to pretend away among the Ceians, too. I attended half a dozen dinners that first week, and was welcomed with smiles into the homes of what Ceirran called Ceiao's quality, where it became apparent at once that Ceiao's quality had a significant fondness for Szayet's things. Whether Twentieth Dynasty statuary or Thirty-First Dynasty jewelry or even Ostrayeti tapestries, there was no house in the city that did not contain some fragment I knew at a glance had come from the shores of Alectelo or Zhivatselo or any of the other ports under my rule. There were a hundred different ways to politely ask after provenance, and I worked my way through at least ninety of them before the variations on *What a wonderful question, I'm sure I don't know* began to grate past tolerance.

Besides this habit of mistruthing, the conversation I could not call worse than Szayet's—growing up at home, if I did not want to talk to some member of my guard or my church, I had been left with either Zorione or my sister, each in their own way profoundly difficult—but it was surprising how uneducated the Ceians seemed to be. Or perhaps not uneducated, precisely, but unexpectedly provincial. I had thought myself, Sintian in name and in ancestry but tens of thousands of light-years from that famous planet, to be desperately far from the center of human intellect, and it was bewildering that so many Ceians themselves seemed to hardly take an interest. In that first week I was introduced by Ceirran and Flavia to those considered Ceiao's best, many of whom had been educated in Sintielo—but to the vast majority, the city seemed less a source of science or philosophy than a source of other Ceian friends.

There were a few with whom I could converse. Ceirran was among them, of course, and there was a poet I particularly liked, Jacinta, who even told me the names of new writers, which I duly passed on to the Library in a data packet the morning after. And besides this there was the sharp-eyed Cátia Lançan, who seemed to feel that her employment of Szayeti in her factories established a point of connection between us, and who made up for a visible disdain for theater or poetry with an obvious fondness for philosophical debate—though she had a habit of sulking badly when she lost. The rest would speak Sintian with me, and often even with one another—it signified that they had sufficient wealth to obtain such fluency, I understood—but the learning I had obtained at the Library as a girl was transformed here to a disquietingly pretentious streak in my character, and I was forced for the sake of charm to turn the conversation to local Ceian matters with an unfortunate regularity.

But there were Ceian matters, too, which caused me more than a little frustration and which I had no desire to discuss with even those Ceians of quality who were counted among Ceirran's friends: the destruction of temples on outposts near Sintia, the state of the colony on Belkayet. I accounted myself lucky that Ceirran so disliked discussion of the death of Quinha Semfontan in his presence. The worst matter was the most provincial of all: the police raids across the city, ordered by Ceirran's enemy Thiago Veguion, for any books or objects that suggested worship of any kind. It was entirely unclear what contraband these raids had discovered. Those Ceians who Ceirran called his enemies said dozens of conspiracists had been arrested, those who he called his friends said that some innocents were held awaiting trial for the crime of merely owning heirloom Kutayeti candlesticks, or old shawls with Sintian writing embroidered on them, or books that mentioned the old Ceian priesthood without decrying it. At first the raids had been entirely among the slums, and the gangster-ridden neighborhoods, but in these latest weeks, even houses in the Inner City had woken to find guards rapping at their door.

"You might count yourself fortunate that they haven't raided *you*," said Alekso as I watched the street through the window. "You knew you were coming to a barbarian city. What did you expect?"

"I won't count myself fortunate," I said. "I'll count myself entitled to privacy in my own house. Why is it you can act so cavalier, Lord? This is a campaign against those who worship in your name."

"Is it?" he said. "I understood from *him* that the purpose was to arrest the people that like him best. I don't see where I come in."

There was no point asking who he meant by *him*. "No one has ever put the two of you in competition, Lord," I said.

"Yet," he said, and vanished; and no matter how I tapped the Pearl, he refused to reappear.

I did not like the food very much, either. Ceirran would hear none of this when I tried to tell him: "*Every* food is here in Ceiao," he said. "No matter what in the galaxy you want, someone is selling it. That is the point of an empire, my dear." But among themselves, the Ceians only seemed to eat pickled beets and pickled cabbage and salted pork and jellied pears. Persimmons and apricots were always too firm when I got them, and tasted of clay. And the fish was not the same, either: It was always carp or catfish at Ceian households, and whenever Zorione found squid in the markets the texture was unnervingly like rubber, and I regretted it after I had taken my first bite.

The wine was, admittedly, very good. "At least Ceiao is skilled in something besides war," I said to Ceirran, after we had finished one particularly fine bottle, and he said, "But we're so *very* good at war," so pleasantly that I choked on my soup. The baths were good, too, and much the same as they were on Szayet, though Ceirran was openly jealous of the cedar and myrrh oils I had brought along with me, and I suspect would have stolen a few bottles if using them at home would not have been an open insult to his husband.

It was my own house that I found the greatest annoyance. It was not that I had expected a mansion, of course—the size was nothing to speak of, but Ceiao was a dense city, and only a handful of families had the luxury of size given to Flavia, Ceirran, and the like. Neither was it the style—I recognized it as a newfangled sort of Ceian design, one Ceirran told me was becoming very popular among the sort of up-and-coming traders and profiteers whose grandchildren and great-grandchildren would someday sit on the Merchants' Council. It was beautiful in itself, with three floors filled with wide white-painted rooms, and a courtyard in the back where a chestnut tree spread friendly limbs over a red-and-blue mosaic of a dragon. In other circumstances, with Ceirran to visit me and Zorione to attend on me, I would have been very happy there.

The trouble was twofold. Firstly, the house was extraordinarily far away from everything I wished to do: Parties, theater, marketplaces, libraries, private baths, public baths, singing, dancing, even casual conversation with Ceirran's friends and acquaintances, all took an hour or more to reach even at my litter's fastest clip, and it made it a great inconvenience to be invited anywhere at all. Secondly—and it was to my fury that I learned this from an offhand mention of the subject by Jonata Barran at dinner, rather than from Ceirran himself—the inconvenience was entirely deliberate. Szayeti were not allowed to live within a twelve-mile radius of the city's center.

"It isn't *just* Szayeti, my dear," said Ceirran, when I confronted him. "And it isn't as if you're forbidden from traveling closer, after all. The city itself is entirely open to you."

"I don't think you even believe that," I said.

He gave me a considering look, folded his hands on the table, and leaned forward. We were playing one of those endless dice games they adored in the city, which always seemed to spark a round of reminiscing about military school whenever two Ceians were in a room together. He was winning by an astonishing amount. "No," he said, "I don't. Keeping the part of the city within the Step exclusive to Ceians has brought me nothing but trouble. It raises property prices, stifles the movement and wealth of my supporters, and allows my enemies to offer very poor work for very cheap wages. What's more, it all but ensures that the Merchants' Council will remain made up almost entirely of my potential rivals and outright enemies as long as I live. If it were just Ceian citizenship that restricted them, it would be one thing, but the list of qualifiers—three generations of planetside inhabitation, fourteen years of military service per household, an income of *twenty thousand* dekar per annum, just for a beginning—that list is so prohibitive I wonder any new residents move in at all. I consider it in line with the scarcity of officer commissions: a measure allowing the current men of quality to more easily keep their wealth and to more easily shape the city as they like."

"And you would like wealth spread to the deserving poor?" I said dryly.

"I don't care where the money goes," said Ceirran, "as you well know. I am not one of those councillors who pretends at being the defender of Ceian virtue. It so happens that the people in Ceiao with the most money tend to reflexively avoid my friendship. If they ever changed their minds, I expect I would feel differently, but as things are, when I am in a position to aid the people they despise, I tend to take it."

"Then buy me a new house, Commander," I said, and shook a handful of dice out onto the glowing tablet. It made a soft pinging noise, and the part of the board representing my score went from pale blue to a dull, unhappy red.

"That, I'm afraid, is still against the law," he said.

"You let me wear the Pearl," I said. "Isn't that against the law? The first law of the city, if I recall correctly."

He scooped up the dice and rolled them back and forth along the crease of his palm.

"It is," he said, "and it isn't. The raids notwithstanding, the fact is that, except for real idealists like Jonata, no one very much cares if the queen of Szayet brings what they think of as her computer into the city. Or—they care—but the fact is that they aren't particularly confronted by it. They know you to be a woman of faith, but they also know you to be the ruler of a planet far from Ceiao, whose culture is markedly different from Ceiao's own. And they don't mind that as much as they might if Szayet and Ceiao had—a different sort of relationship."

I opened my mouth to ask what on earth that meant, and then stopped. I had met the Ceians of quality. I had shaken their hands. I had known them well enough already, from the way they spoke to me, from the way they clasped my hand and stared at my ear and said my name with a kind of peculiar pleasure. I had known their love was not really a thing less poisonous than their hate. Nevertheless, I felt for a moment like a child: as if I were watching my father, standing bareheaded with blood on the tips of his fingers.

"It isn't about you," said Ceirran, and when I looked flatly at him: "It is about you—but it's about me, too, my dear. Thiago Veguion, for one, would see any movement toward opening property within the Step to foreigners as not only a sign of my corruption by foreign elements, but a blatant grab for power. And I can hear Cachoeiran now: *How long, Ceirran, will you patiently wait before filling every lieutenancy and captain's chair with a tattooed Muntiru?* Though he cares far less than most."

I said nothing for a while. Then I said, "You have a Pearl of the Dead. You will be a living deity in this city."

"Yes," he said. "When I'm ready."

"When will you be ready?" I said. "When will you tell Ceiao what Szayet has done for you?"

He hesitated, and then he at last threw his dice. They scattered in all directions, and his score shot upward in a clatter of pings: blue, blue, blue as the sky.

We went to Flavia's the next day, though not for the sake of Flavia herself. Anita, to my bewilderment, seemed to have no fixed abode of her own: She stayed now at one friend's, now at another's, sometimes even on Ceirran's own couch. "My only home is the battlefield," she said when I asked her, and smote her chest with a dramatic flourish. Ceirran said she was stone broke. This week she was staying at her sister's, and we sat on her sister's couches and drank good wine and talked blandly of nothing for twenty minutes until Flavia said, "Oh, for Fortune's sake, what kind of a boor do you think I am? Are all your councils contained to people who have lived on Szayet these days?"

"That," Ceirran said mildly, "is unkind."

"You," she said, "are unkind. Oracle, my apologies! Your patience *must* be divine in order to put up with him—ah." She was looking at Ana's face, eyes gleaming with triumph. Ana's expression had gone abruptly very blank. "*Divine*, is that it? I knew I'd hit on something eventually. You should have seen your face."

"Keep talking that way, you'll make him think I'm a liability," said Ana. She was smiling, but it didn't reach her eyes.

"Only to me," said Flavia, and patted her cheek. Ana looked deeply skeptical, but Flavia, paying no mind, said to Ceirran, "Religion, then. Well, is it about the raids? But what kind of secret would you need to hide from *me*? I thought I knew all *your* finances back to front, Matheus"—both Ana and Ceirran winced at this, which she ignored—"you can't be afraid that you'll be raided?"

"Me! No," he said. "You might watch yourself, Flavia—you, and your circle. Veguion's stomach for sending his guards into the houses of my friends grows bigger by the day."

"He's my friend, too, Matheus," she said pleasantly.

"Forgive me," I said, "but I thought you were commander of all troops on Ceiao. For what reason do you lack the loyalty of the city guard? Can't you order them to stop?"

Flavia's bright gaze swung round to me, and I wished I had not spoken. "So it isn't about the raids after all," she said. "You can't know enough about the guard to have been counseling on them for months, can you? Then what affair on Ceiao could you possibly be privy to? No offense meant, of course, Oracle! It can't be anything on Ceiao at all, can it?" She turned her head. "Matheus," she said, smiling, "you can't imagine that *I* wouldn't be a safe harbor for conspiracy. If I didn't know better, I'd say you'd forgotten Teo and Sérgio entirely—"

"Are you quite done?" said Ceirran.

For a moment I did not recognize the look in his face, it was so hard and cold. Flavia met his gaze for one second, two—and then she looked away. Her smile didn't so much as twitch, but she said:

"I apologize, Madam Oracle."

"No offense was taken," I said slowly. I was not quite sure what had occurred, but when I glanced at Ana, her shoulders were easing down.

"To answer your question," said Ceirran to me, "I have the oaths of every guard and soldier on the planet and in the stars."

"More importantly," said Flavia, settling back against the couch, "he has the purse strings to their salaries."

"But he can't control who bribes them," said Ana cheerfully.

Ceirran sighed. "It's a matter of incentive," he said. "I was given the title of commander in order to restore peace and order in the city, after Quinha—when the war left domestic soil. I cannot punish our men for upholding the law. But neither can I control where, how, or for whom the law is enforced—and if Thiago Veguion takes it upon himself to privately offer a thirty-dekar reward for every conviction, I cannot stop him. All that *would* stop him is a public reprisal by a respectable councillor—and there are very few councillors who are widely respectable, especially after the war. I might, of course, offer the guard bribes of my own, but besides the basic indignity of the situation, my personal treasury is not infinite." He shot a look at Ana. "Especially after my recent time away."

"That's the trouble with spreading yourself thin, I say," said Ana, looking not the least bit sorry. "You know what Veguion's got that you don't? Focus."

"Do you know what you have that he doesn't, Matheus?" said Flavia sweetly. "Friends you can trust."

He narrowed his eyes, and I tensed, but that swift terrible coldness didn't return to his face. Instead, he chuckled, and if I had not already been looking so closely at Ana, I would not have seen the minute relief in her expression. "Don't think I'm not glad to have friends," he said. "Perhaps I *have* forgotten a little how to trust, after all these years. And don't think I'm jealous of your friendships—even if they are with my enemies."

"Of course you're jealous," she said, and patted his hand. "I wouldn't get very far these days if I hadn't decided to find it charming. The point is—"

"The point is," said Ana, "if I'm made to live any longer with this woman huffing and pouting at me every time I walk into a room, you'll have another jailed sister on your hands. Tell her, Szayet."

But I did not tell her. Rather I leaned forward and said to Flavia, "What, exactly, do you think of Túlio Cachoeiran?"

She looked shocked, then thoughtful. "He asked after you the other day, as a matter of fact," she said. "He's felt dreadfully left out that everyone's met the foreign queen but him. Don't tell me *he's* privy to Matheus's secret plans! I really will be jealous then."

"Not at all," I said. "I was thinking of sharing them with him."

They exchanged looks. I was momentarily certain that Ceirran would at once tell me *no* and confirm my worst fears about his secrecy, but instead he said slowly, "It is not the worst thing you could do."

"You haven't met him?" said Ana. "Truly?"

"Not once," I said. "I used to read his works as a child. What *do* you think of him?"

"He is—a neutral party," said Ceirran.

"He's a little prick is what he is," said Ana, amused. "There's no one in the city who can look at him without wanting to shove him into the river for the pleasure of hearing him squeal. You certainly won't manage it."

"He is highly respected," said Ceirran, looking pained, "in the majority of the Crossbar, and certainly among all our peers on the Merchants' Council—"

"He isn't respected at all, he's a lawyer," said Ana.

"—and his writings have even been praised in Sintia," Ceirran said. "And, as the Oracle says, as far away as Alectelo. He is not, ah, sympathetic to our cause. But if he could be made to be—"

"He's certainly never had any great love for the military," said Flavia, "and especially the military acting on behalf of private interests. It was an early point of contention between him and Teo Pulcron, as a matter of fact. I'm surprised he hasn't spoken against the raids before now—but before now they haven't been coming into the Inner City, of course. But, Matheus, you *have* been trying to persuade him for ages, haven't you?"

"Ah," said Ceirran, looking awkward. "He might be more amenable to the plea from—another source." He glanced at Ana, who smiled without humor. "Patramata," he said to me, "I don't deny that he would be a significant asset to the cause. And I know that, ah, you admire his reputation. But you have heard me speak on him."

"Then I will court the reputation, and not the man," I said. "He isn't truly your *enemy*, is he? He might have taken Veguion's side against you, if he had wanted to?"

"If you were to ask him, he has no side but the will of the people," said Flavia, smiling a little.

"Amazing how often the people's will is the same as his personal grudges," said Ana, and they shared a brief look I could not read.

"If you want any support from the Merchants' Council when you reveal my gift, and our arrangement, you must begin somewhere," I said to Ceirran. "Why not someone who has already asked to meet with me? Perhaps I may even like him."

"Cachoeiran does so *very* badly want to be liked," said Ceirran. "It is his first weakness. If anyone can bring him to sympathy for my objectives, Patramata, I expect it will be you. But my hopes are not high."

I exhaled. "Then you may as well know," I said to Flavia. "It would make me a boor indeed to share this with Túlio Cachoeiran and not with the commander's own friend."

But Flavia only raised her eyebrows thoughtfully when we had explained what I had brought into Ceirran's city. "How fascinating," she said. "You built it yourself?"

"I did," I said, "with the aid of Alekso Undying."

Flavia's eyes flicked to my ear, and her mouth twisted. I could not tell whether it was a smile.

"Well," she said, "you might want to leave that part out."

"She seems very calm about it," I said to Ceirran, later, in my bedroom. We had left the sisters' house together, and he had ridden with me all the long way to my house in the Outer City, which I appreciated for the sentiment, if not for any practical help that it gave. When we had arrived I had invited him upstairs.

He smiled, a little. "You should not take it as an insult," he said, "or as any kind of ill sign. Flavia is not easily impressed, though she pretends to be. To hear her speak, you'd think she was as lighthearted as a bird in the morning, and if I hadn't seen her once raise a mob in the streets and march it to the council's meeting chamber, I would believe it. In some ways it is a great pity she never became the ordinary kind of soldier."

"I should hope that Cachoeiran will be a more impressionable audience, then?" I said.

He laughed. “Cachoeiran,” he said, “if he had become the ordinary kind of soldier, would have put his hands on the controls of a ship exactly once and flown it into a tree. He prefers to be performer, rather than audience—though what Ceian doesn’t?”

“It will go well,” I said, after a moment. “I can manage him. We can charm him.”

“I hope it does go well,” he said, “but I’m afraid you will have to do it without me.”

“Without you?” I said.

“I am going to Far Madinabia,” he said. “Some of Quinha’s old friends have begun a pirate colony there, and I’m afraid it must be put down. I don’t know how long it will take, though I can’t imagine it will be longer than a month—these are very ill-funded men.”

“Far Madinabia!” I said, and closed my eyes, trying to picture it. It was a planet in Madinabia’s system, so named because of its wobbling, highly irregular orbit around Madinabia’s star. At any time, it might be far enough away that water could barely rise above the freezing point, or close enough that the oceans began to bubble up into continuous rain. Often it even passed near enough Madinabia that some of the outer moons were pulled away from their orbits. “Where is it now?”

“Sextile to Madinabia, and very nearly habitable,” said Ceirran, “though growing warmer by the day, I believe. When I visited during the campaign, the people were making pilgrimage from their poles to the equator. Now, I imagine, they will be traveling the other way. The pirates make their home on the great roads and harass travelers for their keep.”

“Very frightening,” I said skeptically.

He stretched. “Such a long time I’ve been at peace,” he said thoughtfully. “I hope I haven’t forgotten the knack.”

“But you won’t be in any danger,” I said, “surely. You’ll stop on that road for a few days, sort it out at once, and return to safety, I imagine."

"Almost certainly," he said, and turned and murmured something against my shoulder, which I thought with alarm might have been *More's the pity*.

I said abruptly, "Would you give me back the Pearl before you go?"

"The—" he said, glancing to my ear, and then understood, and frowned. "Why?"

"To show Councillor Cachoeiran," I said. "Flavia may not be easily impressed, but she takes me at my word. This is a stranger, and a respected Ceian. I am afraid to go before him without proof."

It was that last that made his brow smooth over, as I had known it would. "Don't be afraid," he said. "Very well. Come to my house tomorrow in the early morning, before my lieutenants flock there for preparations. I'll loan it to you."

I hesitated and at last said: "Thank you."

"My pleasure," he said. Then, a few moments later, "In any event, I'm afraid I will be entirely out of contact. The orbit makes sending data packets nearly impossible." He frowned. "That won't hurt the Pearl, will it? To have its recorder so far away?"

"Not at all," I said. "One day, the recorder will need to be near the Pearl to transfer memories into its artificial intelligence, so that your soul might be preserved—but that day is far, far away. For now the Pearl only waits."

He was silent. I had seen his face change at *soul*. "Very well," he said at last, with forced good humor. "Will you be able to entertain yourself, these next few weeks?"

"Oh," I said, "certainly."

He grinned up at me. "I think that ought to worry me, my dear."

"Most likely," I said, and leaned over to kiss him. "I suppose you'll try to restrain me."

"If only you would let me," he said fondly.

I took that for what it was, but I paid attention to how he enjoyed it.

CHAPTER THIRTY

CEIRRAN

It was a long way to the outskirts of the Shieldmirror, and the journey no shorter for being much more peaceful than the last time I had made it. I had only petty officers for company, having left Anita behind to act as my substitute on the Merchants' Council. This was more an act of deliberate provocation than anything else: I was nearly certain that it was Thiago Veguion who had orchestrated the motion to send me to clean up the pirate problem personally, and I intended to make him suffer for it.

The Merchants' Council had of late become a great irritation. After the long and brutal rhythm of war after war, it seemed absurd that we should all return to various little rooms at the top of various Ceian towers in our finest blue cloaks and discuss the price of grain on Itsaryet, as if it were a sensible way to go about running a society. Each of us had spent our seven years in the military—though only some of us had seen combat, of course, and we all knew it—and each of us knew that governance could come from the end of a gun as well as it could come from a motion passed with two-thirds majority. More than this: Each of us knew that the power I possessed, the sole command of the fleet and the veto for all motions that it bestowed upon me, shaped the quality of that governance as no man's power had shaped it for—though they did not dare to say it—one hundred and fifty years. *I cannot run an empire on my own*, I had told Anita once on Szayet, but the prospect of governing it through these hundred petty men and their thousand petty squabbles grew increasingly exhausting. Nevertheless—these were the illusions that kept meetings peaceable and Flavia's parties pleasant. More than this, these were the illusions that banished the monstrous, grinning memory of civil war, which otherwise squatted at the ends of our beds in the small hours of the morning, and stared until we could not sleep for dreaming of its face.

It was very nearly a pleasure to crawl out of my ship and into the broiling heat of a Far Madinabic evening. My army had set up camp nearly a week earlier, and the tents were scattered from the river where we had landed down the great yellow slope of a hill, where grass curled and lay dead against the hard earth. On the horizon, the last sliver of the sun was trembling red and fat against the swell of what had once been a green field.

"In your most pessimistic estimate, Captain," I said to Galvão as he led me down toward the command post he had set up six days earlier, "do you anticipate this taking beyond a month?"

"Frankly, sir, I don't anticipate it taking beyond a week," said Galvão, and looked alarmed when I sighed. "Is that wrong?"

"Not at all," I said, "only that Thiago Veguion's excuses for delaying the vote on the worship allowance motion grow increasingly tiresome. I'm sorry, Captain—that much is none of your responsibility. I look forward to shortening those few days as best I can. Have you a map of the area of operations?"

He did, and he and the other lieutenants and I gathered in the cool yellow light of the command post and pulled the holo wide and debated this or that formation and this or that time of attack and this or that weaponry, while outside the ensigns carried great crates of food to the mess tents, and guns to the weapons tents, and raised standards before the command tents and hammered at tent poles, and the crickets sang as if this were a true summer rather than only an ominous heat. The pirates were at a disadvantage, in that they had deliberately pinned themselves to a planet, and we knew exactly where they were. Even cleaning up Gracia's enemies in the atmosphere of Szayet had been more difficult—they, at least, had had the good sense to stay out of satellite range. But the pirates were at an advantage, too: They knew we were coming. This meant that they would try to flee, for the most part, and go to ground as best they could, and it was this that we were trying to prevent. I had no interest in having to return to this planet again.

Galvão followed me out of the command tent after, toward my tent. "Are you going directly to dinner, sir?" he said.

"I should think so," I said, bewildered. "Is there a reason for me not to?"

"Your cousin is here," said Galvão. "I'm sorry, I don't know his name—the boy. He came with the other lieutenants in the initial assault."

"Otávio!" I said, stopping dead. "Otávio Julhan! But I wasn't told! He can't be a lieutenant already?"

"He's been in the army these four years, sir," said Galvão, "according to his captain. The report is that he's a quick study, sir, if a little sickly. His commanding officers speak well of him."

"And so they should," I said. "Where is he now? I want to speak with him."

He was among the camp followers. No matter how varied the battles may be that you fight in the galaxy, whether in the Swordbelt Arm or the Shieldmirror or the Crossbar or Arqueiran or the edge of the Black Maw itself, whether on ice or water or grass or sand or in the howling bombardment of an asteroid storm, with destroyers or with cruisers, with mines scattered over an atmosphere, with nothing but yourself and the other man and two charged guns, there are camp followers. When the whole universe goes to war against itself molecule to molecule, and crumples and snaps and collapses into a single point of heat, there will be camp followers. I nearly admired the principle.

He was not doing anything untoward, though, only speaking around a campfire with a couple of line-faced women and two soldiers, which surprised me somewhat less than it did Galvão. I knew from my grandmother's letters Otávio Julhan had shown no interest in women, men, or anyone else over the course of his short life, and I was becoming increasingly certain that he never would. He had been a quiet boy when I had last met him, and a thoughtful one, and his commanding officers at the academy had spoken highly of him at first and then ceased to speak of him at all, which I recognized well enough as a sign of a student who had surpassed what they could teach. Good. It made me glad to know that Ceiao still produced such soldiers.

"Otávio," I said, and raised him to his feet and kissed him on each cheek. "What are you doing out here in the heat? I had no idea you were at war."

He let me embrace him with no particular stiffness, but when I had let go of him he saluted with the crisp perfection of a boy at the academy. "It's an honor, sir," he said.

"Sir!" I repeated, laughing. "Call me cousin, if you cannot call me Ceirran. Do you know the last time I saw you, you were nearly this high? And how is your mother?"

"Well, sir," said Otávio, then, "Well—cousin. She told me to ask after you."

"I have no doubt she did," I said, "and I wish you had." Otávio's mother lived by the ocean, many miles from Ceiao. My grandmother had taken the whole family there while I was still in military school, not long after her wife's death. Ostensibly this was to benefit the boy's health, but I had long suspected it had been so that she and Otávio's mother could escape the shame of my mother's disgrace. "You didn't think I would want to see you? Come to my tent and eat dinner with me, and I will see what you have learned the last ten years. I can promise you it will be a good deal better than soldier's food."

Otávio followed me across the whispering grasses in near silence, and then said as we approached the tent and my standard raised before it, "I hear that Captain Ana Decretan eats her meals with her men, and is accounted a great leader for it."

"Ana is a very particular case," I said, "and it would take a very particular man to follow her example. Is this what you've been doing while I've been on campaign—studying the habits of my officers?"

"No," said Otávio.

From anyone else it would have sounded defensive. From him it sounded startlingly plain, as if he did not know how to say truth otherwise. "I'm glad to hear it," I said, and ducked through my tent flap. The mess cooks had prepared hare, and lentils with coriander, and a sweet nut tart. I gestured Otávio to the other seat across my desk, pulled my tablet out from beneath it, and flicked the holo of the map to life.

"Tomorrow we will set up roadblocks, here and here," I said, "and stop all travelers along the road, in the expectation that some pirates will attempt to disguise themselves as pilgrims. Tell me, what are the disadvantages of this plan?"

"Local reaction," said Otávio at once. "The populace won't want to have their journey to the poles delayed, and they'll resent our army for doing it. That's the second-worst danger."

"And the first?" I said.

"False positives," said Otávio. "If any of our men should

mistake a pilgrim for a pirate, and take him from his friends or family—or kill him. Or worse, if our men should become afraid that the pirates will attack rather than stop, and decide to eliminate threatening travelers through sniper fire. The locals would turn on our men instantly—they prefer theft to perceived physical danger."

I noted how he said *Our army* and *Our men*. It was not with the fierce pride of loyalty that I had heard from some soldiers, Anita among them. Rather it was with a proprietorial indifference, an unconscious kind of possessiveness. At first I thought it reminded me of Gracia, but then I remembered the way Gracia had said, *I want to know everything about your people*, and dismissed the thought.

"Tell me," I said impulsively, "why were you with the camp followers?"

Otávio's face went absolutely blank for a few moments. At last he said, sounding uncertain for the first time: "I wanted to know what they had to say."

"About what?" I said.

"About the health of the army," said Otávio.

When I caught his gaze, he looked back, unflinching. It was easy to see my mother in him: her pointed chin, her full mouth, the flint in her eyes. In another sense, it was easy to see my own face.

"Very well," I said. "Tell me how we might overcome the roadblock's disadvantages."

He was right about the resentment, which we stymied almost entirely via bribes; my pockets were noticeably lighter when the next two days were done. The danger of false positives we overcame by killing no one whatsoever and taking all prisoners back to our camp, where we tied them up in one of the smaller tents and put it about that they were being terribly tortured. In point of fact we were not torturing any of them, a result that greatly disappointed a number of my officers in my tent that night, but I said, "I wager Otávio can tell me why."

"There's no point," he said. "We don't want to learn anything from them. We want to make their comrades angry, and we want them to dig in their heels and attempt an ambush."

"Quite right," I said warmly, and ignored my officers' looks. On his way out of the tent, I caught his arm.

"Stay with me tomorrow," I said. "I want to see how you fight."

Galvão looked alarmed at this, but Otávio showed no expression at all.

"It would be an honor, cousin," he said.

It had been many months since I had waited through the night before a battle. I had long since lost that young soldier's habit of blending terror and excitement, feeding on each until I was dizzy with them. Still, my body, which knew it was about to face death even as certain as I was that I would come out of the next day well and breathing, suspended me between boredom and adrenaline; whenever I settled into the first with enough comfort to close my eyes, the second would come roaring back into my blood like gunfire. Accordingly I found it difficult to sleep, and rather than stay up tossing and turning and looking over my battle plans as if they would dissolve the enemy if I read them closely enough, I slipped out of the tent and went into the dry grasses to look at the stars.

At this point in Far Madinabia's orbit, even nightfall failed to banish the heat. The sky, on Ceiao and Szayet so clear with stars that I might have reached up and plucked them down like berries, was here more and more obscured by the mist, which rose from the distant ocean and spread over the globe like a mushroom cloud.

On Ceiao, we resented the severity of our winter and summer, knowing them to be the product of a great and terrible man whose followers had done such small and terrible things. But this was a part of the galaxy that Alekso of Sintia had never conquered, and it was strange to remember it—to remember that there was strangeness in the universe, astonishing strangeness, and brutality, and beauty, which occurred for no other reason than the whims of Fortune herself. Back and forth these pilgrims went, poles to equator to poles again, and it felt so bewildering that there should be no reason for it. It felt so strange and so rare that there should be no one to blame at all.

In all the years through which I had risen through the ladder of offices, from ensign to admiral and at last to this highest honor, which no one since Valquíria Barran had held, I had received correspondence from my grandmother exactly once annually, at the New Year. She asked after my health. She informed me that my aunt and cousins continued well. She told me nothing of their lives. I wrote back to her, perfunctory: I had my health, and I was glad of hers. Did Otávio and his sister need anything from me? Did she? One year, after I had become an admiral, she invited me to visit her house—but she was in ill health when she did it, and she died before I could take her up on the invitation.

I accounted myself a man of infrequent anger, but I was angry then—brutally, terribly angry—at my grandmother for keeping my cousin from me. I was angry with her for writing rather than visiting. I was angry with her for inviting me to stay and not coming to Ceiao. I was angry with her for having left in the first place. I was angry that she had not stayed with my mother, and suffered disgrace with her, and lost everything. I was angry that she had not stayed with me.

There was no point to the anger, and there was nothing left of her but ash. I was no Oracle, and I could not speak to the dead. But it seemed such an injustice that any of the living who might ever love me should be kept from me now.

CHAPTER

THIRTY-ONE

GRACIA

"Try threats," said Alekso.

"You're very funny, Lord," I said.

"I'm not joking," said Alekso. "Threaten him; it's what he'll understand. Tell him that if he doesn't make whatever alliance it is you want him to make, you'll make sure he can't buy goods anywhere in the Swordbelt Arm. Tell him you really will have the captain shove him into the river."

"Do you know," I said, "your home planet is considered across the galaxy to be the center of civilization, education, and refinement?"

"As well it should," he said, stretching his legs out along the sofa cushions. "What does that have to do with anything?"

"Imagine, if you like, that you wanted this man to think well of you," I said. "To respect you, even. Would you begin with compliments? With a gift? With sycophancy, or apology, or humor, or modesty? Would it be best to speak first on the subject of Szayet, or Sintia, or Ceiao? Should I reveal the Pearl after some time, when I have put him at his ease, or at once, to throw him off-balance? What authority should I tell him that I possess? What concessions should I be prepared to give on Ceirran's behalf?"

"You don't want him to think well of you," he said flatly. "You want him to do what you say."

"Lord, will you give me *any* advice on how to go about this in a civilized way?" I said.

"If you had any decent power, *civilization* would be whatever you happened to be doing at the moment," he said. "What you want advice on is being a sentimentalist. Was that the door?"

Túlio Cachoeiran proved to be a small, square-faced man, with a shaved head that made him look alarmingly like a priest. He was wearing a snow-spotted black overcoat a little too long for him, a pair of thick glasses, and a collection of silver rings. His skin was pale enough that, when he held out his hand to shake, I could see clearly where they had left green marks on his fingers.

"What a pleasure," I said, and pressed his hand. "Please come in. May I offer you something to drink?"

"The pleasure is all mine," he said, shrugging off his wet coat to a maidservant. He did have a pleasant voice, high and clear, and his Sintian was entirely without accent. "It would be greatly appreciated. Have you any wine?"

"Indeed I do," I said, leading him into the cool white room that sufficed as the house's parlor. "There is a vintage from thirty years ago from an island west of Alectelo, of which we are very proud. Might I—"

"My apologies," said Cachoeiran, "I should have said: I only drink Ceian wine. You will find—if you have not already—that now you are in Ceiao, the quality of grape here is far above anything grown on one of the outlying planets. Have you anything from the lands just over the river?"

This so threw me that it took me several seconds to respond. Cachoeiran misinterpreted: "If you have nothing of the sort," he said, "of course you should not feel me to be put out at all. I will happily drink water, or if you have some, ah, some sort of cultural liquor—"

"Not at all!" I said. "Of course we have Ceian wine. The commander brought over a case the other day that he praised greatly. Casan Ribeirvidon, 102 *dapousto da theomaquían*—was that it, Zorione?"

"Oh," said Cachoeiran, now looking uncomfortable, "madam—I'm afraid Commander Ceirran may not have informed you that particular vintage is, mm—extravagantly priced. I can assure you that some provincial beverage will be perfectly—"

"Why should cost be an object to Szayet?" I said cheerfully. "Zorione, could you fetch us a bottle?"

Cachoeiran settled himself on one of the long red couches I had had carted in and cleared his throat. "I was so pleased to receive the introduction from Flavia," he said. "I'm afraid you must find it very dull here in the Outer City with the suburbanites and foreigners, after the—luxuries—of your palace on Szayet."

"Not at all," I said. "I have been to parties in the Inner City a dozen times already. You have proved such a hospitable people! I am entirely surprised at your generosity."

His fingers twitched, counting back from when I had arrived in Ceiao, and then the corners of his mouth turned down. "You have been a popular guest," he said, now in Ceian. "I can only applaud both the diligence of your society and the attractiveness of your company. May I ask to which events you have been invited?"

I had thought that his Sintian was very good, and I had been right, but it was apparent at once why he was called the master of the Ceian language. There was a formality and a fluidity to his speech in that tongue, which revealed itself in three sentences the way it had not in half a conversation in my own. I thought then of speaking with Alekso on the destruction of Ostrayet—the sensation of being tested, and failing.

"My apologies," I said politely. "I should have said: I don't speak Ceian."

Cachoeiran looked startled, and then his mouth pinched. "What a shame," he said. "As the poets say—*when in a man's home, do as*—"

"But they do say it in Sintian," I said thoughtfully, "if I recall correctly. And you are, I think, in *my* home—unless I'm mistaken about the state of Szayeti sovereignty? Or unless you cannot speak Sintian well enough? We could try Kutayeti or Cherekku. My Belkayeti is not what it once was, but please—whichever is most comfortable for you."

Blushes showed up very clearly on Túlio Cachoeiran. This one crawled up his neck as if he were allergic to his coat. "Of course you are not mistaken," he said. "I can assure you my Sintian is very adequate, madam. I was educated in Sintielo. Thank you for your concern."

"How impressive!" I said. "I'm afraid I was only educated at the Library of Alectelo, but I have always found it adequate for my purposes."

That made him sit up, though a moment later he assumed an expression of nonchalance as thin as linen. "The Library?" he said. "I know it, of course. I have never, regrettably, had the opportunity to visit—I have always wanted to. I planned to, before the civil war, but of course afterward..."

"You may visit whenever you like," I said, genuinely pleased at last. "Of course the war is long over now—the Library sees visitors from every arm of the galaxy. We would be delighted to receive such a distinguished guest."

I had meant him to be flattered, but his look of satisfaction was near unreasonable. "Oh," he said modestly, "not so distinguished. Though I'm afraid I'm a very busy man, and I simply don't know when I'll have the time. But if I should ever be able to get away from my legal work—"

"Or if there's any book that you might want," I said, "only say so."

At this he at last could not hide his delight. "Might you," he said, sitting upright again, "might you have a copy of *Wisdom of de Arajada*? Would it be preserved there? The Sintian libraries have lost it—I spent weeks scouring them when I was younger—but I *know* it remains somewhere in the galaxy, and wherever I travel, I hold out hope—"

"Of course we do," I said. "I have read it myself. I will write at once to the priests."

I had expected another elated outburst, but at this, his expression collapsed. "Ah, yes," he said. "The priests."

This insufferable stumbling block again! "I hope I haven't offended," I said. "It will not be possible to send you the book unless the priests are the ones who fetch it. They are the keepers of the Library, you see."

"I know who keeps the Library," said Cachoeiran. That pinched look had returned. I waited, uncomfortably aware that I would not like whatever he said next, and a moment later he burst out with: "Do you not think, madam, that the care of the Library of Alectelo ought to be placed in the hands of those who might be more responsible?"

I blinked. "I find my priests very responsible," I said. "It was with their aid that the Library was built, in the first instance. In the second, they have kept its contents preserved for three hundred years, under very difficult circumstances."

"Difficult circumstances," said Cachoeiran at once. "Yes, difficult circumstances—and one might ask, for what reason are those circumstances difficult?"

"In a seaside—" I began.

"I will tell you why they are difficult," said Cachoeiran. "It is because the Library sits by the sea, when under any other circumstances it would be on a high mountain in a very dry plain. It is because Szayet is made a wasteland, when under any other circumstances it would be a green and pleasant country. It is because the priests are the priests of a man who had no care for learning, madam, and no love for knowledge. That is why circumstances are difficult, and that is why, rather than kept under the purview of those whose priorities will always lie elsewhere, the Library ought to be given over to an entity who will care for it, or failing that, a newly created—and secular—branch of the Szayeti government."

When I understood his last sentence I felt myself go nearly as red as he was. "You might remember," I said, "that the Library was built by the love of that man's life, who was his first disciple and the carrier of his living voice."

"Ah," said Cachoeiran. "Yes. The famous Pearl of the Dead. For which, I hear, you have received special dispensation. May I see it?"

"No," I said.

Cachoeiran looked not at all perturbed by this. "The Pearl," he said, "is an extraordinary machine, with an extraordinary artificial intelligence, built by an inventor of extraordinary talent. I don't deny this. I rather give the credit for the Library, Madam Oracle, to your highly accomplished ancestor, rather than any computer—and certainly rather than the memory of your ancestor's lover."

I said, "Caviro Orakolo would have disagreed with your opinion of Alekso Undying quite vehemently. So would the Szayeti people, whose Library it is."

At this, Cachoeiran leaned forward on the couch. If there had been any playfulness in his argument, it was gone now, and his eyes behind their bottle glasses were deadly serious.

"Alekso of Sintia committed genocide, madam," he said. "He may be your god—you may think him as undying as you wish—but what he did was a genocide. No flattery or eloquence will make it anything else. If he had lost one battle, he would have been reviled across the galaxy as a monster. As he did not, those unfortunate planets populated by his advocates view him as a god. Very well. I cannot change that. But you cannot convince me to do the same."

"I have no intention of trying," I said.

"I doubt that," said Cachoeiran, "with all respect, Madam Oracle. I have found very rarely that worshippers of Alekso are content to worship him privately. No matter how emphatic they are that their love of the man is an individual one, it always comes out that one must tolerate this or that unreasonable custom, that one must celebrate this or that holiday for the sake of the peace, that one must not speak ill of him in public. This is one of the reasons, madam, that the custom of Ceiao has held so strong against worship for so long. I understand that to you we must seem intolerant. No, I am by no means ignorant of that! But tolerance turns in on itself, more than many of the tolerant understand, and in order to preserve any kind of freedom—in order to preserve any kind of disestablishment—there are steps we can take, *must* take, which may appear restrictive on their surface but to an eye of any clarity are as vital to liberty as oxygen to the blood." He stopped, breathing heavily.

My heart was thumping hard. Looking at this little man with his flushed cheeks and heaving chest, whose works I had pored over with such care in my father's ship as a child, I felt a kind of pity, and was reminded not for the first time how close pity was to disgust.

"You know very little of religion," I said, "and less of gods."

"The faithful tend to say so," said Cachoeiran. "But I can assure you that all that can be read of Alekso I have read. What is more—"

"Did I speak of Alekso?" I said. "I said *gods*. Do you believe there is only one?"

That made Cachoeiran stop dead. His mouth worked and flattened. At last he said, "And what do you mean by that?"

Temper had surged hard in my throat. I swallowed it down. It was only once before that I had loosed my fury before a Ceian whose reputation I admired, and that had been the day I had come out of the carpet. Perhaps some part of me had thought honesty might be rewarded again.

If so, it had learned its lesson. "You say it yourself, Councillor," I said. "In order to preserve any kind of liberty there are steps your city can take—*must* take, which on their surface may seem startling or even repulsive, but when viewed by the trained eye, by the educated eye, by the eye of great wisdom, reveal themselves to be both necessary and vital. What liberty is left in the city when the city lives in fear of the army arriving at its doorstep? What is *freedom* to Ceians when freedom's careful preservation requires the exchange of one tyranny for another? To treat priests as a threat"—I smiled, to cover my feeling at saying it—"to treat priests as a threat is one thing; to treat men of wisdom as a threat is quite another. Men of wisdom like you."

"You speak of the raids, of course," he said, settling back in his chair.

"Of course," I said. "Councillor, I am not coming to you with an argument from faith. By reason alone you must see that your city"—what was it Ceirran had said about how Cachoeiran thought of Ceiao?—"your highly illustrious city, which has stood for centuries as a beacon of liberty to the galaxy, must *act* as a beacon of liberty to the galaxy if it wishes to stand for centuries more. A principle cannot be cast aside in the name of present danger. It is like the keystone of a bridge: It must be bolstered by supports of weight and merit, supports like reputation—like public speech—like friendships with men of power."

At that his smile slid wide, squat and content. "You are well-spoken," he said, "for a Szayeti queen."

"I was educated at the Library of Alectelo," I said coaxingly. "There is more wisdom there than that of de Arajada, Councillor. I am trying to tell you that there is wisdom from Szayet that could be shared, wisdom that *has* been shared. Wisdom that could be shared with *you*, Councillor, if you were only willing to stand on the side of liberty."

His face had flattened into bluntly hungry curiosity, which I might have under other circumstances found charming. "What wisdom?"

"Will you agree to speak against Thiago Veguion?" I said. "And to meet with Ceirran, perhaps, when he returns?"

His nostrils flared. "Is this a negotiation?" he said. "I thought it was a conversation between like-minded people."

"Of course," I said, startled. "Is this not Ceiao? Might it not be both?"

"If it were Ceiao," he said, "we might speak the Ceian tongue," and smiled coolly at me. "Why should I have faith that a friendship with Szayet would offer any wisdom at all?"

I would tell myself, later, that I had had to use my best judgment, and I had meant to show him anyway. And it was true—it was true, of course it was true. I had meant to show it all along, and it was best judgment that drove me, and not temper, or pride, or anything left of the child I had once been.

"Look," I said, and took the second Pearl from the sleeve of my robe.

Cachoeiran looked at it. Then he laughed.

"How marvelous," he said. "Does it work as well as the first?"

"It is exactly the same," I said. "It is the same make, and it has the same maker. It is a receptacle for the human soul. With one exception: It is currently empty. The one who will occupy it is not yet dead."

"Of course," said Cachoeiran, smiling. "You, I suppose?"

"No," I said. "Not me."

His eyes rolled up in thought, and then he chuckled again. "Extraordinary," he said. "Does the commander know?"

"He knows," I said. "He keeps it in his house."

For a while he only looked at the Pearl, and laced and unlaced together his fingers in his lap. His face was very thoughtful and very still.

"This is the wisdom of Szayet," I said. "This is the next three hundred years of power. If you were to befriend the commander, this would be the next three hundred years of your friendship. This is a principle, Councillor, if you would defend it."

His fingers twitched toward it and then stilled again. I shifted in my seat. "What do you think?" I said at last, when the silence had stretched on too long.

He shook his head. "You have, truly, made a wonder," he said, "and I think you even know it. It is nothing but a shame that the strictures of your queenship force you to call it a receptacle for a—a *soul.* In a better world you would be praised as an extraordinary engineer in your own right, and perhaps in a century you will be. I am only sorry that you must claim that it makes a man immortal in this one."

"I am not lying," I said. "This is a Pearl of the Dead, as surely as the one in my ear. The one who lives within it will live as long as the Pearl itself."

He smiled at me with great tolerance. "But, madam," he said gently, "if you really believed you had the technology for immortality, you would never bestow it on Commander Ceirran. Much as I understand your feelings for him are—ah—"

"They are fond," I said, "but nevertheless, I am queen of Szayet and have a duty to that people. Is that what you mean to say?"

Cachoeiran made an apologetic face. I smiled. "I understand perfectly," I said. "Perhaps you should not ask why I have done what I have done, but rather what the next generation of *Dom* Caviro will do."

"What will the next generation of *Dom* Caviro do?" asked Cachoeiran.

"They will take up the next three hundred years of that friendship, Councillor," I said. "They will carry his Pearl. They will be the commander of Ceiao's living voice."

His lip curled, then, and he sat back in his chair.

"What a shame, madam," he said. "A computer is not an heir, however much Alekso of Sintia might have wished it so."

Ice slid into my stomach. "Then you will not be our friend," I said.

"A man that keeps Ana Decretan as his intimate, who is sick over the tables of her entertainers while Galvão Orcadan fights her battles in Far Madinabia, might well consider degeneracy a type of friendship," he said. "You, who keep your people in bondage with madness or with lies and call that government, might well consider going to your knees a type of friendship. But Ceiao is of a different substance—and what you hold in your hand will always be anathema to it."

He could not have known the full scope of what that insult would mean to me, but my knuckles went white. "To your council, you mean?" I said. "I don't doubt it. But have you inquired with your people recently?"

At that, his face went as flat as a painting.

"What an interesting theory you've raised," he said. "I'm afraid it's getting late."

"You may be right," I said, and smiled widely and politely at him. My heart was beating hard. "I hope you enjoyed the wine?"

He glanced at his cup, which was almost full. "Greatly," he said. "Thank you for receiving me." He stood. "What a stimulating evening this has been."

"One last thing, Councillor," I said. "The commander's

friendship may be anathema to you. So be it. You understand that by this you make yourself an enemy to liberty?"

At that he laughed openly. "If you like to say so," he said. "But the Ceian people would certainly—"

"The Ceian people again!" I said. "How kind they are to you. How lucky they must count themselves to have you as one of them. And you really will be one of them, Councillor, if you speak to anyone of the second Pearl of the Dead." He looked blank, and I said, heart pounding, "Do you think Thiago Veguion is the only person capable of ordering raids on the houses of his enemies?"

He went scarlet at once. "You cannot—" he said.

"Of course *I* cannot," I said. "Who is it that was given ownership of the Ceian army?"

Behind his glasses his eyes were as flat and empty as stones. "Your master," he said, "has turned the galaxy into his gaming table. Fortune will be his reward."

"Please get home safely," I said. "I will send you the copy of *Wisdom of de Arajada*. Do let me know if there is anything else I may do for you."

When he was gone, I lay flat on the couch and became hysterical. A few minutes later, I said, "Oh, dear," and sat up.

"Shall I write to request the book he asked for, Holiest?" said the maidservant timidly.

"Please don't bother," I said, pushing myself upright. "I don't see that there would be very much point. Ever-Living God! I had better write to thank Flavia for the introduction. I can't imagine Cachoeiran will be particularly inclined to do it. *What* in the world was he thinking? What was *I*? Oh, Flavia will laugh..."

I put my face in my hands. "Ceirran will laugh," I said, muffled, "until he bursts. At least there's some good in that! Oh—do pour out his wine, I won't drink it. Split it among the servants, if you'd like to. *The quality of grape here*—oh—what a way to win an argument—" And I had to lie down again.

I woke the next morning, threw my mantle over my shoulders, and came down the creaking flight of stairs for breakfast. Rather than bread and honey at the table, though, there was only Zorione. Her arms were crossed over her chest.

"Good morning!" I said. "I feel I'm about to be told off for staying up past my bedtime. What's wrong?"

Zorione said in dire tones, "There's a *man* outside the door, Holiest."

There *was* a man outside the door, who was six foot tall and looked as though he had been built out of concrete. He was dressed in the dark blues of the city guard, and he was standing directly on our stoop, staring at it without blinking. It had snowed last night, and it was going to snow, but the hood of his cloak was not over his head. He seemed so much like a statue I wanted to watch and see if he might let birds land on him. "Hello," I said. "Can I help you?"

I saw his eyes go to the Pearl in my ear and his mouth curl down. "Sergeant Reube," he said. "The city sent me, ma'am. Want to make sure you're following city regulations, ma'am, regarding cult objects."

"How kind," I said. "I am. Good morning."

He pointed to the Pearl. "That's a cult object."

"For which I have special dispensation by Commander Matheus Ceirran," I said. "You may ask at the customs bay."

The sergeant hesitated, and I knew then who had sent him, and why he was there, and it was all I could do not to slam the door in his face. "May I ask," I said, "whether you were sent by the city as a whole, or by one man in particular?"

"I don't see how that's any of your business, ma'am," said the sergeant.

Damn the man! I had taken Cachoeiran for a coward, and I

had not been wrong—but I had not accounted for this. He might adhere to the letter of the law I had given him, but he knew well enough how to have me harassed without alerting any other member of the council to why. "Then please," I said in my politest tones, "don't let me detain you."

The sergeant said, "I think I'd like to take a look round the house, ma'am," and began to climb the steps.

"No," I said.

He stopped and blinked. "Ma'am," he said again, "I'd like to take a look—"

"Certainly I understand you would," I said. "The house, and my person, are Szayeti possessions, and under Szayeti sovereignty. You may not. Was there anything else?"

The sergeant blinked again and cleared his throat. "Yes, ma'am," he said. "I was told that, if you wouldn't consent to a search, I should let you know, ma'am, that in the city's official view, it might be safest for you and your household to remain in the Outer City from now on."

I said, slowly, "The city said what?"

"The city says it's best for your household not to cross the Step," said the sergeant. "Not with that thing in your ear. That's from the whole city, ma'am, not from—not any one person. That's policy."

"That is absurd," I said. "I have left the Outer City a dozen times already. I have walked down the center of the Avenuan Libeirguitan."

"The city says it's for your safety, ma'am," said the sergeant. "We don't know how the people might respond to seeing that kind of thing, ma'am. The conspiracy, and all. People might mistake you for one of those criminals they keep finding. You might be attacked in the street."

I stared at him—then I *did* shut the door in his face, and whirled down my hallway, toward the dining room. "Get

Matheus Ceirran on a holo," I said to Zorione. "Get him immediately."

They tried for half an hour. It was exactly as he had said: Far Madinabia, the Ceian satellite operators informed me, was completely out of holo range, and it did not come closer no matter how I shouted at them or tore pillows or hissed threats into the tablet. At last I calmed sufficiently to restore my presence of mind and messaged Flavia, whose head appeared on my tablet a few minutes later, frowning.

"I'm afraid there's nothing *I* can do," she said. "You really can't get hold of the commander? No? What a pity. Heads will roll when he's back, I'm sure."

"They had better," I gritted out. "You can't talk to anyone at all?"

"Do I look like a member of the Merchants' Council?" she said. "I have to admit, I'm impressed by Túlio. I never thought he had this kind of spine. You really told him Matheus would—? Well, I'm sure his face must have been a picture. I'll visit you sometime soon. Please don't get too bored."

Before I could tell her what I thought of Cachoeiran's spine, she was gone. When I looked outside, the sergeant had multiplied: There were now three blue-suited guards, loitering along the street. I stomped upstairs and swore until my mouth was dry.

"Barbarians, all of them," said Alekso.

He sounded uncommonly cheerful. "This must make you feel very important," I said peevishly, collapsing into a chair.

"I don't need Ceian lawyers to tell me I'm important," he said. "How does it feel to be a prisoner again?"

"I'm not a prisoner," I said. "I can go anywhere—except—"

"—except anywhere interesting?" said Alekso. "Incidentally, do you think this is the last time you're going to get into trouble as soon as your pet barbarian isn't here to protect you? I told you that you were being shortsighted. You ought to have learned by now who you can actually rely on."

"Yes," I said. "I am learning it more every day."

He drifted closer and climbed up onto my bed, where he sat cross-legged with a thoughtful look on his face. "You know why they behave like this, don't you?" he said. "Insist everyone act as they do, believe as they do, enter into their wonderful liberation? They're a lonely people. Seeing someone without their ideals frightens them. They want to embrace him, to bring him into the fold. But however far they spread their thinking, the loneliness never goes away."

I had no interest in replying then, but if I had, I might have told him that I had been lonely for many, many years.

If he asked me today, I might answer differently.

CHAPTER

THIRTY-TWO

CEIRRAN

We had made our camp on a wide, flat plain ten or so miles from the great road, with mountains surrounding it on three sides. This made matters very convenient for the pirates who intended to kill us.

The morning dawned low and humid, and as I sat at my desk holding Gracia's recorder in my palm, the heat itched at my neck like a tongue. I nearly wished I had not left the Pearl with Gracia, so that I could take it out now and turn it over in my hand. To our good fortune, though, there was cloud cover. It was a great inconvenience, having to begin battle at the enemy's invitation, and it was a greater inconvenience having to pretend we did not know it was coming. I meandered through camp as if I had nothing better to do, and spoke with my captains and their lieutenants, and meandered back. It was enough to make me wish for an officer who might crack a ribald joke into my ear, or needle me with her ill-conceived notions of strategy, or go round collecting on some awful bet she had made with one of the enlisted men. It would have been a pleasure to have someone to speak bluntly to.

At last, when it was coming up on nearly three hours past sunrise, I heard a high, sharp series of whistles from across the camp: One of the men on surveillance duty had spotted the gleam of metal in the hills, and there was nothing for it but to draw our guns and withstand the fire.

Otávio fought rather well, at first. I had wondered whether he would. Being clever was one thing, but many clever Ceian minds had died before for want of a body that could keep its calm. But he was as coolheaded as his commanding officers had said, and took cover with me behind one of the tents, where we kept our heads below the hail of red light and I occasionally murmured to him "There," or "Now," where I spotted a pirate who had left his sight lines open.

The pirates were also, to my annoyance, slow, and trickled like honey down from the hills into a circle around our tents. They came in with only enough speed to replace those of their comrades who we had killed. I supposed I should be grateful for it—if they had had any initiative, we might have had to work at holding the standoff.

"I ought to have put the men in shifts," I said to Otávio at last, after a little while. "The day is too hot. Tell me, if you were to organize a ration—"

There was a short, sharp *crack*, and my right eye exploded into stars.

The ground was under my shoulder. That was a surprise. There was a rock digging into my arm, which was an irritation. The whole side of my body stung. I had fallen down.

"Sir?" said a very distant voice, and then, "Cousin?" and then there was a warm, metallic taste on my lips—water. Water, from one of those awful canteens. The world was shifting direction. I gulped it down, not knowing what I was doing, until what had been colorlessness swam, and I became aware that I had eyelids, and could open them.

Above us, the firefight was ongoing. Otávio was crouched above me, eyes wide.

"*Hell*," I said, and sat up, with effort, and wiped at the side of my face. "What happened?"

Otávio pointed behind me. I turned and looked down, and saw a wide, heavy plank of wood, painted gold on one side. When I looked up, I saw the standard it had come from, half-broken: my own.

"Damn!" I said, and looked back at Otávio. I judged him startled but not afraid. "How much—" I had drunk half his water, but there was nothing to be done, and he showed no recognition that I had deprived him, let alone anger. "Did anyone else see?" I said.

"No," said Otávio. "You don't want—"

"No," I said. "My own standard! Bad enough that the men will see it broken." Otávio looked blank, and I said, more shortly than I meant to, "Superstition, boy, don't you know it?"

"But our men are Ceian men," he said.

"No matter what men believe, they all swear by something, and don't ours swear by fortune and misfortune?" I said. "And misfortune is all we need—being knocked unconscious by my own standard is as ill an omen as anyone could ask for." Damn and hell! I felt along my jaw again, where the stinging was worst, and my hand came away wet. "Is there much blood?"

"Yes," said Otávio.

I cursed again and dabbed at it with my hand. It was on the other side from the scar; the mockery from my enemies on the council that would go with a matched set was all I needed. "Is it very deep?"

Otávio was silent. Then, to my surprise, he tipped his canteen onto the edge of his cloak, and raised the hem to my face. I stared at him, and he drew it away.

"No," he said. "It's done bleeding now."

Galvão, seeing me bloody, would have asked me for my orders. Jonata would have gone pale. Anita would have mocked me, and then she would have shot the next man she saw. "Good," I said. "And as for the standard—"

"Sir," he said, nodded, and shifted his gun up. "They're still coming," he said. "Can you see?"

I could, and after that it was hours more of the heat, rising and crouching, crouching and rising. The water in my canteen was draining, too. I had not fought so long after unconsciousness before. I looked at Otávio out of the corner of my eye, when I could, though I often could not. "Can you see any more?" I said to him at last, after what must have been the fourth or fifth hour of steady fighting. He shook his head mutely. His face was pale.

There was no point in rushing the matter now and paying for it later. I watched the hills, fired, fired again, looked back at the hills. They stayed bare. The pirates, in their loose circle, were beginning to shrink in, to press closer to one another. At last I saw, through the tents, one exchange a glance with a man I couldn't see, and then he stood, raised his gun, and began to run toward us.

"Now," I called to Galvão, and Galvão shouted "*Now!*" down the crowd of fighters, and the men beside and beyond him took up the shout until finally, through the crowd, I heard a sharp crack, and then a red flare rising into the humid morning. I held my breath. Ten seconds—thirty—a minute—

—and then, appearing from the haze like lightning, the ships: ten of them, twenty, fifty, swooping down and low to the ground so that the men leapt off them with ease. Downward and downward they came, from every direction, until they were in a great ring around the plain.

If the pirates had been wise, then, they would have pushed inward, and they might have given us trouble for the first time all morning and even made an attempt at capturing me. But they were not wise. My men would not have been able to surround them in any battle where the enemy had air support of their own—they would not have been able to do it against a competent enemy—but there was no shame in humiliating fools.

I bared my teeth and rose. "Come," I said to Otávio, "let's have you taste real blood—"

But he was lying on the ground beside me, his own empty canteen in his hand.

By the time the doctor had pronounced it dehydration and sunstroke, the remainder of the fighting was entirely over, and I had missed it all. I was not so much irritated as afraid. I did not like to sit in a cool medical tent full of beeping machines and sleeping patients, away from combat that my men had seen. I was not one of those commanders who gained his men's love by sharing in all their petty discomforts—I preferred, rather, to award them great shares of plunder at the victory—but no soldier in the galaxy respects a man who hides from danger.

When I left the tent, though, I was surprised to discover a pile of golden items waiting for me in a small glittering heap. When I picked one of them up and turned it over, I was surprised further: It was the shape of a human being. "What are these?" I said.

"Sir," said Galvão. He must have been waiting outside the tent door. "From the pilgrims, sir."

"The *pilgrims*?" I said. "What—are they here?"

They were, masses of them. They were waiting on the far side of camp, huddled in loose white robes. Many of them, I noted, wore the blue tattoos I had last seen when I was driving from moon to moon on Madinabia itself.

"Greetings," I said to them politely, "from the Empire of Ceiao to the province of Far Madinabia. Has your governor sent you?"

There was whispering, and some shoving. At last an elderly person stepped out of the crowd, tattoos so thick on their skin that their limbs might have been dead of frost.

"It is not the governor, Commander," they said in accented but passable Ceian. "It is just us."

"May I help you, then?" I said.

They nodded fiercely. "You helped us," they said. "With the thieves—you helped us."

"It was my pleasure," I said, feeling vaguely that I had entered into a farce. "Can you tell me what this is about?"

They bent down to peer closely at one of the gold statues in my open palm. "Do you know what these are, Commander?" they said to me.

I shook my head, amused. But the tattooed person did not look amused at all.

"These are the guardians, which we brought from Murajil," they said. "Do you know Murajil? You call this a part of Madinabia, the tenth moon of your Madinabia. It's the guardians of our nation. The guardians belonged to our head. This was our commander, who has died. He was killed. Do you understand me?"

I shot a look at Galvão, who shrugged slightly. "I'm sorry," I said, "I'm confused. You're angry? You would like me to return them?"

But when I tried to press one of the little men into their hand, they pushed it away with great force. "No!" they exclaimed, and among the Madinabic there was a flurry of head-shaking. They took my hand—Galvão twitched, but I shook my head at him minutely—and closed my fingers around the piece of gold.

"This is tribute, Commander," they said. "This is tribute. Do you understand me?"

It was with a sense of deep disquiet that I returned to the medical tent. Otávio was looking better: The unpleasant paleness had gone from his face hours ago, and when I pressed my hand to his forehead, he was no longer cold. As soon as I pulled it away, his eyelids flickered.

His eyes were clear and cool, and showed not the slightest hint of confusion. "It's over, isn't it," he said to me.

"It is," I said. "You did well."

To that he only shut his eyes. At last he said: "Cousin—if I were to ask you for something—"

"For what?" I said, startled. He had asked me for nothing in any of the days we had been on this planet.

I heard him exhale through his nose, hard. "I have a friend, now living on Sintia," he said, at last, "whose father fought with Quinha Semfontan."

"They're forgiven," I said at once. "Let them come home." It made me glad to say it, an easy gladness, as simple as the pleasure of drinking cool water. I did not think about how it was like or unlike the feeling of holding the little golden idol in the curve of my palm.

"Thank you," said Otávio. He did not look at me. I could hear the sound of his heartbeat, low in the monitors.

He was up and walking the next day, and we went together to see the prisoners, through the winding paths of the tents in camp. Scattered irregularly along the side of the paths, as if dribbled from the hand of a giant, were a number of oddly shaped lumps, which resembled rocks from a distance. It was only when we came within a foot of them that we could see they had once been skin and bone. In the wet heat of the air their features had deteriorated rapidly, but even if they had not, I do not think I would have recognized them. All of Quinha's friends who had been citizens of any quality were now my enemies in the Merchants' Council.

"Whose work?" I said to Galvão.

"Some of the new captains'," he said. He was looking warily at me. I supposed he expected me to be disgusted. I coughed into my elbow and stepped over one of the heads, which had rolled to rest facedown in the dust by my feet.

The woman who had captured the pirate leader was tall and square-shouldered, with peculiarly Madinabic features and an unhappy curl to her mouth. "Sir," she said, saluting.

"Well done, Sergeant," I said, and clapped her on the shoulders and kissed her on the cheek. "You'll be well compensated for this." At this her frown inexplicably grew, and she gestured to a blunt-faced corporal who was pinning the pirate's arms to his sides. They had gagged him with a strip of cloth, doubtless torn from some soldier's cloak. He was no longer struggling, but I could see the whites of his eyes.

"Show the commander," she said.

The corporal grinned and shoved the pirate down, so that he sprawled sitting in the dust.

After a moment I recognized him: one of Quinha's closest friends, a man of no particular name or money, and who certainly had no seat on the council. I had only ever seen him at her side, fetching her drinks and asking her for petty cash. *Why do you keep* him*?* I had said to her petulantly once, after she had swiped at Anita once too often, and she had laughed and said, *Matheus, you must learn to begin surrounding yourself with people who you think little of; they will never disappoint you.* Which I had only thought many years later that I might have interpreted as an insult.

Sebastião, that was his name—Sebastião Pombal. "Bastião!" I said. "Is this what it's come to for you, without the admiral to ask for petty cash? What a shame. You were once so well respected."

He grunted through the gag. "Take it out," I said to the sergeant. "Were you afraid that he might bite?"

The sergeant said nothing, but the corporal said defensively, "He'd try anything, sir," and knelt to untie the blue rag from the pirate's head. The moment it was gone, the pirate tried to spit in my face, and found that his mouth was too dry.

"Yes," I said, "it is difficult, isn't it. Galvão—take him and put him in the hold. We'll decide—"

"Cousin," said Otávio suddenly. "May I?"

I was surprised, but who was I to deny him now? And I was pleased, too, pleased that the ruthlessness was in him as well as the intelligence, pleased to know that he counted himself the enemy of all the enemies of his family. I had very little family left in the world.

"You may," I said.

Otávio saluted briefly. Then he squatted before Sebastião. It was an ungraceful motion, but he did not seem ungraceful doing it, like a bird stooping in the dust for its food.

He cocked his head—I was reminded bewilderingly again of Gracia on Alectelo, two fingers pressed to the lobe of her ear—and looked thoughtfully into Sebastião's eyes. Then, without ceremony, he forced Sebastião's jaw open with two hands, slid his gun between the man's teeth, and pulled the trigger.

CHAPTER

THIRTY-THREE

GRACIA

It was a long time since I had worn trousers, least of all the tight, ugly Madinabic leggings that were the only type available in the city on short notice. Zorione helped with the strings at the ankles, and I laced up the ties through the rows of eyelets at the waist as best I could. "Are you sure they're easier to climb in?" I said dubiously.

"Very sure, Holiest," she said. "The woman at the market said they were warm, too."

That much I didn't doubt. In the heat of my bedroom, with the woolen Ceian coat over them, they were stifling. "Fine," I said. "I only hope I can walk straight. If I don't return by morning, send a messenger to the council to contact Ceirran on Far Madinabia, and don't let them stop until they've found him."

"Holiest," said Zorione, "you're sure you don't want to hire a bodyguard?"

"I'm afraid it would spoil the point," I said. "Are you quite sure the Pearl is well covered?"

She inspected the braid, which had taken the better part of an hour to carefully craft around the right side of my face, running across my temple and down over the shell and lobe of my ear. "Invisible, Holiest," she said at last. "You'll be safe? You'll be careful?"

"I always was on Alectelo," I said, and when she looked bewildered, I laughed and pressed her hand. "You may go. Thank you. Remember—a messenger to the council."

It was a great deal easier to maneuver myself out the window of my house in the Outer City than it had been in my father's palace. For one thing, it was much closer to the ground, and for another, the chestnut tree had great spreading branches I could cling to. They were damp with last night's snow, but not slippery, and once I had hold of one I could climb down and down until I reached the tiled courtyard below me. From there, it was easy enough to scale the wall behind where loose bricks stuck out at a dozen angles, and to drop down to the sidewalk on the other side.

I had expected to feel triumphant, or smug, or elated at my own athleticism. Instead, to my surprise, I felt like a child, and I wished to walk through my own front door. But I was out in the cold now, and there was nothing for it but to hail a litter. I tried, when its legs skittered over the incline that the Ceians called the Step, to feel some kind of pleasure at it.

After half an hour of wandering I was informed kindly that there were no Szayeti bars in the city—indeed, there were hardly any Szayeti at all—but the neighborhood that lay adjacent to the Kutayeti section of the Outer City had a few spots where people might dance, or perhaps the Cherekku quarter, if they would let me in? I thanked the woman I'd spoken to and asked directions to the Kutayeti bar. It was a cold night, and a ways to walk, but anything was better than going home.

The Kutayeti bar was loud enough to rattle my bones from

their sockets and smelled of orange-flower water and sweat. I thought at first that the orange flower was a deliberate affectation, and realized it was not when my boots stuck to the floor. The sweat was from the dancers—the bar was built to fit fifty, but there must have been a hundred of them, and only a third Kutayeti, if that. Most were Ceian, but I recognized Belkayeti clothing, and Medveyeti, and even the tall white boots of a Muntiru, kicking up in a rapid high-step with her partner. The girl behind the bar was Sintian, and held out her hand for my few centonos before she would push a glass of the orange-flower water at me, mixed with some clear liquor whose bottle was unlabeled. I tossed it back, grimacing at the taste.

The people did not seem to know what they were dancing to. Nor did I, of course—but at home we had at least known the names of our dances, and this dance did not seem to have any name at all. Most were using it as an excuse to artlessly grope one another; the rest were flailing in a failed effort to do the same. I turned to the girl behind the bar for another drink, and when I turned back, found my eye arrested.

There was a lithe, muscled woman in the center of the crowd. I noticed her first for the way she moved—in all that fumbling mass, it took no practiced eye to see her comfort in her own body, her shoulders and ankles and hands, how her hips moved against those of the young woman in front of her. She was wearing sandals whose straps laced up to her knees, and a little pleated cotton skirt barely covering her thighs, and a bright pink feathered coat of such enormity that it was impossible to tell if she was wearing a shirt underneath. Her dark head was flung back in pleasure, and though I could not see her face, I could see a thin trickle of glitter running down the edge of her neck.

I was staring at her so openly that it was no wonder that, when she looked down again, she spotted me at once. Her eyes went wide. There was glitter under them too, little golden rivulets of it, and still more gold in streaks along her cheekbones. She mouthed incredulously, *Szayet?*

I stood at once, my face hot. It was too late, though: Ana was pushing over to my place at the bar, her face shining with glee. "Szayet!" she called, over the music. "Dance with me!"

"No!" I said, or thought I said. Ana's warm hand had closed over mine, and it only occurred to me after I was already on the floor that I could easily have tugged it away.

I had always hated Kutayeti music. The song was just noise, all trumpet and cymbals, and I could feel it shuddering straight from my ankles to the base of my skull, and I was pushed into Ana by the crowd, tugged away, pushed again. I had meant to say something to her—to ask her about my exile from Ceiao proper—but I could not think of it suddenly, could not speak. She had caught my free wrist with her other hand, and now she was swinging me into some kind of four-step—no, this at least I knew; it was Sintian, but when I had learned it on Szayet we had been methodical, eagle-eyed, counting our turns and heel strikes in time, and here in this packed hall one of Ana's hands had slipped to my waist, and in the wrist of the other I could feel her heartbeat, and against my neck her breath.

"What in the world are you doing here?" she shouted into my ear.

"What are *you* doing here?" I snapped back.

"Wasting time," she said, and whirled me away from her and back into her arms, so rapidly that I nearly tripped. She had *meant* to trip me, I realized a moment later when she grinned, and I viciously attempted to replicate what she had done at once—but she was a soldier, of course, and held her ground with ease. Her smile widened.

She leaned in and shouted: "*Now* are you enjoying yourself?"

I stared at her as best I could through the patterning lights and the warmth of her hands on my lower back. She looked entirely different, I thought, with her eyes made up. That flash of cruelty that I knew so well in her face was more distant, and there was a sort of animalism in her, a violence that had nothing at all to do with soldiering. Her hair was falling into her eyes again, and she was wearing some bright, sharp perfume, pine resin and a sweetness whose name I didn't know. Paint her eyes with kohl, and she might have been any noble I had seen at court. She might have been an Alectelan born.

"I am," I said.

"What?" she shouted.

I shouted back, into her ear: "Why do you always mock me?"

Ana grinned at me blankly a moment, then she tilted her head and called, "Let's go outside."

The street in front of the bar was uneven with snowbanks, colored up dull yellow grey beneath the sodium sky. Ana patted the pockets of that enormous coat and produced a battered tin of seeds, which she offered and, when I declined, tipped into a little piece of paper in a long black line.

"Are you really still angry about it?" she said thoughtfully as she rolled the paper up. Her blunt, calloused fingers moved with a surprising dexterity.

"About what?" I said.

"Oh," said Ana, "what I said to you when I was fourteen."

I looked sidelong at her. In the dim light, that wildness from the bar faded. It was easier to see the features of the sharp-faced, smiling girl from those many years ago, the one who had laughed when I told her my father was an Oracle.

"I didn't know you remembered," I said.

"Szayet, Szayet," said Ana, and tucked the tin into her pocket and leaned back against the wall of the bar. "You're a hard woman to forget."

The cigarette smelled sharp, like pepper, and the flame made her brown fingers shine red through cupped hands. She shut her eyes and sighed smoke out into the air. When she tilted her head back to rest against the brick, the streetlights gleamed rain-white on the glitter at her throat.

"In any case," she said, "you remember, too."

I said, "I remember everything."

"Of course," said Ana, and smiled around the cigarette. "Prophecy."

In that winter wind the little stone in my ear felt very heavy, and very cold. "Captain," I said, "do you believe the Pearl has a soul inside it?"

Her hands went still. She blinked—a slow, dark sweep of eyelashes—and said, "No."

"I see," I said, and pulled my coat tighter over my shoulders. "Thank you, Captain. If you don't mind, I ought to catch a litter to the Outer City. I'll see—"

"Do you?" said Ana.

I had begun to move toward the curb, but now I stopped. "What kind of question is that?" I said.

"The one I'm asking," said Ana. "Do you believe in the man in the Pearl? Not that little thing you keep in your house for the commander. I mean the Pearl that lives in your head. Do you think a king is alive in there?" She exhaled smoke. I could not see her eyes. Her voice said, unreadable: "Do you think he made himself a god?"

After a moment I said, "Yes."

But I had taken too long.

Ana didn't laugh this time. She said, eventually, "Why did you pray for the boy?"

I hadn't thought she had even known I had done it. "That is none of your business," I said softly.

"It is my business," she said. "He was my kill."

There was a kind of heat in my chest, which curled up among the heat of the alcohol and mingled in my blood. "All right," I said. "All right—tell me this, Captain: Why are you here? Why aren't you on Far Madinabia with him?"

She began, "He ordered me—"

"He's left you behind," I said. "He's left you behind again. He always leaves you behind."

The reflection of the ember was flickering in her eyes. "Be careful," she said quietly.

"And one day," I said, "one day you'll go running after him, because that's what *you* always do—and you'll find he's gone somewhere you can't follow. And that will be the end of it—and you won't ever see him anymore."

Ana stood up straight, dropped the cigarette on the street, and ground it out with the heel of her sandal. When she leaned in toward my face, her eyes were half-lidded and utterly blank.

"He'll never tell the city that you made him a Pearl," she said. "Never. And do you know why?" Her tongue flickered over her lips, and I flinched. "We're the same," she said, "you and I. You think he'll leave *me* behind? Watch your back, Szayet. He'll never tell the city you made it for him—because he doesn't want you to be his Oracle."

The world went very quiet at the edges.

"He'll never say the thing you want him to say, either," I said. "He'll never say it to you."

I really thought then that Ana would hit me. I could see it in her body: how she turned, how her eyes went bright. I raised my chin, ready for it. But after a moment she unclenched her fist, finger by finger, and worked her jaw, and shut her eyes.

I had no desire to remain on that cold and snow-stained street any longer than I had to, if she was not going to speak to me anymore. I turned to go.

"We work very hard at hurting each other, Szayet," she called out behind me, when I was a few feet away.

I said without looking at her, "I am sorry to tell you that it takes no effort at all."

CHAPTER

THIRTY-FOUR

CEIRRAN

It was Jonata who greeted me at the foot of the stairs at the tower where we were to hold our council meeting, six hours after my ship had settled on the edge of the Nevede under the swift blue winter light of sunrise. "I'm so glad you're back," they said, "but, Matheus, you should know—"

"I know already," I said shortly. "I received data packets from Túlio Cachoeiran and the queen of Szayet as soon as I entered the atmosphere." I had also received a package brought by courier to my front door containing a little black leather case and a Pearl, the knowledge of which Jonata could be spared. "Don't worry," I said, "I intend to resolve things swiftly."

"No," they said, "you should know—Matheus, I voted for it."

I stopped with my foot on the first step. "You—voted?"

"I thought you would want to hear it from me," they said. "Matheus—I heard all of Cachoeiran's arguments for putting some sensible limits on where the Oracle can bring that thing she claims to be Alekso of Sintia, and I want to *talk* to you about them. You have to understand how popular it was in the council—"

"Popular!" I said, thunderstruck. "Jonata, were you brought up to do what is *popular*?" They began to reply, and I waved it away. "It's no matter—I'm not angry with you. We'll talk after I've dealt with the matter. Sit next to me in council."

"You don't intend to *repeal* it?" they said.

The procedure for repealing a council motion was difficult and complex. Any attempt to repeal had to, legally speaking, be the first subject brought up in a meeting, so that the remainder of the council's time could be devoted to debating it. This time was dearly needed, as in the ordinary course of things, a two-thirds majority was needed to either successfully repeal the motion *or* to keep it on the books, and council business could grind to a halt entirely for days while each side strove to convince their fellows of how dire the need was to vote yes or no. Valquíria Barran, being appointed commander in the disestablishment's very early days and being a leader for desperate times, had been made free of this burden: A commander of Ceiao could repeal a motion without the council's vote.

I was not so lucky. "I don't intend to repeal it," I said, "and could not if I wanted to. The secretaries are entirely bought by Thiago Veguion, and I have been conveniently denied the first speaker's slot each time I have asked."

Jonata looked relieved at this and followed me up the winding stairs, past window after window through which the Libeiracópolan's white bulk loomed like a giant's peering face. I could see the silhouette of some Diajundot tourist or Ceian on her day off, filtered through the red window glass. "But I do think we ought to talk," they said. "Cátia and I have been discussing worship, and she has some really intelligent things to say about the whole danger of the thing, Matheus—"

"Of course I want to talk to you," I said, as we reached the top of the stairs. "You ought to come over for dinner one of these days. Before Barran's Feast, if you can manage it. I'll speak to Celestino. Come, we're already late."

The council meetings tended to move from tower to tower, based on petty squabbles, new construction, fashion, or proximity to whichever councillor was most powerful or most irritating in his complaints. For nearly a decade before I had become commander, it had lingered in the vicinity of Túlio Cachoeiran's house. Now it was in a tall, narrow building on the Avenuan Libeirguitan, as near the Libeiracópolan as any building could be that was not a mansion. Its top floor was a great flat room, where hundreds of wooden chairs had been arranged in awkward concentric circles. There was no central seat; in this space, we were ostensibly equal. Neither were there any steps or raised daises or differing levels to the space, which might have caused one Ceian citizen to bow or stoop to speak to another.

Most of the council had already arrived and were sitting on the outskirts of the circle, muttering to one another. After a few moments I spotted Anita's face in the crowd. She was sprawling between two pinch-mouthed councillors, and both of her feet were up on the chair in front of her.

I made my way toward her, and she jerked her chin at me in a nod and took her feet down so that I could sit. The chair she'd saved for me was in the front rows of the circle, not quite at the center. "Barran," she said, to Jonata behind me, grinning. "Met any nice girls lately?"

Jonata made an expression that was probably intended to be a smile and sat next to me, arms crossed. "Matheus, though I love you, I won't have dinner with you if *she's* there," they whispered in my ear.

The council secretary stood before I could reply and cleared her throat. "The Merchants' Council recognizes the honored merchant Rafaela Bazeirron," she said, "on a matter of proposed changes to the provincial tax code."

"Fortune preserve us," whispered Jonata, and gave me a horrified look when Anita chuckled.

The councillors were interminable, but they were always interminable, and knew no other way of living. After the excitement of Far Madinabia, though, it was less endurable than usual to sit among them and wear a placid face and pretend they were as intelligent as they believed they were. The only bright moments were when I shifted or cleared my throat, and every one of them glanced at me at once with wide eyes and frozen expressions. Then, at least, I knew they were bothering to paying attention to what came out of their mouths.

The afternoon, as usual, was given over to the more prominent councillors, and the length of the speech-giving doubled, and then tripled. "When Commander Ceirran was given governorship over the Madinabic peoples," said Cachoeiran, "this venerated council looked upon such an appointment as a great fortune. Who better, after all, to bring civilization to these masses than the man who had spent so much time among them? And when Commander Ceirran returned from Madinabia in order to pursue, hmm, other purposes—noble purposes! Virtuous purposes! It was, nevertheless—I shall say *surprising*, for rather than waste the time of the council by relitigating feuds long past—"

"Fortune forbid we do *that*," muttered Anita, behind my ear.

"Hush," I said.

"—than what greater surprise," Cachoeiran was saying, "to discover that the Madinabic peoples had themselves come to *our* planet; which, rather than to effect the flow of wealth from those well-conquered provinces, as others have done in, for example, Belkayet or Cherekku—"

Anita made a low noise. Quinha was the one who had conquered both, of course. "Hush," I said again.

"I do not seek to accuse," Cachoeiran said, "and may I be prevented by all sensibility and reason from doing so! Rather, as a

Ceian and businessman, I simply seek to question: Why, discontented with the quality of Ceians at home, does Commander Ceirran seek to change our population? Why, on a map that since time immemorial—"

As we wound our way down the tower staircase, after the speeches had concluded and the meeting had broken up, Anita said meditatively: "If I had a planet of my own, I think I'd ban lawyers."

"I had no idea your ambitions were so high," I said. "In Arqueiran or the Shieldmirror?"

"Whichever you can spare, I'm not fussy," said Anita. "Just make it warm. How long has this winter gone on? I'm so damned tired of freezing half to death whenever I take off my tunic."

"Try leaving your tunic on," I said.

"Why?" she said. "Oh, hello, Túlio."

He was waiting for us at the bottom of the stairs, arms crossed over his chest. "If what you wanted to speak to me about is the Szayeti woman," he said, "I am sorry to inform you that it was not *my* decision, but the decision of the council as a *whole*—"

"Who said anything about the Szayeti woman?" said Anita merrily. "Not at all, Túlio. What you and I need to talk about is money."

"Money?" said Cachoeiran. He looked abruptly hunted.

"Money," Anita confirmed. "What a lot of trouble it is, isn't it? Especially if you haven't got any—*especially* if you spent all your military service stamping papers and never had any plunder! I know Flavia had all sorts of problems before her marriage. You aren't married, though, are you, Túlio?"

"I have never had that pleasure," said Cachoeiran stiffly.

"No," said Anita, "you strike me as someone who hasn't."

"Captain," I said reprovingly, and caught the edge of her grin. She knew this game well enough. "Councillor," I went on, "I would like a word with you. Jonata tells me you gave a very passionate speech in favor of the motion against the Oracle. I don't doubt that if it was your oratory, it was magnificent."

The sad thing about Ceiao's greatest speaker was not that he was easily flattered, but that the same flattery worked every time. He uncrossed his arms. "Well," he said modestly, "I might say it was one of my better ones—but no, I tell a lie. The refutation was lacking in the fourth section, I think."

"Not at all," I said. "But what a shame that your talents should be manipulated to such ends! When I think that, rather than carrying out Thiago Veguion's vendettas and feuds, you might be made the soldier for a better cause—"

But that made him cross his arms again. "I am no soldier," he said.

"Not at all," I said, mentally cursing. "Forgive me. The metaphor sprung to mind. I only mean to say that, were you in the service of something greater—"

Cachoeiran glanced from me to Anita and back again. "I am in the service of nothing at all," he said reedily, "and I must tell you and your—captain—that I'm not desperate enough for *money* to sell my opinion on"—he glanced at the passersby, and waited until they had drawn out of earshot to continue—"the actions of the queen of Szayet. I tell you I have been baldly threatened. I should think my dignity is worth more than a few dekar."

"Don't be absurd," I said, now irritated. "What politics are you playing, Councillor? Speak plainly. What reward would assuage your *threatened dignity*? Is it property you're angling for? Some motion you're missing votes on that I've overlooked?"

Cachoeiran's mouth worked.

"I don't wonder that you don't understand it," he said at last, "because it is a matter of principle."

CHAPTER

THIRTY-FIVE

GRACIA

I'm not shocked," I said.

"I'm shocked," said Ceirran heatedly, and paced back to the other end of my sitting room. "Have I not just returned from defending Ceiao from her foes? Is my triumph not in another month? A matter of *principle*, he says—as if he has any principle besides pride!" He stopped himself halfway across my carpet, and tucked his hands behind his back, and bent his head formally toward me. "My apologies, my dear, it's you who should be insulted."

"I've already been insulted," I said. In the last weeks, after that single night of dancing, I had hardly left the house. The adrenaline had carried me home and no further, and when it drained away it had left me as empty of purpose as a town under tide. Hanging golden bracelets over my wrists and smearing kohl onto my eyes had felt as if I were doing it to a doll. "I am insulted, of course. I'm not shocked. If he says it is a matter of principle for him, I believe it."

He drew closer to the couch, head tilting. "I'm surprised," he said. "Frankly, Patramata, I expected that you would tell me to reveal the Pearl to the city at once, claim divine right, and institute an Island of the Dead a mile down the Nevede."

I smiled at him as best I could, but his words made me think of what I had most been trying to forget, and the smile dropped. "Do you know," I said, "he told me he wished the Caviros had never allied with Ceiao in the first place?"

"He?" Ceirran said, and then realized who I meant, and laughed uneasily. "Did he? Should *I* be insulted?"

"If you are insulted," I said, amused, "I'm sure he'd be pleased to know about it."

"You haven't spoken to him in a while," he said.

I looked at him sharply, but his face was friendly. "No," I said. "Well—you haven't seen it. You've been away."

He shrugged. "I have," he said, "but even before."

I turned my answer over on my tongue thoughtfully. "I've been queen a longer time," I said at last. "I need to ask him for less, I suppose—the same way one might need to refer less and less to a dictionary, as one learns a new language."

"Is he a dictionary?" he said, smiling. "I thought he was the source of all authority in Szayet."

I returned the smile at once—that was easy, rote and reflex, like jerking back a finger when burned. "You're right, of course," I said. "My mistake. I ought to speak to him more often."

His eyes narrowed, then he sat beside me on the couch. "You're angry," he said.

"Of course," I said. "As you said—I have been insulted."

"Not at Cachoeiran," said Ceirran. "Patramata, are you angry at me?"

For a moment the breath caught in my throat. I stood and crossed to the other side of the room, where the sky hung heavy and grey through the window glass.

"I've—" I hesitated. "I have been thinking."

"About what?" he said.

It was difficult to find the words, difficult in a way it had not been since those first days on Szayet. "You are the commander of the city of Ceiao," I began tentatively.

"You *do* want me to claim divine right and install an Island of the Dead," he said. "I might have known."

I whirled. "Do not mock me," I said. "Ceirran, you are the commander of the city of Ceiao. You are the first to hold all its armies since your hero who killed its gods. You are the most powerful man these last three hundred years have known."

"I know that," he said, frowning.

"Do you?" I said. "Then why do you sit in my parlor stymied because you have failed to talk a lawyer away from his *principles*?"

"You failed, too," he said. The laughter had disappeared from his face entirely.

"I had nothing more than talk to work with!" I said. "Why do I neglect my god? Ceirran, why in the world would I want to speak with the source of all authority on Szayet when it is the source of all authority on Ceiao in whose hands my fate rests? I have given you a gift—"

"And have I given you nothing?" he said, standing. "Is that all that lies between us, Patramata? A catalog of mutual debt?"

"Don't misconstrue me," I said. "I am trying to say that I have invested myself in you, and now I have paid a price for it, and I want to know whether you—" *He's left you behind*, I heard, in my own cold voice, and my stomach twisted sourly. "If *I* were commander," I said, "if I had a seat on the Merchants' Council, if I had Ceiao's ten million ships—"

"You mistake my position," he said.

"I do not," I said.

"You do," he said sharply. "You think because my authority is extensive it is infinite. You think the whole mechanism of the empire is a single man. You might have thought of that before you offered a threat on my behalf, without stopping to ask me if it would be convenient for me to follow through. My office is not a sword you might use to cut through every knot. I cannot—"

"I am not ignorant of the empire," I said. "I have never been ignorant of your empire. *Cannot?* What is *cannot*? You *will* not, either because you are afraid"—he made a low noise in his throat, which I ignored—"or because you do not think it worth the effort, because you do not think my exile worth dulling your *office's* precious blade on—"

"What am I meant to do?" he snapped at me. "You are only a client queen!"

The silence lingered.

"I am sorry," he said, at last. "That was ill said."

I said, "There is no need to apologize for telling me the truth."

"I think there is," he said, and sat down heavily. "Patramata, I am sorry. It was crude."

I turned to look out the window again. There were crows on the building opposite the street, two of them, one with its neck stretched, the other preening at the back of its companion's head. The winter light picked them out in two stark tones: black feather, white sun, black beak.

"I missed you," he said, "when I was away."

I turned back. Under the light he was two-toned, too, and abruptly I saw him as I might painted on a wall: not a face, but only lines and flat shapes, arranged against one another to provide the illusion of a man. Then he tilted his head and was himself again.

"I missed you, too," I said.

His brows drew down, but he did not ask me whether it was true. I do not know now whether I am glad of it.

"Will you forgive me?" he said.

I closed my eyes. It was a small thing to say.

"I will," I said.

He exhaled. "If I return tomorrow," he said, "will you meet with me for dinner?"

"Where else would I be?" I said.

CHAPTER

THIRTY-SIX

CEIRRAN

Gracia's words lingered when I left her house, and they lingered when I climbed into my spider-litter, so much so that I hardly saw the Outer City pass by around me. After half an hour's travel, I tapped the front panel of the litter to reveal a standard-issue tablet and stylus, which I removed and woke with a pass of my hand. It took me some time to find the event I was looking for—I received at least a dozen party invitations every day—but it was short work from there to open the holo I wanted.

There were bags beneath Anita's eyes when she fuzzed into clarity before me, and her expression was uncharacteristically cold. "Are you well?" I said, alarmed. "You aren't sick?"

"Ill? Me?" she said. "Not at all," and after a moment, grinned. "Saw your location. Thought you might be someone else. It doesn't matter. What do you need?"

I hesitated, but I had never known her to keep any secret from me that I truly wanted, and it was often safer to let her have her little lies. "If you are well," I said, "I thought I might attend a party in the Inner City, and I don't intend to go alone."

We met an hour later at the door of the house, a narrow-windowed little thing with a few lanterns stuck along its front steps, blinking the unpleasant yellow of cheap chemicals. Nearly every event I had attended in the last three years had been somewhere along the Avenuan Libeirguitan. It was an unpleasant shock of nostalgia to recall how drab and tedious the other parties were, and only the surprise at my arrival dulled the inanity of the conversation. Anita drifted along at my side, glancing at me with amusement whenever any piece of flattery fell particularly flat, and with her company I kept myself alert and smiling until I heard a familiar thin voice and swept toward it.

"Joaquim Nequeiron," I said, "what a pleasure."

"Commander! The pleasure is mine," said Nequeiron, but he said it to Anita, who was behind me, looking like a cat that had caught a bird. His cheeks were dark, I realized, with more than drink.

At once I discovered the overwhelming need to be elsewhere. "All my apologies," I said, "I see a colleague at the bar. If you'll excuse me—"

As I moved, though, Anita caught my sleeve. "Commander," she said, and when I bent my head to hers: "You were right: He is in debt. Desperate."

"For money?" I murmured dryly and, when Anita grinned like a shark, shook my head infinitesimally. "Attempt discipline, Captain, if it's not too much trouble. How much?"

She named an amount, twice what my expectation had been. "I'll sign any papers," I said, "if you bill my household the arrangements. Captain? It's all to go to Nequeiron directly. Do you understand?"

"Perfectly," she said, by which she meant that when she poured half of it away on wine and clothing, she would not let herself be caught, but it amounted to the same, for my purposes.

"And I hope that he will have the inclination to attend the council meeting tomorrow," I said, "if he finds himself sober enough. Do you understand *that*?"

Her grin widened. "Perfectly," she said. "Thank you *very* much," and brushed past me to catch Nequeiron around one narrow hip. "Joaquim, Joaquim," she said, "when was the last time you went out dancing?" He went still redder, and she laughed and patted his thigh, at which I turned firmly around and went to the bar to inter myself in an endless conversation about my own calendar reforms.

I had entirely forgotten how slow this part of the year was in the city, without the mayhem of civil war and foreign conquest to distract me from the empty time. The only calendar day of any real import for months was Barran's Feast, a month before spring, which every worker and layabout outside the Inner City celebrated by drinking themselves half to death, marching from the Step down along the Avenuan Libeirguitan waving flags and singing patriotic nonsense half-remembered from school, and stuffing themselves with the free sweets handed out by the city. I enjoyed it well enough ordinarily, but just now the thought of it irritated me—a distraction from my business, exactly the kind of dead sentiment that men like Cachoeiran thought the city should love best—and when I looked for Anita, so that I might tell her so and hear whatever mockery she thought would puncture my mood, she had already vanished into the night.

A good night's sleep did a little to repair my humor, but I still sat alone in the council room the next morning, and smiled and shook my head at Jonata when they waved me over. It was a little while before all the councillors were filed in, and then the secretary stood, brow furrowed.

"There's been a recent change to the agenda," she said. "The Merchants' Council recognizes—Joaquim Nequeiron?—on a matter of regulation for the gem trade?"

Nequeiron pushed himself up, his dark head barely visible over the crowd.

"I wish—" he squeaked. "I wish the council to know—that my matter has been resolved out of session."

"What a relief," said Thiago Veguion loudly. He was staring directly at me. I was very sure he did not know what was happening, but he was, as little as I liked to admit it, no fool. Nevertheless, at the sight of his face, the remnants of my ill temper vanished like candle smoke. I smiled pleasantly at him. "Who's next?"

Nequeiron made a noise like a deflating balloon and waved a hand weakly. The secretary cleared her throat. "Next—" she said.

"Excuse me," said Anita pleasantly. "Did the honored merchant yield his time?"

Somewhere to my right, I heard Cátia murmur something like *Oh, for—* "I believe," the secretary said doggedly, "that the next scheduled speaker is—"

"I don't believe the honored merchant *did* yield his time," said Anita. "Did he?"

"Erm," said Nequeiron, who was looking as if he greatly regretted taking the nine-hundred-dekar loan he had asked for. "I—"

"He's certainly not sitting down," said Anita. "Were you done, Joaquim? Or was there something you wanted to tell the council?"

Nequeiron glanced down and seemed to discover to his own discomfort that he was still standing up. "Erm," he said again. "As my matter has been resolved—I wish to yield my time to—to the honored commander of Ceiao, Matheus Ceirran."

There was a great groan from the council at this. One woman shoved her chair back and left the room, muttering something. I glanced at Anita, who gave me a grin that said, *Yes, I know her name.*

"Thank you, honored colleague," I said, standing, and looked around at the councillors. Barboulethan looked bewildered. Cachoeiran looked murderous. Jonata only looked concerned, and I pulled my eyes away from their face. Anita wasn't smiling, not yet, but her gaze was as unblinking as a snake's.

"As I have the good fortune to act as first speaker today," I said, and ignored Cachoeiran's snort, "I invoke my privilege as commander to pass a repeal."

Thiago Veguion muttered something that had the word *surprise* in it. "Please," said Cátia, her voice dry as a bone, "enlighten us."

"I repeal the motion to restrict the movement of Altagracia Caviro Patramata to the Outer City," I said. Cachoeiran sneered, but his face froze when I said, "Furthermore."

"Furthermore?" said the secretary, sounding as if she had never heard the word.

I have invested myself in you, I heard in Gracia's voice, *and now I have paid a price for it, and I want to know whether you—*

"Furthermore," I said, "I also repeal all motions banning cult objects within the territory of Ceiao. I end restrictions on the possession of idols, mats, books, lights, food or drink, smoke, or other substances and materials that may be used for prayer. Nor are there any restrictions on the carrying of religious objects publicly, or the wearing of religious clothing. No motion shall be passed by this council which acts to punish the users of cult objects. Any such motion that has been passed is, from this moment onward, null and void."

For a moment there was absolute silence. Then the council room burst into shouting.

I shoved my chair back and stood, and swung my cloak over my shoulders. Anita stood, too, and strode swiftly through the shoving councillors toward me. Now she was smiling, and it was not a snake's smile but a tiger's.

"Ceirran," Cachoeiran was saying into my face, "Ceirran, you can't—"

"The commander is leaving," said Anita, and turned that smile into his face. When Cachoeiran tried to push past her, Anita shifted her feet and sent him stumbling across the floor, and before I could see whether anyone had bothered to lift him up again, she had me out the door.

We were silent for some time as we made our way down the stairs, and the white dome out the window receded below the buildings. Then, as we were crossing toward the door of the building, Anita snickered—hiccuped a laugh—and, as if a dam had burst, started laughing so hard she needed to sit down on the floor. I waited patiently for her to finish, but I was smiling, too.

"Commander," said a voice behind me.

I turned. It was Cátia, poised on the stairs.

"You won't be able to do that again," she said. "Tomorrow your colleagues will come prepared."

"Is that a threat, Councillor?" I said.

Her face didn't move. "I would never threaten you," she said.

"No," I said, "I thought not," and rounded the corner into the street.

CHAPTER THIRTY-SEVEN

GRACIA

Ceirran was gone to the Merchants' Council the day after our argument, and it was Flavia who caught me in the morning, in a spider-litter that skittered up to my door as sleet heaved itself down from the heavens and the wind howled through the branches of the chestnut tree. "What a terrible day to try to cheer you up in!" she shouted, tugged me from my front step through the door of the litter, and pulled it shut behind us. "If I were one of the common people, I'd call this ill-fortuned from the start. How *are* you?"

The inside of the litter was full of heat, golden light, and the smoke-treacle scent of her perfume. "I'm well," I said. "I'm very well, honestly—you're generous, but there's no need to spend your day coddling me. The commander has done his best."

"Nonsense," said Flavia briskly, and tapped on the brass panel behind her, so that underneath us the engines jolted into life. "He knows very well I can outdo him, and he would never forgive my failure. Should you go back to Szayet complaining of *every* Ceian's hospitality? Besides, I've already paid for the litter." She pushed back one of the curtains on the window to peer out and winced. "Though I fear his idea about picnicking is a doomed prospect."

That startled a real laugh out of me. "Picnicking?" I said. "In the dead of Ceian winter? Did he really expect that would bear fruit?"

"Oh, the two of you have both had more ill-thought-out ideas," said Flavia, so gaily that it nearly took the sting out of it. "In any event, we can make it a little ways north of the river, and see some of the scenery—which is more than plenty of Ceians ever do, you know!—and which ought to distract you from the places you *can't* go, or if it doesn't, I certainly hope my conversation can." She settled back into the cushions with a satisfied sigh. "Besides, I was told the storm ought to end in an hour or so. Though if it doesn't, I'll be asking *you* to pass on my complaints to the responsible party, Madam Oracle."

I laughed again, since she meant me to, and let myself relax a little. Despite her artfulness and perspicacity, despite the sharp, unpredictable edge of her wit—despite the tightness that came to my throat when I thought of her sister—there was still a real comfort in Flavia's company, her effusiveness and studied charm, and her conversation did carry us from my house all the way to the Nevede, where she tapped the brass panel again and brought the litter sliding to a stop.

"I don't doubt the river can bear this little beast," she said. "It's frozen as thick as a Madinabic skull, but I was hoping—ah, yes!" She popped open the litter door. "The snow's stopped. For now, anyway. Come out and admire it, won't you?"

The air was still bitterly cold, but the clouds had thinned, and the sun was a pale ring of light. The river, which I had last seen roiling grey through the Gate of Shattered Chains, had frozen as flat and bright as a tablet. Along its surface and beneath the bridges, wrapped up in great coats and bright scarves, Ceians of all ages slid and spun and whooped. To our left and our right, more than a mile down the river in each direction, I could hear the engine rumble of ships about to depart, whose predecessors' fading smoke still hung in the air in thin streaks.

"I don't suppose you've ever been ice-skating?" said Flavia to me.

"Never," I said. "It hardly snows at home. Do you intend for me to learn?"

"Not in front of half the city," said Flavia, laughing. "I wouldn't like to damage Szayet's dignity so badly! But you and I might slide across, and the litter can go over the bridge without us—what about that? Here—" She pulled a wrapped foil package from the pocket of her coat and unfolded it with gloved hands, fumbling only a little, to show me one of the raisin-studded buns they sold from stands on Ceiao's streets. "It's only a little of the promised picnic, of course, but it's from my own kitchens. Will you have half?"

The bun was still hot from the foil, and it kept my hands warm as I watched Flavia push herself gracefully onto the ice, sliding a few feet forward on her boots before her momentum ran out. "You'll be a natural," she called back to me. "Come try it!"

It did come naturally, at least after my first uncertain steps. My boots were far from appropriate for the snow, but over the ice they sailed as smoothly as a swan, and once I had stopped trying to keep my movement entirely under control I even began to enjoy myself. When I caught up to Flavia, her nose was red with cold and she was smiling.

"Is the bun good?" she said. "Yes? Are you suitably cheered up?"

"I am," I said, laughing. "You have done a great service to Ceiao's hospitality."

"And they say Matheus brings home victories!" said Flavia. And then, when we had slid a little ways farther out onto the ice: "I heard you spoke with my sister recently."

I skidded to a stop and nearly slipped, but she caught my arms and steadied me on my feet. "Don't fall there, I think," she said. "The ice isn't so thick in every part. Szayet's dignity isn't the only thing that might be in danger!"

I nodded my thanks without much grace and pushed forward again. "I did meet Ana," I said. At once I disliked conversing in the cold like this, the way my words puffed into the air, pale but unmistakably visible. "I didn't know she had mentioned it to you."

"She didn't say much," said Flavia behind me, "only that she had seen you dancing. She said you danced well." And, while I was trying to think of how to answer that, and trying to think whether she might be lying, she slid up beside my shoulder and said, "Why don't you call her Anita? She wouldn't mind."

I looked straight ahead, where the far white bank with its straggling black pines was growing before us. "I suppose I have never thought of her that way," I said.

She made a thoughtful noise, but she reached the bank before me, and we were straight away both caught up in the business of climbing up onto dry land without ruining our robes and mantles. At last we were both on solid ground, only a little worse for wear, and Flavia leaned one hand on a pine tree and dusted the remaining snow from her boots, huffing. "Well, I can't think where the litter's gone," she said. "These things are so cursedly slow when the streets are iced over. But there's a little copse beyond all this, and a good view of the mountain."

All this was a narrow, cracked grey road just through the pines. Across from the road sat an enormous brick building, with white letters on the side too faded for me to read. There was also a pervasive, unpleasant chemical smell, which I had half noticed while we were crossing the river but which here was heavy and undeniable. I stepped out through the trees, scraped my shoes off as best I could on the road, and tilted my head up. There were three great chimneys on top, trickling white smoke into the air. This must have been the source of the smell.

"What is this?" I said.

"Oh, this?" said Flavia, behind my shoulder. "That's just Cátia Lançan's factory. Isn't it awful? There's more like them all along the river. One of the reasons land within the Step is at such a premium, of course. If I had to breathe this in all day, I'd sell my own tongue to afford another house."

"Could we see inside?" I said.

"Inside?" she said doubtfully. "I don't see why not, but I don't see why you'd want to. Are you sure? Well, all right. Let's see if there's a staircase. I don't think you want to walk in through the machinery!"

There was a rickety metal staircase around the back, and at its top a wooden door that led to a bewildered doorman, a long, poorly lit hallway, and a highly flustered factory manager, who shook our hands with a kind of gallant panic and offered to show us around his office. "I'm afraid I can't go into too much detail about the books, of course," he said, "but if you like, I could call Captain Lançan, and she might tell you the details herself?"

I understood the ubiquity of the Ceian officership, of course, but it was unsettling to encounter *Captain* before Cátia's name. "There's no need," I said. "I don't think it was the books I was interested in, anyway." I hesitated. "Is there any chance we might go down on the floor?"

He gave me a startled look, as did Flavia. "Yes," he said, "yes, of course, I—Kadlec? Kadlec, can you come into the office, please?" A tall, dark Medveyeti appeared at the door, frowning down at us. "These ladies would like to look around the floor," said the manager, slowly and very loudly. "Can you help them?"

The Medveyeti led us down another flight of stairs in the hallway in near silence. It would have been difficult to speak even if he had tried: The noise of metal scraping metal was audible as soon as he opened the door, and by the time we reached the bottom it was deafening. In every direction were machines, whirling and swinging and stamping and shoving themselves up and down with frightening force, throwing off sparks at angles that sent me flinching into Flavia, and where there was not metal there were people, packed shoulder to shoulder, tugging on controls or staggering under great pieces of metal or deep in the guts of one of the mechanisms. They were dark-cheeked and sweating, dressed in faded tunics, hair braided back or tied into cloths. They were so intent on their work none of them looked round at us, and those who did only wove around us as if we were an obstacle like a dropped tool or a shrugged-off coat.

"We make parts only," the Medveyeti called to us, over the terrible shriek of the machines. "They make full ships in different factory." He eyed us with visible uncertainty. "You want to see something? A machine you like?"

Flavia, who was lifting the skirts of her robe delicately with one hand and picking her way over the floor with care, glanced back at me and mouthed *Can we go?* I hesitated. I had not known why I had wanted to see the factory. It had been an impulse so unexpected and so powerful that I had not thought further. "I think—" I began, when there was a shriek so terrible that Flavia and I both clapped our hands to our ears—and then silence.

The Medveyeti said something in his own language, which I did not understand but whose tone made its meaning plain. "One moment," he said. "Please stay here," and he shoved his way through a mass of people toward an enormous crane-like steel monster, from which I could now see a bar was dangling like a broken limb.

I turned uncertainly toward Flavia, who was making a face of disgust at me—and then saw a woman over her shoulder, head bowed and hair wrapped in a linen kerchief with Sintian letters stitched along its borders. Sintian letters, I thought in confusion, but not the Sintian language—and then I understood what language it was, and finally knew what urge had driven me here.

I pushed past Flavia, whispering a frantic excuse. "Madam," I said to the woman in Sintian. "Madam—hello. May I ask your name?"

She opened her mouth, and then she took in my ear, and her eyes went wide at once. They were ringed with kohl. "Holiest," she said, and she made a small and terrible noise, and covered her face.

"Madam!" I said, surprised, and reached out to touch her hand, at which she squeaked again. "I'm sorry—please let me see you. Have I hurt you? I only wanted to know your name."

She lowered her hands, slowly, but she would not meet my eyes. "Franciska," she whispered. "Franciska Kolody."

"Franciska, you don't know how glad I am to meet you," I said, and meant it. "Might I ask—are they treating you well here? Is this—are you happy? Are they paying—" But I stopped, then, because she was shaking her head frantically, her hands creeping up toward her face again.

"Holiest, forgive me," she whispered in broken Sintian. "I can't. They would not allow."

"There is nothing to forgive," I said, automatic, but she shook her head. She was trembling.

"Forgive me," she said urgently. "Forgive me that I don't humble myself in front of you."

I stared at her, how her throat worked, how her eyes were wide and fixed on the floor, and I swallowed hard. If I had been on Szayet, I would have pressed two fingers to my ear at once. But I was not on Szayet—and, to my own surprise, I did not want to touch the Pearl at all.

"I forgive you," I said in Szayeti, and took one of her hands and kissed its knuckles. "I forgive you. You have come before the face of the king, and in His sight you are welcome and your children are welcome, from generation to generation."

Her shoulders jerked, and her hands went to her face. "Holiest," she said, and I believe would have said more, but I turned as quickly as I could and walked away, so that she would not see the look on my face.

Flavia tucked her arm through mine when I rejoined her and smiled quizzically. "Well," she said, "have you seen all you wanted to see?"

"I have," I said. "Thank you for indulging me."

"Think nothing of it," she said, in a tone that made me sure she would be thinking it over more than I liked.

The litter was waiting for us outside at last, in a low blue wintry light against which the pine trees and the city lights stood out like jewels. Flavia slid in, tapped at the front panel until it popped open, and pulled a tablet from it into her lap. "Well, we'll be a little while crossing back from the river," she said. "If we hurry, we ought to get there before real nightfall, though Fortune knows that's a challenge this time of year."

"Not at all—I didn't mean to ruin your plan for the day," I said. "I am sorry, Flavia. If you'd like, we can go farther. Was it a copse of trees you were speaking of?"

"Oh, no, I've been told to get you back home well in time for dinner," she said, tapping with the stylus at the tablet. "Our commander has something he'd like to tell you, though you didn't hear it from me."

My head snapped up, the factory entirely forgotten. Flavia was looking down, but her mouth was curling up at one edge. "Do you mean to say—" I said.

"You didn't hear it from me!" she said. "Let him break his own news, for once—though you may want to avoid Túlio's company for a while, I think. And perhaps Jonata Barran's, too."

The spark of happiness inside me fizzled. "Jonata?" I said. She inclined her head, and I said, "I am sorry to hear that. I know the commander is—fond of them."

Flavia set the tablet aside on the cushion and smiled at me thoughtfully. "He is, isn't he?" she said. "And I don't suppose he's ever told you the reason?"

"I didn't know there was a reason," I said, startled.

"Oh," said Flavia, "there is. He was in love with Sílvio, Jonata's older brother."

I tried to keep the shock off my face, but I did not succeed. Flavia looked as satisfied as a cat with a bird. "This was long ago, of course," she said. "Do you know that Jonata's parents died when they were very young?... No? Well. Sílvio was fifteen, luckily, and he took care of them until Jonata was of age and could go into school. It kept him away from any real promotion or plunder, but what's to be done? The two of them were inseparable. You never found one without the other. Ceirran would have courted Sílvio, if he had had the money at the time. He didn't, and Sílvio married another, a Sérgio Catílion. But they still wrote each other love letters for many years—very passionately, I believe. Matheus was made to read one aloud in a council meeting, once, when Túlio was first beginning to grow paranoid about people conspiring against him. It was a terrible scandal. He's never forgiven Thiago Veguion for it."

"But where is Sílvio Barran now?" I said. "Surely not in the city."

"No," said Flavia, "he certainly isn't. Sérgio lost his fortunes, and his seat on the council, and it happened that Túlio was right: He conspired to raise arms against the council. He promised the people he would relieve all debts. He was shot in the square. Quinha and Matheus only narrowly escaped being implicated themselves, and after that they pledged allegiance, and Matheus went to Madinabia. But Sílvio wasn't so lucky. He was disgraced, and rather than be forced into exile, he swallowed hot coals."

She paused. "I thought for a while that Matheus would never forgive him for it."

"Forgive him?" I said.

Flavia seemed not to hear me. She said, quite quietly: "That was when my husband was killed, too."

That struck me silent, at least for a while. "I hadn't heard you were married," I said at last.

"I'm not," said Flavia. She did not look at me, but she said to the window of the spider-litter: "Teo was much older than me, in any case, and balding, and rather full of himself. But the people loved him."

"And you, of course," I said.

She raised her eyebrows. "Me, of course?" she said, but after a moment her expression softened. "You mustn't think I'm cold-hearted," she said. "This is Ceiao, Oracle. The question isn't what you *feel*—anyone can feel, and I wish all fortune upon those who do. The question is what's to be *done* about it."

"Still," I said. "I'm sorry."

Flavia leaned back on her cushions and pulled aside the curtain. Outside the clouds had scattered at last, and the snow was beginning to trickle into the gutters in dark rivers.

"I don't wonder he hasn't told you about it," she said, almost apologetically. "I would be surprised if he even thinks of it now. He forgives easily, and forgets easily. You know him."

"I do," I said. "I do know him."

CHAPTER

THIRTY-EIGHT

CEIRRAN

Gracia burst from her house like a ghost when my spider-litter came to meet her and nearly flew across the street, her robe fluttering behind her like an insect's wings. "I heard," she said. Her face was alive again and glittering, though whether it was with triumph or relief or amusement I did not know.

"You haven't heard all," I said. "I am going to move you out of the Outer City."

She shut her eyes and smiled. "You are," she said, and stood on her tiptoes to kiss me through the litter window. "Have you already picked out a house?"

"I have," I said. "It is on the Avenuan Libeirguitan."

She kissed me again, more deeply, and when she pulled away, her eyes were shining.

"Is this only out of spite?" she said. "You can say yes."

"No," I said. "A little—yes. But in the most part, no. It is absurd to deny it to you. You are the queen of Szayet, and you are the Oracle. Beyond this, and more importantly than either, you are the commander's guest. You should be beside me because I ask it, and the council should need no other reason."

She covered her mouth with her hand. "Does that amuse you?" I said.

"Yes," she said unrepentantly, and then, relenting, added: "The council amuses me more than you do. Come out of your carriage, and have dinner with your cultist queen. Have I asked you yet about Far Madinabia?"

We took dinner in her rooms, and she did ask me about Far Madinabia, and laughed when I told her how we had routed the pirates, and raised her eyebrows when I told her about Otávio. When I mentioned the little idols the Madinabic pilgrims had given me, her face went blank.

"What does that mean for you?" she said.

"Nothing at all, as far as I know," I said. "Quinha accused me of being Madinabia's priest, once, but even she knew it was only talk. Nothing like this has ever happened to me before. Why—are you jealous on behalf of your Pearl?"

"Jealous?" she said. "No, of course not," but she hesitated, her eyebrows furrowing. "Ceirran," she said at last, "you liked it, didn't you?"

This startled me. "I hadn't thought to put it that way," I said at last.

"No," she said. "I thought you might not have." Her face was still a picture of concern, and I smiled and lifted my hand to her forehead to smooth it away.

"You *are* jealous, Patramata," I said. "What about this: Shall I commission a statue of you?"

That made her laugh. "Of me!" she said. "Of course, and why not? Install it in front of Cachoeiran's house, and send him to an early grave!"

I had been half-serious, but her face was so bright that I could not bear to press the matter. I lifted the platter with the remnants of our dinner onto the bedside table, and kissed her, and drew her against me.

She shut her eyes when I pushed inside her, a little later, and I caught her face in one hand and pressed my thumb gently into the soft place under her eye. "You don't want to look at me?" I said, without meaning it.

She shook her head, so that her long hair fanned out black against the pillow. "I want to remember this," she said breathlessly. "I'm trying to remember this."

And so I shut my eyes, too, and breathed in sweat, and her perfume, and the distant smell of snow. And I mapped with my hands the shape of her face, of her shoulders, of her thighs, of her breasts—as if I were molding her from clay, as if I could pour bronze over her with a touch, thinking: *Remember this, and this. Remember I was here.*

Later, when the streetlights had blazed into life and the shadows of the tree in her courtyard were shifting over our ceiling, she sighed and curled against my chest.

"You know there are people," she said, "and I expect Cachoeiran is among them—there are people who would call this the end of Ceiao."

"There will always be people calling what I do the end of Ceiao," I said.

She stretched and rolled away. I watched the shape of her body shift under the bedsheets. "And are they right?" she said.

I caught her wrist with my hand. "Do you believe it's true?" I said. "That this is a breaking of the disestablishment? That a city I command is no liberated city?"

She stilled, then, and said distantly: "I met a Szayeti today."

"A Szayeti?" I said. "Do you mean one of your ministers? Is everything all right at home?"

"Not one of my ministers," she said. "An ordinary woman. I suppose she must have come here to work, once, and stayed.

It doesn't matter—it's only that you said *no liberated city*, and it made me think of her. The way she spoke to me. That she said she wished to kneel before me. It made me think of your pilgrims." I could hear her exhale, though I could not see her face, and after a moment she said, "It wasn't the truth, after all. I have never been only a client queen."

I waited to see if she would continue, and then, when she did not, said softly, "Did you like it?"

She turned her head. In the darkness her eyes were flat coins. "No," she said. "It made me feel small. It made me feel humbled before her."

I ran my thumb over her knuckles, left to right, and back again. "Patramata," I said, still more softly, "may I ask you a question?"

Her eyes shut at once, and her hand went tight in mine. "Just ask," she said. "I'll tell you the truth."

I wanted to say it to her kindly, even with gentleness. I could not. It was not that I thought she would not accept it. It was that there was no gentleness in the question to give her. I had reached the end of my power.

"When did you learn which heir the Pearl had chosen?" I said.

"As soon as I put it on," she said. "It was the first thing the god ever said to me."

Her eyes were half-shut, and her hair was a dark curtain over her face. I reached for her and tucked a strand of it gently behind her ear.

"What did you think I would say, if you told me?" I said.

She breathed in my arms, for a little while.

"Do you know that before I heard you had come to Alectelo," she said, "I almost went to Belkayet, and asked them to make me queen?"

I had to work hard to keep my initial feeling off my face: A part of me very much did not like to be told in bed that I had been a second choice. "But you didn't," I said at last.

"I didn't," she said. "I would have had to publicly abandon my claim to be holy. I would have had to say before the Szayeti people that the god of my fathers did not want me, and that even so, I was forcing Szayet to be mine."

"And then you did exactly that," I said, running my hand down her hair. My heart had settled. She had chosen me on purpose, after all. "Patramata, do you want me to absolve you for it?"

"I didn't do that," she said, "not exactly," and then, before I could think over her words and parse what she had not done, "Ceirran, I don't think I want you to be a god of absolution."

I laughed, a little startled. "I don't think that's up to you."

She was quiet a long while then. I thought I heard her murmur something against my neck, but she was warm in my arms, and the snow had begun to fall through the window, and before I could ask her to repeat herself, or ask if she had even said anything at all, I was asleep.

CHAPTER

THIRTY-NINE

GRACIA

Yes, I lied.

"Three hundred years," Alekso said. He was watching me from His coffin in His tomb on the Island of the Dead, eyes half-lidded. "Three hundred years of Caviro's endless, pointless children, sons and daughters and all the rest stretching generation and generation further and further, and do you know how patiently I have waited—do you know how carefully I have waited, Caviro's daughter, to choose an Oracle who had the courage for conquest?"

"Lord," I said, and stopped.

"There's nothing to do about it now," Alekso said, and sighed and lay back on the coffin, His arms folded behind His head. "Sending a transmission as difficult as a dream to your sister nearly overloaded the circuitry—but there's nothing to do about it now. I could depose you, if I had a body. But the body I wanted is, I don't know, sunk in the harbor, or strung up on the palace walls, or in prison—you might've been coward enough to keep her in prison—and now there's only you." He looked sidelong at me. "You could give up the throne, of course."

Ceirran's breath was slow and regular in my ear, and his heartbeat was steady against my curled hands. From within the circle of his arms, I watched the lights bob on our ceiling, back and forth, cast by the lanterns of passing litters. The branches of the chestnut tree were whispering against each other outside, rubbed bare in the frozen wind.

I had said to him, because I thought he would not hear it: "If you think that, you understand very little of gods."

Freedom at last! Freedom at last: freedom of the city, freedom of the Pearl. It had seemed such an enormous thing, while he was at war. Now that he was returned, it felt smaller.

But many things felt smaller, when he was beside them.

I felt then, at once and very powerfully, that the whole of Ceiao was held deep within that winter night, that every mile of the hemisphere was under it, subject to it, sunk deep into its power, and only in this small room by the chestnut tree could be found warmth, and living human bodies, and the capacity for light. Then it passed, and I was in the darkness again.

In the cold light of the next morning, the inside of the Libeiracópolan was a great, swollen emptiness, with a flat tiled floor on which our footsteps echoed and a roof that arced high enough that the crossing and crisscrossing staircase obscured its apex. Its windows were visible only in the sunlight that shone through them, dappling the whole floor with stained-glass shadows in soft reds and blues.

"The admirals decided quickly that it should remain a memorial," said Ceirran. "Perhaps too quickly, in my opinion. None of them had seen inside it before, of course. No laity who came in went out again. I imagine they must have been curious." He strolled away from me, toward the curving wall. "They might have turned it into a public arena, for example, for games. Or they might have simply razed it like the Wall. These days, few ordinary Ceians have interest in visiting."

The walls were lined with dozens of clay vases stacked atop one another, most chipped, all painted with scenes I almost recognized. I saw ships in motion, descending upon planets and moons. I saw dozens of tiny figures, faceless and indistinguishable, on their knees before a man who pointed the barrel of a gun to the sky. I saw a boy holding lightning, reaching out to another boy in a soldier's cloak, standing in the clouds with a golden circle painted carefully behind his face. I didn't recognize them, at first. After a moment I realized: At home, of course, Alekso's life story was nearly always painted by Szayeti, and all the years of Sintian rule had changed that art only a little, adding some curled hair here, a counterpoise there. Here the black figure of Alekso ran and fought and flew in a style entirely Sintian, his name scribbled in the Malisintian alphabet over his head.

"I'm astonished these weren't smashed during the theomachy," I said.

"They are the only piece of worship that survived," said Ceirran. "The priests held them in low regard, and therefore so did the people, low enough that they would not destroy them. The cathedrals—the statues—the mosaics—the street names, of course, were easy to replace. The Nevede at one time ran white with fragments of limestone and marble."

Ana was on the other side of the chamber, peering at the scrollwork on the pillars by a tall stone arch opening into darkness. "The high priests' chambers," said Ceirran, misunderstanding my gaze. "Not very much left now, I'm afraid, only empty rooms. The people dragged out the furniture and tapestries and burned them, or stripped them for gold and copper. A good mile of the wiring in the city might be from Luĉjo la Senkompata's vestments alone."

I watched how Ana moved. She was out of uniform today, but she was wearing soldier's colors: a blue tunic and a long coat of deep indigo, vivid against the blackness of the tunnel. She was not looking at me.

"Come look at this," said Ceirran. I followed his pointing finger to the amphora, where another black figure of Alekso stood, his face and his clothing scratched out in fine white. He was standing over a deer, painted with equal delicacy, which he had seized by the antler. Its head was thrown back and its tongue fell sprawling out of its mouth. Beside him, on the other side of the deer, was another man, lifting an axe above his head.

"The deer is a symbol," said Ceirran. "Representing some local population or another, I expect. You'd have to ask your priests of the Library which one. But look at this," and he brushed the Malisintian above the second man's head, where some long-ago painter had written Alekso's companion's name.

"My father said—" I said, as if saying it would make it not be so.

"Your father was a milksop and a lying fool," said Alekso Undying. "All he did was scrape and bow, plead with these Ceian savages as if they were his betters—as if they were mine. *He told me the same thing you told your sister, you know:* We can't leave Alectelo. *Do you know how many Alectelos I've built? How many I could build, given the chance?* Will *you give up the throne?"*

By the eighth flight of stairs I was beginning to grow winded, and by the fifteenth I was panting. Ceirran smirked at first, but by flight twenty-five was himself short of breath: "Take pity on me," he said pathetically to Ana. "I'm an old man."

"You're barely twenty-nine," said Ana mercilessly without looking back. "Go to war again, it suits you."

I made the mistake on the thirty-third flight of looking down. I was not afraid of heights—it would have been difficult, growing up in the palace—but it made me dizzy immediately to see the thin railings spiderwebbing in a hundred directions below us, reaching all the way to the gleaming red floor below. It was impossible not to think at once of how easy it would be to tumble over one of those railings—how your body would hit each step, each iron bar, flight over flight. And then it was impossible not to think of how easy it would be for someone to creep up behind you, and shove—

"It would have been easier to go down instead of up," said Ceirran, as best he could through his panting. "But the dungeons have been closed for a hundred and fifty years."

"More's the pity," said Ana.

"I don't know that I agree," said Ceirran. "I wonder whether it might not be better this way . . . to allow the people to forget."

It grew colder as we climbed, and by the time we reached the fortieth flight I was shivering. The stained glass windows grew and grew, and when we at last stopped on the fiftieth set of stairs, they dwarfed us entirely: Each was nearly a hundred feet wide, and against them Ana and Ceirran were black figures themselves, scarcely visible except when a piece of red or blue light glittered off a buckle or pin or their eyes. Ceirran was feeling his way slowly along the wall. "Here," he said at last, and I saw his silhouette bend and tug, and a little square of marble swung open so that clean white daylight fell in and sprawled over the iron stairs.

Outside was a low flint sky, and a keen, biting wind, and a balcony with a railing, and the city of Ceiao, spread out as neatly as if drawn on a tablet. Mauntan Bau was a craggy silhouette on our left, now scattered with snow. From this height I fancied I could even see its peak above the huddled clouds. Below lay the flat white curve of the river, and the grey arched gates. At the peak of the river's arc, the golden one they called God's Crown winked in the pale sun.

"This is the view of the city the priests wanted?" I said, expecting another speech, but Ceirran said:

"I don't know, but I like it."

Ana had gone ahead and was circling along the balcony, her black-gloved hand trailing along the rail. She was singing faintly, a soldier's song I had heard in the street: *Citizens, grab hold of your wives*... Ceirran was watching her, his mouth curved. "She'll freeze her fingers," he said fondly.

I leaned over the railing and looked down. The Avenuan Libeirguitan lay to each side of us, a sword blade. At its north bank were rows of trees, crooked and bare of leaves, and strips of harbor, and a few squatting silver ships. From here we could only see half of the Inner City, the wide roofs of its mansions stretching in a semicircle before us like a blue sunrise.

"Can you see my house from here?" I said.

Ceirran squinted, and pointed to one roof. "That one," he said.

"Can you really tell them apart," I said, "or are you seeing if I'll catch you out in a lie?"

That made him laugh. "Far be it from me to try to put anything past you, Patramata," he said, with great solemnity. And then: "Someday you'll be able to point it out yourself."

I let him stand there awhile, watching his city. There was a peculiar light to winter in Ceiao, not quite dim but not really what on Szayet I would have called daylight, and beneath it his features had a kind of softness that did not seem at one with the rest of him. I had thought once that how he held himself made him seem bigger than he was, more dangerous. In the low light of that sky he seemed distant, too, as if filtered through static. The air smelled sharp again, like metal.

"Someday?" I said gently.

"Soon," he said.

"Tell me what more there is," I said, though I did not want to. "What more does the city need? When will they know what you are becoming—what we are going to become?"

"Conquest," he said. "After the triumph—the city needs another prize, before it will swallow a god. More good news. More victory."

I said nothing, but I looked down at the mosaic of blue roofs, and pressed in close to him so that his heat was against my side and my hip. After a moment he sighed and wrapped an arm around me. His fingers were as cold as the snow.

"It will be Kutayet next," he said. "It must be next, no matter what the council says. And the land reforms *will* go through, and the Kutayeti will take advantage, and there will be more of them in the city, more Aleksans, more people who have no love for the disestablishment or for the council or for my enemies—and the city will change. Things will change. Change is what things *do*."

"For the better?" I said.

"Forever," he said, and turned his face into the wind and closed his eyes, so that the first flakes caught in his lashes and stayed there. "Even a planet knocked off its axis turns toward tomorrow. It has no choice."

Ana was coming back toward us along the balcony, her cheeks red. My gaze caught on her chapped mouth, and I had to jerk my eyes away. "This wind bites like a tiger," she said. "Let's go back downstairs, eh?"

I was ready to leave that hunger behind, too, but Ceirran said, "Give me another minute. I want to look at it awhile more."

*"*You *were the one who wanted to build an empire," I said at last.*

"We could have done it," Alekso said, "if we hadn't had you *to deal with. Well—you did get the throne, in the end, so you can't be wholly useless." He shrugged. "And you weren't bad at the ground fighting. But that was against Arcelia, and she could hardly hold a formation. The spirit, as they say, is willing. I certainly was, anyway. Against anyone else, I don't think your dying would even be very fun to watch."*

He sighed. "Caviro understood. He was never so attached to things. *Things for their own sake, crowns and wine and fine clothing, planets and cities. He left me a legacy—that was what he cared about. He knew what needed to be immortal."*

"What needed to be," I said.

"Yes," said Alekso, and he sat up on his own grave and smiled at

me, utterly without warmth. "If he *had lived forever, I might have had a world worth being immortal in."*

As we crossed the tiled floor, I saw a pair of silhouettes through the door at the end, standing on the sidewalk outside the Libeiracópolan. It was Jonata and Cátia, heads bent together, whispering over a tablet Cátia was holding. When we crossed out through the doorway and into the sunlight, Cátia turned at the noise and smiled coolly.

"Commander," she said. "What a surprise to meet you here."

"A surprise?" said Ceirran. "Why should it be? Jonata—what a pleasure to see you."

Jonata let him kiss their cheek and press their hand, but their eyes were on me. When Ceirran drew them in to link arms, they pulled away. "I'm sorry," they said, "I have to run—Cátia, I'm sorry, too, I'm awfully busy. Will I see you both at council later?"

"No need," said Cátia pleasantly. "I'll stop by your house. Take care."

"Take my invitation to dinner!" said Ceirran as they turned away, and I saw him frown at their retreating back, and then nod at Cátia. "It was good to see you, Councillor."

Cátia was smiling slightly. "How good to see you," she said. "I'm sorry, Commander—with all the excitement, I don't think I ever congratulated you on your victory in Madinabia. I'm sure I meant no insult."

"Don't worry," said Ana, "you can cheer at his triumph with the rest of the crowd."

Cátia's nostrils flared briefly, and she turned to me. "Madam Oracle," she said, "what a pleasure to see you in the Inner City again. I heard you visited one of my factories while you were—occupied elsewhere. What a compliment. I didn't know you were interested in my little enterprise. Perhaps you and I could discuss business at some point."

"I'm afraid it's only your laborers I was interested in," I said, ignoring Ceirran's startled look. "So many people from the Swordbelt Arm in this city, and yet I see so few! I can't help some curiosity about my neighbors."

"What good Ceian would discourage curiosity?" said Cátia, nodded to us, and moved away. Ceirran stared after her, frowning.

"I don't know why Jonata should keep putting me off," he said to Ana, sounding melancholy, as we continued down the street. "Are they courting her, of all people? Even if they are—"

"You know why," said Ana, quietly enough that I thought I was not meant to hear it.

"They *know* Celestino bears no grievance toward them," Ceirran murmured back. "I've told them a hundred times. Why would he care? No one could still feel jealous of a man years dead, much less his sibling. If they would only—" Then he paused, and cleared his throat. "Patramata," he said, "tell me about Kutayet. Have you traveled there yourself?"

I glanced involuntarily at Ana. She was looking back, one eyebrow raised. I expected her gaze to be mocking—she certainly believed I didn't know what Ceirran meant, and it was an opportunity to mock me for it—but instead there was no humor at all, and even a kind of recognition. Heat flared unpleasantly in my cheeks.

"Not myself," I said, turning back to Ceirran with some effort, "but I have heard from my spies on the planet—" And the conversation carried us all the way to the door of my new house, where Zorione was waiting for me with a long list of items for purchase.

Ana left us, then, but Ceirran stayed, and gave me amused advice on all of Zorione's questions, and followed me upstairs when she was at last satisfied. The new house was enormous—I had not begun to explore all of its rooms—and consequently its current emptiness of furniture and decoration felt starker, its silences louder. The snow had begun to fall outside the window in grey soundless sheets, and if the street had ever been visible from the little window in my bedroom, it was not now. But my servants had laid down a mattress and a dozen pillows, dyed in deep, rich reds, and I smiled at Ceirran and said, "I'll sleep like a conquering soldier."

"Is this what you think conquest is like?" he said, laughing.

"I don't know," I said. "Why don't you show me?"

Ceirran looked at me awhile. His eyes were dark, unreadable. At last, when I was about to ask whether he had forgotten how to speak, he lifted my hand to his lips, and he kissed my knuckles, one by one, and then the back of my hand, and then the inside of my wrist.

"Oh, that's how conquest is done?" I said. "One inch at a time? But, Commander, at this rate, you must grow very bored very quickly."

His mouth pressed brief and hot on my forearm, on the inside of my elbow, on my shoulder. He nipped there, and I jerked, shivered. "Are you asking for flattery?" he said.

"Oh, is that what you think I'm asking for?" I said, laughing a little. "And you were doing so well."

"I could never," he said against my neck, "never grow bored of conquering this."

I shivered a little again, and not entirely pleasantly.

"Come here," I said, and caught his face in my hands, and lifted it to my own. He went easily enough. "I don't have your patience," I said, and let myself sound a little pleading, a little desperate. "Lay me down, please."

At that last he smiled. "Anything you like," he said, low and very satisfied, and I bent my head to his again and let him lick his way into my mouth.

He took his time opening my robes, and then he took his time touching me: my sides, the curve of my belly, my breasts. At first I watched him carefully, trying to figure out whether I was being teased, whether I should grow desperate, whether I should beg—but he seemed entirely content to touch his fill. When at last he pushed first his fingers inside me, and then himself, he was slow there, too, so slow, eyes closed, and after some time there was almost a dreamlike quality to it, an unreality, his solid weight on me, around me, inside me, and the steady rhythm of his hot, heavy breath.

The snow had not stopped by the time night fell. In the light from the streetlamps it was a sunset gold, visible for a moment where it passed through their beams and then vanished again into the dark. I curled my body against Ceirran's chest.

"And after Kutayet?" I said.

"I can't say for certain," he said, his voice rough with sleep. "My men will be wealthier. There will be Kutayeti refugees, as I say. But all the peoples Kutayet has conquered will come to Ceiao, too. If a rumor were to start among them about some kind of immortality—"

"I don't mean the Pearl," I said, and shut my eyes.

He sighed against my neck. "No," he said. "You don't, do you. You mean, after Kutayet—where."

I said nothing, only listened to his breath, to his heartbeat against the bare skin of my back.

"Tell me," he said—I could feel him rumble against my rib cage—"tell me, Patramata, what should I do? What worlds are left to conquer?"

I curled away from him, gently, and propped myself up on one elbow.

"Commander," I said, "are you asking me for a prophecy?"

He sat up. In the shadows, his eyes looked like Ana's—and then not like Ana's at all: his were deep, living things, like pools, and there was nothing hard or untouchable about them, nothing untouched.

"If I did," he said, "would you tell me the truth?"

I reached out and ran a finger over his cheekbone, along the bow of his lip. "Ask me," I said.

His mouth curved under the pad of my thumb. "Holiest," he said. "Holiest—please."

He did not go to his knees. He never would, as long as I knew him. He was always a Ceian in that. It did not matter to me then, in any case. He had learned to worship well enough.

Much later, in the deep of the night, I lifted my hand to my ear. Alekso's body at the edge of the bed was barely visible. I rolled away from Ceirran gently, so I would not wake him, and padded to my window, where the snow was still coming down thick and fast from the yellow sky. "I saw you today," I said.

"You saw an image of me," he said. "Can't you tell the difference?"

"I believe I can," I said. "I am your Oracle."

"Are you?" he said.

I closed my eyes. "I bear your Pearl," I said at last. "Whatever else is between us, there is nothing untrue in that. It is a matter of plain fact."

"A fact today, yes," he said. "But one day you'll bear his. And on that day, you'll finally give my soul to the woman I wanted to have it in the first place." The snow was a low hiss of static in the darkness. After a moment, he said, "You agreed to that bargain."

"I know, Lord," I said. "I proposed it."

"You may be my Oracle for a while," he said. "But I have seen a dozen Oracles, and compared to the length of my memory—compared to the length of my legacy—your time with me will be a drop in the sea. Remember *that* the next time your barbarian asks you for a prophecy."

"He meant nothing by it," I said. "He was only laughing at me. Even if I had really seen anything, even if I had had anything to tell him, he doesn't believe."

"Do you?" said my god.

I let go of the Pearl, and he dissolved into a grey swirl of snow. There was nothing beyond the window but storm. I could feel the cold seeping through the glass, like breath. I stood and watched it for a long, long time.

Of course I lied about who was heir to the Pearl of the Dead. What would I have done but lie? What other road would I ever have taken?

Zorione told me once, on a little satellite that is now dust and ashes, that Alectelans had died in my name. They did not die because they aimed to be heretics, she told me. They died because they believed that my cause was true.

It has been a long time since that night, when I lay in the dark between Matheus Ceirran and the image of my god. I have thought of it often since, trying to make sense of it, of how vividly it stands out in my recollection. As I am telling these memories to you, I am turning them over in my hands, I am holding them up to the light. It is in memory that I am trying to find some kind of truth, if truth is anywhere to be found.

There is a Sintian play I have always loved, long learned by heart by restless children across all that territory Sintia once conquered, which tells the story of a king's daughter who is the prophet of an imaginary god. This god himself is invisible, untouchable. He never appears in the play. There are no monuments to him, no statues. Nevertheless, as she goes to war and returns, counsels her royal father and fights with him, every word the prophet says is proven again and again entirely true.

The scholars ask: What are we meant to understand from this woman who speaks with a voice we cannot hear? What are we meant to make of how she sees and touches a wisdom that cannot be seen or touched?

But I always thought: It would make little difference, if the voice of the god was audible to the audience, if the things he said to her were said by an actor. He would be no more knowable than before. Nor, I suppose, would she.

And, after all, perhaps there was no god in the first place. Or perhaps there was something—a voice, a light, a holy certainty—but she learned she could not trust it. Perhaps she thought she had faith in someone, and then decided that the thing she had faith in, the thing she held hard in her heart and loved and could not let go, was not a god at all.

She dies, in the end. So many of those Sintian plays seem to end that way. Sometimes from the fault of the heroes, but more often from the fault of the story. There is always some terrible fate crouching at the end of it, like a lion with its mouth open. This is what Ceians call Fortune, and speak about the way they used to speak about gods. And when you are educated, when you have read enough stories and when you know enough about the story you are listening to, you grow to expect the death of the hero, and when death comes, the end of anticipation is even a relief.

I think a liar is a kind of teller of stories.

But this is not what I am trying to tell you. And besides, that much you have already learned. I was there the day you learned it.

The prophet in this play, she dies because her prophecy is disbelieved. Her father the king locks her in a dungeon, and when his city is burned from within, she hangs herself rather than be made a prisoner of war. In Sintia in those days, of course, the kings and the prophets were two separate people.

It seems very simple to live that way.

CHAPTER

FORTY

CEIRRAN

I had forgotten that moving house in the city was no easy matter. When I had come to the Inner City, shortly after Quinha had made our pact to divide the galaxy and not long before we had gone to war with each other, the logistics had been primarily military ones. The campaign was hardly half over, then, and everything that mattered in my life was in Madinabia save Celestino. At that point we had been married four years, and I knew him well enough to trust he could handle my domestic affairs better than me. It was Quinha who had advised me to take a spouse. I had felt it to be rather a chore when we had wed, but I thought then that at last I understood how such a thing might benefit me beyond connecting me to Celestino's family's wealth.

How young I had been! It was almost amusing to think of it as I watched the servants lift beds and couches above their heads, and wheel boxes and trunks through Gracia's door and into the long tiled hallway. How young, and how small the world had seemed in its possibilities.

The servant at my hand, carrying my tablet, coughed politely. I startled—I had been paused before Gracia's house for nearly ten minutes. "Come," I said. "Let's arrive at the meeting with enough lateness to be fashionable."

The Libeiracópolan was an altogether different sort of space from any the council had met in before, and I was glad at once that I had ordered them to do it. It had not been hard to close the memorial to the public for a day at all—I had not received one complaint. In that great chamber every whisper, every scrape of chairs, rattled up to the stained glass and came back magnified a hundredfold. After only a few minutes the councillors ceased to murmur altogether and only passed glances and raised eyebrows, which came to a halt when the secretary stood.

"The Merchants' Council recognizes Túlio Cachoeiran," she said, "on a matter of—personal concern?"

I groaned under my breath, but what followed was dead silence. At last, when it had stretched to such a length that a few brave councillors had begun to whisper again, I saw the curly head of Thiago Veguion emerge from the crowd.

"I'm afraid Councillor Cachoeiran's personal concerns have arrived sooner than he expected," he said pleasantly. "He has asked me to convey that he has gone to his house in the country. He will apprise the council of when he intends to return."

That caused a stir, and another near-deafening flurry of whispering. Someone called out, "Does he yield his time?" and there was a ripple of uneasy laughter.

"If the honored councillor is absent," I said, above it, "we will have to continue without him. Who is listed next?"

"The Merchants' Council recognizes Emiliana Barboulethan," said the secretary dubiously, "on a matter of scheduling."

Someone groaned at that, too, quietly enough that in another of the towers we likely wouldn't have heard it. Barboulethan, who had been rising to her feet, went scarlet. "Erm," she said, and began to speak with some confusion about the history of the Ceian calendar, the names of assorted Ceian historical admirals, and the nature of spectacle itself, which was a story that appeared to have a beginning centuries before Alekso's conquest and which proceeded from point to point in the manner of a concussed pigeon. When she had made her way through the first two centuries, the councillors began to fidget, and by the time she was up to the year after the theomachy there was audible yawning. I saw Narcisa Cipon surreptitiously tap her tablet. Her eyes popped, and she mouthed *Only fifteen minutes?!* across the room to someone I couldn't see.

"...This is why it is certain," Barboulethan said at last, nearly twenty minutes later, "not only certain but definite, and not only definite but self-evident, that any cavalcade can and must, erm, coincide with a greater commemoration; because commemoration, in its nature, the word itself reaching to the Malisintian *memoru*—as the poets might say, *to remember in perpetuity*, though the poets, if I recall correctly, referred instead—"

"Hold," said Thiago Veguion. "Was that a motion? I heard a motion in that. You wanted something, didn't you?"

"Erm," said Barboulethan again. "I only mean to say that, to my mind, the unity of memory with remembrance stipulates that Ceiao might wish, for the purposes of uniting in time—"

"What fortune, it was," said Veguion. "I vote yes. Yes? Can there be a motion?"

There was an uncertain flickering of hands. I kept mine down. Veguion had enough spite to reject even the smallest item I seemed to support, especially after the repeal of the worship ban—but he was both easily distractible and highly impatient, and I knew it better than he did, and so his followers' hands went up, and a few of mine too, and at last the secretary said:

"Motion passed. The triumphal processional for the recent

conquests of Matheus Ceirran is to be held in ten days, along the Avenuan Libeirguitan."

There was a brief pause. Cipon was counting on her fingers, mouthing the days of the week. Cátia rolled her eyes and bent to whisper in her ear, and then Cipon rolled her eyes, too.

"If this little piece of theater is done with," said Veguion dryly, "perhaps we might move on to the business of governance? Yes? Is that function still left to us? *I* have a motion, in any case, which would establish a customs bay on the satellite of Novytis entirely free of tax..."

Jonata caught up to me as the meeting broke up, and fell in at my side as I emerged from the Libeiracópolan and into the shade of the snow-laden trees. "Hello," I said, pleased. "I apologize for Barboulethan. I'm afraid she has her uses."

"Uses?" they said, confused, and then shook their head. "It doesn't matter."

"Something matters, Jonata," I said, clapping their shoulder. "What's troubling you?"

Today their hair was pulled back in a mass of ponytail, and their chin was a bundle of blue woolen scarf, which looked as if someone had knit it painstakingly and not very well. They looked very young—almost young as they had when I had first met them. "It's only—no one has held a triumph on Barran's Feast before," they said. "Not along the Avenuan. Are you canceling the holiday?"

I turned to them, surprised. "Are you insulted?" I said. "I should have thought—I've offended you. You ought to be in my processional, Jonata. I'll talk to the lieutenants—"

"In the processional!" they said, looking more horrified than before. "Among all the—people? With their shouting, and—no—I only wondered—"

"You were very wise to wonder," I said. "We *will* honor your ancestor at my triumph, as best we can, and even if you won't show your face, you ought to come and tell the planning committee how you'd like them to do it. When was the last statue built to her? I'll commission one. There ought to be one on the street where she made her famous siege—or no, in front of the Libeiracópolan, so the people can come and pay tribute. We might even give it your face! What does a holiday matter compared to that? Does that seem like an appropriate honor?"

"Appropriate," said Jonata faintly, and then shook their head. "Matheus, I'm sorry, I have to go, I promised Cátia I would have dinner with her. I'll send you a message—" Then they were gone, shrinking into the mass of councillors pouring down the street from the Libeiracópolan.

Flavia's house was nearer the great dome than mine, though on an adjacent street. Anita herself greeted me when I knocked, leaning against her doorframe in a silk morning robe only loosely tied around her waist. "Good morning," she said, utterly unembarrassed.

I knew she knew what time it was. "Are you a servant now, attending your own door?" I said. "Why were you not at the council meeting today?"

"Did you need me for it?" she said, surprised. "Didn't Emiliana bore them to death all right?"

That brought me up short. I hadn't thought whether I had *needed* her. "Did you not want to come?" I said.

"To the *council*? Never," she said. "That can't be a surprise to you? In any case, they'll all see me soon enough."

"I don't know that I like the sound of that," I said. But I only half meant it, and she knew it, and stretched her arms above her head and sighed happily.

"So will you," she said. "So will everyone. In my opinion, it's past time Ceiao learned to appreciate a bit of theater."

CHAPTER

FORTY-ONE

GRACIA

Festivals were more common on Ceiao than they were on Szayet, for no particular reason I could see besides how inordinately the Ceians seemed to enjoy them. They called this Barran's Feast, of course, but if there was any great difference between the cheering and drinking and parades on Szayet for the Feast of Alekso's Crown and those here, I failed to see it. It was, in fact, in the multitude that I felt my worship of Alekso least strange. At least, amid the carousing crowd, no one was looking at me.

I was not amid the crowd now. Ceirran had reserved me a sort of box to watch his processional, which stretched from the Libeiracópolan all the way to the edge of the Inner City. Along the avenue, between the mansions and the linden trees, his workers had built a series of creaking wooden towers. I disliked the noises they made in the wind, but I rather liked being able to watch the whole population below me, moving in swirls and currents like the sea. It was his money that had sponsored the whole endeavor. It sponsored such a lot of things on Ceiao these days. The whole city seemed to be in debt to him, for one reason or another. This, too, made me feel particularly Szayeti, in that I felt a vicious sort of pleasure about it. I was glad that I should not be alone.

"What a monstrous lot of noise the crowds make," said Flavia. "I would call that a good sign."

Nor, of course, was I alone in the more literal sense. I did not know whether Ceirran had arranged for Flavia to ask if she could watch the parade with me—it seemed like one of his machinations, but he was so busy these days with other governance—but nevertheless I was glad to have someone beside me, not least someone who understood a little.

"Would you?" I said.

"Oh, of course it's terribly ugly," said Flavia easily. She had come in all her finery, and she was wearing the golden hairpins Ceirran had sent from Szayet, which made me glad. "But you shouldn't mistake ugliness for ill fortune. They're delighted enough to deafen each other, and all for his sake. What could be a better omen than that?"

"High-spirited, yes," I said, "but delighted—I don't know. I've seen crowds in high spirits before."

"Oh! I'm sure you have, Oracle of Szayet," said Flavia. "Terribly sorry to offend!"

"That's not what I mean," I said, a little embarrassed. "I have seen crowds who were angry—frighteningly angry—or grieving, or afraid."

"Yes, I'm sure you have," she said again. "So have I," and the tone in her voice made me turn to her. She was only smiling, though, just as pleasantly as she had been smiling before. I remembered, then, something Ceirran had told me: that she had once raised a mob in Ceiao's own streets, and led it all the way into the Inner City.

"The mistake is mine," I said, and her smile curled into something almost genuine. "But aren't you afraid of crowds? The violence they can do?"

"I'm afraid of plenty of things," said Flavia cheerfully. "They say your god rode lightning once, don't they? Do you think he was afraid of rainstorms?"

Before I could think of a reply the screaming grew, impossibly, louder. She leaned forward in her seat, over the railing of the box. "It's coming," she said.

"It?" I said.

It was an enormous banner, nearly reaching up to the floor of our box, carried by thirty soldiers with poles lifted above their heads. It was a deep green and showed a series of thirteen silver crescents arranged around a great circle. After a moment I recognized it: Madinabia's flag.

The crowd screamed, and when the banner had drawn close enough to us that I could see behind, I understood why: The Madinabic prisoners followed, dragged in chains. Our box was opposite the box of some councillors—I recognized Cátia, and Ceirran's old enemy Veguion, and others I didn't know—and Cátia leaned forward at this, face intent, to watch the warriors trip forward. And they were warriors, that first wave of them: I could see their tattoos, their muscles. They were dressed in their native costume, leggings and leathers, and I wondered at that: Had they been allowed to change clothing since they had come to Ceiao? Had Ceirran's people kept the clothing they had been captured in, and returned it to them when it was time for this display? Had they sewn Madinabic leggings especially for the purpose?

And behind the warriors more Madinabic prisoners stumbled, but these had no tattoos, and I knew that they were not warriors at all. I saw women as old as seventy, and children as young as ten. I saw one woman clinging to another woman's hand, a swollen belly under her leather shirt. They were staring up, wild-eyed. Next to me, Flavia was applauding.

"Not very many," she said, "but I suppose when you have three stages, they can't go on all day..."

The next banner came, green again with a golden slash through a circle I did not recognize, but I recognized the prisoners that came after it: They were not tattooed at all, and they wore the same robes as those I saw every day on the street, albeit dirtied and torn. The flag must have been Far Madinabia's, then. The crowd's cheering dimmed noticeably at this, and it was clear that the pirates noticed. As the soldiers pulled them forward, one pirate called out, in clear, unaccented Ceian: "Go home!"

At this the soldier beside him struck him, hard, and he was silent. But the crowd was silent, too, and I heard Flavia sigh.

"He would insist on showing our men as if they were barbarians," she said softly. "He'd like to believe his people don't think of Quinha as one of their own anymore, I expect."

I hesitated. "I thought he—" I said, and did not quite know how to finish the sentence.

"Loved her?" said Flavia. "Of course he did. She was his dearest friend. He *will* persist in forgetting that other people had the gall to love her, too."

I did not know what to say to this, but luckily I was not required to reply. Flavia exclaimed and pointed. "You ought to cheer for this!" she said.

I had known they were coming. I had myself supervised their loading onto the Ceian ships. Nevertheless it was a shock to see them pulled along in chains: those guards who had taken up arms against me those many months ago.

Ceirran had done me the courtesy of leaving out the Szayeti flag. But the guards were dressed in their red cloaks, and someone had shaved their heads, as if they were our priests. The crowd had come back to life again, and shouted, and chanted

Ceir-ran!—the noise rolling down their masses like waves. I applauded mechanically, but my eyes followed the guards as they went. At this distance, I did not know if I recognized them. At this distance, I did not know if they recognized me.

After this came legion after legion of soldiers, for which the crowd roared with equal enthusiasm in every new wave—returned veterans, home at last. Then there were dancers, and then marching musicians, and then acrobats, and then, borne with great solemnity by a line of bulky soldiers, an enormous painting of a hawk-nosed woman with a great cloud of grey hair and a somewhat pinched expression. Even if the crowds had not been screaming her name, I would have known her at once: I saw a dozen replicas of this same painting in miniature, whenever I ventured far enough south to see the Rouan Valquíria Barran.

Flavia seemed particularly interested at this. "I didn't think he was showing Barran's face," she said. "He must be indulging Jonata."

"He likes to," I said, and immediately regretted it. It was too late to take it back, though, and Flavia was smiling at me.

"Have you seen them today?" she said. "No? I wish you could—I spotted them climbing up the stairs to their tower, looking green as a leek. The rumor's that they would've rather not come."

I scanned the towers, trying to spot a familiar head of fair brown hair, but the street was so long and the crowd such a mass of noise and color that there was no hope. "I'm surprised you didn't tell me they're indulging him," I said.

"Oh, that's not news," said Flavia. "What do any of us do these days but indulge him? Fortune knows you certainly did."

"I did what?" I said, startled—but she was on her feet, deaf to me.

"She's here!" she said, pointing. "Stand up! She's arrived!"

I already knew the *she* that must be meant, but I leaned over the railing nevertheless. Ana was, of all absurd things, on a horse, and she cantered down the street, her hand lifted in a wave. I had thought when I first met her that she looked like something out of propaganda, and then forgotten it. Now, seeing how she sat straight-backed and smiling, how the crowd roared her name, how her face was wiped clear of any sly black glances or temper or hint of vulnerability, I saw again, and with a curious disappointment, its plain and very ordinary handsomeness. They seemed to love seeing her, too, though not in quite the way they had loved seeing the prisoners. I heard laughter, now, mixed in with the cheering. Someone below us had begun a song whose lyrics made me raise my eyebrows.

"Hallo-o-oo!" Flavia bellowed down, and waved. The call was swallowed up in the noise, but Ana saw the wave. She turned that grin up toward us, saluted, and—it was impossible to be certain at this distance—had she *winked*?

She stopped a little way down the street, not quite at the edge of our field of vision. "Will she ride with him to the end?" I said to Flavia.

"I'm not sure," she said uncertainly. "She must have something in mind."

I held my tongue on that and glanced across the street to where the councillors were sitting. They, too, were looking at Ana, and whispering together. One of them, a pouch-faced man who looked very like Jonata Barran, met my eyes and sneered. I looked away.

It was not difficult to tell when Ceirran was approaching: The chants of his name were audible for nearly a full minute before he came into view. When we did at last see him, striding down the street with a complement of soldiers at his back, Flavia gasped in delight. I stared. He was painted in a long red stripe down the center of his face, with dots along his cheekbones reaching to the place on his temple where the Pearl's wires would have entered on mine. His hands were painted, too, in curls and wavering lines. He was clothed all in white, his robes gleaming in the winter sun like a snowfield. It made him look to my eye like some very ancient painting, by some miracle not yet worn away.

"Is this particular to how you celebrate triumphal processions?" I said to Flavia.

"You mean the paint?" she said. She was half hanging over the railing, applauding hard. "Not at all—it's for Barran's Feast. Ordinarily half this crowd would have it on. They say it's how the priest was dressed, when she burned him—*Hello! Helloo-oo!*" She was not so lucky with Ceirran as she had been with her sister: He only had eyes for the cheering crowd.

"Help me," she said, looking back, "he likes to look at *you*—"

"I think I had better not—" I began, feeling my face grow hot, and then, in a very different tone of voice: "What is she doing?"

For Ana had slid off her horse, and she was striding toward Ceirran. The crowd didn't understand, either. The people below me were murmuring in confusion. Ceirran's face, though, was clear: He did not look in the least surprised.

"She didn't tell me—" Flavia began, and then went silent. Ana had reached Ceirran and stopped. The crowd was utterly hushed.

"Captain Decretan," he said.

"Commander," said Ana, and she went to one knee, and pressed her lips to his hand.

When I tell you a gasp went up, I do not do it justice. It was more akin to a scream. Ana did not seem to hear it; she remained perfectly still, statue-still, kneeling at Ceirran's feet. Below me, a woman was trembling so badly that I feared she would faint.

Ceirran was frozen a few moments. Then he said, in a low voice that nonetheless carried: "My Anita," and he went to his knees before her, took her arms in his, and lifted her to her feet.

Had I thought the crowd screamed before? *Now* they

screamed, wild and frantic: *Ceir-ran! Ceir-ran!* They were shoving one another, clinging to one another, weeping. I heard one call, "I knew—" and a second, "He would never, never make us—" and a third, "Raised her up! Raised her to her feet! On your feet, you sons of misfortune, on your feet for the great man of Ceiao!" Not since my coronation had I seen such a clarity of joy.

There was a prickling feeling at my temple. I looked up, across the Avenuan, to where the Ceian councillors were watching the spectacle with wide eyes. Only one was not: Cátia, leaning forward intently. She was staring directly at me. When I caught her gaze, she went still, and then nodded deliberately and tapped twice at her ear.

I did not know what she meant. I nodded back. She smiled thinly and sat back, and bent to murmur something into another councillor's ear.

It was in a pensive mood that I returned home that evening, and it lingered through all the unpacking of carpets and soaps and oils and the hanging of tapestries and the airing out of new quilts and blankets that had yet to be done in the house in the Inner City. It felt like nearly an hour that I stood deciding where to arrange my paintings and alabastra, and when I was startled out of my reverie by a knock on the door, it was a surprise to discover that it had hardly been twenty minutes.

It was Ceirran there, dark-eyed. There were flecks of red paint still along the bridge of his nose and at his knuckles and by the corners of his eyes. He stooped to kiss me in the hallway, which I let him do with pleasure, and then, at my acquiescence, he backed me up step after step against one of my new stone walls and cupped my face in his hot long-fingered hands, and drank me in as if I were wine. "Oracle," he murmured against my mouth, and bent to kiss my jaw, my neck. "Oracle—"

I would not be able to recall, afterward, where the servants had fled to, where Zorione had gone. The world had narrowed down to my own skin, my own heartbeat, and then they were not even my own any longer but wild animals, straining toward the heat of his mouth. It was only by extraordinary effort that I opened my eyes, and even then I barely ruled myself enough to say, half laughing, "Upstairs—quick, upstairs, before we lose all propriety—"

"Why should I?" he murmured against my neck, his thigh pressing hot between mine. "Why shouldn't we do anything we want?"

"*You* may want—" I began, and then said breathlessly, "Oh—" as his hands began to work at the ties of my robe.

"I do," he said, muffled against my collarbone, my breasts. "I do, I do. I do."

When at last we were in my bedroom, he fell upon me like the lightning, and I wrapped my legs around him and urged him onward, in. I held on to his shoulders, kissed at his face, hungry and thoughtless. The paint on his face had the clean metal taste of coins.

Afterward, contrary to his habit, he did not slip out in the late hours to slink home to his own house. Instead, he ate supper with me, and wandered around my house in a sort of strange delight. There was an aura to him that I had not seen since some of the islands we had visited on Szayet, and there it had been a weak, watered-down thing, which I had read only as his usual mixture of exuberance and thoughtfulness. Or no—I had seen it in him once before, but only once, and that had been in a room in my palace many months ago, when he had cocked his head at me and asked if I was trying to seduce him.

For all that it had brought me every one of the things that now shaped my life and my queenship, I did not like to remember that moment. No, this was not quite true—I did not like to remember who I had been, empty-handed and alone. I did not like to remember, when he had said, *I have been looking at you*, what it was that he might have seen.

Nevertheless he now recalled it to me. There was a solidity to his body, which seemed at once more present and more intangible than any of ours, and a distant light to his face, as if he was feeding from some great wellspring from which the rest of us had not drunk.

"What are you thinking of?" he said, when he caught me watching him.

"You," I said, entirely honest, and stood on tiptoe to spread my hands over his broad shoulders and nip at his mouth.

Still—I remembered it. The sound of that scream...

He brought me upstairs again, after we had eaten. There I undressed him as one of my servants might have, unpinning his cloak and draping it over my chair, hanging his tunic in my closet, wiping the last of the paint from the corners of his eyes. When I was done he lay back in my bed and sighed in contentment. I sat on the end of the bed and watched his breathing slow.

There was no chestnut tree behind my new house, but there was a tall lattice along which ivy was meant to grow, if you had the time and discipline to cultivate it. I clambered down step by step, swung myself to the soft ground at the last, and landed with a thump.

Last time, riding in my spider-litter toward a forbidden bar, I had felt like a child. Now I walked, as though I were neither queen nor child but a Ceian citizen. The way was shorter this time, but the weather was colder. I was glad for my workaday brown woolen cloak, and my hair braided over my right ear.

It was easy enough to find one of the poorer districts. They were not even very far from the Inner City. No one turned when I slipped into the tavern, but when I asked for a cup of wine, the weather-beaten woman at the bar next to me turned at once.

"You're new," she said. "Just come to the city?"

The accent! The people of the Inner City never commented on it, but hers was faster, her *r*s only half-rolled. There was no point lying now. "Yes," I said. "I'm a tourist—I'm here to see the Barran's Feast celebrations. I'm from Sintia."

At that her face opened up a little, pleased and smug. "So!" she said. "The Sintians come here to admire *us* now, do you? I'd say it's about time."

"Oh, yes," I said, "and there's so much to admire. So many peoples in the processional! Your commander must be quite a conqueror."

A sleepy-eyed woman, farther down the bar, said, "What would you know about it?"

"Oh, that he won all of Madinabia," I said, "and could win any other nation he intended to, I expect. Only I was surprised—his, what was it, his captain? His lieutenant? When she kissed his hand—"

At that quite a lot of people seemed to look up at once. "And what would you know about *that*?" said the first woman, the one who had asked about my accent.

I opened my mouth to reply, but another Ceian, very red with drink, said, "You want to talk to a Sintian about him? You want to get another, another name-dropping scholar with her nose in the air, speaking Sintian at us about *him*? You haven't heard all that kind of drivel in the council holos enough already?" They shook their head. "You know who's speaking Sintian about him?" they said. "Right now? Every councillor in the Inner City, that's who, talking *history* and *philosophy* in their, in their, in all of their mansions. Oh, they're speaking Sintian, right. *Oh, the commander's too kind, he's too popular, he's too generous, he cares too much about people*—how do you say *that* in Sintian?" They thumped their glass on the table. "You know why? Because none of *them* could ever make anybody get on their knees for them in the first place."

"And nobody should," said a man, a little uncertainly.

"Doesn't matter whether anybody should," said the speaker, mostly to themself. "He didn't *let* her, is the point, and all *they* do"—this seemed to mean the council again—"is tear their hair trying to work out how to keep their big ugly houses closed for another hundred years to anybody who didn't go to their *Sintian* schools, and do you know, do you know, if Cipon raises rents twenty dekar again, I'll have to move off of Ceiao?"

"We all know, Carmo," said the sleepy-eyed woman. She was drunk, too, I realized. "The way you talk, you're the only person who ever signed a lease with Cipon in the whole system."

"See if you keep that tone when the commander stops *all* them raising rents again," said the drunk person confidently. "See if you keep it when me and all those foreigners they threw in jail get our plots of Ceian land, over across the ocean. Fortune's coming for everybody who ever showed him they loved him, right? So see if you laugh at me *then*."

"You believe that story, do you?" said a bald man sitting farther down the bar.

"Course I believe it," said the drunk person. "Why wouldn't I believe it? We need it. As soon as he can work out how to get it past the council, he'll do it. He's going to raise the dole, too, you see if he doesn't. He's going to make all the moneylenders start giving loans to people like us—"

"We get loans," said the sleepy-eyed woman.

"Oh, yeah, we get loans," said the woman who had first spoken. "Just the other week my niece took a big old loan from from that Kutayeti by the Minor Gate, great terms. All you have to do is promise that when you can't pay interest, you won't kick up a fuss when his boys come and cut your hand off."

"If Pulcron were alive, he never would've stood for that kind of thing," said a voice from somewhere in the back of the bar.

"Yeah, Pulcron would've had his boys cut off your whole arm," said the bald man, and there was a ripple of laughter.

"But they *are* jealous," said the drunk person. "They're jealous of how—how—how *good* the commander is—" The tavern grumbled at that, some in agreement and some disagreement, and they said, "They're jealous of how *great* he is—of how *easy* it was for him to come back with, with money for us, land for us, markets for us—they're jealous because none of them could ever manage it if they tried—they're jealous of how much he's *loved*."

"I think you love him enough for about twenty of us," said the first woman, not unkindly. "Isn't your wife waiting?" They brushed off her friendly touch to their shoulder and sneered, and she pursed her lips. "Well, I'm going," she said. "You stay here and sing him a serenade."

"As if that'd bother *him*," said the sleepy-eyed woman. "Princess of Medveyet."

There was a rise in the grumbling at that, and even a few gasps. I set down my drink. "What does that mean," I said, "Princess of Medveyet?"

She smirked. "You don't know *that*?"

The child in me bristled at that, but I was no longer a child. "No," I said. "Will you tell me?"

The woman made a crude but evocative gesture using her hand and mouth. I raised my eyebrows, but the bald man said wearily, "Andreia, hold off awhile," and shunted her with his shoulder down the length of the bar. "You haven't heard the rumors?" I shook my head. "I'm not surprised," he said. "It's not civilized. We ought to keep our ears clean, if we ever *do* want to have a hope of being people of quality." This seemed directed at Andreia, who shrugged and made another rude gesture. He turned back to me. "Still. You have heard of Medveyet, I suppose?"

Medveyet's system wasn't far from ours. We bought iron from them, mostly, and they glasswork from us, though we were by no means close friends. It was only recently that our trade had stabilized. Medveyet had been a republic, about thirty years before I was born, then a war zone, then a monarchy, then a loose confederation of sects. Now it was a colony, and among Ceiao's most loyal. "Yes," I said. "He fought against the rebellions there?"

"Maybe," said the man. "I think he was stationed at the right time? It was when Mauro Monteiron headed the council—"

"You tell a lie," said Andreia, "it was when Manoela Ameidon headed the council. The summer we had the earthquake, remember? Me and my dog got stuck on a bridge."

The man shot her a look. "As I say," he said, "better for us to contemplate *that* sort of question, instead of...in any case, he was stationed in the court of the queen there—Jozefa, Justina, something like that. Her son was around the same age."

"Older," said someone down the bar.

"Older," the man allowed. "Five years. Maybe six. The kind of boy who—well—he's been married thrice now, if I recall. And back then our men were in trouble in that part of the galaxy, some—some fanatical nonsense, I don't know, their country was holy and we were terrible dirty heathens, the usual ideas, the point is: We were losing men, it was as dangerous as all hell, the queen was no help, hated Ceians like fire, even the rich merchants couldn't do business there anymore—anyway, Commander Ceirran gets put in this prince's personal guard."

"And I mean *personal* guard," Andreia put in cheerfully.

The man rolled his eyes. "He was just a lieutenant, for Fortune's sake, what could he even have done? He was barely in his manhood, so—anyway, the queen's policy changed. Ended up putting down the fanatics, in the end. And afterward, people said he'd—well. As I say. It's not right to speak of it." He hesitated. "He raised her up from her knees," he said a moment later. "That means something. He loves the city. I believe that."

"Princess of Medveyet," said Andreia. I had thought her tone mocking, at first—and it was. But I had assumed a bitterness in it, a dislike. Now I thought I had not read her correctly. "That's *right*."

I went home that night through a cool, clean rain, which collected white and grey on my raincoat and slithered to the ground like serpents. When I slipped in through the servants' door, I hardly noticed Zorione fussing over my damp slippers. I only padded up the stairs to my room, where Ceirran was sleeping sprawled and shirtless, one hand thrown over his eyes.

He stirred when I slid between the sheets next to him, and when I kissed him he rumbled. "Where have you been?" he murmured when his hand found my wet hair.

"Everywhere," I said, and kissed him again, more hotly.

He laughed. I always loved to feel him laugh. "You're a mystery, Oracle," he said indulgently.

"Really?" I said. "I think I understand you perfectly," and climbed on top of him.

CHAPTER

FORTY-TWO

CEIRRAN

The last days of winter were always the slowest on Ceiao, and the most difficult to wait through, knowing that the heat was about to burst over the city like flowers. But Gracia was so near me now that it alleviated the boredom as well as the impatience. I found myself sleeping in her bed more nights than not, and waking to the sight of her brushing her hair, or reading her reports from home. It was almost as if we were on a ship on Szayet again, but for the noise of clattering trains and spoken Ceian in the streets outside.

Because of the holiday there were no council meetings, and would not be until just before spring, and I saw very little of those councillors who were not already my friends. There had been a flurry of jostling for power when I had first defeated Quinha and made myself the first man among them, when every lieutenant had wanted to be my captain, every councillor my confidant. Now they came to me rarely. When they did, it was not to pull themselves into my affection when they did not have it, nor to convince me of some loyalty which they had never cultivated till they feared me, but to beg for things: favors, pardons, promotions, words in the ears of judges. These I granted with pleasure. It made me glad to think that some kind of peace had returned to Ceiao, that an order had established itself, and that from that order something new at last might grow.

Jonata did accept my invitation for dinner at long last, which made me gladder. Celestino could not eat with us—he had a prior engagement at some friend or other's—for which I apologized to them, but Jonata said it was no matter.

"It's you I want to speak to, anyway," they said. "Matheus, Cátia told me you want to go on campaign again."

"Did she?" I said. "She's quite right. I intend to leave with Anita and Galvão once spring has come and the river is melted."

"Without council approval?" they said.

"I don't know that I need it," I said. "In fact, I wonder how Cátia heard at all. Though please don't think I don't care about *your* opinion, Jonata—you're welcome to come along, as a matter of fact. Would you like to discuss a little strategy?"

They smiled, a distant, uneasy smile. "I'm not sure where she heard," they said. "She told me—well, I wanted to know—what will happen to the Oracle?"

"What will *happen* to her?" I said. "What a funny way of putting it. She'll return to Szayet, I expect. She's already been a rather long time away. And then, once my victory is sure, I may follow her there. Did Cátia tell you that it's Kutayet I intend to go to...yes? Well, as I'll be in the Swordbelt Arm, it seems only sensible to pay her a visit."

"But that's such a long time away from the city," they said. "What will the council think of that?"

"I'm growing rather tired of wondering what the council thinks," I said, and leaned forward. "Jonata, you *ought* to come with me. You ought to see Szayet. The people there are—well—I want you to see them. I want you to see how they talk to Gracia, how they behave around her. And I want you to see the ruins, I want you to see the world they've made with what they've been given. It *is* different from how it's been done on Ceiao. When Kutayet is ours, and my empire's borders are secure—well, I want you to see what beyond Ceiao is possible."

They leaned forward over their plate of lentils, intent. "Then what is Ceiao?" they said. "What is Ceiao to you—to the council—to any of us? The empire has grown so much, Matheus, and that's such a victory—we've brought change to the galaxy, real change. We've replaced blind obedience with education. Better yet, with virtue. There are freedoms we offer, and culture, Sintian poetry and philosophy met with Ceian governance, as it ought to be. And this all used to only be a light in one small part of the Crossbar—and now you can carry a centono from one spiral arm to another to another, and buy an apple wherever you go—civilization! But does it only go one way? Can Cherekku and Diajundot and—and Madinabia understand our ways without—without—"

They stalled, and their hand, which had been gesticulating with such emphasis that it had nearly knocked over their wineglass, went to their mouth uncertainly. "Without what?" I said mischievously, and then laughed when they frowned. "You don't have to answer that, Jonata. What a surprise! I thought you had learned all your oratory by the book, and left the passionate rhetoric to others."

They blushed. "I mean it," they said, a little shyly.

"I don't doubt you do," I said, and picked up my glass of wine and turned it so it caught the light. "You know," I said, "your brother had that kind of zealotry, too." They looked startled, and I added: "Only for his friends—never in public. He was no politician, not for his own sake. He would never have been a demagogue."

"Not like—" they said, and bit their tongue. I swirled my wine. They meant *like Flavia Decretan*, of course. Sílvio had never done for his husband what Flavia had done for hers.

"How did Cátia hear that I wanted to go on campaign?" I said, to change the subject. "Was it so easy to guess?"

But at that Jonata frowned and leaned forward. "Matheus, I've heard another rumor, and I want to ask you about it," they said.

"Cátia guesses too much," I said, smiling. "Has she heard Celestino and I will be moving house?"

"Moving house?" said Jonata, startled.

"Yes," I said. "I expect Celestino will be made to handle the bulk of the work again, if I am on Kutayet—but I don't know that it can wait. I think it's time we came to the Libeiracópolan."

Jonata said, "The Libeiracópolan?"

"You look pale," I said, alarmed. "Are you quite all right?"

"Yes," they said. "Of course, only—are you sure?"

"Oh, Jonata, you saw how happy the people were," I said. "Why shouldn't I be somewhere they can come and go, and ask me for whatever they need, and—and tell me what kind of satisfaction I might bring them, or do bring them? And it seems more convenient, if the council is to meet there more often from now on—and I intend it should. The council has been far too removed from the people, too. Does it not please you?"

It seemed to take them a moment to understand they were meant to reply. "Ye-es," they said, and, "Yes—of course. I only—no." They tugged at their hair, a little absently, and at last looked up. "I'm sorry, I think I'm a little ill after all, I need some water," they said. "Your kitchens—"

"Of course!" I said. "Downstairs, along the hallway," and watched them leave, frowning. They took a good deal of time returning. When they did, they hesitated behind the couch, their fingers curled around its back.

"Matheus," they said, "tell me something."

"Anything," I said.

They drew a deep breath in, then blew it out. "Do you think," they said, "do you think—I know that Sérgio conspired against the council. I know he meant to kill people. I do. But do you think, if they hadn't had him executed, if the council had shown him mercy—do you think Sílvio might have decided to live?"

I had said *anything*, and I had meant it. I looked aside for a while, though, trying to breathe. When at last I could, I said, "Yes. Yes, I think he might have."

They nodded, without meeting my eyes, and said: "Do you think it was still the right thing to do?"

"Ah," I said, and rubbed a hand over my mouth. "Fortune preserve us, Jonata, you don't go easy on me. Do I wish the council hadn't done it? Of course. Of course I do. What else could I wish for? How could I not want to see every law and all good reason laid aside for his sake?"

"Every law and all good reason," Jonata echoed, and looked away—then they smiled, swift and unexpectedly sweet, and circled around the couch and bent to kiss my cheek. "I'm sorry, I didn't mean to make you sad. It's getting late, Matheus. I'll see you again soon."

"Please don't be sorry," I said. "And *do* come back soon," and stood to escort them out.

They did come back, a week or so later, for a party at my house—Celestino's birthday, but naturally it was my friends and allies who made up the attendants, and Celestino busied himself in the kitchen by telling the servants what mistakes they were making, only rarely letting himself be drawn by a smiling Cláudia Pulcron into a few steps of a formal Sintian dance. Jonata didn't speak to him, but they hardly spoke to me, either; when they arrived, I was caught up in a flurry of flattery from

Barboulethan and a few friends of Nequeiron's, and it occurred to me only hours later how few of Jonata's friends—Cátia, Cipon, their cousin—were actually in attendance at all.

By that time I could see them nowhere in the room. I went to my front door to peer out into the street, looking for their silhouette along the low golden lamps—perhaps they had stepped out to smoke sílfion?—when I was startled by a touch on my arm.

"You're letting the wind in," said Gracia. "You're not enjoying yourself?"

I had hardly spoken to her that night, either. I turned to lean against the doorframe and smiled down at her. I had not thought I had drunk very much, but at that moment I was so warm and so light I forgot words entirely. It was enough to enjoy her gaze on me, thoughtful and bright.

"Why wouldn't I be enjoying myself?" I said. "A city at peace and a room full of people who love me. Was the Undying himself ever quite so happy?"

She looked at me unreadably. "Would you like me to ask him?" she said.

"No," I said. "No, I don't think we need his opinion."

Her mouth moved up at one end, not quite a smile. "I don't think I'm going to stay much longer, you know," she said. "I should fetch my coat."

"Oh—be sure to say goodbye to Celestino!" I said, momentarily distracted. "I think he's still in the kitchens."

Her eyebrows went up. "Whatever you like," she said, and turned to press into the crowd inside.

She was right; I was letting the wind in. But I made no move to follow her. Instead I pulled the door shut and sat down on the front step in the cool hollow of light beneath my door lantern. The air was cold and very clean. Before me was the distant clatter of spider-litters, behind me the faint indistinguishable chatter from my sitting room and entrance hall, the laughter of my guests, the faint chink of my glasses and silverware.

A minute or so later, the door opened again. Gracia paused, and then closed it and sat down beside me on the step, fingers brushing mine. I leaned over to kiss her, which she accepted but did not return.

"That might be reckless, Commander," she said, when I had pulled away. "It is your husband's party, you know."

"There's no one on the street," I said, gesturing to the Avenuan, empty except for the lights. "And even if there were—" I shook my head, wanting to express it and not knowing how: the lightness in me, the surety, the fading warmth of her mouth against mine.

"You are happy," she said quietly, "aren't you."

"Profoundly," I said. "Aren't you?"

She was silent for a minute.

"When the river unfreezes," she said at last, "and you go to Kutayet, and conquer the peoples there, and the peoples that they themselves have conquered... When you call yourself a god before the Crossbar and the Swordbelt Arm, and you lift me up beside you as Oracle to your divinity—when that day comes—"

The wind had picked up. A strand of hair had worked itself loose from its braid, and whipped across her forehead, but she made no move to brush it away. "Yes?" I said at last. "What about that day? You're tired of waiting for it, do you mean?"

"Oh—I don't know," she said. "I was just thinking of the sunrises on Szayet, out on the water. How I'd think about preserving them in glass bottles, in amber..."

"Are you homesick?" I said. "I was just telling Jonata that they and I should visit your planet again. Your people, the love they bear you—it's not a Szayeti lesson, I think, but a lesson for the empire. For all the galaxy." I hesitated. "Sometimes I feel very fortunate that I found you."

She leaned forward and hugged her knees to her chest, uncharacteristically graceless.

"You asked me once whether I wanted your absolution," she said. "For blasphemy, I suppose. For defying Alekso—for seizing the throne. For keeping Arcelia imprisoned for trying to tell the truth."

I looked at her, startled. Her face did not move.

"What would you tell me if I said I wanted absolution now?" she said.

I leaned forward and brushed her hair from her forehead and tucked it behind her ear, searching her face for some signal, some clue. At last I sat back and laughed.

"I'd call you a liar, Patramata," I said. "I don't believe you're sorry for anything."

She tilted her face up to the sky and smiled at it. Then she curved her hand around the back of my neck and pulled me in. I let myself be kissed, hot and sweet, and then she was standing, brushing off her coat, smiling down at me.

"Go back to the party, Commander," she said. "Your people must be missing you."

I had one last visitor that winter, on a grey and blustery afternoon when the morning's snow had turned to ice that pattered on the rooftop like the footsteps of dormice. The servants were building a fire in the sitting room, so that the crackling mingled with the rattle of the pipes in the walls, and the room filled up with heat as swiftly if it were one of the public baths.

Anita swept in along with a gust of sleet and spent nearly ten minutes dripping over my carpet while Celestino politely attempted to stop her from stripping naked in the entrance hall. At last they compromised on her boots and coat, and she padded in socks to my sitting room and took the wine he offered, and kissed his hand with great ceremony, and grinned at him as he disappeared upstairs.

"Will you persist in causing as much discomfort as you can manage to my husband?" I said, not entirely amused.

"Grant me your indulgence," she said. "I've had a long month."

Her hair was dripping into her eyes, and there was melted snow glittering on the tip of her nose. I considered her. "Tell me why it's been long," I said at last, and her face lit up as she bent forward to speak.

She hadn't had a long month, of course, unless you considered the usual litany of ill-advised affairs and iller-advised financial schemes worth noting. Nevertheless she was and always had been a pleasure to watch as a storyteller, full of animation and delight, so that even the worst of her sins were a cause for commiserating laughter, and the best of her triumphs for celebration. I noted that she, too, had seen very little of the councillors, which was no surprise—it was not as if she had ever been particularly popular among them, and Jonata in particular held her in great disdain, which disappointed me to no end.

"But before long we'll go to Kutayet," she said at last, "and all of this nonsense will be behind us."

"You aren't the only one impatient," I said. "Gracia said just the other night that she was tired of waiting."

Her smile flickered. "How is the Oracle of Szayet?" she said.

"She's well," I said. "It's not war she dreams of, of course."

"No," said Anita. "It isn't, is it. You are—doing it? Recording your—memories?" She said the last with a sort of distant disgust, as if she were describing a monster in the Black Maw from a storybook.

"I am," I said. "Each day's, and it takes the memories of the days before, too, and keeps them. I wonder if by now it remembers all the way back to Madinabia."

"And after you take Kutayet—" she said.

"After I take Kutayet," I said. "Yes. I'll tell the people."

She pushed her damp hair back from her forehead, so that it

stuck up at sharp angles. Then she said, "Why are you so comfortable in delaying it, Ceirran? Why do you put it off for month after month? I know it's nothing to do with her—I've seen what you've done for *her* sake. And I don't think you're afraid of what the council might say, or the people. How long's it been since you were afraid of anything? I want to know—"

She exhaled sharply. I leaned forward.

"What is it?" I said. "What do you want to know?"

"What do you believe?" she said, and held up a hand when I began to answer. "Don't ask me what *I* believe. I admit it's worked before, but not now. What do you think the Pearl does, Ceirran? Does it make you immortal? Does it make you—" She bit back the last words, and when I raised an eyebrow, stared back in near defiance.

"What do I believe?" I said. "I believe—" and stopped.

Gracia had told me, once, about the first Pearl of the Dead. She had said, *You think of divinity as a list of set qualities: infinite knowledge, infinite destruction, life everlasting. He was a god later...*

"I don't know whether I believe in the immortality of the human soul," I said. And then, at Anita's face: "I don't know. That's true, Captain. But perhaps I do believe—in the immortality of a man's name. Might that be the same thing?"

"No," she said. "It isn't the same thing at all."

I exhaled. "Then I am sorry," I said. "I don't know what more I can offer you."

"Ah, I'm melancholy," she said, and slouched back on the couch, and grinned a little, an animal's grin. Whatever brightness had been in her eyes had slipped away again, and her face was cool and amused, herself in her fullest. "You're indulgent. Bring me more wine. I'll be better company and make you laugh, and we'll plan to conquer the galaxy."

She was, as promised, altogether bright and brilliant for the next hour, and told me terrible gossip she had heard from Flavia, which I accounted only half-true. When the sun set the servants brought in dinner, roasted duck with leeks and turnip and soft cakes after. Celestino came to eat with us, sat steadfast while Anita cheerfully attempted to charm him, and disappeared at once when the food was gone, which made her laugh again. I went to the little stone room in the back and brought out another bottle of wine, which she drank the better part of.

After some time the conversation turned, as it often did, to Madinabia. Tonight she recalled a tribe from Madinabia D, one of three great nations on that moon, who had spent the preceding fifty years making war on their neighbors and conquering the bulk of them. "Do you remember," she said, "they wouldn't retreat? They didn't even *have* real warships—just thousands and thousands of those little fighters—do you remember how they'd pile up on the ground after dogfights? They were like anthills."

"I remember their chief," I said. "What an enormous man he was—we might have made truce with him! Only—"

"Only," said Anita, "he took insult at a teenage girl coming to negotiate—and threw me in chains—" and burst into hiccuping laughter, of such length and force that she fell sideways on her couch. When it died, she exhaled. Then she climbed off the couch, crossed the room, and settled again on the floor beside my feet.

"You've had more wine than I thought," I said to the top of her head, amused. "Perhaps you ought not walk back to your sister's."

"I'm not that drunk," she said. "Just—" The sentence seemed to have no end to it. She leaned back against the foot of my couch and tilted her head back so she was staring up at the broad red ceiling, and sighed contentedly, her eyes sliding shut.

"You look like a street cat come in from the cold," I said. "Should I give you a pillow so you can lie before the fire?"

Her mouth twitched, but she said nothing. I let myself look at her, as I so rarely did: the sharp bones of her face, her rough hands, the wiry muscles of her shoulders and arms. For some time I even thought she had fallen asleep, until she murmured, "Matheus?"

I hummed in answer. Her eyes didn't open, but she said:

"Did I do right?"

I knew what she was asking about. I took a moment to answer, though. I could see the swell of breath in her chest, how it quickened as the silence stretched. At last I reached down and rested my hand on her shoulder—and felt all the tension slide out of her at once, like a river into the sea. I had meant to answer her, to tell her the truth: how I felt about what she had done at the triumph, how I felt about our time together on Madinabia, how I felt about—but at long last, I had run out of words.

What do I believe?

I believe she knew, anyway.

She left near midnight. The sleet had turned to rain, and the silver sheets of it glittered through the streetlamps like stars. She walked like a street cat, too, long-limbed and swaggering, without an umbrella. Within moments she was soaked to the skin. She didn't look back. I watched her silhouette grow smaller until it turned a corner and disappeared.

I fell asleep that night to the clatter of rain on the roof like stones. When I woke, the storm had ended, and I could see spilling over our bedspread the clean white light of day.

Celestino was staring up at the ceiling. "Matheus?" he said without looking at me.

I hummed and sat up. My recorder was waiting for me in the bedside table, as well as my tablet. I settled one in my palm, tucked the other under my arm, and climbed back into bed beside him. He hadn't moved.

"I've had a very strange dream," he said.

"Oh?" I said.

"Very strange," said Celestino. His voice trailed off. I woke my tablet with my free hand and began to flick through the paperwork Anita had sent me overnight. Joaquim Nequeiron wanted yet more money—that was all right; we would find money to spare. One of Barran's distant cousins wanted another distant cousin freed from prison—that was absurd, an abuse of my generosity.

"You were sitting in the Libeiracópolan," said Celestino.

"What?" I said.

"In my dream," he said. His hand was resting on his ear, though he did not seem to be conscious of it. "You were sitting in its center—or a statue of you was, an enormous statue. It must have been a statue, because it was all over white, like it was made of marble, or pearl. And two people came along, and they reached up to its chest—" His mouth moved wordlessly. Then he said: "Its chest cracked in two. They pulled out its beating heart."

I blinked. "How grotesque," I said.

"It was," said Celestino. And then, sounding as if the admission cost him: "It frightened me."

"Frightened you?" I said, startled.

He looked up at me. He had once been a beautiful man, my husband, though I had lived with him long enough now that I rarely remembered it. Even now, his eyes were wide and as brown as the river, and his mouth was a set line.

"If I asked you," he said, "if I asked you—to stay with me today. Would you do it?"

I hesitated. These last months, Celestino had not asked me for anything. He so rarely asked me for anything; and I had, though I had worked very hard to avoid thinking of it in those terms, asked him for a great deal.

"If you could give me some excuse," I said, very gently.

"But I don't have one," he said. He sounded nearly as bewildered as I felt. "I only think—" He shook his head. "I didn't think. I only had a feeling. I don't know the logic of it. I can't tell you any good reason why."

I let go of the recorder. "I'll be back from the council in the afternoon," I said. "If it would please you, we can talk further then about your dreams."

Once I was dressed, as I opened the door, I glanced back at him. He was looking fixedly back at me, almost unblinking, as if he were trying to remember something.

When I stepped outside, there was a slim, dark figure waiting a few yards away. I squinted against the sun. "Jonata?" I said. "Are you coming to the council meeting with me?"

"I thought I might," they said. "Would you mind?"

"Not at all," I said, and linked my arm through theirs. "You look worried. What's troubling you?"

"No trouble," they said slowly. "No, only—you're a little late. I was worried you might not come to the Libeiracópolan today."

"I didn't know today was important," I said, smiling. "It's only a domestic matter. I wish I could promise that this is the last time the council will have to wait on my private business! Do you think they'll forgive me?"

Their mouth flickered quickly, not quite a smile. "I'm sure they will," they said.

"And you, too, Jonata?" I said.

They glanced at me, and then looked away, and then briefly laid their head on my shoulder. Surprised, I reached round to pat them on the arm. "I don't think you've done that since you were a child," I said. "Why did you come to fetch me, in any case? Is there something you wanted?"

"Just your company," they said. "Just for a little while."

I glanced back before we turned through the entrance of the Libeiracópolan. The sun was glittering on the trees. The Avenuan Libeirguitan was become a hall of diamonds, and the concrete was dark with icemelt. Only six days left until spring, now.

I could feel it breathing, deep beneath the earth. The daylight was creeping up, closer and closer, licking at the bounds of the morning to see if the morning flinched. The prison of the frost, cracking to let the wild things out.

"Matheus?" said Jonata, tugging at my elbow. "Come on. Everyone's waiting."

CHAPTER FORTY-THREE

GRACIA

I had a dozen fires to put out that morning. None of them, to my great irritation, was worth my time. Every packet from Szayet seemed to contain some new crisis: a spy gone missing, a shipment of grain vanished into the ether, a diplomatic agreement I had thought done and dusted suddenly returned with a hundred corrections, and every time I sat back to wonder what to do with the rest of my day something else would appear, blinking a dangerous red. I even tapped Alekso for aid once or twice on some of the particularly tedious problems, but he had gone cold and unresponsive, and only a few flickers of color in the corner of my eye told me that he was not vanished altogether. It was late in the afternoon before I was finally able to get up from my desk and come downstairs to ask the servants for some lunch, and before I had even managed that, there was a knock at the door.

It was Cátia Lançan. She smiled very warmly, and I knew at once that something was wrong.

"Madam Oracle," she said politely. "May I come in?" and did

not wait for an answer. "What a lovely home you're staying in. Do you know the provenance?"

"I cannot say I do," I said.

"Sérgio Catílion," she said. "A fine soldier—very fine. Dug himself into a mountain of debt, I'm afraid. Plotted to raise arms against Ceiao. Our mutual friend Cachoeiran had to denounce him in front of the council. And yet for all that, a very fine soldier. One of our best." She looked up at the sprawling mural in the entrance hall. "And before that," she said, "long, long before that, it was owned by a priest called Nathália Xicaran. Does that mean anything to you?"

I hated Ceirran for a moment. Of course he hadn't told me. He wouldn't have thought I would find it funny. I didn't. It seemed only sad, extraordinarily sad, that I should be standing in the house which in a different world might have been his husband's.

"I'm afraid not," I said. "May I offer you something to drink?"

The servants had cleared nothing away from the sitting room, but it was not as if they had had time. We settled ourselves on those long Ceian couches and waited for them to attend us, during which Cátia commented politely on the pillars, the furniture, the tapestries.

"I always mean to tell you how lovely it looks," she said, and gestured to my ear, where Alekso's voice sat silent and cold as the grave. "I've been thinking of making investments in quicksilver pearl myself. I don't suppose you've been to see our oyster crop on the coast?"

"I'm sorry to say I haven't had the opportunity yet," I said. "I've had such a great deal to do in Ceiao. You might have heard as much."

"What a shame," she said, reaching up for the cup of wine from the maid. "It's strange to think that, if Szayet had never offered Ceiao her friendship those centuries ago, the species might have become altogether extinct. Don't you agree?"

"Strange indeed," I said. "Why are you interested in pearl, if I might ask? I was under the impression your factories were doing rather well."

Her thin mouth curled. "They are," she said. "This is a new venture. Based on—insider information. And I was very much taken with a piece recently obtained by a friend, which they were kind enough to lend me. You must be something of an expert on the stuff, I suppose?"

"Oh, only as far as any Szayeti is an expert," I said politely. I could not read her face, which disturbed me. If it had made any sense, I would have thought that she was really trying to be friendly. "I'm sure you know that we are sentimental about quicksilver pearl, at home. It is a religious matter."

"How charming," said Cátia, "these local customs. I've brought my friend's pearl with me, as a matter of fact. Perhaps you'd like to see it?"

"Please," I said automatically, and then my mind caught up to my mouth, and I half rose from my seat—but Cátia already had the second Pearl of the Dead in her hand, and was holding it up to the light.

"Ah," she said. "I see you're interested."

My first instinct was to spring at her and throw her to the ground and seize it from her hand, as if we were on Szayet and I had a hundred guards outside the door. I suppressed this at once. My second was to throw her out of my house—but this too I forced down. The Pearl—Ceirran's Pearl—winked at me from her hand. I could not afford to let it out of my sight.

My third, long-belated, was confusion. She could not possibly have mistaken it for an ordinary pearl. Whoever had stolen it for her—whatever *friend* she had spoken of—would have had to take it from Ceirran's house itself. So why would she speak as if she were ignorant?

What kind of lie was she trying to tell?

I let myself sink back against the couch. "I'm curious," I said. "You would like my—expertise?"

"So you do have some," said Cátia. "What good fortune. Would you judge it to be valuable, then?"

I reached for it, but she pulled her hand away, watching me through half-closed eyelids. I sat back, sipping at my wine, and weighed my options. I wanted to play her game, if only to see what lay at its end. But what moves would she allow me to make? I could ask her where she had found it, a question she would hardly answer—I could invent a provenance out of thin air, and thereby tell her bluntly that she could not trust me—or I could say only that it was very valuable indeed, and tip my hand.

"Why are you asking for my opinion?" I said. "There are thousands of merchants and assessors in the city. Some of them are even Szayeti. What can I offer you that they cannot?"

She tucked the Pearl into her palm and sat forward on the couch. "You know," she said, "I don't think you and I have been very close friends."

I stared at her open-mouthed for a moment before I recovered myself. "I'm sorry," I said. "I didn't know you had desired my friendship."

"There's no need to apologize," she said. "It's not the past I'm thinking of, but the future. Even Ceiao's future, if you'll forgive a little rhetoric. I'm sure you, too, have heard that change is coming to the city. Yes?"

"So I've heard," I said slowly. "An invasion campaign of Kutayet, yes?"

"Yes," she said. "Among other things. It's important to the council, Madam Oracle, that Szayet and Ceiao's friendship should outlast all change. No matter what happens in the Swordbelt Arm—or in any other part of the galaxy."

"Is there any reason I should not continue to extend it?" I said.

"You mistake me," she said. "You asked what you can offer

me. Please understand: I am making an offer to *you*. I am prepared to be generous." She leaned forward. "I am prepared to be your friend, Madam Oracle. Will you tell me the value of this pearl?"

An insult would not have surprised me. An open threat would have sent me to my feet to call my guard. I should have guessed at this, the most Ceian and the most obscene of maneuvers: an attempt to buy me.

Long ago, Arcelia had said to me, *I thought: There must be something left even she wouldn't do.*

"I'm afraid your eyes have deceived you," I said. "It's pretty, of course, but quite ordinary. I would expect it to fetch hardly eighty dekar on the open market."

Cátia looked at me unblinkingly. "Are you sure?" she said.

"Very sure," I said, smoothing my skirts. I needed her out of my house, the sooner the better. Ceirran's friends would need to know about this. Ceirran would need to know—this was as blatant a move against him as his enemies had ever made. Was the Pearl meant to be blackmail—leverage—evidence against him in a trial? Did she mean to ask for a bribe, or some change in policy? It did not matter. He could call the city guard into Cátia's house and seize it, if need be, and find some excuse for it—or perhaps this would even force his hand, and he might reveal it for what it was—"May I make you an offer?" I added, as an afterthought. "Ninety dekar, perhaps. As I said: We Szayeti are sentimental about these things."

"Yes," said Cátia. "I recall. A religious matter." Her head tilted briefly, like a bird's. Then she said: "Well—if it's worth so little—"

I flung out my hand at once. I was too late. She had tossed it into my cup of wine.

Our ancestors, when they named the pearl after mercury, did not name it aright. It does not flow, when dissolved.

From within its center, rather, the rust erupts. First one dark splash licks up, and puddles outward in waves; then the next, spilling and spreading onto the pearl's surface, brown and scarlet and dark as a kiss on someone's neck, unfolding and coagulating in circles one after another until there is no silver left. The rust thickens and mats, and bubbles atop itself. The reaction becomes so rapid that it is invisible to the human eye. The pearl has at this point grown to twice its previous size. Its surface is now thick, and rough, and heavy with its own death. This is in the first two seconds after the alcohol touches the stone.

If the wine had only been spilled over it a little, it might have been subject then to the oxygen of the open air, and survived longer. It had not. The rust shell cracked, instantly, like glass. When it fell apart, it shattered on impact with the cup, and the redness bubbled upward, just as living blood once had. Then it settled to the bottom beside the dregs. Beneath it was a small, hard thing, knobbly and brown as a walnut. It was of roughly the same worth.

I sat, and looked at the lump of stone in my glass that had, fifteen seconds ago, held Matheus Ceirran's immortality.

She hadn't needed it to blackmail him, after all. She hadn't needed it to arrest him. She hadn't needed to hold it as leverage. There had never been any leverage necessary.

I said, very quietly, "You have been careless with something beautiful."

"I'm sorry," she said. "Have you reconsidered?"

I stood. "Please leave," I said. "I have some preparations to make."

I packed my robes, when Cátia was gone. I packed my shoes. I packed my tablets and my carpets and my robes and my jewels and gowns. Then I went upstairs and sat on my bed, and wept until my eyes were sore.

Night fell, as I did this. I had expected as much. Noise rose, which I had expected, too. I listened to the screams and to the clatter of metal with a distant ear. My windows were covered with thin curtains, through which the light faded. Shortly afterward, it began to grow again, flickering, low and red.

On that little western island with Ceirran, with the whole pulsing universe scattered above me like water and salt, I had tucked my head against his chest and closed my eyes. And when I had opened them, my father had been standing beside me. He was smiling, and his arms were outstretched, and I leapt into them, and shrieked in delight as he lifted me high into the air.

We were in my nursery. Outside I could see the glittering ocean, and the curves of the harbor, and hear the low hushing murmur of the servants, just where they had always been. But my bookshelf reached higher than it had in the nursery—many times higher—and it was filled with Szayeti books, Ceian books, Kutayeti and even Cherekku books, and I tugged my father toward them, because I could explain these books to him now, I could tell him everything he hadn't understood, I could tell him everything I knew.

Sweeting, he said, and laughed. He knelt and kissed me on the top of my head. Then he opened the door of the nursery, and light spilled, so bright that I could no longer see what lay beyond it, and I watched as he walked through the door into that blinding sun.

I had awoken long before dawn. Ceirran's face had been barely visible above mine. I had watched it for minutes, for hours, as the broken moons moved in shadows over his face. I had thought of him rolling my ancestors' Pearl of the Dead along his palm on the ship, in the privacy and warmth of our bed. Such a small thing, I thought, to have survived so long, to have caused so much bloodshed. Such a small and ordinary thing, compared to a living man.

Now I left my bedroom, and went to sit in the entrance hall.

Zorione was speaking to me, her voice far away. I heard only *not an hour ago*, and *grave danger*, and *Holiest*, and *Are you hearing*— and *Please*—She left, after a while, and came back with bread, and shoved it into my hands. I ate without tasting. They seemed so great, those mechanical efforts of biting and chewing and swallowing down, and I did them until the bread was gone, and there was nothing left but the sight of my hands.

There was a banging at the door. Zorione cried out, and waved to a guard to bar it, but I held up a hand. "Open it," I said.

"Oracle—" said Zorione, desperate.

"Open it," I said. Her eyes wide with fear, Zorione unlocked the door and pulled it open.

I hardly recognized the figure there at first. I had seen her in war and in peace, with a smoking gun and a drink in her hand, silver-tongued and sleek—but I had never, in all the time we had known each other, seen Ana look as if she were not in control.

She staggered forward. Zorione caught her, though Ana's warrior's bulk was enough that she stumbled beneath it. Ana's cloak was half-torn off her shoulders, and there was a streak of something beneath her eye—blood or mud, I could not tell. I could not tell whose.

I stood in a swift movement. "Get her water," I said to Zorione, "and wine—something to wash her off with—"

"I don't need *water*," Ana spat, and then spat again, this time blood.

I felt myself begin to tremble and did not know why. It was not as though I had not seen blood before. "Sit down," I said.

"I won't," said Ana. "I'm not here to stay. I came to warn you—"

"I already know he is dead," I snapped.

Zorione turned to me, her eyes wide as saucers. Ana shrugged her off, unsteady on her feet. She was looking at me as if she had never seen me before.

"You already know," she said.

I looked away. My heart was beating very fast. "Who was it?" I said.

"Jonata," said Ana. "And Veguion—and Cipon—but it was Jonata, they were the—" She stopped, shook her head like she was underwater. "They had *knives*—like barbarians—it was Jonata, it was all—"

"Where was his body?" I said, over her. "Some council tower? No, the temple, of course, the Libeiracópolan. Did you guess it that quickly?" She tried to speak, but I stepped toward her and said, "Had he already bled out by the time you managed to reach him? Could you have saved him if you had found him sooner?"

Ana's chest rose and fell. She said, very softly: "I ought to let them drag you into the street and rip you limb from limb."

"Get her water," I said to Zorione again. "Go."

She hesitated, but she knew me, and fled. Ana took a step forward. Her hand was on her gun.

"Do you think this is a game?" she said, even softer.

I looked steadily at her. Her hand was curling around the grip—her finger twitched toward the trigger—then she let go of the gun and reached for my body, and pulled me toward her, and I dug my fingers into the nape of her neck and swallowed her gasp before it left her mouth.

I had thought once that in peace she had grown soft. I had been mistaken. There was nothing soft in her now, in the muscle of her arms, her teeth in my lip, the hard outline of her gun against my hip. She pressed me toward the wall—I thought, briefly and wildly, of Ceirran kissing me against this wall, and I shoved her away. She stumbled back. Her eyes were as dark as wine. On my tongue I could taste the sharp, heady metal of her blood.

I reached for her throat. Her eyelids flickered, but she didn't move. I curled my fingers around her captain's pin, and in one swift, graceless motion, ripped it free. She flinched. Her cloak slithered to the floor.

I had thought to take her tunic next. But in the end it did not matter: In every way that counted she was naked already, and an animal. She bared her teeth, and leapt for me.

How can I make you understand what she was to me in those half-shadowed hours? What would you believe? There had been moments, those last months, when I had thought that were I to so much as brush my hand against Ana Decretan's, I would go up like straw. It was almost a shock to discover that I might touch her and live. It was almost a shock to discover that she might touch me—that she did touch me, was touching me, warm hands and hot mouth, that she had a grip like steel, that her throat had the taste of salt, that her hair had the texture of cornsilk, that her body under mine was hot and alive and inside its ribs there was a heartbeat and on its tongue was the sound of my name.

On the bed she pulled the weight of my body over herself, working herself urgent and breathless against me. Her hands on my hips gripped hard enough to hurt, and she leaned up again and again to seize my mouth. She could not seem to stop. Even when I said, "Hold—let me breathe, let me," trying to pull back and look at her laid muscled and tousle-haired and naked beneath me, she only nodded mutely and then tugged me desperately down to kiss her again. At last I wound my fingers into her hair and yanked her back, and she cried out. I looked sharply down at her, expecting to find maybe anger, maybe shame, maybe an attempt to hide her reaction altogether—but she only stared at me, and her tongue came out to wet her lips.

With my free hand, I reached down, and when I touched her between her legs she shuddered and went still. Her gaze flickered to my mouth.

"Do it again," she ground out.

I pressed my fingers into her again, where she was soft and

hot and very wet. The column of her throat moved. She made no noise.

"That?" I said. She was silent. "Or—" And I dragged my nails down the back of her neck, almost hard enough to draw blood, and she gasped and rocked down against my hand, eyelids sliding shut, mouth moving wordlessly. And then it was not wordless at all, and I covered her mouth with mine, bit hard at her lip, muffling her *please, please.*

She lay beside me, afterward, still as earth, an arrangement of loose muscle untethered from purpose. I would have thought she was asleep, if I had not been able to feel against my arm the birdlike quickness of her breath. In the dark I propped myself up on my other elbow and let myself drink my fill at last of all the small particulars of her face: the ink-stain lashes, the square jaw, the hard flat shadows at her mouth. There was a bruise at the base of her neck. I could not tell whether it had been left there by some Ceian on the street or by my mouth.

At last she said, without opening her eyes:

"When he spoke—"

I said nothing.

"When he spoke," she said finally, "it was like the world cracked open."

I tore my eyes away from the bruise and said, "It's cracked open now." My voice felt hoarse.

She didn't reply. I let her have her silence, there in the dark. Her body was so warm beside mine, nearly feverish, as if what ran in her wrists and temples was boiling water rather than blood.

After some minutes she said, "There'll be a will. A funeral... all of it. Ceremony."

"There always is," I said.

"The sun should stop in the sky," she said. "How's that for ceremony. Every ship on the planet should see its engines die and choke on dust—how's that for ceremony. The people of the city should open their veins and let their blood run back into his body until he stands upright and alive again—how's *that* for ceremony?" A muscle in her jaw tightened. Then she said, without emotion, "You ought to leave before the funeral."

"My bags are packed," I said.

"Fortune's eyes, you really did know," she said, faintly marveling. "How? Ah, don't tell me: prophecy."

"Something like that," I said.

"Fine," said Ana. She sounded now only very tired. "Fine. I won't see you again."

She turned away from me, and I heard her slow, shuddering exhale. I rolled to one side and swung my legs off the bed, and padded naked to the door. That awful, warm insensibility had passed, and my restored faculties felt uncertain, sore. I did not know that I could bear to look at her face again.

As I turned into the low white lamplight, I heard her say, so softly that I barely caught it, "Thank you."

I remembered that, afterward. It was the first time she had ever managed to surprise me.

PART IV

CHAPTER

FORTY-FOUR

GRACIA

I know that he would have told you at length what happened on Ceiao next. But he and I were not really of one mind, no matter how we wished it. There was only one war I was ever interested in.

Suffice it to say that the City of Endless Pearl was wet and cool with winter when I returned to her. My people clustered to meet me in the streets, their breath white in the air, and I reached out my hands to them and let them kiss my knuckles and reel away starry-eyed. The palace was quiet. I might have expected it to be quiet. How long had I ever spent in it without Ceiao occupying its quarters and halls?

How long had I ever spent without Ceiao, as queen?

How long was I going to spend without it, the days and weeks stretching out ahead, summer into winter into summer again? How long was it going to last me—this, the rest of my life?

I tell you I was disinterested. I am perhaps, even now that there is at last no longer any need of it, a liar. Or rather a half liar: I could not have been interested even if I had wanted to be. It was almost like being a child again. I had known that diplomacy happened, that wars happened, that empires were made and broken in the sky above me while I played in the sand, but they were so far above and I was so small, the earth like a coin and the sky a drop of water, which gathered on its surface and would not burst. I had letters from Ceiao, from what few faithful spies remained. Cachoeiran had turned up dead on the Rouan Valquíria, three golden hairpins through his tongue. Otávio Julhan had come from Far Madinabia to join the captain in the city, and was deep in her counsels. Barran and Cátia had made camp in the Swordbelt Arm, not far from Belkayet, and were preparing their armies for battle with Ceirran's mourners. There had been a funeral, after all. A will. Ceremony.

In no particular order this news came, and I dismissed it with no particular attention. There was always some other thing to focus on: a matter of palace staffing, of steel shipments, of religious delicacy, of taxes raised or abandoned or uncollected. There was always something else to read, and the world was so wide and empty above me, and beneath it I was just as small as I had always been, and whenever I put down the papers, I was in my own mind again, entirely alone.

I attended to these matters very late after sunset, in my cold bedroom, with the curtains open and the windows wide to the night. I always meant to sleep. It was just so quiet in Alectelo. I could hear the silence, every time I closed my eyes.

Of course the war did come to Szayet in the end. Ceiao always seemed to, given enough time.

What people remembered of the proscriptions was fragmented after they had finally ended. I was never able to draw an explanation out of traveling Ceians with any lucidity. When the narratives were clear, they were repetitive, rote, the same words and cadence I had already heard used by their countrymen in earlier interviews, as if they had gathered in conspiracy to bear false witness.

I have never been able to understand why. I did not believe they were lying—but I did not, and I do not, believe they were speaking from their hearts. I am not sure even now whether it was confusion that barred them from using their own words, or fear, or shame. Or perhaps there is a certainty in the discussion and argument they passed among one another on Ceiao—a certainty, when memory is so savage it becomes impossible to retain, in a well-worn story.

The story they told me was this: that Ceirran's killers had been put on a list, and the people on the list were condemned to die. Any who had known of the conspiracy, but said nothing, were condemned to die. Any who had aided them during that period of unrest in Ceiao afterward were condemned to die. Any who aided them now were condemned to die. Any who tried to save any man on the list were condemned to die. This, I should note, I needed no Ceians to explain to me. In the first place, a suspicion of being caught in the net of some policy like it was why I had left Ceiao so quickly—so entangled had I been with Ceirran's affairs, so little did the Ceians trust me. In the second, it was what I would have expected Ceirran to do, had he lived.

Had he lived! When they weren't speaking of themselves, it was all they spoke of. Had he lived, he would have erased all debt; had he lived, he would have by now appointed a dozen priests to wait on his every need, and put up a statue of himself in the Libeiracópolan; had he lived, he would have killed Jonata Barran with his bare hands, and hung their body from the Libeiracópolan's door. Had he lived, Far Madinabia would have fallen into open rebellion. Had he lived, Kutayet would have been at that moment a smoldering wreck. Had he lived, he would have been a tyrant to the Ceian people. Had he lived, he would have been the savior of the Ceian people, who had been the only ones who truly knew him.

What the Ceians said, and what they said with such certainty and automation, was that it was not all political affiliation that had placed these people of quality on the lists of the walking dead. The money and belongings of the executed were stripped from them and awarded to the state. Or—and here the Ceians lowered their voices—to those two people who had, these last months, become all of the state that was left. And at this they would nod at me, and at one another, and perhaps murmur something about *the captain* or *that boy*, if they were very brave.

Here is what the Ceians did not say: Anyone—citizen or immigrant, councillor or factory worker—who delivered the head of a proscribed man to the government would be awarded ten thousand dekar.

I did not ask these travelers where they were going. I did not ask them how they had found the money to travel to Alectelo, so far from home.

But all of this I heard after the war had ended. What arrived on Szayet arrived on a late white morning, when the mist had come up from the harbor at dawn and shaded all our buildings and horizons into a pencil-scratch grey. I was at my desk, working on a piece of the land management statutes that the new spring would force upon us, when some bright thing flashed in the corner of my eye. I glanced up and stared. Over the faded ocean, barely visible through the fog, was a falling piece of flame.

It slid onto the beach fifteen minutes later, belching smoke, before a whispering crowd of Alectelans. My ministers and I were at their head. All of us had run down from the palace, and some were still in their morning robes—I had barely had the presence of mind to put on my crown.

It was easy enough to tell the beached ship was of Ceian make. What was more unusual was its coloring: Though the shape and the quality of the steel would have been recognizable from orbit, it was missing that blue stripe along its side, which would have identified it at once as military. This was a private vessel.

The hatch on top burst open and a woman tumbled out. I did not know her at first. She had a round face and close-shaven hair, and she was dressed in damask robes, which had once been fine and which were now ragged and streaked with grease and dust. When she fell to the sand by her ship, reached out for my hand, and said in antiquated but clear Sintian, "Oracle—Madam Oracle, please," it was only then that I recognized her: Jacinta, the poet, who I had met when I had first come to Ceiao in the winter, many months ago.

I took a step back involuntarily. She scrambled to her feet. "Oracle," she said again, faint. Her eyes were dark with exhaustion, and there was a faded cut on her forehead. "They're coming after me—you have to help me. Please help me. I'm on the lists."

I stepped back again. "What have you done?" I said.

"Nothing," she said, and she reached out for my hand again, and this time caught it and held. "Nothing, I've done nothing—I have money, I don't know, maybe it's money—my wife pleaded for me, they caught my wife—please, they're right behind me. Please. All I'm asking is the Library. Just let me sleep in the Library until—" She shook her head wildly. "Just let me stay. Please. I'll give you whatever you ask for. Oracle, give me sanctuary."

I shook her hand off. My ministers were staring at me, and my foreign minister was even faintly shaking her head. I shut my eyes. "I cannot grant you sanctuary on a whim," I said.

"Please," she said. "Please don't let me die."

At once the words were tight and hot in my throat. I swallowed hard. "I cannot grant you sanctuary on a whim," I repeated. Then, when she shrank into herself: "But neither will I turn you out into the black to die on a whim." She reached for my hand again, and this time I let her. "You are on Szayeti soil," I said, "under Szayeti sovereignty. That is not a matter of my will, but a matter of galactic law. If you have done wrong"—I held up a hand to her exclamation—"if you have done wrong, the Oracle will discover it, and we will mete what justice we are able. But until that time I have no intention of taking action based on the laws passed in the Empire of—"

But before I could finish the sentence, there was a roar in the distance, low and animal, and then a high-pitched hum, which grew louder and louder and broke when a large Ceian ship sped onto the beach and docked itself beside the poet's.

She made a small, awful noise. The hatch creaked open, and a head emerged. This time I did not know his face. It was only his clothing I knew: his blue cloak, and the golden pins that held it to his throat.

"Jacinta Corelhan?" he said.

"Is the City of Endless Pearl a customs bay?" I said sharply. "State your name and business, stranger, and then return to my exosphere and wait to be processed. Or better yet, come forth from your ship and make obeisance before the Oracle of Szayet, and beg mercy for your discourtesy."

He looked at me: my robes, my crown, the glimmer in my ear. Then he climbed out of the hatch and swung himself down onto the beach, and dusted off his knees and his jacket and the belt that hung from his hip.

"Did you hear me?" I said. "State your name and business at once."

"Otávio Julhan sent me," he said to the poet in Ceian. Then he pulled the gun from his belt and fired.

At this point a great deal happened at once.

I screamed. The crowd screamed, too, and scattered in all directions, tripping over one another to get away. Those few soldiers among them shoved through, toward the man, and seized him by the shoulders. He stumbled back with a look of almost comical surprise. Jacinta the poet took a step forward, and fell into my arms.

I had seen footage, of course, of the body. I did not want to see it. It did not matter what I wanted. It came with each letter, with each data packet, with each report of the war. There was no moment that the world did not show it to me, did not demand it be shown. I had seen his body in the blue stained-glass light of the Libeiracópolan, I had seen his body under the shroud. I had seen his body with the shroud thrown off. I had seen his torn mantle, and his wet dark blood. His hand flung over his face. His eyes, closed by the gentle fingers of some unknown mourner, twelve thousand light-years away.

I knelt and lowered the corpse carefully to the sand. Her mouth was a little open. I could see the broken place where she had been worrying at it, only a few moments before.

After some time I became aware of a noise, and then, a little while later, of a touch. One of my guards was bending down, her hand on my shoulder. When I lifted my head, she sprang back and bowed.

"Holiest," she said, "what shall we do with the murderer?"

I stood. The living Ceian was staring at me, open-mouthed. I did recognize him, I thought, though I did not know from where. It might have been from any street in the city—from the bar, the night after Ceirran's triumph—from the factory floor. In his eyes there was a kind of wildness, and a confusion that sent my heart into my throat.

I said to him in Ceian, "Do you speak Sintian?"

"No," he said, bewildered.

I wanted to curse like an Alectelan and spit on the ground. I was not an Alectelan. I was a queen, and he had done what he had done in front of the Szayeti people.

"I am going to speak to his admirals," I said, and turned away. "Bring him to the marketplace, and have him shot."

But there was no speaking to his admirals. It took me nearly a day to determine this—every official I spoke to sent me to another, who sent me to another, who gave me excuse after wandering excuse until I could determine at last that neither of Ceiao's new powers was able to speak to the queen of Szayet—or, if either was able, neither was willing. "Admirals Julhan and Decretan are at war, Madam Oracle," said one captain to me. "If either comes planetside in the next several weeks, I expect they will be occupied with that unfortunate business."

There was a careful politeness on her face that I wanted abruptly to dig my fingernails into. I ended the holo call and buried my head in my hands.

The fog, which usually dissipated in the clear heat of the day at this time of year, lingered at the harbor-gate, and by late afternoon was a golden haze through which the distant shorebirds fluttered and scratched at the beach. I stood, paced toward my balcony and away again. When I had first returned to Szayet from Ceiao, I had found a smallness to my bedroom I had never noticed before. I had slept in another bed, and then another, and in every one I had woken just before dawn, gasping at the closeness of the walls.

My tablet made a soft, clear noise. I turned and tapped it at once. "I thought I would never see you again," I said, and then jerked back.

"I can't say I expected to see you, either," said Cátia Lançan. "How times change. Do you have some time to talk?"

I opened my mouth to snap *No*, and then closed it. She looked tired, too. There was a puffiness to her eyes, a sharp slant to her mouth, which had not been there on Ceiao, the day she had thrown my Pearl of the Dead into a cup of wine.

"What if I do?" I said. "What do you want?"

"What do I want," she said. "In honesty? The same thing I

wanted the last time we spoke. I'd like a friendship between Szayet and Ceiao." She propped her pointed chin in her hand, and her eyes narrowed. "And I'd like to invest in quicksilver pearl."

"Was our last meeting an overture of friendship?" I said coldly. "I didn't realize."

Cátia's lip curled. "It might have been," she said. "I told you then I was being generous. If I offer to be generous a second time, will you decide again to act so hastily?"

I hesitated, and then pulled my chair out from my desk and sat before her, so that the gold of the growing evening in the window shone through her hands and her cold brown eyes. "You accuse me of acting hastily?" I said. "I recall that you offered *generosity* with as much confidence as if it were you who had walked in triumph down the Avenuan Libeirguitan the previous month, all while Commander Ceirran still lived."

"Commander Ceirran died not a minute later," she snapped, and looked at once as if she regretted it, but my lip curled.

"Have the people let you walk down the Avenuan Libeirguitan since?" I said.

A muscle in her jaw worked. "Madam Oracle," she said, with deliberate patience, "I would like to make a deal with you. My— The respected councillor Jonata Barran and I are presently the admirals of a very large army, stationed within the Swordbelt Arm. We are, in addition to this, some of the only remaining living members of the Merchants' Council. On these facts can we agree?"

"We can," I said, after a pause.

"I am glad to hear it," she said. "Admiral Barran and I are in possession of many, many ships and many, many soldiers. What we are not in possession of is money with which to pay them, and to pay for their supplies. It is here, Madam Oracle, that I hoped you might be of assistance."

I laughed, high and hard. "Councillor, I'm afraid you're misinformed!" I said. "Of all the places in the Swordbelt Arm to come to for *money*—of all the places in the galaxy, even—I am terribly sorry that your strategy is based on such a misapprehension. Please feel free to reach out the next time you're looking for a planet without any wealth at all. Good evening."

She leaned forward and said, "We both know that's not true."

The humor left me at once, like a cold wind. I said, "What in the world can you mean by that?"

"You have wealth to send me," she said, "if you're so inclined. What you *are* lacking is the ability. But you may have heard, Madam Oracle, that I come from a manufacturing family. You may even have heard that among the materials we manufacture is diving equipment."

I stood at once, my hand hovering over the tablet.

"I do not know what you think of me," I said quietly, "though I must assume it is very little. You have twice now provoked me to commit an act of personal betrayal, in the first instance against someone for whom I cared deeply, and in the second against my faith and my god. I have already refused you in the matter of a treasure small enough to be held in the hand. I cannot imagine what price you think would induce me to give you the treasures of my home's own oceans. I must urge you not to provoke me again," and I would have ended the holo then, had she not said:

"Sovereignty."

I stopped.

"Is that a threat?" I said.

"No," she said. "No, it's not a threat. Please sit down. You should know by now that news in the galaxy moves quicker than you think."

I shut my eyes, and I sat. "This is about the poet," I said. "I should have known."

"Who?" said Cátia. "Oh—the woman who died? Yes. It's

about her. More to the point: It's about the bounty hunter who shot her. Do you know that it's against the law to aid the proscribed?"

"Ceian law," I said at once.

"Yes," Cátia said. "And it's against Szayeti law to commit murder." She leaned back and tapped her fingers on a table just out of the holo's vision. "Which do you think Otávio Julhan will decide takes precedence?"

I leaned forward, furious, and she held up a hand. "I'm only acting as messenger," she said. "And I'm making you an offer, Madam Oracle. I will send you, free of cost, a freighter full of whatever you might need: seaships, submarine cranes, undersea drones, steel spiders. You send me five ships full of quicksilver pearl—just five! I'll even cover the cost of shipping. And then, when my war is won, you and I can negotiate a treaty to enforce Szayeti sovereignty. We can even give your planet a special status, if you like. Friend of the Ceian Empire."

"What if I do nothing," I said, "and negotiate such a treaty with the admirals who currently occupy Ceiao, should they win your war?"

She sighed.

"I told you earlier that Admiral Barran and I are in possession of many, many ships," she said, "and many, many soldiers, stationed in the Swordbelt Arm." She folded her hands in front of her. "I'm afraid that this part is the threat."

I shut my eyes. In the distance, far beyond the sea, the ships roared.

"I need time," I said. "I need to consult with my ministers."

"Take a day," she said. "Take two, even. I can afford to be generous." She smiled without warmth. "I just can't afford it for very long."

Her image vanished. I stood and picked up the tablet, and whirled and dashed it against the wall.

It shattered at once. Against my carpet, the sparks danced and died. I closed my eyes. Then I stepped carefully over it and leaned out into the hallway, where a guard sprang to attention.

"Please call a maid," I said, "and please have a new tablet delivered to me. I'll be back later in the evening."

I had been a child the last time I had gone exploring in the palace. It took me a long time to find the place I wanted, and for a while I was afraid that it had been destroyed in the explosion. I remembered it only vaguely, the way I remembered dreams. But at last I turned down a hallway I half recognized, and pushed open a door I half knew, and coughed at the dust.

It was an ancient room, filled with old tablets and moth-eaten clothes, and I did not think it had been opened more than twice in the last three centuries. What I was looking for was buried toward the back, under a rusted helmet and a scrap of red feather. It was round, and flat, and gleaming silver. It looked nearly exactly like its counterpart I had given Ceirran many months ago.

I knew how to operate the recorder I had given Ceirran, and I knew how to operate this. I slid my fingers round it, found a warm little indent on the side, and pressed hard.

At once a head appeared, handsome and dark-haired, with cool golden eyes. *I was fourteen years old*, it said clearly. *My father had given me a ship that no living man could fly. And when I cursed his name, you smiled at me, and you said: no living man*, yet.

"I was wondering when you might look for it," said the living Alekso softly beside my ear.

I didn't look at him. He drifted forward a little and bent toward his own face. The holo-Alekso turned toward him blindly, and my Alekso reached out a hand. It passed through his own cheek. "Is it your true self?" I said.

"No," he said, leaning closer toward it. "You know better than that, Caviro's daughter. Your ancestor spent weeks putting its contents into my new body. This thing is only memories. What you carry in your ear is my soul."

"But nothing else went into the Pearl," I said. "Only these memories, and your living blood, when you still lived, and the intelligence to animate them." I swallowed hard. "Are you anything more than that?"

He didn't look at me. "I don't know," he said. "Are you?"

I watched the face over the recorder speak for a little while longer. Then I said, "I want advice on the Ceian war."

"At last," said Alekso, and straightened. "Your Councillor Lançan's overconfident, in my opinion. With even a hundred good ships, and a few decent pilots—"

"No," I said. "Not from you."

He looked at me without expression. Then he said, "You were never planning to give me to your sister, were you."

I set down the recorder, and the low murmur of its voice ceased at once. His living face watched me, unmoving.

"No," I said. "If it had only meant letting her become your Oracle when I became Ceirran's, and my remaining the queen of Szayet, maybe. I might have considered it. But you would never have consented to anything less than kingship. And I would never have let the Szayeti people go."

I had expected him to become angry, to snap, to shout. But he did none of these. Instead, he stood silently, looking at me, and then he turned and went to the door and through it into the hallway.

I set down the recorder and followed him. He walked for a little while without speaking, me a step behind, and then turned and drifted through a pair of glass doors and onto the balcony, which I opened and then shut behind me. There was a cool wind in the air, carrying with it the smell of salt. We stood there for some time, he and I, he looking at nothing, me looking at him.

"I've been expecting this," he said after a while.

"You must have," I said. "Ever since I made it."

"No," he said. "Not because of that. Do you know that every one of your ancestors, from your father back to Caviro's first child, has asked me to restore their dead to life?"

This silenced me for a moment, but at last I said, "But they didn't have a Pearl."

He said, "Neither do you."

"I do," I said. "It might be damaged—of course it's damaged—"

"It's not damaged," said Alekso. "It's gone."

I exhaled at that, slow and careful, and turned my back to the water to look within, at the warm redness of the hallway, the old royal tapestries, my father's favorite paintings.

"Then undo it," I said.

"I can't," said Alekso Undying.

"You *built* it," I said. "You built it with me. You can tell me how to make another one, one that doesn't require the blood of the living man to work with its recorder. You can tell me how to make a Pearl that doesn't need a recorder to work at all. You can tell me how to pull the living man out of the memories. You can tell me how to repair the Pearl that was broken. You can tell me how to make it right again."

"I *can't*," he said. "Think a minute! If I could, I wouldn't care whether you kept *me* safe. You have no new Pearl. If you had one, you would have no living blood to code it to his genetic print. You have no soul to bear."

"You were the greatest inventor this galaxy has ever known," I said. "If every one of my ancestors since Caviro's first child has asked you for it, how have you not yet made a way to undo death?"

"Do you want the truth?" he said.

I turned to stare at him.

"Everything I made," he said, "he made with me. Every

bridge I built, every foundation stone I laid, every weapon I fired was as much his mind as it was mine. He was my hands, he was my voice. He was half my genius. He was half my soul. In all justice the city should bear his name beside mine, and the only reason it doesn't is because justice never mattered to him. I give his children advice, I give them orders, I watch the palace, I watch the harbor and the ships and the sky…but I could make nothing new for Caviro's first child. I have made nothing new since."

I said, with difficulty, "Did my father know?"

"No," he said. "Some of your ancestors might have guessed… but up until you I chose them all. Up until you, I wanted them all. When they looked at me, they saw the king he said I was—the king he believed I was. That was all I asked for."

"Then you really are only the memory of a man," I said.

"It's done, Caviro's daughter," said the dead god of Alectelo. "It will be done whether you blaspheme me or no. I can't undo it any more than I can shove myself out of this pearl and into flesh and bone. You can keep people on this side of death, but you can't pull them back over the line. You can't, and I can't. It would break the world."

"I'm not asking to break the world," I said. "I just want one conversation."

Alekso turned his head away from me and stared across the concrete harbor, into the sky.

"If I could drown your planet all over again," he said softly, "if I could boil it and break it and fill it with locusts and wild dogs, if I could hurtle it ten thousand light-years away from your sun, if I could send the seas out hissing into the void, if I could put a knife's blade to your throat and push, if that would, for one second of eternity, put Caviro in your place—do you think I would hesitate?"

I knew Alekso could not truly see. I followed his gaze, though, up and up, to where the ruins of Ostrayet hung silently over the ocean.

After some time I said, “Then what do we have to say to each other?”

“Do you know,” he said, “in three hundred years, you are the first of his children who has been wise enough to ask that question?”

CHAPTER FORTY-FIVE

GRACIA

"Do it," said my minister of the treasury at once.

"Don't do it," said my minister of the interior.

My foreign minister was uncharacteristically hesitant. "Holiest," she said, "there are a great many risks, and a great many rewards. Szayet's duty to Ceiao—Szayet's duty to her economy—Szayet's duty to galactic law—"

"That much had crossed my mind," I said. "But what is *my* duty to Szayet?"

They looked at each other. At last my minister of war said, "Consult the Pearl, Holiest," as if it were obvious. Perhaps it was.

"Ministers," I said after a moment, "leave me. I wish to speak to the Undying alone."

They stood, but uncertainly. One at the end of the table said, "When shall we return, Oracle?"

"Tomorrow," I said, and the lie came easily: "I wish to speak to Alekso for some time."

One by one, they departed. I thought the war minister cast a suspicious glance over his shoulder as he went, but Zorione ushered him out of the room before he could do more than look and shut the door behind him.

"Holiest," she began, but I said:

"Leave me, too, Zorione. I'm sorry—I'll summon you back, when I'm ready. But I want to be alone."

I watched her go. Then, when sufficient time had passed and I thought they had all gone their separate ways, I stood and crossed out into the hallway, and found the staircase that would take me down into the deepest parts of the palace. I hesitated before the last door. The last time I had seen it, there had been a woman curled up before it, sleeping in her uniform. It took me a moment to gather myself, and to unlock it, and to descend the staircase to a part of the palace I had not seen for eight long months.

The field that separated me from the prisoner was hardly visible: only a faint glimmer in the air, as of heat. I paused a few feet before it, unwilling to draw closer. I could feel the electricity curling off of it, like grass.

The prisoner had no such compunctions. She was less than an inch from the field, standing straight-backed and elegant, as if she were in the center of a banquet hall. She was older than when I had last seen her—of course she was older. How could she not be older? What had I expected: that prison would freeze her not only in space but in time, leave her full-cheeked and glossy-haired, young and lovely and malevolent and dangerous, my same bright-eyed and just-defeated sister?

"Sit down," said Arcelia, and smiled at me with all her teeth. "I would offer you bread and salt, it's only—"

She was thinner, too. Dirtier. They dressed her poorly in prison: a thin shift, brown and sloppily woven. If she had seen it on the street, when we were children, she would have laughed at it. I would have laughed, too, eager for the mixed sound of our voices. Now I stayed silent, and watched her pace like a leopard along the deadly wall.

"I want your advice," I said.

"What am I going to say?" said Arcelia. "No?"

"Matheus Ceirran's killers are at war," I said, "and desperate, and demanding I dredge the oceans. There is much I could gain from them, should I offer them what they ask for. They might forgive all of Szayet's debt. They might offer us a treaty that guaranteed freedom from any Ceian incursion into our space for centuries. Or—" I shut my mouth. Arcelia was yawning.

"How interesting," she said. "It sounds like you ought to help them."

"Or," I said, "they might renege on the deal, in which case I should have nothing at all, and be a traitor to Ceirran's memory besides. And his friends are making lists of traitors, which grow longer by the day."

"Then it sounds like you ought not to help them," said Arcelia.

"And if Ceirran's friends win," I said, "and turn their attention to making Szayet a part of their empire? Or if Ceirran's killers make good on their threat, and come to Szayet with the greatest army we have seen since the Sintian invasion?"

Arcelia stopped pacing.

"So Alekso won't speak to you," she said.

I felt it like a slap in the face. "You don't know what he's doing," I said.

She grinned like a wolf. "Can't I guess?" she said. "You and I both know what he would have advised. You and I both know how little he would have thought of a Ceian military threat against his intelligence. I only wonder that it took so long for him to give up on you."

"You don't know what he says," I said. "You don't know how he feels."

My sister crossed her arms and cocked her head at me,

birdlike. I had thought once, on the other side of this very same force field, how strange it was to see another's emotion on my own features. But those features appeared to me now so distant, so alien, that they might as well have belonged to a woman of another world. Perhaps they did: the world I might have lived in, the queen I might have been, in someone else's history.

"Gracia," she said, "why are you here?"

I had been called *Holiest* a thousand times, and *Madam Oracle*, and *Szayet*. I had been called *Patramata*. It was the first time in a very long time that anyone had called me by that name.

I took a step closer to the warmth of that force field, and then I sat and wrapped my arms around my knees. Arcelia breathed out what might have been a laugh. Then she sat, too, looking into my eyes.

I said to her: "Did you kill our father?"

"No," said Arcelia.

I searched her face. It was utterly calm. "You sound practiced," I said, at last, trying to say it without inflection.

"I am," she said. "I've been waiting for you to ask me for a year."

"I don't believe you," I said.

She laughed. "I didn't think you would," she said, and smiled, wholly without humor. "More than a year since the day he died, and all that time I've been waiting to tell you the truth—more than a year, and a war, and a heresy I never thought you were capable of, and all that time I've been waiting for you to just *talk* to me. Do you remember when you were on the other side of this wall? I came to you, and I said, *Gracia, I want your help; I want you to be by my side*, and what happened then? You left me. You called me a liar, and you left me. Well—I suppose you thought you could do better than me. But now you're alone, aren't you? Again."

"Am I meant to trust your word?" I snapped. "Yes, I remember that you came to me in this prison—I remember you came, and you said, *Our father told me he would make you queen, just before he suddenly fell sick—*"

"But you thought I had killed him before that," she said. "You thought I had killed him from the moment I claimed the throne. You thought I had killed him from the moment I said something you *wanted* was something I deserved. And then you lied, Gracia. I've been waiting for more than a year to defend myself to you. I should have known better. You never cared how our father died."

"Of course I care," I said. "How dare you say I don't care?"

"You don't," she said. "You'll care about the Pearl, and the throne, and ancient books, and ancient buildings, and a pair of embroidered shoes, and all the fine things in the world—you'll always care about *things*, Gracia. But you're a liar. You've been lying so long you don't know anymore when you're lying to yourself." She propped her chin on her fists. Then she said meditatively, "I think sometimes that trying to be your sister is like trying to be sister to the Great Maw. There's nothing inside. And when you try to touch it, it warps, it becomes something unrecognizable. You called me a heretic, Gracia. You let so many Alectelans die for your heresy—and then you took the crown, and you kept it. And you loved it, the way you never loved anybody real." She smiled. "That was why you liked *him*, I think. The first person who ever made it through all that endless, empty ego."

"Don't—say a word about him," I said. "Don't say his name."

She looked at me with what was nearly and terribly pity. "I haven't. That's what I mean, Gracia. You don't *want* to hear what I have to say."

I began my retort, and heard her voice in my mouth. For a long moment I was very still. The impulse was in me, as immediate and palpable as the need to breathe, as strongly as it had ever been in the fine houses and the factory and my own bed in Ceiao: to touch two fingers to my ear, and call up Alekso Undying.

And what would happen if I did? Would I listen to him? Would I obey, or disobey? Would I repeat his words to Arcelia, to my ministers, to my people, or would I lie to them? She knew me; she knew me, and she had known me all along. I was a liar, and I was a blasphemer, and I always had been. So why did I want this? To know, beyond all doubt and disbelief, the will of God?

When I had cleared my throat, I said, "Tell me something."

"What is it now?" she said, still smiling.

"What would our father have done?" I said.

Her smile dropped at once. She pushed herself back from the force field, fast and careless, and the end of her cloak caught and singed. She did not seem to notice. "Why would I know?" she said. "Isn't that your demesne? Isn't that what you call yourself—*Patramata*?"

I had thought it would hurt to hear it, but it was easy, startlingly easy, as if a weight had been lifted from my forehead and set down. And it was surprisingly easy to say it: "You were his daughter, too." And then, even when her face went hard and tight: "You are *Dom* Caviro. You were a prophet, once. Will you tell me what you think?" I made myself meet her eyes. "I'll listen to you."

"I am a prophet, *still*," she said. "I am the only rightful prophet on Szayet. You know that. I know *you*. Lie to the people, if you want, but must you lie to me?"

"You won't answer me?" I said, and when she did not reply, "What would he have thought? What would he have wanted? If I do as Ceirran's killers ask, what would he have thought of me?"

"He's dead, Gracia," she said. "Even if he ever cared about us, there's nothing left of him to care what we do now."

I had thought that would hurt, too.

I got up. "There is a mountain in Itsaryet," I said, "which once hosted the grandest temple in the Swordbelt Arm. It is now home to a safe and secretive prison. When the war among the Ceians is over, I am going to send you there."

Arcelia looked up at me, expressionless.

"You'll be happier," I said. "The jailers are priests, and they are as trustworthy as anyone. You'll have space—and you'll have conversation. It will be a great deal more pleasant than this cell, and a great deal safer for you. I'll send officials to inform you of the details."

"You really are faithless," she said.

"You're right," I said. "I am. But I mean to be a prophet, too."

I turned my back to her and began to climb the stairs. At every step I expected to hear something: a plea, a retort, a last barb or insult. But there was only silence.

CHAPTER FORTY-SIX

GRACIA

At Micavalli," said Barran. "That's where we'll meet them."

It was a system near Sintia, toward the outskirts of the Crossbar. Alekso's father had conquered it, years before Alekso had been born, and it had been a flat, sparsely populated farming planet ever since, filled with rocky fields and grasslands. "*If* you can meet them," I said. "And *if* now is the time to do it—which I am not at all convinced it is. Councillor, you and I are making a bargain—"

"And a good one!" they said. Their hair was sticking out in stretches and tufts, and there was a scab on their lip where they had been biting it. But their smile was the same, hopeful and wide as a moon. "Patramata, Ceiao *will* move forward from this, and when the disestablishment is—is—"

"Reestablished?" said Cátia's voice dryly in the distance.

"The people don't understand *now*," said Barran, "but they will understand, when they're really liberated, when they aren't being poisoned by talk of resurrected gods—and when we've won the war, we'll *restore* Ceiao, we'll make the whole territory of the empire as free as it once was. Now is the great opportunity—for your people as well as for ours! But if we don't cut them off from their supplies, well—"

"Yes, I understand that your enemies are gathering followers," I said. "This is precisely what worries me. Say you do win at Micavalli—"

"Say that *we* win at Micavalli, rather," said Cátia's voice, "as you're funding the victory." There was a click, and Barran's face disappeared, replaced by hers.

"You are funding it, Madam Oracle," she said. "Isn't that right?"

"Five ships of quicksilver pearl," I said. "That only. And you'll send the diving equipment, and you'll handle its sale."

"Certainly," said Cátia. "Jonata is right, as usual." She smiled, a warmth in her pale face that made it briefly unrecognizable. "Now *is* the time for action—nearly. If we win this position, we can block Decretan and Julhan's communications with their supply base. We'll resupply our men, we'll pay our damned mercenaries, we'll watch the would-be cultists starve in Sintia. Then, and very quickly, Jonata and I will retake Ceiao."

"And you'll renegotiate a sovereignty treaty," I said. "Before you turn to other business, please."

"And renegotiate a treaty," she repeated, and narrowed her eyes. "Yes. That reminds me. You won't mind, will you, if I ask you to install a tracking beacon in the ships full of pearl, to ensure that they depart from your shore and arrive at mine?"

"Not at all," I said. "I expected you to make the request. I have installed several already."

"And you do know what will happen if they don't arrive," she said. "Or do I need to repeat the threat?"

"There's no need," I said. "I have a long memory."

She looked at me coolly. "Madam Oracle," she said, "are you sure of this?"

"Would you rather I weren't?" I said sharply.

"Forgive me," she said. "It's just that I'm still a Ceian, though I admit there are few of us left. Asking questions is a habit of mine. You were among those closest to the commander."

"Jonata Barran was close to him, too," I said.

Her face didn't change. "It's a question of practicality," she said. "We're about to become very important to each other, Madam Oracle. All I want to know is whether you're prepared for that. I heard that you and he were happy together. I don't care whether it's true. I'm only asking: Can you be happy in Ceiao now?"

I sat back and ran my hands over my face, and sighed.

"Fine," I said. "If you want it spoken aloud—fine. Yes, we were happy, he and I. And how long would it have stayed that way?"

She didn't answer. I looked away. "A month, yes," I said. "A year, I think so. I think we might have managed that. But Ceiao was hungry, Councillor. I have learned that much by now. It might have been an attack by Kutayet, and my sovereignty demands falling aside in my desperation—it might have been a famine somewhere, and either his people or mine needing more than it was good or right to need—it might have been only time, time moving onward, and one of us growing weary of the other, and your city still hungry. Your city is always hungry. I don't think it knows how else to stay alive... How long would Matheus Ceirran and I have been happy? No. No, you know, too. No one was going to give us forever." I exhaled. "What I do with you is no different than what I did with him, when he landed on Szayet with his army and his empire. It is no different what the Szayeti did when Alekso broke their moon and drowned their world. When you are held in the mouth of a god, sometimes the best you can do is let yourself be swallowed and call it a homecoming."

She was watching me without expression throughout this

speech, but at that last her lip curled a little. I was not sure if she knew it.

Her expression might almost have been one of pity. "In another life, Madam Oracle," she said, "in another life, I think you and I could have been friends."

"We only get one life," I said.

The freighter outside my dock, when I at last came down from the palace and crossed to the harbor, was the largest freighter I had ever seen. It took up so much of the sky that its shadow fell across the whole of the harbor, over the following street, and halfway up the wall of my own palace. It was as large as three city blocks put together. It could have fit thousands of people. It could have fit an army. Its hold was open, where we had pulled out the dredging equipment days earlier. Inside it there were still a few boxes, twice as tall as me, marked UNDERSEA DRONES or DIVE LIGHTS. There was a long blue stripe along its steel: Ceian made.

Beside it, my five ships looked like twigs beside a tree. My dockworkers were darting among them, wheeling transports full of crates, lifting boxes up and into the holds. I nodded to them when they knelt, gestured them up again, and sought out their captain, a dark, shaven-headed woman in middle age named Teresa Kotlaya, whose bow was so crisp and formal that it might have come out of a picture book.

"How soon will the pearl be ready?" I said. "I've told the Ceians we would send it tonight."

"We should make that in good time, Holiest," she said, but she was looking at me out of the corner of her eye, and at last burst out with: "Holiest—some of the men have refused to continue working."

"It's their right," I said. "I wish them good fortune."

"I'm worried that they won't be the last," she said bluntly. "They don't like the work, Holiest. Even if it's Szayeti workers bringing the old world from the water—they say putting it in the hands of barbarians isn't in the spirit of the holy law. I apologize for my candor."

"There's no apology necessary," I said. "I could use more honest advisers. The ships—they'll be manned with a skeleton crew, won't they? No more than a few sailors per pearl-load?"

"Yes," said Captain Kotlaya. "I don't doubt any of those men. But the greater problem—"

"I understand," I said. "Captain Kotlaya—will you let me know when the ships are about to depart? There are some items I would like to look over."

She gave me another sidelong look, but she bowed. "Of course, Holiest," she said. "Whatever you command."

CHAPTER
FORTY-SEVEN

GRACIA

I had had the opportunity to observe war from close quarters, and I had not enjoyed the experience. Nor was I enamored of it from a distance. It was difficult for my ships to send me reports, caught as they were in the void between planets. I received data packets in the early mornings, and reports from Jonata and Cátia's faction in the afternoons, where I updated their captains on the ships' locations and covertly consulted with the spies I had installed among their ranks weeks earlier.

Cátia had not been lying when she had said she could not afford to wait. Her ships were easing toward Sintia day by day, skirmishing with Otávio's advance guard, drawing back again when they failed to gain the advantage. It was a motley assortment who made up their army: their own fleets, of course, those colonials from Belkayet and Medveyet who had volunteered for a chance at glory and field promotion, even veterans from Quinha Semfontan's command who had come back into the Ceian fold under the broad hand of Ceirran's forgiveness but evidently bridled at it. And beside this, to make up the numbers in those task forces that were not at full strength, the assassins had hired mercenaries from Kutayet. It was these mercenaries who drained the bulk of Cátia and Jonata's funds—and these mercenaries who she already owed several weeks' back pay.

At last Jonata called, on the tenth day since I had sent the ships. "We'll be out of contact from now on," they said. "Cátia says Decretan's on one of the Sintian moons, and that awful cousin is closing in fast. I can't think your ships will arrive more than a day before we start the battle proper. Are you sure they'll be on time?"

"They have just entered the Crossbar," I said. "You can check the tracking beacon, if you like. They'll arrive at the agreed-upon port, and your men can unload the ships there. No contact between you and I would be necessary, even if it were possible."

They chewed on their lip. Then their hands curled into fists, and they leaned forward, face intent.

"Patramata," they said. "Altagracia—you're right. He would have made himself into a god. He *would* have. There was no other way it would have ended."

I looked at them. It was difficult to see in those soft brown eyes the fierce, hawk-nosed woman whose image I had watched the soldiers lift over their heads. I wondered if Barran ever thought the same thing.

"Do you believe me?" they said, when I didn't reply.

"I believe you, Councillor," I said. And then, a moment later: "I understand."

The next day there were no holos. There were no messages from the men on the ships I had sent. There was only a data packet from my spies among the assassins' ranks, and it read: *Decretan has made her attack.*

Do I need to tell you what happened next?

My father spoke once, beneath the silver-carved ceiling of a mighty ship, about the business of an Oracle. He said to me: *A prophet's business is a translator's. A prophet's business is to take His words, and to make them into something the world can bear to hear.*

What he meant, though I did not understand it at the time, was that he was a liar.

Or perhaps this: There is something greater than a lie, wider and wilder, which is a dimension of this world as surely as time, and which holds men in its current as surely as the accretion-tide. The Sintians might have called it greatness, and the Ceians glory. The Szayeti might have called it divinity. My father had none of these, but he understood this thing, though he could not give it a name. He understood it, and he called it the business of an Oracle.

And I am his daughter, Altagracia Caviro, queen of the Szayeti and Oracle of the dead, who is named Patramata.

What happened next will be written in tablets for a thousand years, not least because of its simplicity: Admiral Decretan outflanked Cátia Lançan, demolished her scanty and ill-organized defenses in a matter of hours, and came planetside to overtake her camp. With a mercenary force to swell her army's flagging numbers, Cátia would likely have overcome them, or at least made an escape toward Sintia. Her mercenary force had abandoned her. She fled. Her communication lines were cut, and of the thousands of ships she had gathered in the atmosphere, only a few remained. It might have been any of those ships that told her falsely Jonata Barran had been killed. It might have been any of those pilots who agreed to steer her fighter when she aimed it toward the sun.

Jonata lived, of course. But they would not live for long. Over the next day Otávio Julhan spread Jonata's men thin over the atmosphere—what few men remained to them—and drove them down toward the planet. Like their friend, they died rather than wait to walk in his triumph. And I heard that Admiral Decretan took it upon herself, when the fighting was over, to build their pyre, and to watch over their burning body until dawn.

And afterward the admirals took the greatness and the glory and covered themselves in it. And they deserved it—I'll never deny that. It would have been far beyond my powers to do what they did at Micavalli. I like war best, I think, as a story.

What I did was this: Eleven days before the battle, an hour before the ships were due to leave from Szayet, as the dusk was rising up in the eastern sky, I went down to the harbor. One of my guards was beside me, huffing with exertion. She was wheeling a cart on which there were ten large wooden crates.

I caught the first dockworker I saw and lifted him up from his knees. "There's something additional to load into the cargo holds," I said. "Two of each of these."

He looked from me to the ships where they sat clustered around the great freighter. "Holiest," he said nervously, "I'm afraid the quicksilver pearl is already bolted in. Any new crates will jostle in the hold very badly."

"That's all right," I said. "Load it in, as I say. With as few men as you can manage, if you wouldn't mind. I'd prefer it to be a surprise."

He ducked his head. "Holiest," he said, "may I know what it is?"

"It is a gift," I said. "In each ship, forty bottles of Ceian wine."

Something caught my eye against the growing dark: a satellite, blinking across the horizon. I watched it move, and my fingers nearly twitched to my heart, pure Ceian habit. But of course the satellite I was looking to salute had long ago been destroyed, and I was laughing only with the dead.

Alectelo was blindingly bright the morning after the battle ended, and the sky outside the window so blue as to be invisible. I let myself take my time that morning, summoning my maids to dress me and sending them away again, brushing my hair in the silence until it shone in the mirror, and at last descending from my bedroom through the palace and finally toward the harbor. I let myself stand at the steps until the wind picked up, and my cloak caught it and for a moment flared out behind me like a banner. All I could see was the great ship, and the thin line of blue sky above, and the distant twinkle of Szayet's sun.

Captain Kotlaya was waiting on the shoreline, speaking softly with a group of dockworkers. I approached her, and when she came out of her bow, I said, "Gather the people."

"Holiest?" said Captain Kotlaya.

"Gather the people," I repeated. "We are going to need many, many workers. Any builders, any engineers. Anyone who has experience with diving."

"Holiest," said Captain Kotlaya uncertainly.

"Yes, I mean smugglers, too," I said, and let my gaze travel again to that great shadow, which rested against my sky like a children's monster. "They will need something to do now, I think."

"Holiest," said Captain Kotlaya. "I don't understand."

I said, "Cátia Lançan received none of the pearl I had promised her. I am sorry for it. But in order that we might dive for it, she sent us the equipment necessary to dredge our own oceans."

Then I tucked my hands into the sleeves of my robe, and added: "May she rest in peace."

CHAPTER FORTY-EIGHT

GRACIA

We brought up the sunken treasure.

It was not all that Szayet needed. We had hardly begun to dig, for one thing. The usage of the submarines and drones and cranes was a more skilled job than any of us fully realized in those early days, and it would be months before we had the manpower to use Cátia's gift to its full capacity. Besides this, even in its multitude, it was limited: Relying on the equipment we had, it would take us decades to raise more than a fraction of the old Szayet's value.

But we did not have to rely on the equipment we had, because we could buy more.

My ministers said this often. They said it in low tones, as if afraid someone would hear, and take it away again. I might have scoffed at them for superstitious fools, but I did it, too. I could not help it. We could *buy more*. We could buy more equipment, and buy new ships. We could increase the dole, and hire experts to consult on renewing our arable land around the planet. We could lower taxes, and keep ministry budgets at their previous levels. We could build steel bridges from island to island, and cover them with fruit and corn and flowers. We could build ships—thousands of ships—we could ask for scientists to develop *new* ships, faster ones, better ones, we could build better maps, we could build better antimatter engines. We could hold a thousand feasts and never run dry of wine. We could cover every inch of Alectelo with gold—we could cover every inch of it in quicksilver pearl. We could *buy quicksilver oysters* and begin the Szayeti crop again, which had been dead for generation on generation. Perhaps what frightened me was not the possibility that our good fortune might fail. Perhaps it was just that new and gleaming *and*: the terrifying expanse of it, like land, running all the way to the horizon.

It took a while for the visitors to begin to arrive. In part this was deliberate: We could not sell all of our newfound gold and jewels at once, lest the sheer quantity of them overwhelm the market. But not everything that had slept under the ocean relied on the market for its worth. There were books and tablets and even some miraculously preserved pieces of actual paper, which the priests at the Library seized upon at once and vanished into their back rooms for restoration. And when they returned with the knowledge of the world in their hands, so did the scholars of the galaxy: poets and playwrights, philosophers and mathematicians, politicians, orators, nervous and shifty-eyed theologians, pouring into the Library and out again, filling up our streets with talk and debate and laughter. The Itsaryeti began to come, and the Belkayeti. The Medveyeti, too. I was hearing talk among the priests of founding a university.

Most nights, I worked late into the small hours and did not recall falling asleep. When I opened my eyes, Ceirran was propped on his elbow, watching me, and the lights of Ceiao were glimmering on our ceiling, and in their shadows I could see only the edge of his smile. He bent to kiss me, and I caught his face with my palm and leaned toward him, breathed him in. His face was rough, but his lips were warm.

"There you are," I said against his mouth. "I've been looking all over for you." And the sound of my voice brought me up out of the soft foggy darkness and into the coolness of the Alectelan morning.

I got up and wrapped my robe around me and went out onto the balcony. Beneath me were my citizens, moving like insects along the streets, and the white of my city under the sun. The beaches were gleaming with silver again.

There was so much of the world returned to us. There was so much that had been lost, which we had thought we would never see unless some empire came to conquer or to steal it away. There was a clean wind that morning, which swelled up from the ocean, and whispered at my hair and the curves of my ears.

I thought then, clearly, that if I had been a girl again, sixteen and queen of nothing at all, I would have gone to that Library. I would have shaven my head, and become a priest. I would have buried myself in those books, and learned all the world's history, and all her languages, and all her laws.

And I would have understood it then, the whole turning of the galaxy around its waiting darkness—what makes up the moons and the planets and the stars beyond them, what makes men kill and oceans rise, what breaks chains and burns towers and brings empires to an end, what causes death and what staves off dying, what passes between a god and his lover when there is no one watching but the dark. I would have understood everything, and I would have believed in it, as surely and swiftly as I believed in the sunrise. And I would have never needed to come out.

But I was no longer a girl, and I never would be again.

I looked up from the city, into the empty sky. It was clear and vivid and as blue as light. The ocean was a still mirror beneath it, glass over glass. All the sweet fathoms of that blue! I wanted to scoop it up in brimming hands.

The sky was never that color on Ceiao, not even in the highest part of the city.

CHAPTER
FORTY-NINE

GRACIA

She had bought Admiral Semfontan's house. He would probably have thought that was funny.

It was there that they signed their pact, she and Otávio. The holo was of poor quality. I watched it over and over again, trying to make out details: the pins on her cloak, the rings on her fingers. The way her hair fell over her face. When she turned to face me, there might have been a pale line along her jaw—a new scar. Or perhaps it was a glitch in the recording, and I saw nothing at all.

To Admiral Julhan: Arquera and the Shieldmirror, and Ceiao north of the river Nevede, and their governorship, and inspection and taxation of all trade therein. To Admiral Decretan: the same for the Crossbar, and for Ceiao south of the road. And the Swordbelt Arm.

I supposed they would be giving Rouan Valquíria Barran a new name.

The visitors came in, and the visitors went out. Our wealth

grew, day by day. And nearly a month after the pact was made, I received this message, sent not privately to me but to the public tablet used for official occasions:

To Altagracia Caviro Patramata, the queen of Szayet, styled Oracle, from Admiral Decretan, Demipotestate for Confirming the Freedom of the City with Conciliary Power, lady of the Crossbar and of the Swordbelt Arm, greetings.

You are summoned to the satellite Plyusna to issue an account of your actions during the righteous war against the assassins of Matheus Ceirran.

Should you be unable to appear at Plyusna, the Empire of Ceiao looks forward to meeting you at the city of Alectelo, on the planet of Szayet, in the spiral of the Swordbelt Arm.

I reread this letter for a long time. Perhaps, I thought, she really did care whether I had funded Cátia and Jonata before the Battle of Micavalli. Perhaps she had that much sentiment in her. But the visitors had come into Alectelo, and the visitors had come out, and the galaxy knew now the gold that Szayet held in its hands; and I had known for a long time what it felt like to be whispered about by Ceians who wanted something from me.

I glanced up. The sky outside my window was a blank slate, and the candle of the winter sun was burning behind the fog. In the distance was the silver sea, and the harbor-gate, and the hulking silhouette of Cátia's ship.

"Zorione?" I called. She was at the door at once, and I beckoned to her. "Could you fetch my minister of the treasury, please? And Captain Kotlaya. And—find my minister of the interior—tell her to summon the dockworkers. As many of them as she can gather."

We began by plating it in gold. From stern to bow, the ship was two thousand feet long, and seven hundred feet tall. This required a great deal of metal, some of which we melted and some of which we bought from our neighbors on Itsaryet and Kutayet. This was less because we were short on material—the Ostrayeti had left behind thousands upon thousands of mass-produced bracelets and necklaces that they would have thought cheap, wiring in long-rusted tablets and ship engines, chests filled with unmarked ingots and coins—and more for the sake of saying we had done it. There was a certain pleasure, at first, in telling the merchants the quantities, and watching their eyes grow wide. Later, when word had begun to spread, there was a different kind of pleasure, which was the look on the merchants' faces before I had begun to speak.

Ceiao had painted—Cátia had painted—the ship as Ceians always did, gleaming steel with a long blue stripe. This we encrusted with rubies, plated carefully in glass to preserve them against the batterings of gravity and solar wind. The inside we lined with gold too, and gems. We carved every inch of wall and ceiling we could carve. We ordered thousands of tapestries from Itsaryet. We ordered, in total, eighty acres of Madinabic carpet. I arrived at the harbor personally when that shipment came, and said blandly to the dockworkers that I was there to make sure nothing else had come along inside, at which they shrieked in shocked laughter. As for the engines and exhaust ports, we plated these silver. "Holiest," said the captain of the dockworkers, "you may not realize how quickly the chemicals will decay—"

"I do," I said. "We will keep them polished. Hire a hundred additional sailors."

The sailors! Simply to crew the ship required four thousand men. We hired these from every part of Szayet, and paid exorbitant wages for them. Then there were seven hundred cooks, from as near as Cabero Plaza and as far as the Shieldmirror, and all the food they required. "*Must* it be fresh, Holiest?" said the head chef, a little desperately, of the fish and the fruit, and I said, "We can hire tugboats to bring it in from every new port. Just tell the captain what you need." There were musicians, and dancers; there were poets and artists from Sintia, come to visit the Library and caught up in the swell of the growing crowd; there were Diajundot acrobats and adventurers, even a few priests who seemed entirely bewildered to be brought out of their archives.

Into the sides of the ship, we cut windows. They stretched across its sides in long, gleaming rows, like a cat's stripes. The whole lower third of the ship had been a storage chamber, built to hold the seaships and equipment. This we stripped bare, and lined it with pearl at the ceiling and a great black-and-white mosaic of stars on the floor. Along the fore and aft walls we put black basalt pillars, and behind them mirrors. The port and starboard sides we made into windows of their own, great sheets of glass so high that thirty men on one another's shoulders could not have reached the top of them, and we strung that pearl ceiling with thousands upon thousands of little lamps, arranged in swooping lines and arcs. Standing within that great room at midnight, with the harbor lights dimmed and the moons shining in through the glass, the lamps gleamed from every direction, around and against the darkness. Unless I looked at the shadows of my feet, it was impossible to tell that I was not standing within the sky.

"What is it *for*, Holiest?" said the head of the dockworkers.

"Feasting," I replied.

Once out of the lower decks and on the harbor beside the dockworkers and my palace staff, I stood and watched the barge awhile: how the ocean hushed at its sides, how the lanterns twinkled on the seawater. There was one further thing I had installed on its prow, which was nearly invisible in the darkness, except where the window lights glinted off its curves.

Then I raised my hand. At once every light in the ship blazed to life. I was temporarily blinded, blinking away tears, and when the spots stopped bursting, I still had to hold up a hand even to squint at it. The ship was as bright as Alectelo from that distance, turning the water gold for what must have been a mile in each direction. I might as well have been looking at the sun. In empty space, it would shine like a comet.

What I had added to the prow was now as clear as if a spotlight were on it: a great head of green stone, its eyes staring sightlessly forward. Anyone who had known it in life would have recognized it at once for the hooded eyes, or the crooked nose, or the wavering scar, or perhaps for the slight smile on its lips. On its brow it wore a wide golden crown.

"You have built a great ship, Holiest," said Captain Kotlaya dubiously.

"You have done more than this," said Zorione. "You have built a city."

I signaled to the dockworkers, and watched the lights wink out, one by one, until my ship and its figurehead were only shadows again. "At any rate," I said, "I have built something beautiful."

We watched the silhouettes of the Szayeti file out of the ship, row after row. They were black against the remaining gold of the streetlamps, like a Sintian painting. I added, "Tomorrow we take flight."

Zorione woke me the next morning. "It's time, Holiest," she said, and dressed me in my purple gown, and brushed out my hair so it fell in shining waves around the Pearl in my ear. When she had finished, she beckoned, but I shook my head.

"One moment," I said.

"What else?" she said. "All of your things are packed."

"One thing is left," I said.

I knelt under my desk and opened the drawer there, and shifted through the long-discarded tablets, and at last pulled out a little silver disc. It fit snugly in the palm of my hand. That was no surprise. It had been made to be held.

CHAPTER

FIFTY

GRACIA

And here is the last lie.

I did stay on Ceiao, after he died.

Not for more than another day. But I went to his house.

It was already abandoned. The gates were bent open, though they were solid iron, and the walls a tangled mass of blue graffiti, half of it in a Ceian so vulgar I could barely understand it. I had meant to knock and see if a servant remained, but there was no need: The door was off its hinges, hanging like a curtain. It was half-burnt.

I had only been inside a few times, and only for parties. It was Celestino's domain, and I did not envy him it. Still, I looked around the entrance hallway with a blank and distant curiosity: the gold-flaked pillars, the imported carpet, the intricate black-and-red mosaic on the walls. I could hear a dull buzzing, and the smell of something unpleasantly sweet. There was a table not far from the entrance, out of place among all this modern Ceian furniture: It looked old, and was nicked with knife scars and patterned with running wolves. Sitting atop it was a bowl of strawberries and pears, and a cup of wine. Someone had knocked over the cup, and the stain had soaked into the fine old wood. Circling each other lazily above the fruit were a pair of fat-bodied flies.

"Holiest," called Zorione unhappily from behind me.

"Just a moment," I said, more to myself than to her. "It can't be far."

Two flights of stairs, but I passed them by. I was moving more by impulse than by understanding. He would have slept on the ground, I thought, not a staircase, far from an escape route. A soldier's instincts. He would have wanted to be near the front door, but not too near, not enough to be unfashionable. There was a purple mantle lying across the carpet, lovely thin wool, ripped in a long line up the back. There was a brownish mark on a marble table, where something made of silver might once have stood. There was a gleam of something within a darkened room.

I stepped over the threshold. It was waiting on the bedside table, discarded the morning before. I picked it up and slipped it into the sleeve of my robe, where, on a sunny day on an island many years and light-years ago, I had once kept a small and gleaming Pearl.

I had meant to leave in a hurry. But there was the little bedside table, one of its drawers half-open to show papers covered in thin, neat handwriting. There was the wide oak bed with its embroidered pillows, where someone had thrown back the covers and not pulled them flat again. There was a sun-faded painting on the wall opposite the window, showing a flowering tree. Every day, anyone sleeping in this bed would have woken to the sight of that tree, and so would anyone waking up beside him. There was a candlestick by the bedside, which was full of melted wax that had dripped over its rim. I could still smell it, a little, when I breathed in.

The recorder came back out of my sleeve and into my hand without a thought. There was a place on its rim, which I had never bothered to show him. I pressed my thumb to it now, and I watched as his face sprang into life and color in front of me, dark-eyed and smiling.

The recording's head turned to one side, as if looking for something. Then its eyes focused on the empty air in front of it, and it said: *I had loved*—I let it go, and the face vanished. When I pressed it a second, it appeared again. *I had loved*, it said, and said again, and again, until the whole room was an echo: *I had loved, I had loved, I had loved...*

"Holiest," shouted Zorione, from somewhere very far away. She sounded frightened.

I had to shut my eyes before I could call back to her: "I am coming." Then I pushed the recorder back into my sleeve and stepped across the threshold without opening them again.

When I reached the gate of the house, I could see why she had been frightened. The populace were pouring down the streets, long pulsing columns of them, silent and hard-faced. I had not seen such a crowd since my coronation. They were Ceians, nearly all of them, but Sintians too, Itsaryeti and Medveyeti, even a few Madinabic parents holding tight to their children's hands. Some were veiled. Many were shaven-headed. All were dressed in black.

Zorione and I moved as unobtrusively as we could. I thought of Raimundo, but there were no strong-armed soldiers left to watch our backs now—or none in this world—and we crossed over the line of the Wall and down the slow slope of the city toward the steep incline where Ceiao's outskirts began.

The safest way was through the theater district. It was, as I had expected, bare of people. What I had not expected was the face of Jonata Barran, staring at me through a veil, saying through echoes so thick I could barely make them out, *Dear friend*—

"Ever-Living God," said Zorione reflexively.

I turned away. The funeral—the *funeral*—I had wondered about the funeral, I had anticipated the funeral, I had planned for the funeral, but the sight of their face—the hesitant, breathy tone of their voice—I could hear nothing, I *wanted* to hear nothing, words kept breaking through like *I loved* and *weep for* and *my best*, I could not hear them, I could hear nothing, nothing, nothing at all.

Zorione's hand was on my back. She was urging me forward. I let her move me, as I had not since I was a child. It was over. We were crossing the square. We were already gone.

Another voice behind me, thick with echoes, said: "I'm not much of a public speaker."

I had wondered about her, too, as best as I was able to wonder about anything. It was hard to imagine her at a funeral: with her hair cut at last and brushed back from her face, wearing a black captain's mourning cloak, her mouth and her eyes painted neat and bright. It was hard to imagine her, at long last, made to carry Ceian formality.

When I turned and saw Ana on those screens, I knew I had again misjudged her.

Imagine her, if you can—the way she looked on that day. Her hair was still long, as shaggy as if it were peacetime, and her face bare. She was not wearing her captain's cloak at all, only trousers and a loose black tunic. She might have been any woman from the street, if it were not for the way she moved.

Imagine her how I saw her then: in mirror, in multiplicity, prowling in unison from screen to screen, a horde of hands in one gesture, an army of feet in one step. She seemed, in her hundredfold, less a legion than a fractal. She seemed as if she had been split into fragments along her soul.

She said: "Friends—" I hardly heard it. I could not look away.

She paused then, and was still again, staring into nothing.

Her eyes were red. If you had been there that day, if you had been standing beside me in that square, you would have seen how red those eyes were. You would not have been able to help seeing it. You would not have been able to help how you felt for that woman, what you would have felt for that woman, who had been the right hand of all Ceiao and who now stood with her shoulders slumped before the corpse of someone who might have been God and who was now, and who would only ever be, her friend.

Your friend, I should say.

Because after all you were not standing beside me in that square. You weren't watching the hundredfold bodies in the screens. You didn't need to. You glanced into the camera—just for a moment—and I saw then what was in your eyes.

When I knew him, Anita, I knew him as commander, as lover, as Ceiao. But he was your friend first.

We made it to the harbor just in time. Had I thought I was unable to hear? Sound was rising behind us, just as it had the night Ceirran had died: chanting, and under the chanting, shouting, and the breaking of glass. Rising, too, was that low, flickering light. It was the light of fire. Our engine noise rose with them both, in concert, and there was barely enough time to swallow down bread and salt before we were off the ground.

The ship lifted slowly. Beneath me was the familiar shape of Ceiao, as it had been described to me once: an open eye. The long runways of its lashes were dark and empty now. The Nevede was a thick, runny grey, choked with boats and people moving along the boats, and with the glittering sparks of torches. And in the center, in the very middle of the lovely blue-roofed houses and parks, a gleaming white dot: the Libeiracópolan.

The engines were roaring now. The city was growing farther from us, tilting, shrinking, and the Libeiracópolan was a white speck in the center of the eye. As I watched, that speck twinkled, a brief flare.

Then it burst. Beneath it, under the smoke that rose in a roiling cloud to smear the whole pupil into colorlessness, was a hard, rotted red. It was the color of rust.

When I closed my eyes, I still saw your smile.

CHAPTER

FIFTY-ONE

GRACIA

Plyusna was a spiderwebbing network of satellites on the edge of a system near Kutayet, where every ship from the Crossbar on its way to the Swordbelt Arm stopped for a few hours to provision and refuel. It consequently boasted a marketplace a hundred acres in size, which fit nearly eight hundred thousand people on an average day.

It was far from an average day. The lady of the Crossbar and the Swordbelt Arm had not spent her reign idly. She had come up from Ceiao in a hail of terror, and lain waste to every little moon in which Kutayet's claws were sunk. They said that, though Ceirran had left nearly all his money to Otávio that he had not distributed to the Ceian people, she had taken some part of it for herself. If so, she had not poured it into trifles. It was half the Ceian army she had brought to the satellite, and half the Ceian army whose ships lay strewn across it, like barnacles on a whale.

It had been a slow, leisurely journey up the spiral arm. We had stopped at a dozen ports, each time in the blazing light of noon, and at each one the people had poured in to gawk at the ship and its wonders. In accordance with this habit Captain Kotlaya wanted to go down to the marketplace at once, but I shook my head.

"We can wait," I said. "We are not undersupplied." And the light of the barge, like a beacon, was nearly greater than the light of the satellite itself. I wanted to sit there, a second sun in Plyusna's endless nighttime. I wanted to be seen.

In fact it was nearly six hours before we received a ping from the marketplace. The man who appeared on the holo was not one of the Kutayeti officials who typically staffed these ports. Rather, it was a Ceian, blue-cloaked and hawk-faced, and I wondered at what Ana had already managed to do in so short a time there. I wondered what she might manage to do in the future, given resources, and faith.

"Admiral Decretan greets Altagracia Caviro Patramata," he said, "and bids her come down to the marketplace customs bay, where she may be greeted and act as the admiral's guest."

I nodded thoughtfully. "I see," I said, and flicked at my tablet, so that the message waiting there blinked red and chimed. "Then make this reply to the admiral, if you please."

When he read it, he opened and shut his mouth for a few moments. "Oracle—" he said.

"Send it," I said.

He dismissed his own holo with a satisfyingly unhappy look. I propped my chin in my hand, and waited.

I did not have to wait long. Beneath me, from the satellite, began to rise lights, one after the other, like fireflies. After a few moments, the control panel began to ping, and ping again, with requests to board. They were military requests, military ships. They were Ana's own men.

The little silver disc was resting in my lap, where it had been for hours now. I pressed the side of it gently, and watched the face there blink into color for the hundredth time. It smiled at me. Then it said:

I had loved Quinha, more's the trouble.

He was as bright as a jewel. If I had not known better, I might have mistaken him for something alive.

"Is the feast prepared?" I said to Zorione.

"All ready, Holiest," she said. She was watching the spectacle of the ascending ships with a kind of awe, her eyes glittering with their reflected light. But my eyes were still on that little steel spiderweb, sprawled in the void.

Ceirran had told me, once, that my queenship ceased to exist when others ceased to believe in it. He was a true Ceian, I think, even if neither he nor his enemies ever really knew it. To his bones, he had been a man who believed in what could be seen and touched. Even his own Pearl had been an object to him.

At his death I had thought that my grief had made the world seem unreal. It was only later that I understood: All that clear, unbending reality had left the world with his soul. All that was left were the same untouchable things I had brought with me in the carpet, the same things I carried with me now in the barge: lies and beauty, queenship and faith.

Somewhere within that satellite, a man was sprinting along the hallways, on his way to deliver a message to the lady of half the world. It was still blinking softly on my tablet.

The Oracle of Matheus Ceirran Undying invites His beloved Disciple to dine with her tonight.

"Altagracia," said Zorione, and I realized she had said it several times, and turned. She was looking at me, my nursemaid, with an expression of fear that I had not seen since we had fled Szayet over a year ago—and with curiosity, too. She said, "Holiest—what are you going to do?"

I opened my mouth to answer, but before I could, the dashboard of my ship shivered and cleared. Ana's head materialized before me, one eyebrow raised. Her hair was long, still, and her cloak glittering with new officer's pins, and her chin was propped in her hand. Her eyes were that same flat, hot black—as black as the sky.

"Szayet," she said.

I said, "Anita."

Her lips peeled back from her teeth in what I could not call a smile. "So," she said. "That's your game?"

"Is it mine?" I said.

"I'll say this for you," she said, "you've got balls. You use his name? You call yourself his prophet? To *me*?"

I leaned forward. "Would you believe me?" I said.

The smile flickered. A moment later she schooled herself, tried to hide her expression, and said, "You have any idea why you're here?"

"Oh," I said, glancing at the gold in my ceiling and walls, "I know why. Will you stay in Plyusna? Or will you be my guest tonight?"

She looked away. In the distant background of the holo, I could see a window, and the mirror of the distant sparks of the rising ships, and beyond them, a great and glowing light, whose source was my own vessel. Her mouth twisted.

She said, a little hoarse: "When you said *disciple*. Did you mean it?"

"What if I did?" I said softly. "What would you do?"

With Ceirran's death, I thought, some raw brightness had been stripped from her. Now it was returning, like gold into the sea. When I looked at her face, I saw her made up in kohl and finery, as clearly as I had the night we had danced in each other's arms.

"Be *your* guest?" she said, at last, as if nothing had happened. "Szayet, you're mistaken."

"I am not," I said. "Come to my ship. Eat from my table. Drink my wine."

She hesitated. I could see her hesitating. But I could also see, in the viewscreen behind her, the hundreds and hundreds of rising lights. Her troops had already accepted my invitation. If she stayed in the marketplace, she would do it alone. She could feast at my expense—she could live on my generosity for a night, and know it, and have the world know it, too—or she could sit, in the loneliness and the boredom, in a piece of the world where nothing moved and nothing lived. And Ana had never been the kind of woman who cared to withstand temptation.

"How generous," she said dryly.

I let myself smile. "Are you not lady of Szayet?" I said. "Is it not your due?"

"Am I?" she said. "Let's see," and the holo vanished like smoke.

But she had been smiling back. I had seen her eyes.

I had met Ana's lord once as an empty-pocketed pretender, covered in nothing but carpet and false courage. Now I met Anita herself as a queen, wrapped in all the luxury of the living and dead, a faithless prophet of an unbelieving god. I leaned forward on the captain's chair, and closed my eyes, and imagined it as she saw it now: my stolen ship, my burnished throne, my fire from the heavens. Any Ceian worth his steel would have thought me a decadent, and spat. My own people would have thought me a god. Ceirran would have known me at once, and he would have laughed.

"Give me my robe," I said to Zorione. "Put on my crown. I am going to tell her a story."

ACKNOWLEDGMENTS

It is not often that someone comes along who is a true friend and a good writer. Isabel Kaufman is both. It is the reader's good fortune and mine that she is also a spectacular agent. This book would not exist without her dedication, enthusiastic feedback, and merciless cheerleading, and it certainly would not be worth reading.

Thanks are due especially to Michele, who taught me how to think about storytelling like a historian; to Remy, who taught me how to think about it like a director; and to Austin, who taught me how to think about it like a personal attack on your friends. All that is good here is due to their lessons, and all ills are mine. Thank you also to Anna, Elisabeth, and Casey, from whose argument at a picnic I blatantly stole the problem that became the Pearl of the Dead and who first suggested that the problem might be a religious one, and thank you to Anna and Elisabeth's cats, Florian and Flannery, who diligently supervised me as I began to write this book.

Among many other sources, I am indebted to *Cleopatra: A Life* by Stacy Schiff and to the Altes Museum in Berlin for first reviving my love of this period, to *The World Without Us* by Alan Weisman for shaping my imagination around science fiction, and of course to Plutarch, Suetonius, and other Roman historians, some of the original unreliable narrators.

Thank you to Angeline Rodriguez, an extraordinary editor, whose passion, generosity, and dedication in the face of plague and chaos were truly undying, and whose sharp and talented eye made this book what it is now. Further thanks to Priyanka Krishnan, Rachel Goldstein, Kelley Frodel, and the rest of the wonderful Orbit team.

Thank you to my mother and father, who made me love books; to my brother, who made me love arguing about them, and whose impeccable eye for California ecology I did my best to appreciate here; and to my grandmother, grandfather, bubbe, and zeyde, who all found their way into this book in some regard. And thank you to Gina Thompson McKuen for introducing me to Shakespeare.

Finally, and not least of all, thank you to Clair Hamner for letting me borrow a Halloween-costume pharaonic headdress for my sixth-grade presentation on Cleopatra. I promise I put it to good use.